# BUT WHO WILL SAVE
## *The Children*

### DONALD HIGGINS

For information contact
But Who Will Save the Children?
4417 Enterprise Dr.
Bartonville, IL 61607
309-688-2990

www.butwhowillsavethechildren.com

# Table of Contents

Preface                                                        vii

Prologue                                                        xi

Chapter 1: Where Am I?                                          1

Chapter 2: Beginnings                                           13

Chapter 3: Mutations                                            18

Chapter 4: Fingers                                             23

Chapter 5: More Doctors                                        28

Chapter 6: Embarrassment                                       30

Chapter 7: Glimmer Of Hope?                                    37

Chapter 8: Adventure                                           40

Chapter 9: Revelations                                         46

Chapter 10: Are You Nuts?                                      51

Chapter 11: The Quest                                          54

Chapter 12: Into The Abyss                                     56

Chapter 13: You're A Suspect                                   64

Chapter 14: The Circus                                         72

Chapter 15: Why Waving?                                        77

Chapter 16: Evidence                                           80

Chapter 17: Your Wife                                          82

Chapter 18: I can find them                                    84

Chapter 19: Turn here                                          87

Chapter 20: Got a Runner                                       90

Chapter 21: I'm a Hero?                                        97

Chapter 22: Pictures, Faces                                    102

Chapter 23: Please God, Help                                   109

Chapter 24: You Are the Devil                                  115

Chapter 25: Can't Help?                                        127

Chapter 26: Over 30 Missing                                    137

Chapter 27: Not Welcome                           142

Chapter 28: Welcome Home                          170

Chapter 29: We Have a Spy                         172

Chapter 30: Eight Days                            178

Chapter 31: Crazy Russians                        184

Chapter 32: Aleksei's Son                         189

Chapter 33: Help Me Mick                          196

Chapter 34: The Search                            202

Chapter 35: Rushing Home                          208

Chapter 36: Rip Their Balls Off                   213

Chapter 37: Hired By Who?                         218

Chapter 38: Calvary Arrives                       222

Chapter 39: Plan in Motion                        229

Chapter 40: The Russians                          232

Chapter 41: Not Alone                             235

Chapter 42: Gatekeepers                           244

Chapter 43: The Twelve                            249

Chapter 44: I Want Off, Now                       256

Chapter 45: Let's Try This Again                  259

Chapter 46: Bomb?                                 261

Chapter 47: Where To Sir?                         282

Chapter 48: Coincidence?                          291

Chapter 49: Shake My Hand                         314

Chapter 50: Don't You Die, Mick                   320

Chapter 51: The Answer Why                        326

Chapter 52: I've Lost It                          332

Chapter 53: I Need Your Help                      340

Chapter 54: Places To Hide                        343

Chapter 55: Retreat                               367

# Preface

While researching this book I found some frightening statistics. Citing US Department of Justice reports, the National Center for Missing and Exploited Children (NCMEC) notes that nearly 800,000 children are reported missing each year. That's nearly 2,200 a day just in the United States. In China and Russia, the numbers are probably similar, but their reporting is sketchy at best.

A staggering 203,000 children are kidnapped each year by family members. Another 58,200 are abducted by non-family members. Statistics show many others are runaways or pushed out of the home by parents.

Few children are victims of the kinds of crimes that you often see in national news reports. Many abductions go unreported to the police and are handled by the family. The NCMEC states that fewer than 350 children per year are the victims of what most people think of as a "stereotypical" kidnapping, meaning the newsworthy kind. The center characterizes such kidnappings thusly: "These crimes involve someone the child doesn't know or someone of slight acquaintance, who holds the child overnight, transports the child 50 miles or more, kills the child, demands ransom, or intends to keep the child permanently."

According to NCMEC statistics, 57 percent of such crimes end with the return of the child without major injury. The other 43 percent end horrifically. Multiply that by the last 50 years, and it's a frightening number.

This book is dedicated to the families of these victims. Nothing can minimize your trauma or loss. I also dedicate this to the police, FBI, and Department of Justice employees who have to deal with these crimes. My heart goes out to them, for they see the results of the devastation to the families on a daily basis.

I'd like to thank my wife, Michelle, for her patience and understanding. I'd also like to honor, and thank my father, Jerry Higgins, and mother, Margaret Higgins, may they rest in peace. They instilled the kind of work ethic required to write both computer software code, and novels. This book is dedicated to our children, Caitlin, Brett, and Dan, as well as my parents.

To the teachers at Bergan High School in Peoria, Illinois who told me I had a knack for writing, thank you. Your motivation and coaching made a difference in my life.

This novel is based on memories, but is fiction.

*Does anyone know where the love of God goes*
*when a predator turns the minutes to hours?*


*The police all say, she'd have been fine that day,*
*If she put fifteen more minutes behind her*


*She may not have been seen or she may have escaped*
*But he saw her, then hunted and took her*


*And all that remains is the faces and the names*
*Of the parents, the sisters and brothers*


Adapted from Gordon Lightfoot's song called:
*"The Wreck of the Edmund Fitzgerald."*

# *Prologue*

Having a special talent is always interesting; understanding its purpose is the confusing part.

My name is Mickey Anderson. I'm an otherwise normal guy who happens to have an extremely strange medical disorder. It's an embarrassing condition, so I've worked very hard to keep it a secret from others. In the last forty years this disorder was responsible for countless awkward, painful, and embarrassing memories. Out of shear frustration, I've assigned this condition a most fitting name: "Mick's Curse."

While I find it extremely difficult to relive these memories, let alone write about them, it's essential in order to convey the extraordinary journey my life has taken.

One doctor, whose inspiration may have unwittingly saved my life during a particularly depressing period, told me to remember this phrase: "Mick, there'll be brighter days. Please remember that even during your darkest moments, courage and faith are all you need to move forward." I repeat his phrase every day in my head. My life turned out to be a perfect example of his statement. "Mick's Curse" made me contemplate suicide too many times to count. I'm only alive today because during my darkest moments I stumbled onto a new and far more interesting purpose for my life.

In a most unusual twist of fate, "Mick's Curse" eventually turned out to be a special talent, and even a blessing for many families.

# Chapter 1:

## Where Am I?

I awoke with a throbbing headache, unable to understand where I was. A man was shouting. Why in the world was someone shouting? It took a second to understand what he was saying.

The man screamed, "You just wouldn't shake my hand, would you? All I wanted was for you to shake my hand. Is that too much to ask?"

My mind was beginning to gear up, and I was attempting to process the sensory signals coming from my nose, eyes, and limbs. My head was covered by a thick, dark material. I was unable see him, but I'd felt the air move as the man paced back and forth in front of me. There was no doubt this man was extremely irritated, but why?

There was a strong odor of something; what was it? Coffee. Yes, that's the source of the odor; the scent is unmistakable. The smell was so strong it must be near my face, or an extremely potent blend. After a few seconds I'd finally realized why the smell was so strong: my head was covered by an empty burlap bag that I'd guessed had recently been used to transport coffee beans. What the hell was happening?

He yelled again, "Just tell me why, Mick. I need to know why. Why'd you refuse to shake my hand?"

I couldn't quite place the voice, but it seemed distantly familiar. I didn't know what to say, so I whispered, "Sorry, I wasn't trying to offend you."

The covering over my head was ripped off, and the friction of burlap to skin burned my nose and ears. My eyes strained to adjust to the bright lights. A man's face was right next to mine, and the only thing I could think about was how offensive the smell of coffee was on his breath. He screamed, "What? You weren't trying to offend me? You fucking asshole, did you forget that I tried to shake your hand at the coffee shop and after your TV interview, but you just ignored me? Now that you're famous, you don't want to talk to your old friends, is that it? I just wanted to talk to you, shake your hand, and talk about the good old days in high school. Now look what you made me do."

I began to process my surroundings. My hands were tied together with duct tape, not only on the wrists but also around the fingers. Duct tape also was wrapped from my arms down around my legs, preventing me from lifting my arms. I sensed my head and face had been beaten severely from the pain that pulsed with every heartbeat. I could smell and taste blood—my blood.

I saw a work bench with a wall of storage cubicles behind it. Everything on the bench was stored in a pyramid shape. I noticed what appeared to be pipe bombs. For some reason I was able to count them instantly, there were fifteen. These were neatly stacked, five on the bottom, then four on the next row, three on the third level, two on the fourth row, and finally one on the top. Fifteen boxes of ammunition, arranged exactly the same way, were next to the pipe bombs. Scanning a little more to the right, I saw the same number of sticks of dynamite, and blasting caps, all arranged exactly the same. I whispered to myself, "Stay focused, Mick, you need to get out of here." It was a difficult task. I had to prevent myself from feeling hopeless, even though the situation presented few options.

The man was still yelling, but now I wasn't paying attention. I was focused on my surroundings and what I could use to my advantage.

Out of the corner of my eye I saw something move, and I realized we weren't alone. In the corner was a young boy seated in a chair, his back to me. He appeared to be tied up, and duct tape was visible on the side of his face. His hair was blond but had streaks of what appeared to be blood. There was blood on his neck and left shoulder. The back of his shirt was torn and blood stained.

The screaming man removed a shiny object from his waist. It took a second to focus on it. *Holy shit!* I thought—it was a giant hunting knife. It had to be a foot in length, and the blade was now right in front of my face.

The man yelled, "Pay attention asshole! You're going to die today, and I want you to know why!"

*You want to kill me? What the hell did I do to you?*

My thought process was interrupted when my peripheral vision caught something streaking toward my face. It was his fist. The impact was just below my left eye, snapping my head and neck to the side. I was almost knocked unconscious. I heard ringing in my ears, then instant burning pain on the left side of my face. I tasted fresh blood.

"I just wanted to shake your hand and tell you how impressed I was with your ability to find those kids. You didn't even remember me, wouldn't give me thirty seconds of your time, you fucking asshole. This is all your fault."

The man walked over to where the child was seated. He used his knife to cut the duct tape and ropes holding the young boy to the chair. He yanked the boy to his feet and turned him around to face me. This boy had familiar big blue eyes. They were wide open with the frightened look of sheer terror. His mouth was covered with duct tape, and blood matted in his hair; tears streamed down his cheeks.

The man yelled, "Ely, say goodbye to Mickey one last time."

He ripped the tape off the young boy's face, and in a terrified, crying scream, the young boy yelled, "I want my mommy, I want my mommy and daddy!"

I instantly recognized him. Those big blue eyes belonged to Ely, my best friend Scott's eight-year-old son. Ely and I play with his toy cars at Scott's house every time I visit. Ely is a car fanatic, just like me. Ely truly believes I am the coolest guy in the world because I have two race cars. He loves to sit in my race cars and make engine noises. We're very close, and Ely has always called me, "Uncle Mickey."

This entire situation didn't make any sense. *Why does he have Ely, an innocent young boy, and why me? We aren't even related, so what was the purpose?*

I heard the barely audible sound of police sirens far in the distance. *Please, God, send the police to this location so they can at least rescue this young boy.* Reality returned when I heard a sharp cracking sound. The screaming man snapped a magazine into a hand gun. An instant later came the sound I was dreading, but knew would be next. Gun owners know the sound well; it's the ratcheting sound created by a bullet snapping into the firing chamber as the gun is cocked.

Before I had a chance to react, he held my hands to the end of the barrel and said, "Good luck finding Ely now." I realized what was about to happen and tried to jerk my hands away. It was too late. I saw a flash, then heard the explosion from the gun. It took me a few milliseconds to process the realization of what had just happened. The screaming man had fired a bullet right through my hands. The pain was nauseating and rose exponentially each time my heart beat. Blood was squirting out all over the desk and onto my lap. I screamed until I became light headed and then started to black out.

The screaming man slapped me and said, "Stay awake, asshole. You need to hear this!"

The man started laughing, then said, "Remember what we learned at our wonderful Catholic high school about Jesus having wounds in his hands? I have good news, Mick. Now you have wounds that are similar to those of Jesus Christ. But unlike Jesus, you can't save Ely now. So, Mick, do you remember me now, my old high school buddy?" He did look familiar, but I just couldn't place him. How the hell was I supposed to remember someone from twenty-five years ago in a situation like this?

He came back and looked right at me, smiled, then screamed, "Any last words, Mick?"

Recognizing I had few options to survive, my "fight or flight" response went into overdrive. My vision returned, and the will to live quickly followed. His face was only inches away. I pushed my arms down as far as I could, then with every ounce of adrenaline-fueled energy inside my body, I thrust my badly wounded hands straight up into the underside of his jaw and connected. There was an unmistakable cracking sound as his teeth were jammed together. I'm not sure who felt more pain, but I was pretty sure it was me. The man fell backward onto the work bench and collapsed onto the floor. I watched as his eyes rolled back into his head. It appeared that his bottom lip had been between his teeth at the instant I slammed my hands into the underside of his jaw. I could see a row of puncture wounds on his lower lip. Blood poured from these wounds onto the floor.

I looked around, unsure of the next move. The duct tape that was holding my arms to my legs had torn free, but I couldn't move. I was attached to the chair with duct tape around my chest and my upper and my lower legs. I tried to move but couldn't pull free of the duct tape. When I tried to stand, I was unable to keep my footing, and lost balance. The chair crashed back to the floor, moved backward, and almost tipped over. I had used up all my body's adrenaline, and the pain exhausted my remaining energy. I needed the knife to cut myself free.

I looked at Ely, his big blue eyes were now bloodshot from constant crying. I knew it would be tough to get his attention, but I needed Ely to get me the knife. It was our only chance to survive.

I shouted, "Ely, get the knife and give it to me!"

He was crying uncontrollably and violently shaking. Frozen from shock, the poor kid couldn't move. I couldn't blame him; anyone of us would be in shock after witnessing something so vile and evil.

I tried to comfort him but still direct his attention by talking softly: "Please Ely, your Uncle Mickey needs your help. Can you get the knife and give it to me? I need your help as quickly as you can. OK, Ely?"

It took fifteen agonizing seconds before he finally ran over to the knife, picked it up, and ran toward me. He was about two steps away when I saw the screaming man's hand reach out and grab Ely's legs, flipping him onto the floor. I sat helplessly as the knife, my only lifeline, slid away from me. My one hope of escape had vanished. In an instant I felt that my life, and that of Ely's, was now as good as over.

The screaming man slowly pulled himself up and then grabbed the knife and gun. He picked up Ely by grabbing the front of his shirt at the neckline. The screaming man's fist crushed the young boy's throat, preventing him from breathing. I sat there helpless as Ely's face quickly turned a reddish-blue color. Ely was now in grave danger.

The man wiped blood from his face onto his sleeve and said, "Well done, Mickey, but you came up short. I have to admit, that was an impressive uppercut."

I looked harder at the man, trying to determine my next move and figure out who he was. My thoughts were interrupted when I saw Ely's fists valiantly pounding on the man's hand. Unfortunately, Ely's effort was in vain—he was unable to force the man's hand away from his throat. The young boy looked at me with desperate, pleading eyes. Ely's arms eventually dropped to his side as his small body gave up. I was heartbroken, if I couldn't find a way to make the screaming man release his hold on Ely, the young boy would certainly die right in front of me.

*You must know this guy, so focus on him, and figure out his identity.* My mind went into overdrive. It seemed as if I was watching a movie sped up to ten thousand times normal speed. Thousands of images and names started streaming into my mind. I stared at the man for a few seconds, focusing all my senses on memories of high school. It finally came to me, his last name started with a "C". I searched my memory bank for everyone I remembered from high school whose last name started with a "C." *Coughlin, Cruickshank, Cunningham—that's it; his last name was Cunningham. What the hell was his first name? His first name was on the tip of my tongue, and started with a "B." Bob, Bill, Ben,...no—Benji—that's it; his name was Benji Cunningham.*

Vivid memories of Benji flooded my mind. His actual first name was Bartholomew, but we called him Benji. I can't remember why we did, but I think it had something to do with a movie about a dog. Someone gave him the nickname and it stuck, and Benji liked it.

I met him on the first day of high school. He was assigned the seat next to mine in our first class of the day. My initial impression of Benji wasn't favorable. He talked constantly, even when the teacher scolded us for talking in class. It was immediately obvious that he had OCD and other behavioral issues because he stacked his books like pyramids on his desk and constantly took items out of his book bag, then carefully placed them on his desk in a pyramid shape, then put them back in his bookbag. He would repeat these steps every ten minutes. His parents probably knew it as well, but his condition went undiagnosed and untreated. His OCD was far worse than anything I'd seen before. It was so bad that if you rearranged anything in his book bag, desk, or school locker, even if it was in a good-natured jest, he would become so enraged that he wanted to fight.

Initially, I'd felt bad for him because I'd known what it was like to be different than others. I soon altered my perception of him when he started touching several of us inappropriately, slapping our butts, and staring at us taking showers after gym class. Benji laughed it off, but it creeped me out. I couldn't stand to be around him, but during our freshman year in high school, he'd talk to me every day as if we were best friends.

After freshman year I kept my distance. After high school I wanted to forget him, but he still called my parent's home during college breaks. I hadn't seen him since high school and he'd grown a long, bushy beard, so recognizing him had been nearly impossible.

"Benji Cunningham," I said quietly.

The screaming man, now positively identified as Benji Cunningham, rushed up to me. "Good job, asshole. You finally remembered me!"

In his enthusiasm, he finally released his hold on Ely's throat. The young boy fell to the ground. The impact awakened Ely, and he gasped several times trying to refill his lungs.

*Thank God*, I thought; *at least Ely is alive*. My energy level quickly fading, I asked, "Why Benji? Why are you doing this?"

Benji responded, "Mick, I liked you in high school. You talked to me when few others would. But after high school, you were always too busy to talk when I called. Do you remember, Mick? You said you would call me back, but you never did. I tried to talk to you, but you just blew me off. Then yesterday you wouldn't shake my hand. You had to be punished."

I said, "Jesus, Benji, that was twenty-five years ago. Sorry."

Benji didn't reply, so I yelled, "But why Ely? He's done nothing to you!"

Benji nodded, as if he agreed with me, then responded, "That's true, but what I really wanted to do was challenge your ability to track down kidnapped kids. I was going to grab some random kid, then put you to the test. Then yesterday I saw a post on Facebook that changed my mind. Our buddy, Scott, posted that he, and his pretty little wife, would be visiting Chicago this weekend. That post also revealed that Ely would get to see Chicago for the first time as well. Scott even told everyone on Facebook what hotel they'd chosen to stay. People give away too much information on social media these days, don't you think, Mick? Since you refused to shake my hand, I decided to grab Ely to punish you. I followed them to the pool. Here is a little tip, Mick. It's easy to spike someone's drink if you hang around the pool bar. It only took a few minutes to knock out Scott and his wife. I put a little in Ely's drink as well. I just carried Ely out, nobody stopped me, it was so easy."

He paused a second and rubbed his aching jaw, then wiped fresh blood from his lips and face. He said, "It would've been a great test, but now we won't ever know if you'd been able to find him. Frankly, Mick, I've not been that impressed with your abilities. After all, I've been kidnapping and killing kids since I was seventeen. The police were never smart enough to catch me. I never left a trace, outsmarting the investigators every time. Mick, here is a little secret that you can take with you to the afterlife. Do you remember the two little girls with the last name of Fisher? They were twins. Well, Mick, I killed them twenty-six years ago. I put them in two garbage bags and left them in that abandoned ride at the fair-grounds. I found out the ride would move without power by turning a hand crank, so I put them in one of the capsules and spun the ride to the top. I removed the crank, and chopped up the wiring afterward, so nobody could move it anymore. Those girls sat up there, hidden from the world, for a month before anyone found them. If those damn birds hadn't ripped open the bags, they might not have been found until the ride was dismantled. The police never talked to me, even though I lived a half mile away. Hundreds of people looked all over the neighborhood for any sign of them."

He started laughing, then said, "Mick, my old buddy, do you remember that you and Scott helped the police by searching the woods behind your subdivision? I was the one that thought to search the woods, just to keep everyone away from the fairgrounds."

I remembered. I was so angry that I wanted to kill Benji and end this nightmare.

The police sirens were now much louder. Benji said, "I'd love to continue our twenty-fifth reunion party, but I have to go." Benji, now happily whistling our high school fight song, looked at me and said, "Bye, Mick. See you on the other side." He pointed the gun toward me while dragging the near-lifeless child toward the door. This sick son of a bitch was acting as if this was the best day of his life. Beaming with pride, he raised the gun toward my head. I saw a flash of light from the gun, then everything went dark.

Strange images began to appear. I saw my mother and father; they were waving at me to come over to them. Next to them was a table, mysteriously floating in the sky. My grandparents were sitting at the table; with them was Jay, my best friend from grade school. I thought this was strange, because all of them had had died. I noticed we were floating high above Lake Geneva in Wisconsin, a favorite vacation spot of our family when I was younger.

My mother, the eternal optimist, said, "It's really a shame that you had to die to see us again. We've really missed you, so let's make the best of it. Here, sit down next to your mother and tell us all about your life."

I asked, "I died?"

My mother said, "Well, yes. That's why you're here, Mickey. It's OK, you're with us now."

Before I could say anything else, my mother interrupted. "You look great and so happy. Your grandparents are here, and I'm sure you remember Jay, your friend from grade school. We knew you were coming and couldn't wait to see you again." We talked for what seemed like hours about what I did with my life and what they missed about theirs.

My mom then said jokingly, "By the way, Mick, I never got the chance to tell you this: I forgive you for putting firecrackers in my cigarettes." I had to laugh as the memories about that day returned. Our entire family absolutely hated that my mother smoked cigarettes. They stunk up the house and eventually caused my mom's cancer. So, I took it upon myself to do something about it. As a ten-year old engineering prodigy, I'd devised a brilliant plan to improve her odds of quitting. I didn't use a firecracker, although that idea had crossed my mind. After careful analysis of a firecracker's destructive power, my ten-year old mind determined it was simply too powerful and would injure my mom. Plan B was to use something less powerful. I had a drawer full of these Bang Pops, the children's toy that had a few little flint rocks and some gun powder inside a small roll of paper. When you threw them on the ground, they make a loud "pop" from a small explosion. Kids sometimes called them "pop rocks" because that name was easier to remember. They were harmless, unless of course you taped ten thousand of them together. While not as dangerous as my other favorite toy, lawn darts, they were still not the safest children's toy.

My top-secret plan, code named Operation Get My Mom Angry, was to spike each cigarette with four bang pops. It wasn't a simple undertaking. I had to remove the rocks and gun powder from four bags for each cigarette. The next step was to skillfully take most of the tobacco out of each cigarette, put the pop rocks and gun powder inside, and finally refill the tobacco. It was a painstaking process, especially for a ten-year old child. After verifying the quality of my work, I carefully placed the spiked cigarettes back into the pack and waited for showtime.

The memory of that day was so strong it felt like it just happened. I watched my mother remove the first cigarette from the pack. She saw me watching and said, "What are you looking at?" I didn't say anything, just watched in anticipation as my masterful plan was about to be unveiled. I was almost giddy with delight as the cigarette exploded about a minute later, showering her with tobacco and paper. I say "exploded," but in reality it was just a loud pop. Still, to a ten-year-old kid, it seemed more profound. I was astonished that she didn't appreciate the creativity of my work or the humor of the situation. Screaming at the top of her lungs, "You're going to get it," she chased me all over the house, finally cornering me in the garage. In hindsight, sabotaging her cigarettes certainly didn't help to make her quit, but it nonetheless left me with a smile as she whipped my ass. That memory was one of the highlights of my tenth year on earth.

Now my mother held my hand and smiled. "It was funny, young man, but there were better ways to make me quit." We smiled at each other.

I said, "Love you, Mom."

My father said, "By the way, I really loved the poem you wrote for my funeral."

I asked, "What poem?"

My father replied, "The one titled 'A Good Man Died.' You know—the one with lyrics similar to Neil Diamond's 'Morningside' song."

I hadn't read the poem at the funeral, but he was right, I did write one, and it was good. My mom and dad told me they loved the poem, and were proud of me. My eyes teared up. I wanted to cry but was unable. My mom said, "Mick, sadness isn't allowed here—only joy, love, and positive memories."

Dark clouds began to appear above us. My father said in a dejected voice, "Our time with you is coming to an end. Mick, remember we love you more than you can ever imagine."

As the sky continued to darken, a huge wall cloud appeared and began to swirl around us.

My mom shouted, "No, not yet, please. We want more time with him."

I shouted to my father, "What's happening?"

My father said, "Be strong, Mick. Find your way back."

My mother held out her hand, and I grabbed it. She said, "But I don't want him to go yet."

My father said in his most comforting, soft voice, "You have to let him go. It isn't his time yet." Lightning struck nearby, followed quickly by a deafening crackling sound.

My mother had tears in her eyes as she slowly lost her grip. I tried to hold on, but the forces pulling us apart were too strong. I felt my lifeless body plummeting downward through an empty, dark, and mysterious abyss. Then the sensation stopped. I heard a voice say my name, but I was unable to see anything.

I asked, "Where am I?" There was no response.

"Do you see the light?" said a thundering voice.

I shouted, "Yes," but there was no reply.

I thought, if this is heaven, where were all the pretty girls, endless parties, and tropical paradise I was promised every time I went to church? And if it wasn't heaven, where was I, and where would I go from here?

I saw a flash of light, then complete darkness. There were no more sounds. My last cognitive thought was, this is how your life ends, complete darkness with no sound.

*Had my life really ended?*

# Chapter 2:
## *Beginnings*

It's a challenge to explain my body's medical issue. I'm not sure I understand it. For as long as I can remember, my hands and fingers have been strangely hypersensitive.

My earliest memory of these symptoms began around the age of five or six, but it could've been earlier. I remember how puzzling it was to me as a young boy. At this stage in my life, I really didn't understand much of anything, but I knew something was different about my hands and fingers.

My hypersensitive fingers and hands were just a mild annoyance at first. As I grew older these hypersensitivities evolved and mutated, becoming difficult to interpret and conceal. I was forced to keep this condition to myself to prevent ridicule. My mother would always attend any visit with a doctor, so I never brought it up. Even if she hadn't been there, I wouldn't have known how to explain what problems I was having. To be perfectly honest, I was embarrassed and didn't want anyone to know. My parents made us go to church every Sunday, and one sermon in particular seemed to be talking directly to me. The priest's sermon that Sunday morning was about behavior. The main point the priest tried to convey was that every behavior, good or bad, has consequences. When I was young, I believed Jesus used this condition to embarrass and punish me for past behavior. Even though I couldn't remember what unscrupulous behavior I might have done to warrant such a hostile response, it was the only thing that made sense. I hypothesized that Jesus wanted me to improve my behavior, and if I did, the condition would cure itself. I really strived to be the perfect angel—for a while. It was demoralizing when the condition didn't improve.

Unsure of what to do, I usually retreated from social activity in an effort to prevent humiliation.

I was an awkward kid, not able to have a normal conversation. I'd get nervous and embarrassed easily. Even though there were no outward irregularities with my hands and fingers, I was convinced others could sense I wasn't normal. I became so shy that anytime I attempted a conversation, or virtually any interaction, I'd fumble my words and sound like an idiot. I couldn't keep my attention off my fingers and hands and was always looking down at them. Kids are not very nice, and they made fun of me constantly. More frustrating were the adults, several of whom told me right to my face that I was weird. What kind of person says that to a ten-year-old kid?

I developed a mild, stress induced stutter, which you can imagine made interactions with people even worse. So, I became known as the quiet kid, sitting alone, drawing pictures of cars. God, I loved cars. Drawing cars was my escape from reality. I did, however, have ambitious goals, even at an early age. I wanted to be involved with cars. I saw this as my life's destiny. Mostly I drew race cars, but another favorite was a souped-up version of the Flintstones' prehistoric car. Drawing cars allowed me to go unnoticed by the bullies whose one job, it seemed, was to make fun of me.

High school brought more of the same, but I did have some friends. I played sports for the first two years, then realized I wasn't big enough for football, and not good enough for basketball. So again, I was the quiet kid who liked to draw pictures of race cars. I was OK with this; I really didn't need to be part of the "cool kid" clique. I felt more secure keeping to myself or with one or two nonjudgmental friends. Sure, there were times where my feelings were hurt because I wasn't invited to parties, or after school hang outs, but in hindsight it probably saved me further embarrassment. I was still socially awkward, especially when pretty girls were around.

When I was about eighteen, the symptoms caused me to withdraw from virtually any social activity for three or four months. I could no longer ignore these symptoms, so I went to my family doctor first and explained my concerns with my hands and fingers. He ran tests but could find no medical condition. My doctor insisted there could be something seriously wrong and wanted me to schedule an appointment with a neurological specialist in Chicago. However, the following week I was to enroll at Creighton University in Omaha, Nebraska, 450 miles away, so I chose to postpone the appointment in Chicago.

Unfortunately, only two days after arriving in Omaha, I began to have significant concerns. I went to St. Joseph Hospital, Creighton University's teaching hospital, and asked for help. They brought in a nerve specialist who quickly diagnosed the condition. He said, "Mr. Anderson, my diagnosis is peripheral neuropathy." He showed me a medical book that had the symptoms and explanation of remedies. The diagnosis didn't seem to address all of the symptoms. Sure, some of his reasoning made sense, but the doctor was unable to explain why the sensations in my fingers appeared and then disappeared so randomly.

I said, "Really? It doesn't seem like what I experience."

He replied, "I believe it does."

I felt his lack of serious testing, and nearly instant diagnosis, were both lackadaisical and inaccurate. I trust what my body tells me, and I had a nagging thought that there was more to the condition than just this diagnosis. Still, even though I didn't believe the diagnosis, I'd felt I needed to give him a chance. I said, "OK, great. So, explain how you're going to fix me?"

He said, "We're going to apply a small electrical shock to your fingers to see if it helps. This is a simple procedure and less intrusive than blood transfusions."

I thought it was a bit draconian to use electrical shock therapy in this day and age, but I told him to schedule me for the procedure. He said, "I don't think you understand. This isn't a one-time thing; you have to come back each day for a month." Well, shit, that wasn't what I wanted to hear. At this point I was out of options, so I decided to be a trouper and go with it.

The next thirty days were annoying, to say the least. Every day I went to the office and they strapped on electrodes. When the nurse turned the machine on, the initial shock wave made me jump. You know it's coming, and you know it will hurt, but there isn't anything you can do about it. When you get a shot, there's a pinch that hurts and then eventually goes away. This therapy was different; the "pinch" pain didn't go away but just changed intensity. The nurse would sometimes talk to me while the machine caused my fingers and hands to twitch. I felt stupid sitting in the hallway with this machine buzzing. Random people walking by would ask, "What's that thing doing?" I had two responses, depending on who asked. If I didn't know them, I'd respond, "Nothing, it's a conversation starter to meet people." If a good friend walked by, I'd say, "I suffer from Macrophallus, which is an abnormally large penis. This machine shrinks it so it doesn't bulge my pants as much. Now go away, I have to meditate."

After thirty days the doctor said, "Are you all better now?"

I replied, "No. There has been zero improvement."

The doctor was mystified, as were others brought into consult on my case. During those four years at Creighton, they prescribed a treatment plan that included everything from simple anti-inflammatory pills to complex drugs designed for people with rheumatoid arthritis. Basically, they had no clue what was wrong with me. One doctor even thought I had Tourette's syndrome because I stuttered when upset. I was basically a lost cause and probably a nuisance to them.

Treating a disease, or even the symptoms, is impossible without an accurate diagnosis. Turns out there was none. I've come to terms with the fact that my chromosomes have run wild, and I may simply be a freak of nature. I had high expectations that doctors and medicine would resolve my condition; however, they were unable to fix, or even improve, my symptoms. The side effects of some of the drugs were far worse than the symptoms, so I decided to stop the medications.

Although it remained manageable, I could tell the condition wasn't getting better. Once I determined that this disorder wasn't likely to kill me, I tried to forget about it. I started to meet new people at Creighton, which caused my entire outlook on life to improve. Nobody had preconceived notions about me, so I was free to start over with new friends and experiences. My previous depression evaporated as I became part of a wider social circle. I was young and considered myself invincible, so a non-lethal medical issue certainly wasn't going to prevent me from living life to the fullest. Like most young people with a mystery condition, I decided to wait it out. Either it would get better on its own, or it would manifest itself into something the doctors would be able to diagnose. A normal twenty-one-year-old man thinks about boobs, cars, and beer, not hypersensitive fingers. I was finally happy.

During my junior year in college, I met a girl. Her name was Jackie. It seemed my life was complete. Everything was going great. Those sensations that had haunted me for years subsided as the euphoric feelings of a new relationship took over. For over eight months I experienced few episodes. After eight months I began to think my problems were behind me, but that was short lived.

A few minor episodes, which were usually harmless and relatively uneventful, manifested into a full-blown emergency when I had two automobile accidents in one week. My fingers would tingle and throb while I was driving, and I wasn't able to hold on to the steering wheel. To be honest, I was lucky there weren't more accidents. I'd had five or six near misses during that time for the same reason. I drove an old crappy car, and luckily the cars I hit were just as crappy. Jackie was with me during both accidents; she was shaken up but uninjured. After the second accident, she ended the relationship with earsplitting screams in front of my friends. In a flash, the relationship, which had lasted eight wonderful months, was over.

I had no idea what was happening, so I stopped driving for six months. Depressed and embarrassed, I retreated from life for a little over a year, until my desire to live again, and love again, overcame my constant fear of failure.

# Chapter 3:

## Mutations

After graduation I felt uneasy about my future. I'd sent resumés to many companies for computer programming jobs but received no offers. A month later I was contacted by someone from the U.S. Department of Defense to see if I was interested in a job with the U.S. Army. I was completely surprised and perhaps a bit confused when they contacted me, especially since I hadn't sent a resumé. Two days later, FBI agents appeared at the door of my parent's house to interview me. The following day, a colonel named Frank Abraham and a sergeant Harry Wilson, knocked on my parent's door. They spent the next two hours giving me aptitude tests. I was understandably nervous but still felt that I'd failed most of the questions. To my surprise, two weeks later I was hired by the U.S. Army as a computer programmer.

I was assigned to a project called Zeus, which was an advanced weapons project managed by the same two people who interviewed me, Colonel Abraham and Sergeant Wilson. They told me their team's task was to improve the accuracy of the automatic aiming software that was used to control machine guns and cannons on helicopters, personnel carriers, and tanks. They informed me the contract would be for one year, with an option to continue another year if I demonstrated improvements in the system. This job was a dream for an unmarried young man. I had to admit, I was still surprised to be chosen because I didn't feel my skills were as good as many other candidates, but I tried to make the best of the opportunity by arriving earlier than required, and staying later than everyone else on the team. It was a crazy year. Each week we were flown to a different test range to fire and analyze different weapon systems in simulated war-like scenarios.

Six months later, while assessing the damage to a tank that had just been destroyed by one of my helicopters, I was introduced to a woman who worked on a similar project. Her name was Yael and she was from Israel. She wasn't on our team, but worked on a special project to improve Israeli air to ground weapons systems. I tell you this now, as if meeting her was initially a positive thing; it wasn't. We didn't get introduced in a nice, cordial manner. Her first words to me were: "Hey you! Get away from that tank. It was destroyed by one of my airplanes and I need to analyze the damage." I was speechless for a few seconds for two reasons; one, she was really cute, and two, she was wrong. I knew the tank had been destroyed by one of my helicopter's rounds. I knew this beyond any doubt, because I was monitoring each shot fired by my helicopter, and this tank was the only tank with a bullseye painted on the side. I'd painted the bullseye myself to help the pilots aim where the round would do the most damage. I used a method of scoring similar to the game of darts. The pilots competed against each other, and the bullseye was an easy way to score and total points.

She was adamant in her belief that I was wrong, and began yelling at me in English, then, when she couldn't control herself, she also yelled in Hebrew. The managers of both projects arrived to find out what all the screaming was about. I knew the size of rounds we were using were different than the ones her aircraft were using, so I was able to prove it was my helicopter's round that had destroyed the tank simply by measuring the impact point. It was then I realized why she'd been so upset; originally, she'd bragged to the manager of her group that it was her "kill." The instant she realized that hadn't been the case, she stormed away, screaming something in Hebrew.

Afterward, I told the general in charge of our teams that this type of confusion shouldn't exist on the battlefield. He ordered me to write a program to collaborate and share targeting data with her weapon systems to make sure our tanks and helicopters wouldn't track and shoot the same targets as her airplanes.

Now we were forced to work together every day until the program was completed. At first, she didn't like me because she'd felt I'd embarrassed her on the test range. She was cute, so I turned on the charm until she realized I was nice guy. Even though it was expressly forbidden in our contracts, a month later we secretly started dating. It was a carefree time in my life. I was relieved that my symptoms had subsided to the point where I was able to have fun again, and stopped worrying about embarrassing situations.

Our contracts were renewed for another year. The manager on her team found out we were dating and transferred her to a different project. Initially I was angry, but my manager explained that because I was no longer on the same type of project, there was nothing preventing me from dating Yael.

It was another great year. We had fun while still accomplishing the goals the military had set. Once the accuracy of the weapon systems had been improved, our contracts ended. The Army wanted me to continue on another project, but Yael would now have to return to Israel.

Yael agonized about returning to Israel. It was a tough decision but she eventually decided to stay in America. At the same time, I'd grown tired of the politics and ass kissing involved when you work for the government. I decided it was time to start my own software company. In a bold, but not very smart decision, I resigned from a very lucrative job with the Army. Yael and I moved back to Illinois. She became an American citizen and a year later we were married.

Five months later, another strange phenomenon appeared.

I developed an ability to detect changes in temperature with my hands and fingers. You're probably thinking, so what? Everyone can do that; what makes you so different? For one, I could tell you how warm or cold something was from ten feet away. Second, I could sense temperature changes through walls. For the next five years I was a hit at parties. I was called the "human thermometer" by my friends, a nickname I grew to hate. People would test my abilities by standing behind walls, and I'd pinpoint their precise location by sensing temperature changes. Some would bet money that I wouldn't be able to find their location behind a wall. I never lost a bet. I was so proficient at sensing heat that I'd use a dry erase marker to outline where they were on my side of the wall. I had a strange ability to tell if they only put an arm on the wall rather than their whole body, or even if they were crouching down. Everyone who witnessed this ability thought it was fascinating, but they didn't have to live with the side effects.

Everyday events that wouldn't bother a normal person made my life difficult. A cup of hot coffee would be the right temperature to drink but far too hot for my fingers to touch the cup. I couldn't be around a campfire or fireplace because of the discomfort. Even more annoying, I couldn't hold a really cold beer or drink without a koozie or a bunch of napkins wrapped around the drink. Even with gloves on, I was unable to participate in a snowball fight or create crude snowwoman figurines with my friends during the winter. It started to interrupt every aspect of my life, so I finally decided to seek help from the nerve specialist in Chicago. Considered the leading expert in diseases of the nerves, this was the same doctor that I should have seen when I went to college. The down side was this doctor wasn't covered by my insurance, and it would be a struggle to get his fees reimbursed. An additional complication was that downtown Chicago, from where I was living, was at least an eight-hour round trip by car. I didn't have much of a choice, so, out of options and needing answers, I made the appointment.

I thought this doctor would finally be the answer. According to the sign on his door, Dr. Simon specialized in inflammatory muscle disorders and neurology. He wore a large bow tie and a hat that had "World's Best Doctor" embroidered on the front panel, and he told jokes constantly. He loved "knock-knock" jokes, and told at least fifty of them during the visit. These silly jokes did help lower my apprehension, however, after my time there, I never wanted to hear another "knock-knock" joke again.

He asked precise questions and seemed to understand the symptoms. After running a series of tests that took nearly an hour, he said, "I've diagnosed your condition as THORD, or thermal hypersensitivity over-registration disorder." I said, "Dr. Simon, I've done quite a bit of research on this subject, and I've never heard of this condition."

He laughed and said, "Me neither. I just made it up. It sounds official, though, doesn't it? I basically mixed your symptoms together and created a name. The good news is there might be some therapies that can help."

He prescribed two drugs and a topical cream that smelled like a combination of a sports cream and really bad body odor. He told me to be patient with the therapy. I can still hear his parting words: "Mick, don't expect an immediate improvement. Even if the drug therapy is working, it will take at least two months before any progress can be measured." Then he pointed to my head and said, "Some of your symptoms may be created by your mind, fabricated inside your brain for reasons I cannot explain. As part of the therapy, I suggest you see a psychologist to make sure your noggin is OK as well."

The first time I used the cream, my wife said, "Oh, hell no, you smell like a homeless guy. Take a shower and get that stuff off." I explained that I had to use the cream, even if it was nasty, to see if there was any improvement. She was right; I smelled like I hadn't taken a shower in a month. The medication he prescribed caused insomnia many nights, which not only didn't help the problem but, I'm pretty sure, actually made it worse.

After two months and no measurable improvement, I stopped using the cream, and ceased taking the medication soon afterward. My friends and family were relieved my experimental "homeless man with body odor" therapy was over and done with.

I sought treatment from a psychologist. The therapist really thought she could help, especially since medications had absolutely failed. I really tried to work with her, but six months into the therapy there was no improvement, so I decided to end the sessions.

I had the feeling people close to me thought I was a hypochondriac. My inability to properly explain the pain and suffering this disorder caused in my life seemed to be my own fault. I was willing to try anything to help, but now it seemed pointless.

# Chapter 4:
## *Fingers*

L ater that year I was getting new basketball shoes and shorts at Northwoods Mall, the largest shopping center in Peoria, Illinois. As I turned the corner to enter a shoe store, I heard alarms.

My fingers began a weird buzzing feeling.

A man running out of the store collided with me, knocking us both to the ground. He jumped up and ran away. It was pretty obvious that he had stolen something. The store alarms were going off because the anti-theft sensor hadn't been removed from whatever he was carrying. An employee chased after him, but after fifteen seconds he decided it wasn't worth the effort.

My buzzing fingers concerned me to the point that after buying shoes, I decided to go home. When I opened the outer doors to the mall, I felt my fingers change from a buzzing feeling to a throbbing sensation. The best way to describe this feeling is to imagine the sensation you feel when you have paresthesia, which is the medical term for when your arm "goes to sleep." Instead of feeling it in my arms, I felt it in my fingers and hands.

I noticed two police cars driving up and down the parking rows. A police officer standing near the doors quickly came over to me and said, "We're chasing an armed man, and we believe he is the mall parking lot. Could you please go back inside?"

"OK," I said to the officer, but I was unable to move. I felt a weird sensation when I looked at a particular car in the parking lot. My fingers began to quiver. I was terrified of this new sensation, but before I could process this change, everything around me seemed to go into slow motion.

I thought, *Either I just got knocked out, or this is a dream.* Without any understanding of what I was about to say, I pointed to a car and said, "See that silver Dodge Charger about fifty feet away—the one with the dark window tint? He's in that car." I'd had no idea why I blurted out this bit of information to the policeman. I remember telling myself, *Mick, you're dreaming, so go ahead and say whatever comes into your mind.* I didn't want to say anything to the policeman, but I'd had a premonition about that vehicle, and I was simply unable to prevent the words from tumbling out of my mouth.

The police officer clicked his mic and repeated what I'd said. The police cars raced over to the silver Charger. With their guns drawn, they looked inside but couldn't see anything. They tried the door handles, but they were all locked. Again, without thinking, I yelled, "He's hiding in the trunk." Three policemen aimed their guns at the trunk while the fourth policeman smashed the driver's window and used the inside release to open the trunk. For some reason I knew he'd be in that car. Just as I predicted, he was hiding in the trunk. Needless to say, he wasn't a happy camper when they removed him. We made eye contact for just an instant, and I realized it was the same man who had run from the shoe store after the alarms went off. After they cuffed and searched him, he was placed in a police car and driven away.

With all the excitement, I'd forgotten about my fingers and hands. I was relieved that almost normal sensations had returned to my fingers. The slow-motion feeling had also dissipated, and normal sounds and movements returned. I felt like I'd just woken from a dream—that the entire event wasn't real. Sometimes when I wake up from a deep sleep, my mind remembers bits and pieces from a dream, and this was no different. I had to piece the chain of events back into my memory and try to understand what had just happened.

The policeman came back to take a statement. He asked, "How long ago did you see him drive in?"

I replied, "I never saw him drive in. I saw him running from the shoe store, on the other side of the mall, about fifteen minutes ago." Before he could ask another question, an unmarked police car pulled up in front of us, and a well-dressed detective got out. We looked at each other, and I instantly recognized him from high school.

"Mick," he said laughing, "what's going on? Did you get arrested again?"

I replied, "Wow, is that the world-famous Brett Stinson? Nice Ford Crown Victoria. Does your dad know you stole his car?" We both laughed, then I said, "I was just helping the police catch a bad guy. You know, a normal day in the life of Mick Anderson." We shook hands.

He said, "You're a funny guy, Mick. Yep, the older guys get the Explorers and Chargers; I get the ten-year-old Crown Vic."

I'd known Brett was a policeman. His father was a policeman and then a highly respected FBI agent. I remembered his father for two reasons. First, he was one of the police officers who shot and killed an armed man holding a child hostage at a grade school. The second reason was that, as an FBI agent, he visited our high school during a career day. His father made a lasting impression on me that day.

During Mr. Stinson's talk at high school, a student asked, "Why can't the police just shoot to wound someone? It seems so wrong to have to kill them."

Mr. Stinson's response was priceless. He said, "If you wound someone, they can still kill you or an innocent person. A wounded criminal is likely to kill someone just for spite, simply because they have nothing to lose. You don't understand yet—you're still young and naïve—but there are many, many evil people in the world. They don't care about laws, civility, morality, your possessions, or even your life. There are people who will stick a knife into their own child's eye, just for looking at them the wrong way. Statistically speaking, before your twentieth high school reunion, there's a good chance that at least two of you in the audience will have a family member who's murdered by one of these deranged criminals."

The audience gasped, and the sound reverberated around the auditorium.

He continued, "Let me give you an example of why we don't shoot to wound someone. I recently was part of an FBI investigation of a serial killer, whom we believe murdered twenty-two people. His first victim was his mother. While eating breakfast he had an argument with his mother. So, he left the table, then a short time later returned with an ax. He used that ax to kill his mother right in front of the rest of the family. It was a sickening crime. Do you want to know why he killed his mother? They had an argument on how to make eggs the correct way! That's right—cooking freaking eggs. His last victim was a policeman who didn't want to kill the man, so he just wounded him. The murderer was able to charge the policeman, disarm him, then kill the policeman with his own gun. Thankfully, the murderer died in a shootout with police a short time later. There's simply no way to reason with a person like that, so we have to be extremely diligent when dealing with criminals. Too many law enforcement officers never get to see their children and family again because they let their guard down. I've already exhausted every less-lethal remedy to the situation before my gun is unholstered. Once my gun is out, a determination has been made that this criminal is a danger to everyone around them. If that person refuses to surrender or drop their weapon, I must be prepared to eliminate the threat they pose to public safety. We don't unholster our guns otherwise." I liked his answer, and Brett was beaming with pride.

Now, standing at the mall with Brett, I said, "Wow, you're a detective already? That's impressive."

"Yep," he answered. I was happy for him, but part of me thought he was a bit young to be a detective at twenty-seven years old. He smiled, put his hands on his hips in a "Superman" pose and sang loudly, "Here I am to save the world!" He continued in a more civilized voice, "Can you believe it, Mick? Those crazy bastards even gave me a gun—and now they let me put bullets in it." We laughed. It was good to see him again.

The policeman read Brett my statement. Brett said, "OK, Mick, you're saying you didn't see him drive in? Then how did you know which car he was in?"

I replied, "I really don't know. I had a sense he was in that car."

The policeman then stated, "Not only that, but he knew the perp was in the trunk." They looked at me, and I shrugged my shoulders. "What do you want me to say? I have a medical condition that allows me to sense heat better than most, or maybe I saw the car move. Hell, I don't really know."

Brett wrote in his book for about thirty seconds, looked up and said, "A medical condition that allows you to sense heat? That's a new one on me." He continued to write notes and said, "Well, thanks for the help, Mick. We have been trying to catch this guy for several years. He was wanted for at least five murders, and last year he killed his girlfriend just for dancing with another man. He kidnapped his girlfriend's daughter and has been a ghost since then. Now I need to find the daughter of the woman he killed. I'm sure you know that police departments have a 'Top Ten Most Wanted List,' and this guy was number one. Mick, you made my day; an extremely dangerous man will hopefully never be free again."

After a pause to write something in his book, he said, "I'm still curious how you knew which car he was hiding in. Perhaps you and I should get a beer sometime and talk about it."

I knew that probably wouldn't happen. While I got along with him fine in high school, we were never good friends. We shook hands and went our separate ways.

# Chapter 5:
## More Doctors

Two years later my symptoms changed again. Randomly, my hands and fingers would visibly quiver back and forth. I had felt something similar during the mall incident a few years before. This was now happening two to three times a month. My son was born during this time, and holding him became nearly impossible when these symptoms erupted. I went to see Dr. Simon again. I described my symptoms to him and even tried to show how much my hands and fingers moved during an episode.

Instead of his usual joking manner, he stoically said, "Did your parents or grandparents ever have any degenerative motor neuron diseases like Parkinson's or Lou Gehrig's disease?"

I said, "No, nothing like that in my family."

He continued, "The reason I ask is that I've seen these same symptoms in other patients when they're in the early stages of Parkinson's."

That statement shocked my wife, and I almost fainted. "You're shitting me, right?" I yelled.

He told me, "There are no specific tests that exist to diagnose Parkinson's disease, but we need to begin further evaluations. There's one doctor on my staff who's specifically trained in movement disorders. With your permission, I'd like to bring him in to consult on your case."

I agreed, and a few minutes later there was a knock on the door, and another doctor entered the room. He introduced himself as Dr. Zhou. I had trouble understanding him because he had a thick Chinese accent. In the next two days he put me through a battery of tests. Afterward he said that Parkinson's was a possibility, but he refused to rule out other neurological reasons. I was convinced that nobody really understood what was wrong with me, and going from doctor to doctor was just a waste of time and, more importantly, money.

Since the symptoms were so infrequent, Dr. Zhou prescribed three different drugs. He told me that if it was the beginning of Parkinson's, these drugs will show an improvement in my condition. If there was no improvement, he told me to stop after eight weeks. I was to return every week for two months to follow up on my progress.

Even though the dosage was changed every week, the only thing the drugs appeared to do was cause night terrors, projectile vomiting, and the ever-popular diarrhea. I was miserable. My wife was frightened of me because I woke up screaming in the middle of the night. I only took the medications for one month before stopping. They had zero effect on the symptoms. During these episodes there was no pain, just weird vibrations, so I decided to tough it out with no medications.

*Why me? I thought. What had I done to deserve this? Would I ever have a normal life if it continued?* I saw no light at the end of the tunnel, and I was quite sure my wife was tired of hearing about it. I started hoping for a miracle.

## Chapter 6:
# *Embarrassment*

Both Dr. Simon and Dr. Zhou told me my condition wouldn't get any worse. They were wrong.

A few months before my thirtieth birthday, the condition mutated once more, this time in the worst possible way. This turned out to be a particularly difficult time in my life. The vibrating fingers and sensitivity to temperature were no big deal; I found ways to hide these episodes. What I couldn't hide was the inability to control my arms. I guess you could call the phenomenon a "spasm."

The only way I can describe these symptoms is to imagine a combination of hitting your "funny bone" and getting electrocuted, both at the same time. Just one of these events is bad, but the two together will fuck up your life in ways you can't even imagine.

I'll never forget the morning of my thirtieth birthday. Late December in Peoria, Illinois, can be miserable, and this day was no different. When I awoke, the temperature was a balmy twelve degrees below zero outside, with winds gusting to thirty-five miles per hour. The forecasted high temperature that day, with wind chill, was ten degrees below zero! We're off to a great start.

I decided to make my family chocolate chip pancakes. I consider myself an expert pancake designer and baker. The pancakes I create are works of art. Nobody else was up yet, so I made three for myself. While bringing the pancakes to the table, I suddenly felt like I was being electrocuted. Without warning or control, I flung the plate into the ceiling, shattering it into a million pieces. One of the pancakes stuck to the ceiling, one somehow attached itself to a spinning ceiling fan blade, and one stuck to a window.

"What the hell just happened?" I yelled. I had to sit down for a minute to try to understand what just happened. I'd never purposely throw the most amazing chocolate chip pancakes into the ceiling, so why'd this happen? After another minute of self-introspection, I came to the conclusion that, hopefully, this was just a fluke event. A minute later I was busy cleaning the ceiling and the windows. As I cleaned the table, I decided to turn off the fan. The pancake lodged on one of the fan blades fell right onto my face. It was like slow motion; I could see it falling but stared at it thinking perhaps I was dreaming. Splat, right on my face. If I hadn't felt stupid before, I sure did then. I said a few choice cuss words then got busy cleaning my face, the fan, and the floor.

I had to vacuum the plate debris, and the noise woke my wife and our son. My wife found me on a ladder, finishing the ceiling. I had to explain what happened. Her response was, "Christ, Mick, so, on top of everything else, now we have to contend with these new 'spasms'?" She went back to bed without even saying anything about my birthday. After cleaning, I made more pancakes and carefully brought them to the table. There were no problems this time.

The rest of the morning and afternoon were completely normal, but then it got weird. I had been invited to a Christmas party that night at my friend Scott's house. Originally, it was supposed to be a surprise party, for my thirtieth birthday, but Scott accidentally "butt-dialed" me. He was talking to another friend about the party, so I heard the details. I called him and explained what happened. We decided to make it a normal Christmas party and invite our friends.

Scott was thirty years old. His wife, who had just turned twenty-one years old, looked like she could be his daughter. Her name was Emerald. When he first introduced Emerald to us the year before, we thought that was her "stripper" name. Turns out, it was her actual name. All of our friends thought the age difference would be a challenge, but Scott and Emerald seemed happy. She was actually a nice person, and Scott didn't try to act her age. I enjoy giving Scott a bunch of shit over the age difference, so when I had a party the year before, I added an additional note on the invitation sent to Scott that read, "Milk and cookies will be served after dinner." Good friends can do this to each other and nobody gets upset. Emerald was a pretty good sport about the constant ribbing, and Scott was eager to show her off.

Scott had just built a brand-new house, and it was stunning. When we arrived, Emerald met us at the door wearing a long, formal evening dress. We immediately felt out of place. Her dress had a sheer lacey top with a plunging neckline. I tried not to stare, but apparently my eyes told a different story. I felt a sharp pain when my wife elbowed my ribs. Apparently, she'd felt I had stared long enough. "Stop staring. You're embarrassing yourself," she said in a hissing voice.

Scott came bounding down the stairs dressed in a tuxedo and shouted his customary, and excessively crude, greeting: "Mickey Kingston Anderson, so how the fuck are you? So, King, how is that rash on your groin healing?" He immediately covered his mouth with his hand and acted like he hadn't meant to say that statement out loud. Then he laughed heartily.

My friends, along with everyone else I went to school with, are aware that my middle name is Kingston. I can't imagine a more embarrassing middle name than Kingston, and Scott loves to rub that fact in my face by constantly calling me King.

I laughed and responded, "Great, absolutely great! Hey, you still have that yellowish discharge from your dick that you were so worried about? Have you told Emerald how you got it? I'm no doctor, but experts on the internet believe excessive masturbation causes this condition." We laughed loudly as usual. The more obnoxious our greetings became, the closer we got as friends. Sure, we're degenerates, but we enjoyed it.

Scott put his finger up in the air. It was a gesture for me to hold any other insults in check, for just a moment, while he patiently waited for our wives to finish their pleasantries. When he was confident that my wife could hear, he continued in a bellowing voice, "Hey, where's that eighteen-year-old hottie you had over here yesterday?" He laughed loudly, always proud of himself for coming up with new zingers.

My wife absolutely hated our crude greetings. "You two are so childish," she reminded us.

Emerald said, "He will never grow up."

"Hell no, sweet tits," said Scott. "If you don't grow up by thirty, you don't have to, and by the way, you do have sweet tits." It was an awkward moment as we all stared at Emerald's chest—you know, just to be sure. She finally put her hands over her breasts as she felt everyone's eyes converging there.

Scott handed me a red Solo cup filled with some weird and excessively expensive alcohol combination and said, "Here, drink this before it gets warm. It will grow hair on your balls." He started to give me a tour of his new house. Unfortunately, I only made it ten feet before that weird combination feeling of electrocution and hitting my "funny bone" occurred. The resulting spasm caused me to throw the cup into the kitchen ceiling, splashing the drink on everything and everyone, in its path.

"What the fuck, Mick?" yelled Scott. I apologized and told them I had a medical problem and was really sorry. My wife explained the spasm event that had happened earlier that day and said I was seeing a doctor about the episodes. Luckily, no other guests had arrived, so just my wife, Scott, and Emerald witnessed this calamity. I asked for towels and used a chair to clean the ceiling and the fan, table, floor, and cabinets. It took twenty minutes to finish cleaning. Only then did I attempt to put the episode behind me.

My wife stuck her finger in my chest and said, "Whatever it takes, you make damn sure that doesn't happen again."

An hour later, thirty more of our friends were at the party having a good time. Scott was showing everyone his new "man cave" in the basement. His house has the largest basement I'd ever seen. There are two large sides. The main side was eighty feet long, twenty feet wide, and fifteen feet high, complete with a projector-screened Xbox, video arcade games, a small basketball court, and huge TVs at both ends. The second side was the same size, and had a full-size bar that looked like it came right out of the TV show Cheers. It was complete with two pool tables and a ping pong table. This house is a man's dream and simply amazing.

Scott and I began playing a friendly game of pool. Every time one of us scratched the white ball, we called it a penalty shot. The penalty was a shot of tequila. I won, with only one penalty shot. Scott didn't fare as well, with four penalties. Scott loudly proclaimed to everyone that I was the pool champion and handed me another drink in one of his expensive glasses. I didn't even get a chance to take a drink when my spasm happened again. This time it was witnessed by over twenty people.

Imagine trying to explain to someone who invited you to their house, why, for no reason, you threw a drink into their ceiling—not once, but twice. Embarrassing isn't a strong enough word to describe how I felt. I was so distraught that I felt like throwing up. After I'd cleaned up the mess, vacuumed the glass shards, and apologized repeatedly, almost an hour had passed. From that moment on I was the elephant in the room. I could hear the whispers from people about my behavior, and it hurt. My wife was so embarrassed that she insisted we leave. I've never been an emotional person, but I couldn't fight back the tears as we left the party. After this episode I became a social recluse once again. I was so terrified of this new behavior that we didn't even go to our relatives' houses for Christmas. Obviously, I didn't want to go to any parties, but once word got out about my behavior, none of my friends were stupid enough to invite me over anyway. I wouldn't even go to a bar for fear it might happen again. This is when I came up with a most fitting name for my condition. From this point forward I called it "Mick's Curse." Perhaps you can understand why I said this was a particularly bad time in my life.

Depressed and demoralized, I returned to Dr. Simon. I was in no mood for jokes, just answers. He had me admitted to the hospital for additional tests. The first one was something called a high-density EEG. That test revealed unusual, elevated brain activity. He showed me computer printouts from the test and circled the areas of concern. I'm a car guy, and to me the printout looked like my number seven spark plug wasn't firing. The next test was to check for a possible brain infection. I had an operation to drain a small amount of cerebrospinal fluid. Finally, another round of blood testing was performed.

Afterward Dr. Simon said, "Mick, you remind me of a puzzle with one thousand pieces. Everyone here is trying to assemble this puzzle correctly, but now we find out that not only have you lost two hundred of the pieces, you also lost the instructions as well. Without these lost pieces we can't put you back together." He went on to give me the bad news. "There are times when medical science can't answer why the brain acts the way it does, and this is one of those times. Sometimes one part of our body has been over developed at the expense of the other parts. The testing we performed didn't specifically point to one diagnosis; however, the symptoms are not a good sign. I don't want to alarm you and your wife, but I'd be remiss if I didn't tell you that we think these symptoms are most probably from epilepsy seizures."

I wasn't in the mood for guessing and told him, "A few years ago you thought it might be Parkinson's. Now you think epilepsy?"

He told me, "A few years ago you exhibited shaking fingers and hands, classic symptoms of Parkinson's. I'm glad those symptoms have not returned. Epilepsy is easily treatable with new technology and drugs."

He went on to say, "There are new treatments for epilepsy. It's not the end of the world. Should we begin today?"

I said, "I won't take any more drugs. Nothing has worked so far."

My wife proclaimed loudly, "Yes, you will. You will try anything and everything available to stop these episodes." So, I was overruled and agreed to try additional medications.

So, once more, I was prescribed powerful drugs with many warnings on the bottles.

As before, not only were these medications unable to prevent the symptoms, but they made me lethargic and uninspired. I still felt the jolting electrocution feelings. I believed the medications were ruining my life even more, so I stopped taking all of them. I was done with doctors and done being a guinea pig. Dr. Simon, while still disappointed that I stopped treatment, said to me, "Mick, there'll be brighter days. Just remember, even during your darkest moments, courage and faith, are all you need to move forward." He had no idea what I was going through, so at the time I simply thought he was just a blowhard.

I was so depressed my wife thought I was suicidal, and perhaps I was. Life had lost meaning, and I had lost interest in finding a cure. I was in a deep and dark place, with nowhere to go but up. If it got any worse, I truly felt my life wouldn't be worth continuing.

That all changed when my daughter was born. She gave me a new purpose and a new sense of pride. Kids are quite a bit of work, but also amazingly rewarding. As she grew, I became less concerned with my own problems, and just marveled at what we created. While I wasn't whole, I was no longer broken either.

Even though I was originally against it, we also bought a dog. The kids loved him, and he grew on me. Our dog was able to tell when I was having a bad day and do something so cute to cheer me back up. He had a favorite toy that he slept with every night. It never left his bed, except when he sensed I was having a really bad day. Only then would he bring it to me, bark, and push it into my lap with his nose. It's impossible to be depressed when your dog brings his favorite toy to you in an effort to make everything better while your children crawl all over you wanting "horsey rides."

I began to think with a bit more clarity, and study my symptoms with an open mind and a new purpose. I decided to be the kind of man my children and dog knew I could be. First, though, I had to find that person buried deep inside my mind, and find some way to bring him back to reality.

# Chapter 7:
## Glimmer Of Hope?

It took a few months, but finally I started to get a sense of when my new electrocution and "funny bone" symptoms were about to happen. At first, I tried to hold onto to a desk or a table to control them, but that didn't work. When you get shocked, your body reacts aggressively to evade the source of electricity with powerful muscular contractions. My body believed I was getting shocked, so I had enormous strength during these electrocution-like episodes and was easily able to flip large desks or tables. This kind of spasm is impossible to hide and very embarrassing. When you worry about when, not if, a spasm will take place, your life begins to lose meaning.

But then I had an accidental discovery of something that helped me more than any drug therapy.

One day, while shopping for tools, I felt the sensation forming in my body. I was both angry and depressed that this was about to happen in a tool store, with fifty people nearby. I had only a few seconds to decide what to do, so I dropped quickly to my knees and prayed that the event would pass without complete embarrassment. I put my arms around myself and waited for the explosion. The electrocution jolt caused my arms to squeeze tightly for about fifteen seconds. I could hear popping and cracking from my joints as the intense experience passed. Even though it felt like I pulled both shoulders out of their sockets, it wasn't as bad as I had feared. I realized that hugging myself worked to deflect the reaction. I literally wrapped my arms around my body and either sat down or kneeled to make sure I could stay in control. When someone asked what was wrong, I'd say that my stomach was hurting, and I'd be OK soon.

Words cannot express how important this accidental discovery turned out to be. It looked weird, I'm quite sure, but not as weird as throwing things into a ceiling or flipping over desks.

Eventually, Yael decided she'd had enough of the drama, and filed for divorce. She wanted to spend more time back in Israel and to introduce the kids to her extended family. This was a huge setback. The added stress made the sensations more obnoxious and harder to hide, and I became even more self-conscious. Thankfully, my recent discovery meant I had a plan of action I could take to defuse the situation. It was tough, but I made it through these difficult times with the help of family and a few close friends. The fewer people who knew about my medical issues, the better. I found that as a rule, you can rely on only five percent of your friends. Eighty percent don't care, and the other fifteen percent are glad you have problems so they can blab about you to their friends.

I decided to change tactics and went back to playing sports at a more aggressive level. I began to play basketball during lunch, and pickleball at night. I did this every single day. I was pleasantly surprised that participating in sports seemed to really help. Then I had a setback when the number of basketball players at lunch began to dwindle, and many times we couldn't get enough players to make a game. Amazingly, Scott was still a friend, and he wanted a partner to play racquetball after work. We began to play often, four to five times a week. It helped to prevent my quivering finger episodes and basically stopped the electrocution feelings. My depression disappeared as well, and I even started to smile again. The sensations began to ease up, little by little, every year. By the time I turned thirty-eight years old, they were gone. It was a wonderful time in my life because I basically forgot about my disorder for nearly two years.

Then, out of the blue, my condition mutated again. This time it seemed to take on a life of its own. I had an explosive episode so debilitating that I could no longer ignore the symptoms or hide their effects. I'm unable to come up with any catchy phrases to describe that day, so I'll call it "my first hypersensitive adventure." From that day forward, my life stopped being mine. My hands and fingers controlled my thoughts and actions, not the other way around.

# Chapter 8:
## Adventure

I was forty years old and still had no idea where my life was headed. So, I decided significant changes had to happen in my life to make sure I'd have a meaningful future.

I've owned a small computer software company for the last fifteen years. I create computer analysis programs for race cars. Now that my hypersensitivity is reduced, I can really concentrate on writing computer code. Business is booming, but so is the stress level in my life. I'm a workaholic, bound and determined to make my company successful. I'm so busy answering phone calls that I have no time to prepare shipments until late in the evening. So, every night at eight-thirty, my life turns into a comical mad dash to FedEx, DHL, or UPS which are twenty minutes away, so I can ship software discs or weather equipment to customers.

My life is a fine line between chaos and sleep.

I'd had one failed marriage already and didn't really have time for another relationship. That all changed when I met my current wife, Michelle. We met purely by accident. Our sons were in the same fifth-grade class together. We had never met before, but I had seen her at school functions. We were forced to talk to each other because of a boneheaded move on my part. I was coming out of the school cafeteria with my son, and she was going in to get her son. The door could open either direction. I pushed on the door to open it and she was on the other side of the door pushing it the opposite direction. I thought it was stuck, so I put my whole body into it, slamming it open. She was knocked off her feet.

While on the floor she said, "Did you think to check if anyone was on the other side before you slammed the door open?" I repeatedly said I was sorry, probably a few hundred times. It was just an accident, but it didn't stop me from being embarrassed. I helped her to her feet and immediately noticed she was attractive. She was impeccably dressed in a designer suit— not something you get off the rack at Walmart. Her wardrobe made me conclude she was someone's "high maintenance" wife. I thought about asking her name but concluded it would be an awkward question, especially since I'd knocked her to the ground.

A few weeks later I saw her again. I told her I was sorry once again. She replied, "It's OK. You're forgiven." We talked for a few minutes before I realized she wasn't wearing a wedding ring. I was having a great day, so I took a chance and asked her out for a drink. I figured if she said no, it wouldn't be a big deal; nothing would ruin the great day I was having. I had to admit, I'd been a bit surprised when she said yes.

Our first date was the strangest one I'd ever been on. When she told me what she'd planned for our first date, I assumed she was kidding. She informed me that every Saturday she volunteers at her church helping to feed the homeless people who lived in downtown Peoria. This Saturday would be no different, except that I'd be helping as well. I believe she was testing to see if I was a decent person before the relationship went any further.

My original opinion of her proved to be way off base. She was down to earth and genuinely a nice person. She'd had a miserable first marriage, so her brothers were wary of any new man in her life, especially someone like me with their own business. They told her to see if I made any money before the next date. She was laughing when she explained what her brothers had asked for, but I could tell she was really was frightened of making the same mistake with another man. I wasn't rich at the time, but I certainly wasn't poor. I brought a bank balance report to our next date in order to dispel some of her fears.

Michelle has a great job as a senior sales rep for a cancer drug company. She is outgoing, bubbly, and really good at her job. She can talk to anyone, about any subject, with a smile on her face. Unfortunately, my life has been a bit more difficult, so I'm the exact opposite around most people.

If I'm interested in what they're discussing, I'll join in the conversation, but otherwise I'm as silent as a whore in church.

Our relationship grew quickly. She understood my job, went to the race track with me, and supported my career. I tried to help her with her job as much as possible as well.

One of my favorite stories started when she'd had me impersonate her manager, who had refused to come to central Illinois to help her close a large contract. It was a risky decision on her part, but the doctor she was negotiating with was from a foreign country, and he didn't want to talk to a woman about financial matters. I never wore suits anymore, and the ones I had weren't up to her standards, so she and I went shopping for a new suit.

Two days later, we went to the doctor's office. I was introduced as the contract specialist manager. We used her boss's actual name only once, and from that point on, Michelle referred to me as "the money guy" during the negotiations with the doctor. It worked; we closed the deal, and the doctor signed the contract. Afterward, the doctor requested my business card, and of course I didn't have one. "I left them in the car, but if you need to get ahold of me, just contact Michelle," I replied smoothly. I thought this whole ruse was a ballsy move on her part—dangerous, yet necessary to keep another company from stealing her client. Once we left the office and returned to the car, we laughed so hard we started crying. We both knew at that moment that we were meant to be together.

Two years later, we were married.

I had few episodes during this time, so she knew nothing about my medical history. Well, except for the funny stories Scott told her about his Christmas party. He loved to tell her how I threw his expensive alcohol into his ceiling, twice. Everyone who heard the story always laughed, except me. I told him, "Hey, it was a bad time in my life. I said I was sorry, so can you give it a rest?" I still got embarrassed even years later.

She is a perfect partner for me. I have to go to race tracks to see customers, and figure out how to improve my software. Michelle loves racing, and she learned how my software works with the race cars. She is also an excellent salesperson. Another one of my favorite stories about

Michelle concerns a priceless interaction with a customer. The customer said he didn't want to spend $2,500 for my program and a weather station. Michelle said, "Let me get this straight. You have a $500,000 motor home, a $100,000 race car trailer, a $150,000 race car, and you don't want to spend $2,500 to help you win?"

Later on, the man and his wife came up to me, and he said, "Your wife visited us earlier. I'm not sure I need this, but my wife says I need to win more, so I'll take it. Well, that, and the fact that your wife shamed me into it."

His wife said, "He needs something to help him win, so we want your best weather station and also your software. Go ahead and write it up." I knew I had a great wife after that conversation.

Michelle's job requires frequent trips to Chicago, some two hundred miles away from our home, for three or four days a week. This really started to interfere with our life. One of the perks of my job is that I can work from anywhere. We decided that I'll come up to Chicago starting on Tuesday of each week. It worked out perfectly since her company pays for a five-star hotel while she is in Chicago. We get the same room each week which overlooks the popular Chicago expressway, I-55. From the windows in the room you can see several miles in both directions.

The episode that I call "my first hypersensitive adventure" began one extraordinary day in March. I had just returned to the hotel after buying shoes at a local mall. While munching on a snack I decided to watch the news on TV. A reporter was describing a heartbreaking story about a twelve-year-old girl named Stacey Robinson. According to the news, she was missing, and the family was convinced she'd been kidnapped. I figured she ran had run away or had just not returned home, maybe in an attempt to piss off her parents, and would return home soon.

A few minutes later I received a phone call from a customer. At about the same time, the news channel popped up a "special report" banner on the screen. A somber news woman said new information had just been released about the case. Video evidence proved she'd been kidnapped in broad daylight, only two hours before, from a nearby Chicago mall. They showed images of two people, their faces covered, forcing her into an old truck. I thought that was weird since I'd just left that same mall forty-five minutes ago. Then a picture of the little girl was displayed. I immediately stood up. "Holy shit," I said out loud. I was shocked when I realized we'd been standing in line at the Cinnabon store only two and a half hours ago! I remember her vividly because she'd dropped a quarter, and I'd picked it up and given it back to her.

I tried to focus more on the TV and less on the phone call when I noticed my little fingers on both hands began tingling. A few minutes later my ring fingers tingled. Within eight minutes the rest of my fingers and finally my thumbs joined in, but now the tingling sensation was replaced with a powerful throbbing sensation. I hadn't experienced anything this violent before. It was so brutal I was convinced that either my electrocution events were returning, or this was a serious heart attack. According to what I've read on the internet, if you suspect a heart attack you should cough or yell. So I dropped the phone, put my arms around my body and shouted, "I think I'm having a heart attack." The customer on the phone thought I was kidding with them. "I think I'm having a heart attack," I yelled again. He asked if he needed to call 9-1-1 for me. I felt the jolt as the electrocution feeling exploded. I had no control; I just squeezed myself for about twenty seconds. I heard popping and cracking sounds from my joints as my muscles attempted to jerk my arms from their shoulder sockets. I was sure it was a deadly heart attack, far worse than anything I had experienced before. After a few seconds I was finally able to breath, but I was still unable to move my arms. Excruciating pain from multiple pulled muscles made any movement impossible. I had to force myself to calm down to release the tension in my muscles, but the pain was still debilitating.

Thirty seconds later, the pain and unusual vibration in my hands began to subside. I told the customer, "Thank you, but no, I feel better. I'll get my wife to take me to the doctor." The sensation was still strong for another two minutes, but the pain finally relented. Within ten minutes my fingers and hands began to return to normal.

I swallowed two aspirin just in case the condition was caused by blood clotting. I did a few self-tests of hand, eye, mouth, and tongue movements I had read about to check for stroke, and it all seemed normal. I tried stretching and moving my fingers. Only the pulled muscles still hurt; the rest of my arms, hands, and fingers were completely normal. Michelle was working forty miles away that day, so just to be safe, I decided to have the hotel courtesy van take me to a prompt care clinic.

At the prompt care clinic, I explained my sensations. I made the mistake of telling the nurse I thought it was a heart attack. When you say "heart attack," they pretty much attack you with tests. First one was blood pressure, 112 over 72. The nurse said, "Is your blood pressure always this low?"

"I play racquetball or basketball five times a week so, yes, pretty close," I replied.

She said, "Then I doubt a heart attack is your problem." After a battery of expensive tests, they pronounced me as healthy as an eighteen-year-old. After an hour of observation, they released me.

I went back to the hotel. I wanted to take it easy and watch TV. The kidnapping story was back on. Not a hint of throbbing in my fingers. I thought the entire thing was my subconscious fucking with me. I wasn't sure how, or if, I'd tell Michelle. I had to make software changes so I focused on work.

I create complex mathematical equations in my software, and I was able to solve a difficult problem. The excitement of finalizing this formula allowed me to forget about the pain in my shoulders and the electrocution event. Thankfully, immersing myself in work helped to take my mind off the entire situation. Two hours later the episode left my thoughts.

# Chapter 9:
## *Revelations*

That night my wife returned from her daily life visiting doctors in medical offices. Nearly crying, she said, "I had a tough day, Mick. It wasn't fun. A doctor yelled at me because the revised dosage levels hadn't been released yet. I'm exhausted, but hungry, so let's get dinner." I could tell now wasn't the time to discuss a possible medical issue, so I let her decompress.

There was a restaurant nearby she wanted to try. It was pricey, but she has a company credit card for her meal; I just needed to buy mine. I'm a self-described cheapskate, so this is a perfect arrangement.

Many really good restaurants are older, well-established businesses. This restaurant was one of those. It was coincidentally called Mickey's and was established in 1919, so probably not named after me. It was located near an old warehouse district. It took us just under twenty minutes to drive there around seven p.m. We listened to the news on the way.

The top story was the kidnapping of Stacey Robinson.

While we were at a stop light, my little fingers started to tingle. Within forty-five seconds, my ring finger started up just like before. I thought, *Damnit, this isn't good*, and shook my hands trying to get rid of the sensation. The light turned green, and an impatient driver in the car behind me honked. I shook my hand again and heard two honks from the car behind me. I continued to the restaurant. Michelle was on the phone talking to her boss about some new sales tactic and thankfully didn't notice. I decided not to say anything to Michelle. Within ten minutes my hands returned to normal, one finger at a time.

The symptoms started again. My little fingers started to tingle, then the rest of the fingers joined in minutes later. About five minutes later the tingle turned into throbbing as we arrived at the restaurant. When I walked around the car the sensation subsided. I opened my wife's door, and the tingling feeling happened again. I thought, *Maybe the doctor at Creighton was right; it's a nerve problem, and the neuropathy is returning.* I extended my arms again and opened my palms like people do in church. *Almost no sensation,* I thought. *Well there goes that theory, neuropathy would hurt all the time; it wouldn't come and go.*

Michelle said, "Let's go already."

I spun around, hands still in the air, and my fingers started to vibrate again. It seemed like the direction mattered. The only thing in that direction was a large row of warehouses that stretched for about a mile.

*Great, I have a tracking beacon in my hands,* I thought. To my amazement, when I turned the open palms to the farthest warehouse my fingers started to throb, when I turned away, they slowly subsided. I laughed out loud at this turn of events. I was mildly concerned that I might be losing it—whatever "it" was.

Michelle asked, "What's so funny?"

"Nothing, just remembered a joke."

I won't bore you with the dinner gossip; the food was great. We paid and left. Michelle's car was low on fuel, so I stopped at a gas station a mile away. I put her company card in the machine and started to fill the gas tank. I had to monitor the filling process because the automatic shutoff kept kicking off the gas pump. It's really annoying when the pump would run for a few seconds, then kick off, over and over again. After four or five attempts it finally continued to pump, and my mind wandered.

Human brains are amazing organs, at least in most people. My brain, apparently a bit more primitive, brought up images of boobs and cool drag racing cars. Yes, that's a weird combination of thoughts, but that's how most men's minds work.

I felt the tingling sensation in the little fingers first, then within five minutes the rest of my fingers joined in. The sensations grew exponentially every ten seconds or so. This lasted another three minutes, and I was again convinced this was a full-blown heart attack. My fingers began to visibly quiver. I realized the electrocution feeling was about to return, so I put my arms around my body and held on. I felt the jolt. I wasn't sure why, but during all of this drama, I noticed a rusty old Ford van, windowless and covered in gray primer, pulling into a different gas station on the other side of the street about a block away. The electrocution event subsided after about fifteen seconds, but the feeling of hitting my funny bone continued. I turned away from the van to take the hose away from the tank. I figured if I was going to die from a heart attack, at least I'd put the gas dispenser back into place. I was astonished that the throbbing was reduced; it was still really bad, but not overpowering. By the time the receipt had printed, the driver had run into the store down the street and quickly exited. He jumped into the van and sped away in the direction of the restaurant we had just left. In a minute the throbbing subsided just enough to be tolerable. However, if I opened my palms and pointed toward the direction where I last saw the van driving, the finger episodes slowly began again. *What's wrong with me?* I thought.

At that point my wife noticed me and said, "Hey, dork, why are you doing the 'royal wave'?"

I responded, "What do you mean?"

She said, "The queen of England waves like that." She did the same thing, moving her hands without lifting her arms, just to show how stupid it looked. We got into the car and I immediately started to tell her the story of my throbbing hands. She said, "I'm really tired; is this truly important? You wake up at night just when I need to wind down."

I decided to tell her anyway. "I went to the hospital today. I thought you should know. Everything is OK. My hands and fingers were throbbing in a weird way, so I thought I was having a heart attack. They said I was as healthy as an eighteen-year-old and let me leave."

Michelle knows about heart attacks and strokes and insisted on performing a few tests on me in the car. Pushing my hands, making me move my facial muscles, made me say difficult sentences, and other tests usually run by doctors. She said, "I don't see anything wrong either."

I added, "My hands vibrate and throb, then it feels like I'm getting electrocuted. It just happened again and it's driving me crazy."

I was less concerned now about a heart attack and more interested in the van and warehouses. I purposely drove in the wrong direction, back toward the warehouse area. This caused my wonderful, loving wife to dryly say, "You're going the wrong way, Einstein."

This is how strange my mind works. Instead of immediately telling her some story to appease her and make the problem go away, my thoughts fell inward to memories buried deep inside my brain. This will seem weird; however, I'm convinced my brain enjoys messing with me. The strangest memories will pop up at the most random times. What popped into my mind at this point was a radio show called, *Bob and Tom* from the Indianapolis area. The hosts are popular for their extremely funny "Man Humor" episodes.

The radio personalities act like they're a legitimate "life advice" call-in show called *Mr. Obvious.* The caller always begins with, "I'm a long-time listener, first time caller." One of my favorite episodes is called "Moody Wife." This begins with a guy who calls in for advice about his wife's constant complaints. The caller says, "She'll compliment me one minute, then the very next breath, she'll insult me." He continues, "For example, I put this bookcase together and she said, 'Hey, nice going, Einstein,' which made me feel great, like I was smart. But then she follows it up with, 'You put the shelves in upside down, you jackass.' This made me feel bad, Mr. Obvious." The radio host, Mr. Obvious, tries to explain to the caller that his wife was using sarcasm, but the caller doesn't understand. The caller wonders if there's a pill his wife could take to make the "sarcasm" go away and make her "better." It's really funny, but I digress.

Long story short, my wife was using sarcasm. I told her I wanted to drive by a building nearby and it would just take a minute. She didn't believe me; she thought I was just confused, going the wrong way, and refusing to admit my mistake.

My fingers hadn't stopped throbbing the entire time. I put one hand up and started using it like a directional antenna. As we drove near the warehouse park, I immediately started to notice the fingers and thumbs vigorously throbbing when I aimed my palms toward the warehouse farthest away. Michelle was on her phone checking Facebook and some other site and didn't notice. When we came to the stoplight and I could point my hand toward the last warehouse, sight unobstructed, all my fingers went nuts, throbbing uncontrollably. My fingers were visibly quivering back and forth and I could feel the old electrocution event forming. I'm not exactly sure how, but I was able to prevent the electrocution event. I was so focused on this experience that it never materialized.

I saw something gray appear in my peripheral vision. I turned my head just in time to see an older, windowless Ford van. Since there are few vans with a similar primer color, it had to be the same one from the gas station. The van was driving through an opening in the fence surrounding the building. I saw a few people closing the gates behind it. After they had secured the gate, they opened a small door and went inside. A second later the large garage doors opened, and the van drove inside. I was so focused on the van and warehouse that I didn't realize the light had turned green.

Michelle said, "The invitation you're looking for is probably in the mail."

I said, "Invitation to what?"

She replied, "The invitation to keep driving. See that green light? That color means you can go. I promise you it won't get any greener."

I felt a little foolish and kept going.

Michelle already thought I was nuts, so I decided not to tell her about this latest episode. There was no doubt now. The farther I drove away from the warehouse area, the better my fingers and hands felt.

The van and warehouse were the source of my episodes. But why?

# Chapter 10:
## *Are You Nuts?*

The next morning was chaos, and my wife had only a few minutes to talk before leaving for work. She asked me how I felt, and I said, "I feel fine. Hey, remember me talking about my finger episodes last night near the restaurant? I don't think it's a heart attack anymore."

"Good to hear, Dr. Anderson," she said sarcastically.

For no logical reason I blurted out, "I think I'm sensing something going on at one of the warehouses near the restaurant we went to last night." I don't even know why I said this statement, and instantly regretted it.

Michelle said, "Mick, are you fucking nuts?" My wife doesn't cuss, so that made it even worse.

My brain kicked in again. All I could think of was that character Sheldon from the TV show *Big Bang Theory*. Often on the show he says, "I'm not crazy. My mother had me tested."

So I said something similar to my wife: "I'm not crazy. My wife had me tested."

I thought it was funny; seemed weird that she didn't.

She had to leave, but I told her, "Be ready for an interesting tale of intrigue and suspense when you get back from work."

She replied, "OK, dork. Did anyone ever tell you how strange you can be sometimes?"

I told her, "You do, every single day."

She continued, "I think you were dropped on your head too many times when you were an infant."

I replied, "Not sure about the 'dropped on the head thing.' Anyway, how many times can you drop an infant on their head before it's considered too many times?" Again, I thought I was hilarious, but she frowned, kissed me, and left for work.

The local news was still covering the kidnapping. They showed detectives at the girl's home carrying out some of her clothing in evidence bags and placing them in a police SUV. The reporter stated, "Inside the SUV are two special dogs." I get interested whenever I hear the word "dogs" so I listened more intently. The reporter went on to say, "These are special 'scent tracking' dogs that will smell the clothes and try to track where she has been taken."

I screamed at the television, "Good fucking luck with that; perhaps you should try that warehouse park." Then my mind decided now was as good a time as any to ponder the word, "scent": *is it the "s", or the "c" that's silent?* It amazes me that I'm capable of accomplishing anything, especially considering my mind is constantly visiting la-la land just when I need to focus on really important tasks.

I turned off the TV and started making changes to my software programs. Soon my thoughts turned to my fingers. I sensed the little ones almost beginning to tickle, then actually starting to tingle. In about ten minutes my other fingers started to throb and then my thumb. I looked up and half-jokingly stated, "I wonder if that van is on the highway nearby." A minute later my fingers were visibly quivering. The electrocution-like symptoms also appeared, but now in a more controlled manner. I decided to get out of the chair and walk over to the window to see for myself. I about shit myself when an old, rusty, primer-covered, windowless Ford van drove by on the highway. A weird slow-motion feeling occurred, similar to the mall incident years ago. I saw two people in the van through the windshield, then noticed a third man lying down sideways behind the seats. I was positive it was the same one from the night before. It was less than two hundred yards away. I had the same symptoms the day before; it was the reason I had gone to the hospital. Was it possible the van was on the highway yesterday as well?

I couldn't believe it. I had so many unanswered questions. I started to worry about my mental state, even questioning if I really saw this van last night and again today. After careful analysis, I concluded my mind wasn't messing with me. There was no denying that my fingers and thumbs sensed this particular van many miles before it was even visible, and that the van most probably was on that same highway yesterday.

I did some quick math. If I started to feel my little fingers over ten minutes ago and the van traveled at sixty miles per hour, it equals around ten miles. If these events were indeed true, then I was able to sense the van from over ten miles away! Why was I able to do this?

Once the van was almost out of sight the throbbing, and the slow-motion feeling subsided. If I turned my open palms toward where the van was last seen, the fingers started up again. I shouted out loud, "For Christ's sake! What's going on, Mick?"

I wanted answers. So I decided to find some immediately.

# Chapter 11:
## *The Quest*

Even though I really had to finish some software changes, finding answers became more important.

I jumped into my Jeep and drove up to the warehouse park. I had to test my theory—right now. I needed to prove what was responsible for my episodes. The only common denominator was that particular warehouse and van. I arrived at the warehouse district about nine thirty in the morning. I stopped at the beginning of the street and was disappointed to feel almost no sensations. I even drove right in front of the building and my fingers and hands were normal. I turned around, but before I left, I pointed both palms toward the building and got some sensation. I asked myself sarcastically, "Now what, Einstein?"

I drove to the gas station and felt nothing there either, so I decided to wait. I stepped out and stretched—no sensations. I opened both palms and used them as a directional antenna once more. I'd felt something, although faint, when I pointed west. Just like that it was gone, so I moved more south—nothing; east—again nothing. I then pointed north, and picked up a sensation. A few seconds later the sensation was gone. Finally, a light bulb went on inside my head. I said out loud, "Come on, Einstein, obviously the van is moving." I decided it would be better if I kept these thoughts to myself. *Mick, you're nuts. But if this is real, what does it mean?*

I decided to get lunch. About one thirty I returned to the gas station. I started to feel tired, so I took a "cat nap" that lasted two hours.

I was awakened to a slight tingling in my little finger. I got out of the Jeep and stretched. In about three minutes the sensation became stronger and was now picked up by the ring finger. Five minutes later the feelings

54

spread through the other fingers. One minute later my fingers were visibly quivering, and the old familiar electrocution feeling began. I looked up. "Holy shit," I said out loud. There it was, the same old windowless Ford van that I'd seen on the highway, driving down the road about a half mile away!

I watched the van pull into the street where the warehouse was located and stop in front of the fence. Two men jumped out, unlocked the chain holding the fence together, opened the fence, and let the van in. After the van pulled in, one man closed and locked the fence. Once the van drove inside the building, the episode subsided from an uncontrollable throbbing to an annoying vibration.

*Now what, Einstein?* I thought. I drove by the building. There could be no doubt now; the uncontrollable throbbing returned. It was late, time to go back. Michelle would be home soon, and I had plans to make.

# Chapter 12:
## Into The Abyss

The next day, the news was still running stories about the kidnapped child. A dramatic news conference about it was live on TV. They showed the mother and family taking turns crying and pleading for the safe return of the child. Then they showed pictures of the little girl, and it hit me; *Is it possible that this could be related to the van?*

Then a sinking feeling came over me. What if this had been happening for decades and I just didn't realize the throbbing in my fingers were connected to other kidnappings or criminal events? I thought about the shopping mall incident about ten years ago, where the man hid in the trunk of a car. *Holy shit,* I thought. *It all makes sense now. Or does it?*

Then I thought back to when I was young, under ten years old. I was convinced my mother had a kind of sixth sense. I tried to lie to her one day about why I was late and where I had been all afternoon. She put one hand up like a stop sign for only a split second while I talked, then said, "I can tell if someone is telling the truth. All I have to do is point my hand at them. Now why don't you tell me the truth, Mickey?" I remembered my mother doing the same thing when people came to the door trying to sell us something. She held bridge night with her friends every Tuesday, and I saw her do the same thing to friends when they told stories. She would just flash her palm up for a split second every now and then. It wasn't really obvious at the time, but those hands knew things! Too bad she wasn't a poker player; she would've been great.

When my mother felt I was old enough to understand, she told me that I had inherited a blood-clotting disorder from her side of the family called Factor V Leiden. Maybe I inherited hyper senses as well.

Unfortunately, my mother had passed away a few years ago so I couldn't ask her about these sensations. I thought to call my brother and sisters, and ask if they had similar sensations, but I decided that would be weird. That conversation would sound like this: "Hi, Dave, this is your brother Mick. By the way, can you tell when a bad person is within ten miles like I can? You can't? Hmmm, well, OK, great talk, see you soon, bye." I decided to keep it to myself, at least right now.

I was feeling pretty excited, but then I thought about throwing glasses of alcohol into the ceiling a decade earlier. That incident didn't have a criminal connection—at least, none I could understand. I asked myself, "Is it possible these episodes and the events are coincidental?" After considering the possible outcomes, I decided to throw caution to the wind and act on my suspicions.

As I contemplated this, TV stations announced emergency county-wide tornado warnings, and a fierce wind buffeted the hotel. It began to rain hard, followed by an intense hail storm. I felt like this quest to find answers was more important than some silly tornado warning, so unless I saw a funnel cloud, nothing would stop me. I needed to go over to the warehouse park and snoop around, so I hopped into the Jeep and drove over to that area. I had already proved, beyond a shadow of doubt, that the throbbing in my fingers only happened when I was near that warehouse or the windowless van. I was as excited as a kid in a candy store and felt more alive than I could ever remember. If this was genuine, then my life had a new purpose.

I jumped out and approached the warehouse. I started to feel my fingers beginning to throb, which meant the van was returning in the next ten minutes. Tornado sirens were going off in the adjacent town. About thirty seconds later, tornado sirens went off nearby. I was uncertain of my safety, so I scanned the skies. I've been through numerous tornado warnings and probably witnessed fifty tornados actually descend from the sky. This kind of weather event isn't to be taken lightly. When a lightning bolt hit a cell phone tower only a half mile away, I decided God was trying to tell me something. Perhaps tomorrow would be the day to find the answer.

I jumped in the Jeep and drove through the hail storm back to the hotel. I watched a tornado touch down from the window of the hotel twenty minutes later.

I hardly slept a minute Wednesday evening. Thursday would be our last day in the Chicago area. I had one day to find out if there was a connection. I arrived at the warehouses at nine thirty that morning, parked nearby, and acted like I was interested in property. I did the "royal wave" thing again. Since I had no serious throbbing while outside and saw no obvious clues that the people from the van were in the building, I began my investigation.

Right from the start, it didn't go well. I tried to go around the fence in the back of the building. I didn't see the sharp piece of metal protruding through the fencing and tore my pants and shirt trying to slip through. I was fortunate that I didn't get cut, but my shirt was torn about one foot on my back. My pants had the back pocket torn free, and my underwear was hanging out. Great, now I looked like a homeless person snooping around a building. I decided to return to the hotel to change clothes.

Less than an hour later I returned. I continued my investigation of the building. Then I made one of my more intelligent decisions. A voice inside my head told me, *Hey Einstein, just yell her name!* I couldn't remember her name, so I looked it up on my phone's news. I yelled at the top of my lungs, "Stacey Robinson, can you hear me?" I did this over and over, walking around the building, but didn't hear anyone yelling back. What I did feel was my little finger beginning to throb, meaning the windowless van was coming closer. Soon my other fingers began to throb, so I couldn't wait any longer. I returned to the Jeep.

I started the Jeep and drove through an adjacent lot about two hundred yards away just in time to see the van turn down the street. My fingers were turning out to be like Spider-Man's "spider sense." I was impressed with my ability to demonstrate with amazing accuracy the correlation of the van's proximity and the intensity of the episodes.

It was only ten forty-five, and thankfully the van didn't stay long. "Private Investigator Mick" went back on the job. I had a really bad feeling that if my investigation turned up something, I'd have a hard time telling the police about it. More importantly, how would my wife react? I visualized her calling the men in white coats to take me to the psychiatric hospital.

I went to the gas station and did my "royal wave" to tell me if the van was nearby. I had no episodes, so I decided to make another attempt at the warehouse. Perhaps they had a job and stored supplies there, which meant they would return at uncertain times. I drove the Jeep into the parking lot across the street. I decided to speed up my investigation because it was windy, and it looked like it could rain anytime.

I yelled the girl's name, over and over. Still nothing. This time I listened more closely for any noises, not just a child's voice. I was disappointed to hear nothing but wind. I decided to go around back and try again. This time I used a rock as a hammer to flatten the sharp metal piece that had destroyed my clothing. I made sure it wouldn't destroy my clothing again. I carefully slipped inside the fence and walked twenty feet to the far corner of the building. I began to yell, "Stacey Robinson, can you hear me? Stacey, if you can hear me, tap on something metal." I used the rock to pound on the brick exterior to make sure who ever was inside aware of my presence. I wasn't worried about any bad guys; I'd had no sensations in my fingers for some time. Even though this was nearly a deserted area, I still imagined that at any second someone would ask what I was doing or call the police.

I yelled her name over and over for about thirty seconds. Then I heard something that made my heart skip a beat—an unmistakable light metallic tapping sound coming from within the building. The sound hadn't been audible before. The wind made it hard to locate, but there was definitely something tapping inside the building. The sound was new and erratic. There was a flag pole nearby with a steel cable clanging on the pole, but this sound was different. I put my ear to the wall and could hear an echoing, metallic sound that wasn't normal.

So I yelled again, "If you can hear me, keep tapping, and try to tap louder. I'm here to help you, but I need to know where you are." As I ran to the other wall of the building, the tapping noises became louder and more frantic. They were chaotic and rapid, then slower, then rapid again. The sound originated just behind the south wall of the building. This location was thirty feet from the fence, and the farthest point from other buildings and the street.

I was caught off guard. I hadn't really expected to find anything, so I was unsure of how to describe my feelings at that moment. It was a strange feeling, a mixture of surprise and joy, but also serious apprehension. My heart began pounding so hard I heard it in my ears. I had a nagging thought that while this could be something important, it could also be a huge disappointment and embarrassment. I've lived through one embarrassing situation after another for my entire life and didn't enjoy those experiences at all. I was strangely detached from reality as I thought about the decision to move forward. I said a little prayer in hopes that a higher power would guide me to make the correct decision. A powerful voice inside me said: *This is important, Mick. Go ahead and take the risk.*

I made the decision to call 9-1-1, internally wrestling with how to explain this without (a)—being considered a nut case, (b)—being considered a suspect, or (c)—being considered both.

I was reminded of a quote from Nietzsche's book *Beyond Good and Evil:* "And if thou gaze long into an abyss, the abyss will also gaze into thee." At that moment I decided to cross the line from an innocent bystander to being neck deep in a situation in which I had zero control. It seemed my life was balancing on this one decision. I was staring into the abyss, desperately trying not to be part of it. I pulled my phone out and dialed the number.

I heard the phone ringing. Instantly the operator at the other end of the phone said, "9-1-1. What is your emergency?" I felt my little finger start to throb slightly.

"Oh, shit," I said into the phone, immediately wishing I had kept that thought to myself.

The operator repeated her question with a nagging, impatient demeanor. I yelled into the phone, "The kidnapped kid—." Poof, just like that, my mind went blank; I simply couldn't remember her name to save my soul. I yelled again, "I hope to God I'm not wasting your time, but I'm convinced I've found that kid that was kidnapped a few days ago."

I thought the operator would get angry, but she was a professional. She asked, "OK, what's your name?"

I responded, "My name is Mick Anderson."

I heard typing and she said, "OK, that matches the phone number you're using." After more rapid typing sounds, she said, "I have your location on 17th Street, near the warehouse district. Is that correct?"

I replied, "Ummm, not sure. I'm not from this area, and I can't see any street signs. The building number is 5980. I don't know the street."

The operator said, "We're dispatching a car to your location but stay on the line. I need to ask some important questions. Do you understand?"

I yelled, "Yes, but make it quick, I can sense the van is coming back soon." She ignored the whole "sensing the van" thing, thankfully.

I tried to calm myself to explain what was going on, but she had to do her job and directed me to answer her questions first.

The operator asked, "Are you referring to Stacey Robinson?"

I yelled, "Yes! That's her name."

She asked, "Did you see her?

"No," I replied.

She asked, "What makes you think this is where she's located?"

The operator brought up an excellent point. *Exactly how was I going to explain this?* I told her a lie. "I didn't see her. I'm looking at warehouses and heard metallic banging noises from inside the building. What caught my attention is the tapping noises are like Morse code for SOS, three quick tapping noises followed by three slow, then three quick again. Over and over, like someone needing help." I went on to describe how I had yelled, over and over, asking if someone was in the building that needed help. I described to the 9-1-1 operator how the pitch and pattern changed. I was pretty proud of my answer—my lie—especially given the amount of stress I was in and the amount of time I had to come up with a story.

She asked, "Are you in danger?"

I answered, "Yes, when the van returns, I probably will be. I sense it will be about five minutes before that happens."

The operator responded, "OK, get yourself to a safe location, and I'll stay on the phone with you. When you're in a safe location, let me know."

After thirty seconds, I said, "I returned to my car. I'm far enough away. Now what?"

The operator said, "You must not be armed when the officers arrive, so If you have any weapons, secure them now. You're reporting a kidnapped child, which is one of the most serious situations any police officer faces. The responding officers may have their guns drawn and we don't want them to think you're a threat."

I said, "OK, I have a concealed carry permit and I have a gun on me. I'll unload and secure it in my car. Let the responding officers know I'm unarmed."

She said, "Now this is very important. Don't make any sudden or threatening movements, keep your hands up, and under no circumstances are you to go near your gun. Am I clear?"

"Oh, I won't, don't worry," I responded.

My fingers were starting to throb now, so I knew the van was closing in. "I hear police sirens. Is that them? I know the van is close. Hurry them up."

Then the operator asked the question I had been dreading, "Who's close?"

I thought to myself, *OK, Einstein, now what do I say?* I could feel my story beginning to unravel. Even with the best of intentions, I was quite sure I sounded like a crazy person.

I panicked and told another lie. "I heard them say they'd get breakfast and return in a few minutes."

Silence on the other end of the line, and then she said, "Um, alright, breakfast at nearly eleven a.m.?"

I thought to myself, *Nice going, Einstein. Who eats breakfast at 11 a.m.?* The sirens were getting louder, but then I noticed that my hands were now throbbing less and less.

I dug myself a bit deeper into the hole by telling her, "The van is getting farther away." I instantly regretted my decision to say anything because she immediately asked, "How do you know? Can you see the van? What kind of van? What color is the van? How many people were in the van?"

*Mick, you're a dumbass. Get off the phone as soon as possible before you say something even more stupid.*

I told her, "The police are here. Can I get off the phone now?"

She hesitantly said, "Yes."

# Chapter 13:
## You're A Suspect

**I** met the police near the fence. They had guns drawn and told me to keep my hands up.

I wasn't surprised and immediately complied. Again, my mind wandered, reverting to my fire arm training classes. We learned about the golden rule—the one about never having your finger on the trigger unless you were about to shoot. For the first thirty seconds after they exited the police car, both officers had their fingers on the triggers of their guns. I thought, *These officers are breaking the golden rule. They're not practicing safe gun handling precautions.* Crazy, right? Welcome to my mind.

Once they patted me down, I was placed in handcuffs as a "precaution." They asked where I kept my weapon. I told them my gun was secured in the glovebox of my Jeep. One policeman asked for the keys to my vehicle so he could secure my gun while the other one held on to me. Once the other officer returned, the questions began, one after another.

They asked me my name and took my ID. Then they asked me to describe why I thought Stacey Robinson was in the building. I was just going to address this question when I told them, "Listen. . . Do you hear the tapping noises?"

One of the officers said, "No. What tapping noise?"

I said, "Quick, we need to go around the building to the south side so we can hear them better. If you scream her name, the tapping will change." I nearly had to drag the officer with me so we could get closer to the fence. I started yelling, "Stacey Robinson, the police are here with me! If you can hear me, keep tapping, but change the pitch so we know it's you." Sure, enough the tapping changed; it got louder and more frantic.

"Do you hear it?" I asked the policemen as we walked closer to the area where the sounds were the most noticeable.

In an impatient bark, the older officer said, "No."

I realized my ears were trained for this sound, but theirs were still assessing the situation. We were still about twenty feet from the best location, so I kept pulling them that direction. I said, "If we go around the fence you can hear it better." Both officers said an emphatic "No." I kept tugging them closer to the fence until we couldn't go further.

I was disappointed now, because I felt the tapping noise was obvious. Finally, I knew they both heard it when they placed their hands near their ears to pinpoint the location. The older policeman stared at me for about ten long seconds. He seemed to be studying my every movement. I said again, "Do you hear it? Please tell me you hear the tapping sounds. Do you hear how frantic the sounds are?"

He glanced at the other officer, then turned to me and tentatively said, "Yes, I hear it."

I frantically said, "We need to do something right now."

The officer continued to stare at me. He was attempting to figure out what I had to do with this entire situation, and I guessed that making me uncomfortable was part of the strategy. While still staring at me, he grabbed the mic on his radio and calmly said, "Code 30, Officers need assistance. 5980 North Seventeenth Street. Request supervisor to this location ASAP. Send fire and rescue, and we need an ambulance also." His gaze never left my eyes. Within seconds I heard police sirens in the distance, and soon twenty police cars arrived. It was pretty cool to watch the excitement. Their guns were drawn as they jumped out of their cars. I thought to myself, *At least these officers were practicing safe gun handling practices.* See what I mean about my mind? In another minute several fire trucks and an ambulance showed up.

Before I knew it, there was one officer on each of my arms, stopping me from moving any further. I was so animated to get them to listen that they probably thought I was on drugs, or would try to run away. They weren't going to take any chances.

I yelled, "Listen to the tapping sounds. Please, you need to get in there now." The tapping sounds now were chaotic and louder.

They seemed to be waiting on the supervisor to act. An older policeman said, "But we don't have probable cause, or a search warrant yet. This could be anything."

I blurted out, "What you have is someone frantically tapping on something metallic. Whoever is inside is trying to get your attention. I'm pretty sure this is an 'imminent danger' situation and no search warrant is required."

One of the officers said, "Twenty years of *Law and Order* and everyone's a fucking expert." I felt really embarrassed, totally understanding how little I knew about the law.

The policeman who called it in stared into my eyes for about ten seconds. I could tell he had decades of experience. Not releasing his eyes from mine, he yelled to the firemen, "I'll make the decision and be responsible. Cut the goddamn lock off now; let's get in there." I heard another officer say, "OK, you heard the sergeant, let's go."

It was thrilling to watch the fireman cut off the lock to the fence; those saws cut through a heavy chain like a warm knife to butter. The door had an anti-tamper device covering the lock, so they cut a hole in the door to force it open. Ten officers stormed into the building with guns drawn. They had ARs, shotguns, and handguns. I heard them scream over and over "Police department." A few seconds later each of them yelled "Clear."

Several anxious minutes went by before I heard police chatter on the radio, "Building cleared. Young female found handcuffed. Send in fire and rescue with a metal saw." Five fire fighters went in with tools. I heard grinding noises as they cut apart something metal. A minute later, they wheeled a stretcher into the building.

It took another agonizing minute until the paramedics wheeled an obviously frightened little girl out to the ambulance. She was crying hysterically, and her head moved from side to side as she tried to decipher what was happening. Silver handcuffs hung from her hands. The young girl had a red mark across her face where it looked like duct tape had covered her mouth. When they reached the Ambulance, she looked right at me for just a second. There was no doubt this was the young girl from the mall. I smiled at her as a tear streamed down my cheek.

Several paramedics immediately loaded her into an ambulance and did some preliminary diagnostics then radioed the hospital. A minute later they drove her away with a police escort.

I'd asked every police officer nearby about her condition. Each officer stared at me with the look of disgust, positive I had something to do with the kidnapping. They'd refused to tell me her condition, and one officer told me to keep quiet. Something told me she was going to be OK. I said out loud, "I really did it, I found her." I don't know why, but emotions got the best of me, and I broke down and started crying.

A few minutes later, the policeman who radioed for assistance walked up to me and said, "You will be a hero for finding that little girl, unless of course you're the person who kidnapped her. I can't stand people who kidnap kids. So, if you're involved, I'll make sure you spend the rest of your life behind bars. Is there anything you want to tell me?"

I looked up and said, "I had nothing to do with the kidnapping. Thank you for believing in me and doing something about it. That took a lot of courage, officer."

The officer stated, "I'm just doing my job and following my instincts. My gut tells me you're innocent, but I'll be following this case very closely."

The supervisor finally arrived and was briefed. The policeman who'd radioed the initial call in was told by the supervisor to read me my rights, and then put me in the back of a squad car. The supervisor informed me that I would being taken to a police station for questioning. I realized three or four news vans had arrived, and quite a few interested spectators as well. As I was being driven away, news reporters shouted questions and took video. It was a ten-minute drive to the precinct, and the entire time they were firing questions at me. I felt like nobody believed my story. I said, "It's just a case of dumb luck that I found her."

Once we arrived at the precinct, they took me into a room, and two detectives immediately came in and acted like tough guys. One introduced himself as Detective Harvey Miller and his partner as Senior Detective Mike Dooley. Both were fat, but Dooley was damn near obese. Dooley, in a raised voice, said, "You have the right to remain silent. Anything you say here can and will be used against you in a court of law. You have the right to talk to a lawyer for advice before we ask you any questions. You have the right to have a lawyer with you during questioning. If you cannot afford a lawyer, one will be appointed for you before any questioning if you wish. If you decide to answer questions without a lawyer present, you have the right to stop answering at any time. Do you, Mick Anderson, understand these rights I've just explained?"

I answered, "Yes."

Sarcastically, I thought, *Sure, what do I have to hide. After all, I found the girl by using my telepathic fingers. Go ahead, Mick, tell them that. Of course they'll believe you.*

Dooley said, "Can we ask you some questions?"

I said, "OK, but first, was that Stacey Robinson?"

Detective Miller said, "Yes."

I replied, "How is she doing?"

"We don't have an update on her condition," said Detective Dooley.

They had taken my cell phone, my gun, and everything I had in my pockets. They even impounded my Jeep for a forensics evaluation. I wanted to explain to my wife what was going on and asked to use my phone. Detective Dooley coldly replied, "Not gonna happen until it's analyzed."

"But I need to call my wife. She'll get worried if she can't reach me."

He told me to answer some questions first.

Dooley moved his chair right up next to mine and said, "OK, Mr. Anderson. Can I call you Mick?"

"Sure, Mike," was my somewhat smartass answer.

He smiled and stared at me for about ten seconds to let me know he didn't appreciate the answer. "Let's start from the top, Mick—the beginning of it all. What were you doing so far from your hometown? Let's see, it says you're from Mapleton, Illinois. Is that correct?"

"Yes, currently. I come to Chicago three to four days a week because my wife works up here. She sells cancer drugs to doctors here in the Chicago area."

They wrote something in their notebooks, then said, "So where do you stay here in Chicago?" I told them the hotel and address. Dooley said, "That's a good ten to fifteen minutes from the location you were arrested— err, picked up, you know, where the girl was found. Let's talk about the chain of events that brought you to this warehouse."

"So, Mick, what's the reason you would be in this warehouse park?" asked Detective Miller.

I told them I had been to dinner at the restaurant down the street a few nights before with my wife.

Dooley interrupted: "Name of the restaurant?"

I answered, "Mickey's."

They asked what I had for dinner, what I remembered from the menu, and what our waitress's name was. I remembered everything but the waitress's name.

Dooly clicked a button on a panel and the 9-1-1 call I placed earlier that day was played back. They focused on the part about the van and how I knew it was coming back. "We're having a hard time believing your story, Mick," said Dooley.

Three hours and four different detectives later, I was still there. Each one asked a similar question in a different way, trying to trip me up on my answers. I realized it was getting late, and my wife would be getting worried. So, I decided enough was enough, and told them, "I'm done, I need my phone to call my wife. So, either charge me, or I'm walking out of here." They left the room.

About ten minutes later they returned with my cell phone. I called my wife, and as expected, that call didn't go well either. I had no privacy; they sat right next to me during the call. I asked, "Can I get a little privacy?"

Dooley said, "Is she your lawyer?"

I replied, "No."

Dooley said, "Then no, you can't unless she is your lawyer."

I explained to Michelle, who had been trying to reach me for about an hour, that I was in police custody. She responded exactly how you'd expect a wife to react—she was frantic and full of questions. She wouldn't let me answer; just kept screaming at me. Eventually she calmed down enough to let me tell my side of the story. I told her the abbreviated version. Then for some reason my mind changed course, and I wondered why the word "abbreviated" needed to be so long. Why not say "AB," and have it stand for "abbreviated"? Finally, I snapped back. *Jesus,* I thought, *Why is my brain so bizarre?* I told her to come and get me.

When I hung up, I said, "She'll be here in fifteen minutes so either charge me, or let me go. Otherwise I'll call my lawyer."

Dooley said, "How about we talk until your wife arrives. Right now, we're not charging you with anything, but don't leave town until we're finished with our investigation."

Detective Miller told me, "If you're cleared of any involvement, you will be something like a hero to the world and her family. Until then, we, and unfortunately the media, are going to turn your world upside down. Either way, be prepared for your life to be turned into a circus, where you're the only performer."

A fingerprint technician came in and took fingerprints on a digital scanner. After he left, Detective Dooley said, "So, while we wait, Mick, why don't we talk about that van and how you knew about it again? Just to clear things up."

I then had a revelation. "How about we review security cameras and closed-circuit video in the area?"

Miller and Dooley looked at each other and said blandly, "Oh, will you look at that, Mr. Einstein here thinks he needs to tell us how to do our job." I realized they would've already done this and again regretted my outburst. The "Einstein" comment caused the *Bob and Tom* radio show to pop into my mind once more.

Dooley said, "While we review the tapes, tell us again about how you knew the van was connected." I gave them a story similar to the one I gave in the 9-1-1 call. "I just don't believe you, Mick," said Dooley.

Luckily my wife arrived. They had no evidence to hold me on, so they let me go. Their parting words were: "We will be working on this all night and will want you to come back tomorrow morning."

# Chapter 14:
## The Circus

My cell phone rang promptly at seven thirty the next morning. "Mr. Anderson, this is detective Dooley. We need to ask more questions—now. We have a police car at your hotel right now, and they'll bring you to the station." I hadn't even got out of bed when there was a knock at the door. My wife opened the door to two policemen.

"Mr. Anderson, we're here to take you to the station," one of them said.

I said, "Why can't I just drive to the station myself?"

The policeman said, "We need to show you something outside the hotel. Can we come in?"

I said, "OK."

They came in, pulled the shade from the window, and said, "This is why. Take a look." He held out his hand like he was showing me some exciting prize I'd just won on a gameshow.

I looked out the window and my jaw dropped. The parking lot had at least twenty television news trucks with satellite dishes pointing to the sky.

Reporters and cameramen were scurrying around in a frenzy that looked like how ants react when you step on their ant hill.

"Holy shit," I said.

My wife asked, "Is he under arrest?"

The police looked at each other and said, "No, ma'am, we're just here to make sure he gets through the sea of reporters and to the station."

I asked loudly, "How the hell do they know my name and where I stay?"

One of the policemen shrugged and said, "Leaks."

"A bit worse than a leak. More like a broken pipe," I responded.

I got dressed, and then we were escorted out of the hotel. As soon as the doors to the hotel opened, all hell broke loose. Reporters and cameras were everywhere, and microphones were shoved right up to my mouth.

The first question was, "Mr. Anderson, did you kidnap Stacey Robinson?" Then I heard twenty more hurried questions. One in particular caught my attention when a reporter said, "Some say you're a hero. Care to comment on how you found the child?"

I yelled out, "I'm not part of the kidnapping, just a concerned parent who caught a lucky break. We're thankful that the police were able to rescue her." They stuck me in the car and whisked me away. Michelle followed in her car.

The policeman who was driving said, "Be prepared; they're at the police station as well."

The other one said, "If you really just found her by accident, you will be a hero for sticking with it and alerting police, but I don't envy your life right now." He was exactly right; my life was about to turn into a complete mess.

We arrived at the police station to find a sea of reporters. We went around back, bypassing the mob and driving past a police barricade preventing reporters from going any farther. We stopped, and the officers opened the door and escorted me into the building. I heard reporters shouting questions from behind the barricades.

My wife arrived and sat in a waiting area while I was placed in a room with five people in suits, two of whom I knew. They had three TVs in the room, and one had paused footage on the screen.

Detective Harvey Miller said, "Mr. Anderson—Mick, if we can call you that—thanks for coming in. Let's get started. With us today are Senior Detective Mike Dooley, whom you have met. We have Special Agent Stan Holliday from the FBI, and Detectives Bob Mansfield and Bob Natale from major crimes division." I chuckled as my mind thought of the movie *Office*

*Space* and how the main actor referred to the two consultants as "the Bobs." These two detectives definitely reminded me of those actors. I waited for them to look at me and say one of my favorite lines from the movie: "So Mick, what would you say you do here?" I snapped back to reality, trying desperately to keep my mind in check.

The Bobs were fat, just like the other detectives, but Special Agent Holliday was far different. He was tall and very muscular, with chiseled facial features and a pronounced jaw line. He was eerily similar to Pat Tillman, the professional football player who gave up a professional football career to join the US military. I have the utmost respect for Pat Tillman—a man's man, selfless and patriotic. It was a sad day when it was reported that Tillman was killed during combat operations in Iraq.

Special Agent Holliday could've been his twin. He was an imposing figure—I guessed six foot eight inches tall, probably around 270 pounds. When he stood up to shake my hand, it appeared his head was going to hit the ceiling. "Wow," I said, "you look just like Pat Tillman. Anyone ever tell you that?"

The others laughed and said in unison, "All the time!"

I responded, "I thought I was looking at a ghost."

Then I asked what football team he played for, and he said, "Auburn University. I was going to the Chicago Bears, but I injured my knee in my senior year. Now I catch criminals instead of running backs."

I said, "Defensive end was your position, correct?"

He laughed. "Pretty good guess."

I shuddered to think how hard this guy could hit. Standing nearly seven feet tall in full pads and helmet, my guess is more than one running back changed directions rather than find out.

"You remember your rights from yesterday, correct?" said Detective Miller. I said I did, and Miller continued, "OK, great. Do you want a lawyer, or will you answer some more questions?"

"Go ahead, I can stop you anytime but I want to finish this," I responded. "But first, how is the little girl?"

Detective Miller answered, "Thanks to you, she'll be fine. She'll be leaving the hospital tomorrow after another day of observation." I asked Dooley, "Did you find the van and the three men?"

He said, "We found what we believe is the van. The fire department responded to a vehicle fire near the river yesterday. Turns out it was an old Ford van. When we ran the VIN, we found out it was reported stolen nearly two months ago. The plates on the van were from another vehicle reported stolen three weeks ago. Fire destroyed everything inside, but the primer color is consistent with your description. The men are a different story. We're reviewing security camera footage, but there are no clear images. They wore hats, sunglasses, and hoodies to disguise themselves every time they entered a store." Dooley said, "We have some security camera footage to show you." He clicked the play button, and a grainy video began to play.

I spoke up. "For Christ's sake, my old phone from ages ago took better video." They agreed; the images were nearly useless, even after they had been run through some of the special smoothing software to be enhanced.

"Mr. Anderson, you stated you were in the area to go to dinner, correct?" asked one of the Bobs.

I responded, "Yes—Mickeys, down the street from the gas station."

"What time?" said Dooley.

"Seven fifteen to eight twenty," I replied.

They clicked "play" on the other TV screen and showed images from within the restaurant. The time stamp was visible at the top of the screen. Dooley fast-forwarded it from seven fifteen to eight thirty. We weren't visible. "So, care to tell us why we can't find you?" said Dooley.

It took several tense minutes. I was beginning to panic, and then I saw the reason. "Look here, it's dark at eight p.m., but on the video, it's still light. Their time stamp clock is off, probably by well over an hour and a half," I replied. The detectives were unable to confirm my alibi initially, so they didn't believe me. Dooley fast-forwarded the tape, and finally my wife and I appeared inside the restaurant. I said, "OK, there I am with the wife." The timestamp on the footage was off by nearly two hours. *Whew*, I thought. *Question number one has been answered, and proven.*

# Chapter 15:
# *Why Waving?*

"OK, good, so you were telling us the truth about the restaurant," said Dooley. In an aggressive manner, Dooley spun his chair in a half circle and sat down about a foot from my chair. He leaned in toward me, no more than six inches from my face.

"Next question, Mick. Who're you waving to while you were at the gas station?"

I said, "Waving? What the hell do you mean?" He started the third TV with surveillance video from another warehouse, pointing to the gas station. Sure enough, there I was in all my glory, doing the "queen of England" wave. "So again, Mick, who are you waving to?" said Dooley.

I said, "I'm not waving at anyone. My hand went to sleep, and I was trying to wake it back up. Hey, fast-forward the video and you will see the same van I saw leave the warehouse. It's at the gas station across the street."

Dooley said, "Yeah, we know, we have been through the video ten times and know what it looks like." One of the Bobs clicked fast-forward, and sure enough, the van was exactly where I said it would be. In less than forty seconds it was gone, and I was waving in their direction. "So, your hand went to sleep twice?" said Dooley.

I lied and said, "I have sensitive fingers, a condition called peripheral neuropathy."

"Uh huh," said Dooley. "We will review that later; I have more questions."

TV number two was started, and they played the footage from the day we found her. You could see me driving down the street, exiting my vehicle, and walking down the road. They played footage from the day previous, and I was doing the same thing. Then they stopped both images at the same time, where I'm using my hand like a directional antenna but it looks like I'm waving at someone.

"So, Mick, who are you waving to?" said Detective Dooley again. Now everyone stopped what they were doing and stared at me. I'm pretty sure that intense "detective stare" is something they practice. Nobody said a word; they didn't have to. The longer they stay silent, the more uncomfortable the person sitting in my chair will become, until they panic. It's a pretty powerful tactic, and it might cause a guilty suspect to either confess, or say a complete lie.

I didn't miss a beat. Without hesitation I stated, "As I said before, I have a medical condition that causes my hand to throb from time to time, and this is the only way to prevent it. You probably have my medical information from the time I was born, but if not, I'll get it released to you. It will be in those reports."

"Bullshit," said Dooley.

I remained firm. "If you don't have my medical records, give me a release form to sign and we can take care of this right now. My doctor in Peoria is retired, but the records are still available at St. Francis Medical Center in Peoria, and Dr. Simon is in Chicago."

Suddenly the door opened, and someone brought in a medical release form. I signed it, and off they went. Dooley said, "OK, thank you, Mick. We will get that information, but let's cover a few more concerns we have."

Dooley asked, "Before yesterday, have you ever had any contact with Stacey Robinson, or her family?"

I knew where he was going with this question. He must have seen security footage from the mall where she and I had been in line together. I calmly said, "No, I don't know her, and I don't remember meeting anyone in the family before either. However, after watching the TV coverage, I realized our paths did cross at the mall the day she was kidnapped. We were in the same line together at the Cinnabon store, and she dropped a quarter. I picked it up and gave it back to her."

Dooley let out a sigh and leaned back in his chair. I could see disappointment on his face, as well as the others'. They had hoped to trap me, and it didn't work. Everyone wrote in their notebooks for a few seconds with frowns on their faces.

He spun another TV around and said, "Is this you and her together that day?" He hit play and the footage showed me picking something up and handing it to her. "What did you say she dropped?" he asked again.

"Like I told you before, it was a coin. I believe it was a quarter." Once we received our food, the footage showed her going one way and me going the other.

They stared at me for about five long seconds to watch my reaction. I had none. I said, "Yes, that's her and me in line. Never saw her again until they carried her out of the building yesterday."

# Chapter 16:
## *Evidence*

"We executed a search warrant on your hotel room and vehicles," said Dooley in an obviously annoyed tone of voice. He referenced his small notebook, then said, "We found a ripped pair of pants and a ripped shirt in the garbage can. Care to elaborate on this?" This one caught me off guard, but I told the story about trying to get behind the fence and tearing my clothes. This would be supported by the video evidence, and I asked to have them play that day again. No cameras were pointed the correct direction. Only one camera caught me moving toward the building before I disappeared and came back with ripped clothes.

This didn't impress them. Dooley said, "Were your clothes ripped because she put up a fight when you went to see her?"

"No, don't even go there, Mike. You know my clothes were ripped by the fence," I said. "Check the fence. There's probably torn fabric attached on the back corner."

Dooley said, "We already did, and yes there was fabric evidence retrieved." I started to panic a little about the word "evidence." I didn't like how that sounded.

They played the 9-1-1 call again where I told the operator they were going to get breakfast and would return. Dooley looked at me and said, "Mick, none of the cameras caught the van and you nearby at the same time. Matter of fact, the van left almost an hour before you arrived. We see the van return, but you're nowhere near it. You want to tell me how you knew they were going out to breakfast at, what, eleven a.m., when you weren't even in the video? Who goes out for breakfast at what, eleven a.m., Mick? That's your voice, Mick, correct? Why'd you lie to the 9-1-1 dispatcher, Mick? You couldn't have heard them; you were too far away. The only way you would've known when they would return is if you were in contact with the people in the van."

I replied, "I was worried that the people in the van would return, so, yes, I told a little fib trying to get the police response to be quicker. But I had nothing, and I mean nothing, to do with the kidnapping."

They started the "good cop, bad cop" stunts. The FBI agent, Stan Holliday, moved close to me, and gently said, "Listen, I believe you. I really think you're the hero here, but we need to convince the rest. Can you help us do that? We need to understand how and why you picked this building." I told another small lie. "We may want to move up to this area, perhaps put my business into one of these buildings. I wanted to check out if any of the buildings had any "for rent" signs. I don't need the whole thing, just a room for a small office with some storage. Guys, it really was just dumb luck that I found her. My curiosity took over when I heard the banging sounds."

Dooley said, "Interesting; you just called it 'banging' sounds, but you told us it was tapping sounds before. Was it banging or tapping sounds you heard?"

A red light went on inside the room, apparently a sign someone else wanted to talk to them. I didn't like being alone with the TVs, so, just for giggles, I clicked "play." Instantly one of the Bobs came back in and said, "Hands off the equipment." I was nervous and needed something to do. I had a good chuckle; seriously, what did they think would happen?

# Chapter 17:
## *Your Wife*

In a few moments all the detectives came back in and quickly sat down.

Dooley spoke first. "We just had an interesting talk with your wife."

Adrenaline shot through my veins and made me jerk up. I screamed at Dooley, "What right do you have to talk to my wife?"

"Easy, partner," said Dooley. "She agreed to speak to us just like you did."

I had no idea my wife was in the other room being interrogated. Now I was pissed. *Why would they talk to her? She didn't know anything relevant to the case.*

Dooley consulted his small pocket notebook, and after about ten seconds he said, "Care to explain your throbbing hand thing?" He continued, "According to your wife, you two discussed a 'throbbing feeling' in your hands when you—what did she say? Yes, there it is—looked at the last warehouse on the street. Mick, that was her exact quote. She said you told her something was going on in that building." He stopped for a few seconds to catch his breath, then continued, "So cut the shit, Mick. What's going on, and how did you know? Just tell us the truth. It will better for you in the end. We know you're connected, Mick, so make it easier on yourself and your family and tell us who else is involved. Nobody just stumbles onto something like this, Mick. There are no 'dumb luck' heroes, just criminals looking to be heroes in the media, when in reality they're trying to get away with something. I'm here to tell you: it'll catch up to you soon enough. We'll get you if we find out you took part in any of this, mark my words."

He paused a second to see if I'd say anything, but I just sat still with my arms crossed trying to control my anger. Dooley continued, "Mick, there will be a lineup when that little girl gets released, and you will be part of it, understand. You better hope to high heaven you aren't part of this. If you go to jail, other prisoners will know you hurt a little kid. There's a code of honor; they'll fuck you up, Mick. They're brutal on child kidnappers. Do you understand me, Mick?"

I calmly smiled back and said, "Yep, I understand Mike. I'll be happy to be in the lineup. I had nothing to do with this, and if you don't believe me, you will soon afterward. While we're at it, let's make everyone in the lineup yell her name, then ask the girl who's voice she heard outside the building. Does that sound like a good plan, Mike? I guarantee she'll say it was my voice she'd heard that day. She'll tell you I was the only one trying to get her home to her mother, even though you fat dumbasses were busy eating all the donuts."

Dooley yelled, "Bullshit, we had all hands on deck on this one. Don't piss me off, Mick. Nobody just stumbles onto something like this. Tell the truth, how'd you find the girl, Mick?"

I was furious, and I lost control of my emotions. In a knee-jerk reaction, I yelled at the top of my lungs, "I have a sixth sense about evil people."

The room went silent for about ten seconds. Then the detectives started laughing. Dooley, still laughing said, "A sixth sense huh?"

I continued, still yelling, "Yes, fat-ass, it allows me to sense really evil people and events. All I have to do is point my hands and fingers toward them." *What the hell did I just say?* I tried to stop myself, but pent-up rage made me powerless against the anger. I blurted out, "Don't be so quick to judge me. It's my 'gift'. I've had it for years. Lucky for you, I saved that little girl using it." Everyone in the room stopped and looked at me, then started laughing again.

"You're seriously trying to tell us that you can tell who's a bad person with your fingers?" Dooley said, laughing.

"Yes, you fat fuck," I yelled, "and I can prove it."

## Chapter 18:
# *I can find them*

I could sense my life was spiraling out of control, going from bad to worse in an instant. So, I told myself, *Screw it, I have nothing else to lose.* I yelled at the top of my lungs, "Listen fat-ass, I'll find the people responsible for Stacey's kidnapping for you. I'll find them without any help from you. To make it more interesting, I'll bet it won't take more than thirty minutes, either."

They continued to laugh at me, which only made me more upset.

"Either I call my lawyer, or you put me to the test. What's it going to be?" I yelled.

Dooley stood up, "Let me get this straight. You think you can find them in thirty minutes using your 'fingers'?"

I yelled, "You're goddamn right!"

Detective Miller stated flatly, "So what? If you can, that just means you're involved with the kidnappers. Doesn't mean shit to us, and it certainly doesn't prove your fingers have any special powers."

"Listen, you fat fuck, let's make it interesting. I'll do it blindfolded. Would that impress you?"

Dooley calmed down and said, "You want to be blindfolded to prove your fingers have the power to lead us to the kidnappers. You guarantee they'll be found within thirty minutes. Do I have it right so far?"

I yelled, "Goddamn right." I took out my wallet and pulled five one-hundred-dollar bills and placed them on the table. "I have five hundred dollars that says I can find them in thirty minutes, blindfolded. If I can, will that be enough to prove that I'm telling the truth?" They all looked at me for what seemed like five minutes. Nobody said a word. I knew I could find them; my little fingers already tingled. I've never lost a bet using my abilities, and I wasn't going to start here.

"Well, what's it going to be, Dooley?" I yelled.

Dooley reached over to the wall and flipped a switch. It appeared the switch was labeled "Mic". I concluded he turned off the microphone. "I might get fired for this, but I'll take that bet. I got five hundred dollars that says you're full of shit, and wasting my time," said Dooley.

He picked up the phone, still chuckling, and said, "Get me a police van and park it at the back door in five minutes. I want one black and white, plus I need a few men and another van as a decoy for the press. I also need a blindfold, a scarf, and duct tape. We have a large van in the back; have someone drive it in front of the press people to block their view of the back door." He hung up. "If you're wasting my time, Mick, I'll come down on you like thunder, got it? Give the money to Holliday. He will hold it so you can't take it back."

I said, "I will. But you give him five hundred dollars too, fat-ass." To my surprise Dooley complied and removed five hundred dollars from his wallet.

Holliday said, "I'm a bit uneasy about taking money from a suspect for a bet."

Dooley said, "Will you stop whining? Just hold the money for a half hour and don't worry about it. Nobody will know."

I said, "Anyone else want to get in on this?" They laughed and looked at each other, but nobody else wanted in.

"You won't be able to see because the van has no side windows, and the five of us are going. There will be a few squad cars, so don't try anything stupid," said Dooley.

"OK, let's make it even more interesting. I'll allow you to put cuffs on me in the van."

Dooley said, "No shit, Sherlock. You think I'd let a kidnapping suspect ride with us without cuffs on?"

They brought Michelle into the room. I told her my plan and that I'd see her in a few hours at the hotel. The stress was really getting to her. I'm sure she thought I was nuts, and perhaps having a nervous breakdown. Michelle tried to understand what I was saying, but it didn't make sense to her. She started to cry; it took a few minutes for her to calm down. I told her everything will be alright.

"Just trust me. I won't let you down." I told her.

We kissed and hugged, and then she was led away.

"Let's go, fat-ass," I said afterward. "Bring the Bobs and the football player with you."

# Chapter 19:
## *Turn here*

Once in the van they blindfolded me, then covered my head with a scarf and taped it over. I couldn't see anything. Then Dooley joined the cuffs already on my wrists with another set to a metal frame. I said, "Let's go."

I held up my palms and moved them around in a slow circle, then came back slightly. I felt it—thank God, I felt it! My little finger started to vibrate slightly, and I said, "They're this way, the way my palms are pointing."

I heard laughter so I shot back, "Start the clock, fat-ass."

We left with a barrage of cars and vans, each going different directions to throw off the media.

Thirty seconds later I said, "Why are we still going left? We need to go to the right, and quickly."

Dooley said, "It's a field, we have to wait for the next street."

I kept moving my hands toward the feeling. It wasn't getting stronger, and we had stopped moving. "Why aren't we moving?" I yelled.

"Traffic is terrible," Dooley replied.

"Then use the fucking siren, fat-ass. You aren't going to win this bet, even if you purposely try to go slow."

Dooley yelled, "I'm getting really tired of you calling me fat-ass."

I replied, "I don't give a shit, Dooley."

The sirens were activated, and we weaved through traffic. I was beginning to panic, but calm returned when my senses finally grew stronger. "We need to go to the right, and quickly," I said.

"Nope, gotta follow the highway, no exits here," said Dooley. We had to drive almost five minutes out of our way before an exit allowed us to go the correct direction.

Ten minutes later I started to get a solid read from my fingers. "Turn left. We need to turn quickly; they're moving to the left," I said.

The driver said, "There's an exit a quarter mile away." As soon as we got off the exit ramp, they turned off the siren.

"They're changing directions; it appears they're zig-zagging or the roads are not straight," I stated loudly.

"West on 95th," Dooley said into his radio. We traveled less than a mile then had to stop for traffic again. I shouted, "Stop! Hold on, they're definitely moving to the right, and getting farther away."

The siren was activated again and off we went. A few seconds later we turned to the right. "The feeling is getting stronger. In my experience this means they're nearly dead ahead about a mile," I said. Dooley turned off the siren. A minute later I yelled, "Hold on!" I was moving my hands to the left; they must have turned in front of us. "They're moving but away now, to the left." We turned to the left. "OK, I'm pretty sure they're moving in the same direction. Keep going straight. We're very close, less than half a mile."

I was still angry, but now my anger was being replaced with excitement. I wish I could've seen their faces. Nobody was laughing or talking anymore. I knew vindication was just minutes away.

One minute later I yelled, "They're turning to the right, take the next right! What just turned up there?"

"There are several cars and a truck that just turned. Next turn is about a block," Dooley said.

We turned, and immediately I yelled, "Within a quarter of a mile—really close." I turned my hands to the left. "Hold up, they're turning to the left again. What just turned left up there?"

Dooley said in an excited voice, "Red truck, looks like a Dodge but not sure." Dooley told the driver, "Run the light." I heard the engine roar, then horns honking and tires squealing as we ran through the red light. "I didn't want to be behind traffic. Now we have some open lanes," Dooley said.

My fingers were quivering back and forth, well beyond the throbbing feeling a minute before. I began to feel the electrocution building inside me. I heard Dooley tell the others, "Jesus, look at his fingers. Mick, what's going on with your fingers?"

"I told you, Dooley, they quiver when really sick and twisted people are nearby. They're close. My thumbs are quivering and that means a few hundred yards dead ahead."

The electrocution feeling was now bothering me, but I controlled it. Twenty seconds later I yelled, "Right turn Clyde!" (That's a line from the movie, *Every Which Way but Loose*.)

Dooley said, "Shit, he's right. That truck turned to the right. Is this bullshit, Mick? You can see out of your blindfold, can't you?"

I yelled, "No, fat-ass, I can't see anything. I told you the truth, I can feel it. Get someone to stop them."

Dooley replied, "For what, making your fingers hurt? We need more than that."

## Chapter 20:
# *Got a Runner*

**D**ooley got on the police radio. "Red Dodge pickup truck just turned right dead ahead one hundred yards; light him up." I heard sirens from a police car behind us. I felt the van move over to let the car through.

Before the police car could pass us, Dooley yelled, "We got a runner." The truck tried to make the first left turn at a high speed and hit a few parked cars.

I yelled, "He is going left."

I heard, "You gotta be kidding me!" from Dooley.

"I don't fucking believe it, but he's right," said one of the Bobs. Just then another police siren sounded ahead of us and to the right. A patrol car, not part of our fleet of cars, had witnessed the accident and did a 180-degree spinning turn in the intersection. The regular police radio sounded: "CF-15 we just witnessed a hit and run. In pursuit of a red Dodge pickup, South 88th Avenue and 95th." A second later I heard Dooly yell into the radio, "CF-15, this is MC-44, we're in pursuit of possible kidnap suspects in same vehicle and are one hundred yards behind you."

"Roger that. Will assist unless you wish to take the lead," the voice on the radio said.

"Just don't lose him," yelled Dooley.

"The damn street is too narrow to let the patrol car behind us pass," yelled Dooley. I yelled, "Turn left, turn, turn, he is getting farther away." The chase was on.

"Damnit!" yelled Dooley.

"What's going on, Dooley," I yelled.

"The patrol car that was chasing him was broadsided at an intersection; someone probably on their phone and not paying attention."

We slowed, and our driver rolled his window down. "Everyone OK?" he called. The answer must have been yes, because we accelerated away at full throttle.

"We lost him!" said Dooley. "That red truck is nowhere in sight."

I yelled, "Right, he went somewhere to the right."

The driver said, "I don't see him."

I yelled back, "Listen, dumbass, neither can I. You don't need to see him; my hands see him. Now turn right at the next street."

We turned, and less than a minute later I moved my hands back and forth until I locked onto the strongest direction. An instant later I felt a super strong throbbing sensation and yelled, "STOP!"

Dooley said, "Are they near?"

I yelled, "Look left, they have to be within one hundred feet."

"Holy shit," said Dooley. "The truck is right there, inside that garage," he screamed.

I'd felt that I'd proven my abilities, so I ripped off the blindfold. I looked left, and not more than forty feet away was a nearly closed garage door. It appeared that the driver of the red Dodge truck had pulled into someone's open garage in an attempt to hide.

They'd tried to close the garage door but the truck was too large to fit. A bright chrome bumper and beat-up license plate were visible where the garage door had stopped. Enough red paint was visible to verify this was a red Dodge pickup. Just to the right of the chrome bumper I saw a man crouching down behind a garbage can. He was trying to see us without being seen, but his bright yellow and red t-shirt gave his position away rather easily. The person near the rear bumper realized he'd been seen, and disappeared from view.

Two seconds later we heard tires squealing, and the half-closed garage door vaporized as the truck smashed through it.

Dooley yelled, "Watch out, he's running again."

The truck nearly got away, but controlling a truck at full throttle, in reverse, takes quite a bit of skill. In a desperate attempt to flee, the driver simply ran out of talent. The speeding truck violently smashed into a parked car on the other side of the street. A policeman accelerated his patrol car and rammed the truck's rear wheel on the driver's side. The force of the impact spun the truck nearly 180 degrees, pinning the truck against another vehicle and preventing escape. The driver tried to get away by flooring the gas pedal, but the rear tires, now badly out of alignment, just spun on the asphalt, producing pillars of smoke. The truck was mortally wounded, even if they'd been able to get away the truck wouldn't be drivable for much longer. Once the driver of the truck realized they were hopelessly pinned, the three men scrambled out of the passenger window and ran in different directions. Police officers gave chase.

I yelled, "Let me out, I can help!"

Dooley looked wearily at me for a second, then told one of the Bobs, "Go ahead. We can use all the help we can get." One of the Bobs struggled to find the correct key, which ended up taking an additional thirty agonizing seconds to get the cuffs off.

I took a second to use my hands to track them. Once I determined where they were, I told the detectives, "One is over there, behind that row of houses on the left, less than one hundred yards away." I spun around to the right. "The other went behind this house. The third one is who we really want, and he is straight ahead." A few uniformed officers ran behind the house to my left, and within twenty seconds I heard, "Hands up, don't move." The other two got away from officers, jumping over fences and running through yards.

Within three minutes the second suspect was located and taken into custody. Two young patrol officers and I were on the trail of the suspect that was the source of the strongest sensation. For a second, I thought the entire thing was pretty funny. Less than a half hour ago these same patrolmen saw me in handcuffs, convinced I was responsible for kidnapping Stacey Robinson. In a humorous, ironic twist, now those same police officers were taking orders from me while we chased the actual kidnappers.

The police officer running next to me yelled into the radio, "We're losing him. Can we request the chopper?"

I told the patrolman, "We won't need the chopper. We can find him ourselves. He is this way, moving to the right."

We were running at full speed, faster than I've run in a long time. The adrenaline my body was producing really helped to give me an extra burst of speed. Out of nowhere, ex-football player and now FBI agent Stan Holliday flew by us like we were standing still.

A patrol car sped past and then stopped about seventy-five feet ahead. A few patrol officers jumped out and joined our group as we ran through backyards. As expected, the chubby detectives were unable to run, so they followed behind in the van.

Two other patrol officers emerged from between houses on my left. I shouted, "Follow us! He is this way." At that moment a man emerged between two houses, about three hundred feet away. The man carried what looked like a large chrome handgun and aimed it at us. I screamed, "There he is. Straight ahead!

He aimed the gun at us, I saw three flashes of light come from his pistol as we dove for cover. An instant later I heard three *zipps* as the rounds went over our heads. Because bullets travel faster than the speed of sound, there was a brief delay between the *zipps* sound and the *bang* of the gun firing. Up until this point I hadn't really been scared. The sounds of the bullets only a few feet from my body changed all that. This was exhilarating and frightening at the same time. The officers near me jumped up and said, "Let's go!" and the chase was back on.

He was sprinting away from us. A few seconds later, he pointed the gun backward and fired twice. We hit the deck again. Holliday was 150 feet closer to him than we were, and he tumbled to the ground in an unusual manner. I wasn't sure if Holliday had been shot, or he just fell. He grabbed his right knee and screamed in agony. The man we were chasing jumped over some hedges and disappeared from sight. When we arrived where Holliday had fallen, it was pretty clear he hadn't been shot; there was no blood. He was cursing loudly. "Goddamn it! It's my fucking knee again." A policeman checked for bullet wounds; he didn't have any. "I'm not hit; now get that fucking guy!" Holliday yelled.

This is the stuff you see on TV shows, not usually in real life. We jumped up and gave chase. He wasn't getting away; my fingers were tracking his direction perfectly. While I was running, a strange sensation came over me. I had felt this before, and it only took a split second to remember what this was. I realized the electrocution feeling was forming inside my body yet again. I had no time for this shit. *Not now,* I told myself. A rage of emotion filled my mind. I'm not sure how, but I was able to channel something deep inside and prevent the episode. I returned my focus to finding the suspect. An instant later I saw the man jumping over a fence about one hundred feet away. I heard dogs barking as he ran through their yards. He acted like a terrified, wild animal, searching for a way to escape. This went on for about three minutes, then I saw him dive over a large hedge row and disappear from view.

I heard a woman screaming a second later. As we got closer to the home I heard, "No, I have a baby. Help me! Oh God, help me! Help! No, don't hurt my baby!" My heart sank. This sick bastard would use anything to escape, even a baby.

When we were about fifty feet from the house, we saw the suspect pushing a young woman toward the back door of the home. His gun was in her back. She was holding a baby in a child carrier wrapped around her neck. He looked back and saw us. Quickly wrapping his arm around her neck, he pointed the gun to her head while dragging her inside. We sprinted toward the house. The policeman radioed his location for backup.

This was a real-life hostage situation, far different from what you see on TV. Sure, when there are hostages involved, you try to talk through the situation. However, unlike on TV, the police never drop their weapons to save the hostages. I counted six police officers near me, and all had their guns trained on the suspect. They fanned out to prevent his escape and get a better line of sight. One of the officers yelled, "Watch your crossfire!" The suspect was breathing hard and looked exhausted. I don't think he could continue to run. This situation was going to end soon, one way or another.

Another group of officers arrived and entered the house from the front, unnoticed by the suspect. Through the window we could see the suspect and woman in the living room. They were focused on us, unaware that officers were approaching from behind. The officers moved to within fifteen feet of the suspect. What happened next was chaos.

The suspect must have heard something behind him, because he spun around and fired at the policemen who entered the room. He hit one officer right in the chest. The force of the bullet knocked the officer onto his back, and his gun fell to the floor. The woman spun away from the suspect and dropped to the ground, covering her baby. The suspect started shooting in different directions, then ran out the same door he came in, directly at us. I saw several flashes from his gun, followed quickly by *pop, pop, pop.*

I instantly felt pain similar to being punched in the gut. At first, I believed another police officer accidently plowed into me. I was spun around and tumbled to the ground. I was having trouble breathing. I'd had the wind knocked out of me before, so I assumed that was the problem—It wasn't. I looked down to see an almost foot-long stream of blood squirting out of my chest and side, landing on the ground next to me. I saw something sticking out of my shirt. It didn't take long to realize I'd been shot. I heard at least twenty gunshots, then after a short pause, then two more shots. For reasons I cannot fathom, my mind brought up my high school career day with FBI Agent Stinson. All I could think of was, *This is why the police don't simply wound a crazed gunman. You eliminate the threat.*

The policeman near me shouted into his radio, "Shots fired. Suspect down."A second later I heard, "Hey, this guy is down." He meant me; I was "this guy." I was horrified. Blood was everywhere, and I couldn't tell how badly I was wounded. The sharp, stinging pain made it nearly impossible to breathe. It seemed that I was unable to get any oxygen. Now that I was in full panic mode, my breathing became very rapid, and I started to hyperventilate. My vision closed down to a small percentage of normal sight. This tunnel vision scared me more than anything. A person can live without a lot of working body parts, but I didn't want to lose my eyesight. Dizziness set in as the world seemed to spin around me. I feared my body was shutting down. For a few seconds everything around me was in slow motion. I reflected on my life and thought, *My God, is this the end of me? What would happen to my wife and kids? If it was the end, what would they remember about me years from now? Had I really accomplished anything in my life worthwhile enough to remember?* I tried to say a prayer but was interrupted by someone shaking me and yelling, "Stay with us, Mick."

The last thing I remembered was Dooley, huffing and puffing while yelling into his radio, "Get a bus, NOW!" Then I blacked out.

# Chapter 21:

## *I'm a Hero?*

I awoke while still in an ambulance. The paramedic was talking on the radio about heading to Mercy Hospital. To my surprise Detective Dooley was riding next to me. Every bump we went over caused me to grimace in pain. I tenderly looked over and said through the oxygen mask, "I won the bet, fat-ass. Do you believe me now?"

Dooley said, "I can't even begin to understand this whole situation, and I thought I told you not to call me fat-ass. Now take it easy, you got shot, looks like you took three rounds. The good news is it appears the bullets have gone through and out. You lost a lot of blood. You wouldn't happen to know your blood type, would you? Got three or four other ribs as well, that's gonna suck. There's a large exit wound on your side. One of your ribs was sticking out of your body about two inches." He removed his phone and fumbled with it for a second. Then he said, "Never seen that before; mind if I get a picture of it? The good news is you will recover, but it won't be quick." He eagerly took a few pictures then continued, "How could you know where they were hiding? Seriously, I have to know."

*I'd like to know how it works as well, I thought. Apparently, I do have some sort of bad guy radar. How long have I had this? Could this be what has haunted me for so long?*

I replied, "I told you the truth, Dooley, though I'm not sure how it works. Takes a special case. Only the really evil and twisted kind of people make my senses explode."

I had to pause for a second because of the pain, then said, "Dooley, I guess I've got a special talent. I have no control over when it will happen, but at least now I understand the reason for it. All I know is I can sense something that only the sickest criminals radiate, and my fingers and hands tell me where they are. I don't know how else to explain it. I said it would take less than thirty minutes, so you owe me a million dollars; that was the bet."

Dooley responded, "Umm, no, that wasn't the bet. Now relax so I can get another picture." I was in a lot of pain, of course, but I wanted some answers. "How is the mom and baby? How is the cop? Did you find out who they were?"

Dooley responded, "Woman and baby are fine. Cop is OK; bullet proof vest saved him. Don't really know the names or stories of the people we were chasing, yet; the one you were chasing is DOA so he can't tell us anything. The others had no ID. We're working on it."

Through the EMT radio I heard that permission was granted for the paramedic to give a pain medicine injection. My pain level was a 15, on a 1 to 10 scale so this was welcome news.

Dooley persisted. "We would've driven right past that truck in the garage if you hadn't told us to stop. I don't understand how you found them. Mick, there are bad people everywhere. Why were you able to find these guys? Can you do this for other cases? If so, we could use your help."

After Dooley had finished taking pictures, he patted my shoulder and said, "Think about it."

The paramedic gave me a shot, and I immediately felt better, not a care in the world. I looked at Dooley and said, "I have no idea, fat-ass, no fucking idea." Then I passed out.

It seemed like an instant later I woke up. In reality, six hours had passed. The doctors were waking me up after surgery to check my progress. My wife was there, and it was pretty obvious she'd been crying. The emotions finally overcame me, and I started crying like a baby. We hugged and cried for several minutes. She said my kids and family members had been called, and they're coming up from Peoria. Then she said, "Mick, I don't even understand what's going on. Exactly how do I explain this situation to our families?"

I replied, "I don't know. I guess we will figure it out soon enough. Let's not worry about it right now." She brought me some racing magazines and my computer so I could try to get some work done when I felt better. I hated to tell her to stop hugging me, but I had to; the pain was too much to handle.

Then Detective Dooley, the Bobs, and Holliday arrived. Holliday was on crutches. With them was a guy carrying a briefcase. I guessed he was a lawyer for the city. They didn't say anything at first, just shook their heads and smiled. Dooley talked first in a tone that sounded like he was reading a script, "Our chief of police and our captain about had a heart attack when they found out we involved a civilian in an active shooter situation. This is completely against damn near every single rule and regulation in the department. We were sent by the chief of police to personally say we're all very sorry about what happened to you. We hope you won't hold the department, or any of us, legally responsible. In exchange, the city will pay your hospital bills. We have also been authorized to make you an offer of twenty-five thousand dollars in compensation for pain and suffering, in exchange for signing these release of liability contracts."

Even though I was in extreme pain, I tried to laugh. I said, "Make it one hundred and twenty-five thousand dollars, fat-ass, or no deal. You put my wife and me through hell. I was the only person who had the ability to find and save that girl. Then I did your job and found those responsible. Also, you need to reimburse my wife for hotel expenses while I recover."

They looked at Briefcase Man, who nodded and said, "Mr. Anderson, we will accept your terms. We will deliver the contract for your signature within the hour." Then he left the room.

Dooley said, "You know, you could've gotten two hundred thousand dollars."

I replied, "I know, but I'd have taken fifty thousand and not complained, so it's a win-win situation for all of us."

"Special Agent Holliday, I believe you have one thousand dollars you're holding for me. I found the suspects in under thirty minutes, just like I predicted." Holliday came forward and held out his hand with the bills. I pointed to my wife and said, "Give the money to my wife. She deserves it after what you put her through."

After a few seconds to catch my breath, I said, "Hey, Dooley, I could get used to catching bad guys for fun and profit." I tried not to laugh.

Then I changed my tone and said, "Listen, Dooley, I want a press conference in the next few days. The world needs to know that I had no part in the kidnapping. I just want to be damn sure everyone knows I was a good guy. I don't want to be a hero; I just won't accept being a suspect anymore. Are we clear?"

"Clear," said Dooley.

A nurse and doctor came into the room. "Mr. Anderson, I'm Dr. Herum, the surgeon who performed your operation. I need to check your condition." He did the normal stuff and checked my vitals, seemed happy enough, then he explained what they did. Turns out I was shot three times. Fat-ass was right; the bullets went through my side and blasted four ribs and cracked a fifth. One of the bullets went across my side, splitting me open for four inches. Another bullet hit a rib just right, and the rib slashed me open from the inside. I was a mess. The surgeon had to remove splinters of bone, then screws and a plate were used to put the ribs together that were shattered in two by the bullets. He told me I had fifty-six stiches. The stitches would be removed in ten days and I'd have some cool scars to impress my friends. He said, "If all goes well, you will be discharged in five or six days. Unfortunately, Mr. Anderson, the rib pain will be severe, and it will last a few months. You will need quite a bit of pain medication for the first two to three weeks."

The nurse finally spoke. "Try not to get hooked on the pain medication, Mr. Anderson."

Outside the room there were two officers, assigned as official security—for me! I'd soon realize why security was necessary. There was a loud commotion outside the room. Apparently, a reporter, dressed as a nurse, had tried to get past the officers. They were able to prevent this woman from getting in the door. She yelled, "Mr. Anderson, how does it feel to be a hero to the people of Chicago and the family of Stacey Robinson?" I didn't know what to think. How was I supposed to feel? In a twenty-four period I had gone from relative obscurity, to being the main suspect in a kidnapping, and finally being hailed as a hero. I wanted to cry, and I wasn't sure if it was from pain or just emotions. My world had changed completely, and I'd never be the same.

About an hour later I had visitors. The entire family of Stacey Robinson, including Stacey, walked into my room. They cried as they thanked me for helping to find Stacey. I tried to hold my composure, but eventually I cried along with them. Stacey's grandmother even baked a cherry pie for my wife and me. I knew this event would change my life, this time in positive ways. I was proud of what I had accomplished, and a bit worried about what would come next. I was mostly glad this case was over and the little girl was safe.

A press conference was scheduled for the next day. Dooley said they wanted to have the press conference quickly so the department would look like heroes as well. The police commissioner, the mayor, and even the governor would attend. My entire family, along with the family of Stacey Robinson would be the honored guests. We would get to hang out with all the cool people I saw on the news each night.

## Chapter 22:

# *Pictures, Faces*

We had been scheduled to give a press conference in the media center at the hospital, but the location was changed because the number of media requests surpassed the capacity. Chicago's large convention center, McCormick Place, was chosen because it had the capacity and was nearby.

My nurse, named Stella asked, "Are you sure you want to do this? You're not healed enough to be moving around."

I said, "This is the most important day of my life. I need the outside world to know I had nothing to do with the kidnapping, otherwise a dark cloud will hang over me for the rest of my days."

"I'm going with you. Just so you understand, if you start bleeding, we will need to bring you back to the hospital immediately." She put me in a wheelchair and led me outside.

Detective Miller, Dooley, Special Agent Holliday, and the Bobs were waiting for me. Dooley looked at the nurse then back at me.

Dooley whispered, "Is it just me, or does that nurse look like Nurse Ratched from the movie *One Flew Over the Cuckoo's Nest*?

Dooley was right; she did resemble Nurse Ratched. We cautiously laughed. She saw us looking her direction and raised an eyebrow, eerily similar to what Nurse Ratched would do during the movie.

I whispered to Dooley, "Those are very challenging observations you made, Randle," which is a quote from the movie. I tried not to laugh, because the pain prevented any laughter.

Once composed Dooley said, "You were right about something. Inside the truck we found Stacey's school ID and book bag."

Nurse Stella fiddled with my IV line interrupting our conversation. Once she finished Dooley continued, "We also found some interesting news about the three people in the truck. The two surviving suspects are brothers, and they're convicted felons with a long rap sheet. Both were convicted of murder when they were juveniles, just fifteen years old. They were released when they turned twenty-one. Since then, they've been convicted on narcotics, robbery, and sexual assault. They had just been released eleven months ago after serving ten years for sexual assault involving a minor, and the minor's mother. They're real pillars of the community."

Detective Miller said, "The dead guy was sentenced for multiple murders and child rape about twenty years ago. He killed a young girl who was only six years old. The girl was shot because she was being used as a human shield by her father, who was the one he really wanted to kill. After killing the father, he raped the mother while the bodies were in the same room. He was such a sick bastard, during interrogation he admitted to fondling the dead girl in front of her mother. I'll never forget the case; he was most evil person I've ever seen. The death penalty was created for just this type of criminal; it was too bad we never got the chance to use it on him. The police were so angry they roughed him up during arrest, and this caused a public outcry. It also resulted in one policeman being fired, and two of my friends demoted."

Dooley said, "At his trial, he would often laugh and whistle when the prosecutor described his crimes. He clapped when one prosecution witness gave testimony about why he shot the girl. The prosecutor thought the case was a slam dunk, so he let him plead to a lesser crime for the pedophilia charges. The case was nearly lost when, on the very day he was to testify, the star witness was killed in a drive-by shooting. We knew this guy ordered the hit but couldn't prove it. The prosecutor lied about the condition of the witness, telling the media and his attorney that the witness was injured but alive. They pleaded the case down to second degree murder and rape of the girl's mother. For reasons we can't understand, he had been released early, after serving only twelve years of a twenty-two-year sentence. All three were in the same cell block and became friends. He had been out of jail for less than a year, and already had arrest warrants for a host of charges, including attempted murder and drug trafficking."

Then Detective Miller said, "We know the guy who died was attempting to become a serious cocaine and meth dealer. We found out the two surviving suspects, and Stacey's uncle, worked for him. About a week ago, Stacey's uncle stole all of the dead guy's drugs then went into hiding. Since the uncle lived with the Robinson family, the dead guy thought Stacey was actually the uncle's daughter. They decided to kidnap her to force the uncle to return the drugs. If they'd found him, both he and Stacey would've been killed. You didn't hear this from me, but investigators found her underwear in the dead guy's pocket. They had planned on using her underwear as proof they kidnapped her, and they were on their way to mail her underwear to Stacey's house with a ransom note. According to the other two, the dead guy was planning to sexually assault her, kill her, and dump the body. Thanks to you, Mick, we found her before they had a chance to finish their plan. We have an APB out for the uncle, and if he turns up, we will arrest him. The building where you found her was abandoned; not sure how they were able to get in."

Dooley shook my hand and said, "You saved that little girl, and we all owe you an apology. I was hard on you, and you proved me wrong."

I replied, "No problem Dooley. All of you were doing your job—no hard feelings. Besides, I made five hundred dollars off you, so we're good."

Dooley said, "You're really going to keep my money after all I did for you?"

I said, "Is the pope Catholic? Does a bear shit in the woods? Yes, I'm going to keep it."

I paused for a few seconds and said, "Dooley, should we make another bet that there are more cases related to the dead guy than just Stacey's kidnapping?"

Dooley said, "No, I don't want to bet you anymore, I learned my lesson last time."

I replied, "Good, because my senses have never exploded like this before. He was sick—I mean like serial killer sick. My guess is the other two were terrified of him. Now that he is gone, they may give you information to help solve a few open cases. That guy was pure evil, otherwise I'd never have found him."

Dooley said, "Yes, you're right about there being more to his story. We took his DNA profile and put it into a new international criminal database. There were hits immediately. Turns out he was in the army twenty-five years ago and served in Europe. During his time in Germany, he was a suspect in some assault cases before he was sent back to the States. German officials told us today that his DNA positively identifies him as the person who committed nearly twenty open child and adult sexual assault cases. Now we're checking every single city where he had been stationed to see how many open cases can be closed."

I asked Dooley, "Do you have a lot of kidnappings in the Chicago area?"

He answered, "We had over five hundred cases in Chicago last year. Child sex trades are especially bad in large cities, and Chicago has one of the worst problems. Many homeless young women and men disappear every year, and a large percentage are never seen again. Less than half are what we refer to as 'classic' kidnappings, where someone other than a family member kidnaps the child. Because of the rise in gang violence, we have seen quite a few children of rival gang members kidnapped. Many of these go unreported, handled by 'street justice'; we just pick up the bodies."

A few minutes later, my family and Stacey's family were brought to a room next to the main part of the building. A woman explained what was scheduled to happen. She said, "Be prepared; the entire room is filled to capacity. It will be crazy." After she finished, we were paraded in front of the press and about four thousand people who wanted to be part of the event.

I was immediately struck by the number of people holding pictures of their missing family members. Mothers, fathers, and even children held up signs asking for help locating missing loved ones. Camera flashes and bright lights were nearly blinding us as the press conference began.

I was hoping to keep my hyper senses a secret, but there had been too many leaks. The top news stories on TV and in newspapers proclaimed I had some special talent to find missing children. I knew most people probably thought my hyper senses were a hoax, but deep inside they wanted to believe. I fully understood that people would be skeptical; hell, a month ago I'd have been the first to think this was a hoax.

The governor spoke first. My mind wandered as usual. Many Illinois governors have been convicted of crimes and gone to prison, so I pictured this governor in a prison jumpsuit and laughed. Michelle glared at me. I didn't pay attention to him; I just scanned the crowd. I couldn't get over how many people were frantically waving pictures.

The mayor spoke next—more mindless bullshit. The chief of police spoke afterward, and gave a rousing speech on the importance of "good old-fashioned police work." He expressed appreciation for the cooperation of the public in solving this disgraceful crime and returning the little girl to her family unharmed.

They brought me and Stacey Robinson up to center stage. I was in a lot of pain, even loaded up on pain meds, but once I was in front of the crowd I forgot about it. More spot lights were aimed at us now. I wondered how famous people ever get used to the bright lights and camera flashes in their daily lives; it was aggravating.

They let Stacey tell her story first, and she wept as she recounted the horror of her kidnapping.

She recalled how scared she felt and then said, "After a few days went by, I had all but given up hope." She paused a second to compose herself, then said, "When Mr. Anderson yelled my name, it gave me hope that I'd be rescued. I was unable to see anything because inside the building was pitch black, and I'm frightened of the dark. I was so scared." She started crying and sobbed uncontrollably for another minute. "I didn't know what to do. I couldn't yell." After another twenty seconds to compose herself, she said, "Then this man, who I believe was sent from heaven, yelled at me to hit something metal faster and faster to let him know that I really was Stacey Robinson. I took those same chains that were locking me up, and used them to set me free." She looked right at me and continued, "You're my hero. I really believe you were sent from heaven to save me."

The crowd erupted, clapping hands, stomping feet, and whistling. I heard, "We love you Stacey," over and over.

I finally began to understand this gift I possessed. I hadn't fully grasped how it might change people's lives until now. I became emotional listening to her story, with tears streaming down my cheeks. Stacey and I hugged and then cried together, quickly joined by my family and hers. It was impossible not to be emotionally affected by these events. Hundreds of photographers snapped pictures, and everyone was standing on their feet clapping loudly.

Once I stopped crying and calmed down, they handed me a microphone. I said, "I'm not a hero, just an average guy who followed his instincts. I'm quite sure I had help from the man above. My family and I are grateful for her safe return and for the help of the police department, specifically fa—." I almost said *fat-ass* but stopped myself. "Detective Dooley and the others who believed in my dedication to locate and rescue this wonderful child. I'm grateful for my wife, who had to endure a few days of misunderstandings, and my family who are joining me on this most amazing day." After a second to let my pain subside, I continued, "For those of you with pictures and signs, I want you to know that, God willing, your loved ones will be found, and you will be reunited. May we never forget those who are missing, and never stop looking. Thank you."

People in the crowd erupted again with clapping, whistling, and foot stomping. It was like a rock concert.

I felt quite a bit of pain and realized I was bleeding. I didn't care right now. It was an amazing event. It was important to me for two reasons. First, I was no longer a suspect but a hero. And second, I knew the strange sensations that had caused countless embarrassing situations were real; not just in my mind. I wasn't nuts after all. What I originally thought was a defect in my body was actually a special ability to help people, a genuine gift. My life had a new direction. I could no longer be depressed about my condition, and I needed to embrace this gift.

With all the excitement, I almost missed the fact that my fingers were buzzing again.

# Chapter 23:
## *Please God, Help*

O ne lady came out of the crowd with a large sign. On the sign was a picture of a young girl.

The sign read: "Please Help Me Find My Little Girl." She was stopped by security, but her sign made me focus, and my fingers started to vibrate. While still on stage I asked Michelle to get Dooley. When Dooley walked over, he said, "Mick, thanks for the recognition."

I told him, "You're welcome, but that isn't the reason I needed to talk to you. The lady with the sign with giant letters that read, 'Please Help Me Find My Little Girl'— I need you to find her."

Dooley said, "Really, right now?"

I told him, "I feel it, Dooley. She was the only one in the crowd I felt. Let's find her little girl."

He got on the radio and said, "All units be on the lookout for the woman with the large sign at the end of the press conference. If you find her bring her to the staging area."

When we returned to the staging area, the nurse saw the blood. She insisted on examining my wounds. "Mr. Anderson, you're bleeding, badly. Blood has soaked your clothes and is on the wheelchair. I'm taking you back to the hospital."

I told her flat out, "No, this is important. A dangerous criminal who likes to harm children is free. We need to capture him, so patch me up as best you can, but I'm not going back to the hospital until this is finished."

She said, "Your stiches are torn. You're bleeding all over. But what would I know? I've only been a nurse for thirty years."

The woman with the sign was led into the room. "Am I in trouble? I just wanted some help finding my daughter."

I said, "No, of course not. We want to find your daughter as well. What's your name?"

She told us her name was Cynthia Pederson, and her child's name was Rebecca. Dooley had a laptop and pulled up her files. Her case was more than five years old, making it officially a cold case.

While in the hospital, I had been thinking about my new found talent. It seemed I could "connect" with a victim only if I had been in contact with them. I had put a quarter back into Stacey's hand, which appeared to be the trigger in that case. I had no recollection of ever seeing Cynthia and couldn't have known Rebecca. Did this mean my sensations were mutating again?

She showed us pictures of her little girl. We discussed the facts of the case and compared that information with what was in the file on the computer. I wasn't sure how our paths had crossed until she showed us some clothing the child had worn the day before her disappearance. She said, "It was reported on the news that you touched something and magically found the missing child, so I brought some of Rebecca's clothing with me today."

One of the items was a dancing outfit. My daughter used to have an outfit like it when she was younger, which she wore in dance competitions.

I asked Cynthia, "Did your daughter ever come to Peoria to the D&D dance competitions?"

She had a stunned look on her face and said, "Yes, twice. How did you know?"

I told her, "My daughter had a similar outfit, and she used to be in those competitions." I was doped up pretty good to quell the pain but still felt my little finger throb. "Let's go, Dooley, and bring her along. I have a hunch that someone nearby has the answer."

Dooley was surprised and whispered to me, "Didn't the doctors and Nurse Ratched tell you to rest?"

"Let's go Dooley," I said. "I need to use this gift while I still can.

Dooley put together a team of eight policemen and two detectives. We left in a five-car procession. I let my hands and fingers direct us, and within fifteen minutes I had all my fingers throbbing. Five minutes later my fingers were quivering. I told the driver to turn into an old neighborhood. We crept down the street until my fingers and an electrocution event told me we were very close. I told them to stop at a small brick house with a garage painted in tan and gray. It was a nice, older house with impeccable landscaping. There was an elderly woman in the front yard who appeared to be planting flowers.

I asked Cynthia, "Does this house mean anything?"

"No," she said.

Dooley typed a few things on the computer and had the owner's information up on the screen. "Geneva Keating is the owner on record, sixty-seven years old and no priors, Mick."

I asked, "Can you cross reference the husband and children to see if they have a record?"

He typed a few keystrokes on the keyboard and said, "Husband deceased fifteen years ago; he was clean." He typed a few more things then said, "Wait a minute, this is interesting. She has a son, Jack M. Keating, forty-five years old. Mick, he is in the system, a registered sex offender. Released six years ago for aggravated sexual assault of a child. City records report he is a carpenter—home building, and renovations." A few keystrokes and his picture appeared.

Cynthia Pederson gasped, and then said, "I remember him. He worked for a construction company that did the work remodeling our bathroom about eight months before she disappeared." Dooley and the officers exited the cars. Dooley walked up to the woman and asked, "Excuse me, ma'am, is Jack Keating here?"

She pointed to the house and said, "What did he do now?"

Dooley and the officers approached the house. A second before they were about to knock, a man matching the picture opened the door. He was wearing painting pants and a paint-stained T-shirt that said, "Fuck Off." He had a beer bottle in one hand and a cigarette in the other. We had definitely surprised him. The all-too-familiar electrocution sensation began to form again inside my body. I was able to channel my mind and prevent any embarrassing convulsions. Once this sensation stopped, my mind wandered as I realized these electrocution events were happening alongside my hyper senses. I know it sounds crazy, but all I could think about was the day of my thirtieth birthday when I threw pancakes and beer into the ceiling. I reminded myself to investigate that date later. And what about the tool store episode? Then I snapped out of it and returned my focus to the case.

Before anyone could stop her, Cynthia jumped out of the car and ran toward him screaming, "What did you do with my little Rebecca?"

The man at the front door ran back into the house, slamming the door behind him.

Dooley said, "I cannot believe this is happening again."

One of the bigger officers, who looked like a bodybuilder, smashed the door open with a quick snap of his foot. Guns were drawn, and they went in after him. The rest of the police went around to the back and sides of the house to prevent his escape. On the radio we heard, "He went out the back door." The chase was on.

Dooley was waddling toward Cynthia Pederson to make sure she didn't try to attack Mr. Keating again. In about three minutes the radio crackled, "Suspect in custody." He was led out in cuffs and put in a patrol car.

Cynthia Pederson was crying and pleading with Dooley to let her go. "Let me talk to him and ask where my little girl is," she screamed.

The excitement was over for now. I felt conflicted. One side of me was happy a suspect was captured. The other side of me was full of despair, for I couldn't assist in finding the whereabouts of her child. It appeared that I couldn't find the victims; my talent was finding the depraved and sick people responsible for the heinous crimes.

As I sat in the patrol car, I thought, *But who will save the children? I've found the sick and twisted criminals, but I need to find the children—before it's too late.*

Regretfully it didn't turn out well for Rebecca and her mother. A mountain of evidence was found in the house and garage that linked him to several missing children. Keating eventually confessed to raping and killing ten-year-old Rebecca. Her body was located—buried under the garage floor of a house he had remodeled.

Dooley told me the worst part: he was on a list of suspects since he was a sex offender. He had an alibi that was never checked out, eventually getting lost in the shuffle of paperwork. The remodeling job Rebecca's mother requested was paid in cash, so it probably wouldn't have been recorded anywhere. Since she was taken eight months later his name didn't attract as much attention as it should have. According to Keating's statement, she was dead days before he poured the cement. Evidence collected indicated he was responsible for other missing children around the area as well. Some humans are just evil and sick, and there's no fixing them. This had been an incredibly sad ordeal that affected me to the core.

It was pretty obvious my senses were heightened by really sinister criminals. Now it appeared that crimes against children were the only thing that brought out my episodes in a way that I couldn't ignore. It was depressing knowing that even when you capture a sick person, you still had to deal with their crimes. There's no worse situation to be in; the families are destroyed, and there's nothing I can do to make it go away.

I didn't know how long these senses would remain in their "hyper" state. I wanted to solve as many of these cases as possible. I felt like this had been my calling for forty years, and I was just now beginning to understand how these hyper senses could be utilized.

It seems strange that my mind would wander at a time like this, but I thought of a song by Gordon Lightfoot, called: "*The Wreck of the Edmund Fitzgerald.*" The lyrics that caused me to reflect about my current situation are:

Donald Higgins

Does anyone know where the love of God goes
When the waves turn the minutes to hours?
The searchers all say they'd have made Whitefish Bay
If they'd put fifteen more miles behind her
They might have split up or they might have capsized
They may have broke deep and took water
And all that remains is the faces and the names
Of the wives and the sons and the daughters

I changed the lyrics to:

Does anyone know where the love of God goes
   when a predator turns the minutes to hours?

The police all say, she'd have been fine that day,
   If she put fifteen more minutes behind her

She may not have been seen or she may have escaped
   But he saw her, then hunted and took her

And all that remains is the faces and the names
   Of the parents, the sisters and brothers

The song seemed a fitting warning of the struggles that lay ahead.

# Chapter 24:
## You Are the Devil

After these two episodes, I was never able to have a normal life again. Going out in public was nearly impossible. Two months went by before the pain subsided enough for me to walk more than fifty feet. It wasn't that I didn't want to help, but I still had to recover and understand my new life. For every real case there are ten thousand crackpots, and I was unable to handle the time required to figure out which was which. So, in an attempt to prevent people from mobbing me, I never went out in public without a disguise. Three months after being shot, I went with my wife to a nice restaurant in Aurora, Illinois, a city about forty miles from Chicago. We were seated in a private area.

We had just finished our meal when a woman approached our table. Based on her clothing, it appeared she worked at the restaurant. She was obviously distraught, nearly breaking down with every word. "Please, Mr. Anderson, please, they say you can find my missing sister. Please, will you help me?" I asked her to sit down because I wanted to remain anonymous, and she was getting louder and louder with every word. She told her story as fast as she could.

She was a black woman, about fifty years old. Her name was Shantell Williams. She was clinging to a picture of two extremely young black girls, obviously twins.

The picture appeared to be old, with yellowing around the edges, and scratches on the frame. "Every day of my life I think of her. I need to know," she said.

Her twin sister, Latisha, was ten years old when she vanished. She placed the picture in front of me. I examined the picture for a few seconds and knew I could help.

She continued, "The newspapers said you needed some of her clothing to help connect to the person you're trying to find, so, when I saw you here in the restaurant, I rushed home to get some of her clothing." She handed me a sweater her sister used to wear. Almost instantly I received a tingling sensation in my fingers and a jolt that made me twitch. Rarely do I get a response like this; it was similar to the first case. Either my senses are getting better, or her sister's killer was within fifteen minutes of the restaurant. I knew I could help her.

I had worked with Dooley for several months trying to solve nearly one hundred cold cases. I've held evidence clothing and personal items from nearly all of the cases. I found out that not everyone who brings me a picture or clothing can be helped. For whatever reason, there's no connection. This case was different, so I called Dooley and said, "We have another case to work. I'm getting a strong feeling about this." I gave Dooley her name, and the name of the missing child, Latisha. He told me he would personally contact a detective he knew from Aurora's police department. He and the Bobs would meet us at Aurora's police department the next morning.

I arrived at eight in the morning sharp. Shantell was already there. Dooley had been there for nearly an hour reviewing the case. He said the Bobs were waiting for me inside. Dooley knocked on the captain's door and went in. We were introduced to their captain, Steve Roggins, and two detectives, Bob Florence and Richard Dittmer.

Dooley began, "I know you have questions about Mick Anderson's abilities. We're here as a courtesy to tell you he is one hundred percent legitimate. If he says he can find the person responsible, then he can. Sure, he is an asshole, but we put up with it because he gets results."

They just stared at me, trying to decide if they believed this was real or some kind of charade. Captain Roggins said, "You have our full cooperation. We don't have any free men for a few hours but can help you after lunch. Here are the case files. These men will answer any questions you need. Fair enough?"

Dooley said, "Fair enough. We just don't want to step on anyone's toes."

They shook our hands and chuckled, "Good luck."

The police had pulled up the long-forgotten case files. "Runaway Kid" was hastily scribbled on the dusty box retrieved from the cold case storage unit. It was immediately obvious from the amount of paperwork inside that they hadn't treated this missing black child with any importance and had closed the case quickly, believing the child had run away.

Dooley said, "Different times back then. It's pretty embarrassing to us now. I'd like to say it's the first time, Mick, but what I see when reviewing old files shocks me. From the 1940s up until the middle 1970s were the worst. Detectives did a quick search and pretty much called most of the missing black kids, "runaways," just like this box. They were too lazy to investigate missing black kids. We didn't have a black detective until the 1970s. Honestly, Mick, I'd like to make this right. Do you think you can help?"

I replied, "Hell yes, fat-ass."

Dooley shot me a look then pointed at me. "Stop that shit, Mick."

We brought Shantell into the room and talked to her for about an hour. I wasn't getting any sensation yet, so Dooley and the Bobs reviewed the evidence with their new computer technology. Once they finished with their review, we put a plan together about the rest of our time. At 11:30 a.m. we broke for lunch. I told Shantell, "Don't discuss this with anyone, understand? Someone you talk to may tell another person; this kind of thing travels fast. It will be far more difficult to catch someone if they know we're coming, and we will be coming in hard."

After lunch we set out. Since I couldn't get a sensation from that many miles, we decided to start near the restaurant I'd visited the night before. Once we were about ten minutes from the restaurant, the vibrations started to show a direction. As we drove closer, I started getting vibrations from all my fingers. I couldn't find a road to help pinpoint the exact location. I knew it was a rural road, but there wasn't an easy way to get there. We would go north and lose it, turn around to gain it back, then lose it again.

"Let me check a map on my phone," I said. "There has to be a road over there, but it shows nothing near." Then I realized the problem; there was an obstacle dead ahead called Jericho Lake. We had to go around the lake to pick it up again. Then we happened on a road that showed promise. A half mile later there was a driveway at the end of the road. It had a mail box with the number 4800 painted on it. I told Dooley, "Hey, I think we're close if the road goes over the hill and to the north. Call it in and see who lives up there."

Dooley called in for information. The radio crackled, "Misner, Thomas J., age 81, lived on this property since 1965, retired teacher, no priors."

That didn't seem promising to me, but I said, "Before we go up, let me call Shantell and see where she went to grade school, just in case he was a teacher of hers. Can you radio back and see which school he taught at?"

I called Shantell and asked what elementary school she attended. She told me, "Let me see, uh, it was Greenman—yes, Greenman." The police radio crackled two minutes later, and the dispatcher said, "Greenman Elementary School."

Dooley and I looked at each other. "Interesting bit of information, fat-ass," I said to Dooley. "Maybe we need to get the rifle or shotgun out." He laughed. I said, "Seriously, you never can tell what people will do, especially those who are used to peace and quiet— and few, if any visitors."

Surprisingly Dooley got out and opened the trunk. He retrieved the shotgun from the trunk. He checked to see how many shells were loaded. "You know how to use one of these, dickhead?" Dooley asked.

"Yes, fat-ass, I know how to use one," was my courteous reply.

He said, "Great story, but there's no way on God's green earth that I'm going to give you my shotgun. I'll let Mansfield or Natale use it, if need be," he said, referring to the Bobs. He put the shotgun between the front seats.

Dooley gave me the finger, then said, "I better call in a county sheriff for backup. Don't want to go into a possible bad situation without additional firepower, and I certainly don't want you accidentally shooting me, so stay away from the gun."

I looked a Dooley with my best disgusted look and replied, "Oh, Dooley, you and I both know it wouldn't be an accident." I started laughing and Dooley flipped me off.

Dooley called in the county dispatcher and asked for backup, and within five minutes a patrol car came down the road and stopped next to us.

Deputy Joe Barnes arrived and introduced himself. Dooley and the Bobs introduced themselves.

"Now, what do you need with old man Misner?" said Barnes.

Dooley said, "Not sure yet, possible cold case and needed another set of eyes."

"And guns," I said.

"You're a civilian. What's a civilian doing here?" said Barnes.

"Long story, Barnes," said Dooley.

He looked at me and finally put two and two together, "Hey, you're that nut job from TV, the guy who says he can find criminals with his fingers," he said laughing. "Detective, is this legit? You really believe this crap?"

"Barnes, it's painful for me to admit this, but his methods are working. He is a royal asshole, though," said Dooley.

I replied, "That was sweet, fat-ass. I didn't know you cared so much."

"See what I mean, Barnes?' Dooley said to Barnes. "Kiss my ass," Dooley said to me.

I told Barnes, "We're the best of friends; don't let him tell you different. He tries to act like a hard ass but deep down he is just a big teddy bear."

Dooley said, "I put people in jail I like better than you, Mick."

"I know, fat-ass, you almost did that to me."

Dooley just rolled his eyes.

We drove along a winding road, and a 1950s style farmhouse and old barns came into view about a quarter of a mile away. We stopped for a minute while I checked the direction with my hands.

"Look at how my fingers are quivering. The person we want is at or near that farm straight ahead," I said.

There was one person walking near the house. It appeared to be an older man. He looked our direction for about fifteen seconds, raising his hands above his eyes to block out the sun. The man seemed to pick up the pace and disappeared behind the house. We continued slowly toward the house. Our cars stopped about thirty feet from the front door, and we exited the cars. The detectives and Barnes scanned the area. Confident nobody was aiming a gun at us, they walked up to the front door.

Dooley knocked on the door, and a woman answered. She resembled my old grandmother, dressed in clothing from a 1950s Sears catalog. She even had an apron draped around her. My mouth started to water once I smelled fresh cookies. My mind now wandered like it always does at inappropriate times. I thought it would be a good time to yell, "*The Andy Griffith Show called, and they want Aunt Bee to return to the set!*" Luckily, I kept my mouth shut.

Dooley said, "Sorry to disturb you, ma'am. I'm Detective Dooley and this is—"

The old lady cut him off and said, "Joe Barnes, how are you? You really grew up, young man."

Barnes tipped his hat to her and said, "Fine, Mrs. Misner, ma'am. And how are you and the family?"

"Just fine, thank you. Now what do you all need? I have cookies in the oven for the bake sale."

Dooley continued, "We're investigating a missing child case, a young girl that went to the same school where Thomas Misner taught."

"Oh, my goodness, well, I'm Elizabeth Misner, his wife. That's terrible. How do you think my husband or I can help you, though?"

Dooley said, "We would like to talk to him, ask him a few questions, that's all."

Mrs. Misner said, "He isn't here, but leave your information and he will try to get ahold of you later. He is an old man, and unfortunately I don't think his memory will be of much use."

I felt the electrocution event beginning and focused everything I had to stop it from happening. In an attempt to diffuse this feeling, I went on the offensive and blurted out, "Oh, he is here, Mrs. Misner. We know that for sure."

Dooley and Barnes looked at me with disbelief. I continued, "So, do you want him to come out now, or should we go and find him?"

"Listen, I told you he isn't here, now you need to leave," Mrs. Misner shouted.

I walked right by her, letting my fingers tell me which direction to go. We walked around to the back of the house to where a massive barn was located. The doors to the barn were closed.

I looked at Dooley and said, "He is in here. I can feel it."

"Thomas Misner, this is the police. We need to ask you some questions," yelled Dooley.

I thought I heard a noise behind the door but couldn't be sure. He didn't come out. Then we heard a creaking noise behind the door and Dooley yelled, "We're coming in, Mr. Misner." He tried to open the barn door, but the handle wouldn't budge. We were just a millisecond away from forcing the door open when we heard an unmistakable noise.

Crack, snap, crack. Anyone who has ever heard the sound created by a pump-action shotgun getting racked knows two things: one, shit is about to get deadly serious, and two, find cover—now! We all scattered and dove for cover. I went around the side then peered out to see the old lady pointing a shotgun in my direction. *Holy shit! Where did that shotgun come from?* I thought.

"I told you to leave—now leave. He ain't here," said Mrs. Misner.

Deputy Barnes tried to reason with her. "Ma'am, we just wanted to talk. Don't make this worse than it has to be. You can trust me; you know me, ma'am, I want the best for everyone. Please put the gun down and let's talk."

Dooley, the Bobs, and Barnes had their guns drawn, but I had nothing to defend myself against this reincarnation of Ma Barker, the gangster Momma from the 1920s. I still couldn't understand where that sweet old lady got that big fucking gun.

*Boom!* The unmistakable sound of a shotgun firing made me dive to the ground. Wood debris was raining down. I didn't dare look where she aimed but I assumed it was the barn somewhere above me.

Dooley, the Bobs, and Barnes jumped up and pointed their guns at Mrs. Misner.

"Drop it now!" Dooley shouted.

Barnes yelled, "Please, ma'am, drop the gun! I don't want to shoot a nice old lady that I've known my entire life."

I peered around the barn and watched. I was pretty sure they might have to shoot her to end this. Then I thought of the cookies. Would I get to try them, or would they be burnt before this episode ended? Slightly burnt would be OK, but really burnt isn't good. Then I snapped myself out of it and tried to focus on the task at hand. Welcome to my mind, yet again.

She held the gun defiantly as Dooley and Barnes went to forty-five degree angles of her, guns aimed right at her. I thought about the shotgun in the police car that Dooley thought wouldn't be necessary. It would've been nice right about now to have it in my possession.

"Ma, honey, don't do it. It's OK. I'm coming out," a voice shouted from inside the barn. I was sure it was the voice of Thomas Misner.

She slowly dropped the shotgun and looked straight at me. Confident the situation was under control, I looked for the shotgun damage to the barn. Part of the front corner, eight feet above me, was blown away. It was far too close for comfort.

A few seconds later she glared at me with demonic eyes and said, "Wait, I have seen you. You are that guy, aren't you? The one that found the girl and those kidnappers a while back." After a few seconds, she continued. "You're ruining a good man. My Thomas is a good man. He has changed. Why are you doing this to us? Why are you destroying our lives? You're the devil. So help me, God, you're the devil."

Dooley and Barnes put handcuffs on Mrs. Misner, and asked her to sit down. Thomas Misner opened the barn door. The Bobs had their guns trained on him. He slowly looked at all of us, one at a time. "I knew this day would come, Ma. It's OK. Well, I'll be darned, it's you—the psychic guy who found the kidnapped girl. I recognize you from the TV. After all these years, how did you know to look for those girls here?"

Dooley and Barnes looked as astonished as I did.

"Girls?" said Barnes.

I had to think of something quick, so Mr. Misner would continue to provide information.

I said, "We had suspicions for some time, Mr. Misner. I followed my instincts; we decided it was time to ask you to come clean. We wanted to give closure to those girls' families. I hope you understand that after this much time their families deserve closure. Don't you agree, Mr. Misner?" Dooley gave me a thumbs-up sign.

Mr. Misner hesitantly replied, "Yes, son, I really do. I don't have many more years to live, and I really want to find forgiveness. I've been hoping to get this weight of shame lifted off me—you know, to try to make things right. I worked tirelessly for forty years to heal myself and help the community in every way possible."

Mrs. Misner was obviously distraught. She started to sob loudly and became combative. Barnes walked over to her and said, "It will be OK Mrs. Misner. I'll make sure you and Mr. Misner are treated fairly." This seemed to calm her down.

After she was calm, he came over to where Dooley was holding onto Mr. Misner. He said, "You're doing the right thing Mr. Misner. Now we need to take you to the police station, OK? I need to put cuffs on you first."

"Do your job Joseph; it's OK," replied Mr. Misner.

"Where are they, Mr. Misner? What did you do with the bodies?" I asked.

He started to weep. After about ten seconds, he pointed a shaky hand toward the floor of the barn. "There, under the floor." He was led away. Just an old man, burdened by the sins of the past. *So many sins,* I thought.

Barnes radioed in and asked for a full forensics team. We were still in a state of shock. Even I hadn't expected this outcome.

Dooley said, "I'll give you the credit for this, Mick, even though it will be better for our careers if we took credit. You did an amazing thing, even if it's difficult to admit your throbbing fingers were the reason we solved this crime."

I replied, "I don't need the credit, Dooley. What I'd like is some of the cookies she is baking. Do we need a search warrant to sample some? I'm thinking of safety here, Dooley. Someone needs to turn off the oven and remove the cookies—for safety. Might as well sample a few while we're in there."

Barnes walked over to Dooley and me. He watched as Mr. and Mrs. Misner were taken away, obviously a bit shaken by the experience. "You really are able to find these kids? I'd never have believed it if I hadn't seen it myself. I knew both of these people since I was around five. I lived about a mile down the street growing up. How can this be? They were like an extra set of grandparents to the children in the area. Nobody could ever have suspected them. Hell, I called them Grandma and Grampa Misner for as long as I can remember. They donated time and money for anything the community needed. She bakes two thousand cookies a year for bake sales. I'm in shock; I still can't believe it."

I told Barnes, "I don't find the kids, Barnes. I find the sick and vile criminals that take the kids. You find their victims." I paused then said,

"My guess is Mr. and Mrs. Misner are making up for being monsters four decades ago. She knew; maybe she was part of it, or maybe she found out later. Either way, she is just as guilty as him. Who the hell knows why evil people do what they do? Perhaps they did change. All I care about is that they take what remaining time they have on this earth to make things right for the families of those kids." I had a feeling these weren't the only children murdered by the Misners, so I said to both Dooley and Barnes, "I think there are more missing children connected to this family."

I told Barnes, "We need to check the Misner's children as well; apples don't fall far from the tree."

Barnes replied, "Wow, either you already knew, or you're a psychic. One of his sons is my age, he is in jail right now! He was convicted for raping an eleven-year-old girl when he was just a teenager; I think he was just thirteen at the time. He was released when he turned twenty-one, and the next year he kidnapped and raped a fifteen-year-old girl from a park in Washington State! Last I heard he was serving a sixty-year sentence. We all felt bad for Grampa and Grandma Misner, and the toll it must have taken on them. Nobody blamed them; we just felt really sorry for them. His other children are fine—just one bad apple, hopefully."

I said, "You have a lot of work ahead of you, deputy."

It took a few days for the forensics team to complete their examinations. One of the bodies had the clothing Shantell described her sister wearing, and there was a book nearby with her name on it. The medical examiner verified it was her from a fracture on her arm and dental records. We were able to tell Shantell that her sister was finally located, and she could find some closure.

Shantell remembered Mr. Misner as one of her teachers. She and her sister liked Mr. Misner because he took extra time to help them with problems. Shantell was pretty sure Mr. Misner would stay late to tutor her sister in math. Obviously heartbroken, she at least felt closure. "Thank you for bringing my sister home to me," she said. "Please locate the families of the other children, so their families can have closure."

Dooley told me there were eight children's bodies under the floor—six black girls and two white girls. I said, "Jesus, Dooley, how did this guy not at least appear on their radar back then?"

"Like I said, Mick, lazy police work. If those detectives weren't so old, I'd love to knock the crap out of every one of them. We're stuck cleaning up their 'ghost cases.' Just a bit of investigative work would've solved these forty years ago."

"Perhaps," I said. "Today's technology would've cross-referenced this guy in an instant. The difference is everyone loved them, so if Misner wasn't on their radar back then, they would never have implicated him—not someone beloved as this guy, at least not without obvious proof."

"I hate to say it, since you're such a dick, but thanks for the help," Dooley said.

"No problem, Detective Dooley. I'm beginning to like you too," I replied.

"Now let's see if we can solve more of these before I lose this gift," I replied.

# Chapter 25:
# *Can't Help?*

I struggle with the fact that sometimes the worst thing I have to tell a family is, "Sorry, I'm unable to help you."

I feel bad for the family, but if my fingers don't tell me something, then there isn't much I can do. If their loved one is dead and the bad guy is too, then I cannot help. There's also an issue with distance. If I'm too many miles from the bad guy, the episodes are either missing or so weak I can't get any sensation.

One day an entire family showed up at a news station where I was giving an interview. The kids held pictures of their mother, and the father held clothes his wife wore the last time they saw her. He said, "My name is Randy Swanson. My wife, Barbara Swanson has been missing for over a year. These are our children—Rylee is two, Carter is four, and Dottie will be six tomorrow." The young girl held up her two hands to count to six and said, "I'll be this many tomorrow."

Randy Swanson had come all the way from Colorado to meet with me. He took a few minutes to tell his story. He was well organized, with files of everything that had happened. The first folder was the initial missing person's report from the Englewood, Colorado, police department. They investigated and found nothing, so he hired a private investigator. He showed me a complete folder from his investigator. According to Mr. Swanson, there had been no sightings of her in over a year, and nothing had come from any investigations.

The third folder contained the computer printouts of multiple lie detector tests. Included was the polygraph expert's printed report, proof that he had passed them all. The fourth folder had names of the detectives and their phone numbers if I wanted to verify.

Since he had heard that articles of clothing were necessary for me to connect with the victim, six pieces of clothing were handed to me by his children, eager to help in any way possible. I held the items he brought. I knew they were innocent bystanders in this disappearance because my fingers didn't throb at all. He owned a computer software company as well, so we had a connection. This family seemed to have it all—wealth, a good life, and still young. The mother had gone missing a year earlier. They'd had three children and a seemingly happy marriage. I was intrigued.

He offered me seventy-five thousand dollars, in cash, that he had in a duffel bag. He handed it to me and said, "Here it is. All I ask is you attempt to find the person responsible for my wife's disappearance and locate my wife." I took the cash and the case.

I was on the next plane to Denver, Colorado. I rented a car and drove the short distance to Englewood. I was disappointed to feel no sensations at all during the flight or drive to Englewood.

I had a scheduled meeting with the private investigator to review his files. The investigator basically told me he didn't think anything bad had happened to her; he was convinced she skipped out of the marriage. He had medical records that showed she was in treatment for bipolar depression, interesting information that wasn't shared by Mr. Swanson. There were copies of police statements from her best friend, Barbara Cass, who thought the husband killed her. The investigator thought Barbara Cass was unreliable, only looking to be the center of attention. He was able to get Cass's medical records, which showed she was a "pill popper" who was being treated for all sorts of ailments and depression. He also showed me how many times Cass brought her children into the emergency room for undiagnosed illnesses. A classic sign of Munchausen syndrome by proxy, he told me.

The investigator was very through. He even showed me an interview tape from a friend who runs a local TV station. It was the complete TV interview, unedited, showing Barbara Cass behaving happy and fine at first, then as soon as she thought the interview was starting, acting suddenly like the world was ending. A terrible acting job, we both thought. Then, when she thought the cameras were turned off, she talked about how much she liked the husband, then switched subjects to what restaurant she would try for dinner. His final comment was, "This woman is an attention whore, lying to make her mundane life have more meaning. It was all about her, not the missing wife of Mr. Swanson."

Mr. Swanson had made an appointment for me with the police. At the station, a well-dressed man introduced himself as Detective John Sterling. He told me, "We have heard about the famous Mick Anderson." He was joined by another detective who didn't bother to introduce himself. They were friendly enough but politely told me to "butt out" of their investigations. The second detective point blank told me, "We think you're a fraud; I don't care what the media says about you." While I understand their skepticism, statements like this really piss me off.

"Give me one of your failures and I'll solve it, and I'll do it within the hour," I said. He chuckled but didn't say anything. "I did a little research before I came here, and saw you have a missing child, Cassandra Cortez. The newspapers presumed she was kidnapped or worse. What has it been, ten days? Let me take a crack at it."

The second detective screamed, "Get the fuck out of here!"

Detective Sterling put his hand up to prevent the other detective from coming any closer to me.

"It's true that most of us think you're a fraud, but I'm willing to give you a try. Stay here for a minute while I discuss this with my chief." He grabbed the other detective by the arm and escorted him through a door.

A few minutes later a door opened and he ushered me into a large room with detectives milling around. They all stopped and looked, some laughing and pointing. At the end of the room was someone I figured was a captain or chief standing in front of a large office. Sterling led me back to this office.

"Chief Ortega, this is Mick Anderson, the one we discussed."

He shook my hand, pointed inside to a chair, and said, "Well, to be perfectly honest, I don't think you can help us, but I'm willing to try anything. Have a seat." He said it loud enough so the other detectives would hear him.

I sat down, and for about ten seconds all he did was stare at me. He pointed at me and said, "I want to make sure I have your complete attention, are you listening?"

I replied, "Yes, sir."

He said, "Good, because most misunderstandings are due to a lack of understanding, and I don't want to repeat myself or have you question the importance of what I'm about to say." He paused, cleared his throat, then pointed his finger at me. "I'll not have my department become a circus. If you embarrass me or the department, I'll personally kick you out of the city, understood?"

I responded, "I see no problem with that, chief."

He leaned back in his chair, paused a second, then said, "What do you need from us?"

I quickly replied, "Clothes, backpacks, toys, or a purse, anything that will allow me to sense her attacker."

The chief nodded to Detective Sterling, and he set four boxes labeled "Evidence—Cortez" in front of me. Each box had a description underneath of the contents. One by one, Sterling opened them and removed bags of clothing and other items and placed them in front of me. The top bag was labeled "Blanket" and held a blanket she slept with every night, according to her parents. I touched it, then put both hands on it for about ten seconds. Next, I opened a bag that had her phone; it was covered in fingerprint dust. I just held it in my hand for a few seconds.

The third bag contained a bookbag, which I took out and held it in my hands.

"Where was this found?" I asked.

"On a street near her school," replied the chief.

I felt a tingle, and I cracked a smile.

"Let's go," I said.

"Go where?" asked the chief.

"Go and get her back," I replied. I felt my little finger tingle just a bit more. "You're about to witness some amazing shit," I quipped.

We jumped in the chief's SUV, and another car with four detectives followed us. I told them where to drive. Eventually we got on the highway and drove for about twenty minutes. We drove past Bandimere Dragway, one of my favorite places to race. "Red Rock is over that mountain, right?" I said to the detective.

"Yes, up the road from the race track."

"Turn at the race track exit," I told them. We drove on Bear Creek Avenue. "Drive past Red Rock." We took the winding road past Red Rock, a natural rock formation that's wonderful for concerts. We drove about five more miles, and I told them to stop between Halfway Rock and Idledale. I started to feel the electrocution event beginning and my fingers were in full quiver mode. There was a dirt path that went downhill.

"I know we're close by. What's out here—does anybody live on the end of this road? Or is this even a road?"

"C1 to dispatch, we need an address check on our location, anybody live out here?" said the chief into the radio.

Dispatch said, "Nothing permanent according to the county records."

I said, "Someone of interest is down the hill in front of us."

We all got out of our cars to explore the surroundings. Then the chief decided to drive down the dirt road. Once we turned a corner, an old RV, similar to what they used in the TV series *Breaking Bad*, appeared. Two old trucks were next to it, and a fire was burning nearby. It appeared they were cooking something. We stopped about one hundred feet from the RV. The sound our tires made must've alerted them to our presence. Three men came out of the RV holding rifles. One in the middle was holding what appeared to be an AK-47. They just stared at us.

We exited the car and took cover. One of the detectives yelled, "Police—drop your weapons now."

Detective Sterling reached back to the storage area of the SUV and retrieved an AR-15 and two magazines. I told Sterling, "That guy, in the middle, the one with the AK-47, he is the one that's giving me the strongest response."

"Drop your weapons. We just want to talk," shouted one of the detectives. Sterling trained his rifle on the suspect and yelled, "Drop it now."

The chief yelled to his men, "Nobody shoot, we need him to tell us where the girl is."

Sterling yelled, "We want the girl. Where is she? We don't want anyone to get hurt; we just want the girl. Don't make it worse for yourself; cooperate and it will be OK for you. Put your guns down." They continued to hold the rifles.

It seemed like an eternity, but finally one of the men—who appeared to be the most scared—threw his weapon down and laid down. The other two glared at him, and the guy in the middle yelled something at him. The guy at the end finally threw his rifle to the side and laid down as well. This left just the guy in the middle with the AK-47 machine gun.

"I'm not scared of you," yelled the man. In an instant he yanked his gun up and started to fire at us. A hail of bullets went both directions. After about one hundred rounds were fired by the police, the chief finally yelled, "Cease firing."

There was no doubt the guy with the AK was dead, but so was the guy behind him. The detectives rushed forward and put cuffs on all three and confiscated their weapons. The chief and Sterling came forward and told the other detectives, "We will guard them; check the RV."

I walked nearby and stopped right by the one remaining suspect. He looked up and said, "How'd you find us?"

I responded, "PFM, buddy. Just good old PFM."

"PFM?" he said. "What the fuck is that, some new technology?"

I responded, "Nope. PFM means pure fucking magic." I don't think he was amused.

"She is here," someone shouted. "She looks bad but is breathing."

The chief said, "I'll call an ambulance."

"Better call a Life Flight; a normal ambulance will take too long," I said.

Once everything settled down and the helicopter had taken off, Detective Sterling took me aside and said, "How the hell did you do that? Who, or what, are you?"

I said, "Sterling, I have a curse and a gift at the same time. I don't understand it—I have no idea how it works or why, or even why I was chosen to possess it—but as long as it does something useful, I'm going to run with it. That guy, the one with the AK, was pure evil. I was able to track him for more than fifteen miles, so either he is the worst of the worst or my skills are improving. My senses are amplified by the worst, most sick and vile criminals. In my experience, with people like this, you will learn he has an extremely demented past."

Fast-forward three days. We had a press conference to announce that the kidnapped child, Cassandra Cortez, was going to be going home from the hospital in a few days. I hadn't asked what happened to her because I didn't want to know. The gang had four members. The police had arrested the fourth after he drove to the scene and was arrested for DUI. The three men at the scene of the shootout were wanted felons who'd jumped bail; they shot up bars and gas stations, and even robbed several banks. In each bank robbery, a security guard was shot and seriously wounded when they burst into the bank. I suspected that Cassandra was in the wrong place at the wrong time and they snatched her. Detectives learned was that the ring leader, which was the guy I tracked, was named Ricky Hilbern. His DNA was a perfect match to five unsolved murders. He was involved with a Mexican cartel distributing drugs in the area and two children were among his victims. He was never going to bother anyone else. The world was a better place without him in it. I knew there were far more crimes associated with Mr. Hilbern, but these were all the police could prove at this time.

Part of the press conference was for the purpose of finding the missing mother, Barbara Swanson. We showed pictures of her while her children and Mr. Swanson pleaded for her safe return. A reward of one hundred thousand dollars was offered for her safe return or information to her whereabouts. I made sure the kids milked the cameras with cute toys and props.

One hundred grand brings out all the crazies, and the phone screeners had their hands full. Mr. Swanson, and his children, were in an adjoining room listening by loudspeaker to each call to try and identify her voice. Nothing useful was learned the first two days. Then a screener took a phone call that took us all by surprise.

"I'm Barbara Swanson, the woman you're looking for," she said to a screener. Randy Swanson was listening to calls and it took him a second before he looked up. He pounded frantically on a window overlooking the screeners. Police tracked every number that came in; this one came from New Mexico.

"You're Barbara Swanson, you say?" said the screener. "We get a lot of prank calls; can you answer some questions to verify?"

"Sure, OK, I can certainly understand that," the caller said.

The screeners had two pages of test questions for any caller who claimed she was Barbara Swanson.

The screener asked, "What kind of car did your mom drive when you were growing up in Chicago?" This was a trick question since they never lived in Chicago.

"We never lived in Chicago. I grew up in Denver, and she drove a big Buick station wagon." *Ding-ding.* I thought; *right answer.*

"What did the door to your bedroom have on it when you were growing up?" said the screener.

"A poster of The Backstreet Boys," was the caller's answer.

*Ding-ding; we have a winner.*

Mr. Swanson grabbed the phone from the screener. "Barbara, is this you?" The caller went quiet. He continued, "Darling, what happened—where are you? Are you safe? The children miss you terribly."

The caller finally said, "I'm sorry. I just got overwhelmed and couldn't take it anymore. I'm so sorry, but I can't do that life, at least not now."

Mr. Swanson yelled, "We can make it work, I promise. Please come home—please."

When the caller said nothing, he handed the phone to his youngest daughter, and she said, "Mommy, is that you? I miss you. Can you come and do the curls in my hair for my birthday party next week?" The caller, now positively identified as Barbara Swanson, just cried on the phone.

My job was done. I had earned the money Mr. Swanson paid me. More importantly, I had earned respect. This weird talent I possess proved to be vitally important. I also learned that I could make a living help-ing people.

I flew home. When my wife picked me up, she informed me there were ten large bags of mail delivered today. The postman said each bag was fifty pounds, so that's a total of five hundred pounds of mail. She told me the bags were sitting in the garage at our old house. That night she and I went through some of the mail. There were thousands of letters from all over the world. Many of them contained pieces of clothing, hair, or jewelry, along with a passionate plea for help locating a loved one. It was hard to fathom how my once-mundane life had turned upside down in a matter of months. I couldn't possibly read and answer each of the letters; there just wasn't enough time in the day.

We had secretly moved to have somewhat of a normal life. Our house was on a private street. Not even our family knew our new address. So, it was strange when someone knocked on the door. I looked through the peep hole to see two exceptionally large men in nice, matching suits. I thought they were police officers, so I opened the door.

The larger of the two men handed me an envelope and said in a thick Russian accent, "We would appreciate it if you would read this—now." The return address was from the Ambassador of the Russian Federation, Washington, D.C. There was no postage on the envelope, and these guys weren't from FedEx, UPS, or the Postal Service. I was pretty sure they were armed. I looked behind them to see a black Cadillac Escalade with two large men next to it in my driveway.

I thought, *OK, a hand-delivered envelope, all the way from Washington, D.C.; you have my attention.* I felt motivated to do as they said and opened the envelope.

# Chapter 26:

# Over 30 Missing

The letter was from Anatoly Antonov, the Russian Ambassador to the United States.

The letter read:

> *Dear Mr. Anderson,*
>
> *We have heard about your remarkable ability to find missing and kidnapped children. I am pleading for your assistance with a current crime wave in the Russian Federation. Over thirty children have been abducted in the last four months. We have not been able to find the person or persons responsible and are asking for your help in this matter.*
>
> *We realize your time is valuable and will offer you US $100,000 in cash to attempt to find them. We will also pay you an additional US $250,000 if you are able to return the children unharmed.*
>
> *I've setup a special phone number, which will be staffed twenty-four hours a day so you may call and discuss this situation. If you accept our offer, we will provide a private jet to fly you to my country. You will have our best detectives and police at your disposal.*
>
> *We need your help, urgently. Thank you for your consideration.*

It was signed by the ambassador. Below his signature was a telephone number.

I asked if the men would wait while I called the number. I wasn't sure this entire operation was legal, but I was intrigued. I called the number; it was picked up on the first ring. "Mick Anderson, we really appreciate your interest in solving our problem. Do you have additional questions?" said a voice in perfect English.

"I don't have any questions at this time. In the spirit of governmental cooperation, I'd be honored to help. I cannot guarantee I'll find the children or end these kidnappings, but I'll try my best to find those responsible."

"Excellent. We will expedite your paperwork, and travel will be arranged tonight. Will your wife, Michelle, be attending as well?"

"I'll ask and call you back," I said. The caller said the first leg of the flight would be to Washington, D.C., where I'd meet with the ambassador for a short time.

"Actually, I do have a question," I said. "Are these children connected to someone high up in your government?"

The person on the other end paused for a few seconds then said, "There have been reports that at least five of the children have parents in the state council. This isn't public knowledge, so how could you know this?"

I replied, "I had a suspicion based on the urgency of a hand-delivered envelope, and a phone number monitored twenty-four hours a day."

I didn't really want my wife to come along. It wasn't that I didn't want to be with her, but I had no idea about the current security situation. We discussed it and decided I'd go alone. I called back and told this to the gentleman on the phone. He told me the travel information and said the money was already in my account. "Damn, you guys move quick." He then told me those men would wait by the house until I was ready to go to the airport. I returned to the men at my front door, and told them arrangements were made. One of the men was talking on cell phone and told the others something in Russian. He gave me a thumbs-up sign.

I was ready in two hours. They drove me to the Peoria airport, where there was a private jet waiting for me. I had never had a private jet fly me anywhere, and I decided I could get used to this. The two pilots were Russian and told me just two things: their names, and how long the flight would take. There was a flight attendant on the plane, which seemed odd at first, but she was nice. Three of the men from the SUV also boarded the airplane. We had almost no conversations, so I slept for nearly the entire flight to Washington, D.C.

After landing the plane went to a private area of the airport where a large limousine was waiting. I counted twelve obviously heavily armed men strategically placed around the limo. One opened the back door and said in a thick Russian accent, "The ambassador would like a word."

I climbed into the vehicle and sat next to a person I assumed was the ambassador. "I trust your flight was good?" said the man in a heavy Russian accent. "I am Anatoly Antonov, and I am the Russian ambassador to the United States. I want to first thank you for agreeing to this mission. It's very important to us that these children be found. You no doubt know that some are children of high-ranking individuals."

Outside there was some movement, and I noticed four black SUVs approaching rapidly. Mr. Antonov looked over and said, "Ah, I see your government people are approaching." He chuckled then said, "We had to contact them to expedite travel plans and to let them know you're not a Russian spy. He could've come alone, but your government likes a show of force."

A procession of people approached the limo, and the door was opened. A man jumped in, shook hands with Mr. Antonov, and looked over at me. In a thick Texas accent, he said, "So, you're the man with the magic hands we have heard about?"

"Depends what you heard I guess," was my reply.

"James P Douglas is my name," he said, reaching to shake my hand. "I know who you are, Mick, and the US government is anxious to get you on your way. As a good faith effort between governments, we have all your paperwork ready to go." He handed an envelope to Mr. Antonov. He removed his phone and told me, "To verify your identity I'll need to get fingerprints. Can you touch the screen, one finger at a time?" I complied, and two seconds later he had his confirmation.

"When you return you will meet with some of my people here in Washington for debriefing. Mr. Anatoly Antonov will contact me when it's time. Do you have any questions for me?"

I replied, "You didn't tell me your job title, Mr. Douglas."

"Yes, that's correct, I didn't," was his reply. Then he tapped on the window, the door was opened, and he got out.

In my best *Ace Ventura: Pet Detective* impersonation, I said to Mr. Antonov, "Well alrighty then, guess I didn't need to know."

He nodded, perhaps a bit unsure what the hell I was talking about. He said, "He is the US government's spymaster, so he checks everyone out who meets with any Russian personnel, especially someone we fast-track out of America. Our governments are wary of each other, as is to be expected, but we get along much better than your media would have you believe. He is, as you say, a 'hard ass,' but they're aware of our situation, and he was instrumental in providing us documents to get you out of the USA in a timely manner."

He looked out the window and said, "Now it's time. I've arranged for another private jet; this one is just slightly bigger." He pointed to a large Russian jet that was taxiing toward us. "There are twenty-two people flying with you. Two of the men and one woman are investigators on the case, and the rest are security personnel tasked with your protection. They'll be with you day and night. Mr. Anderson, what I am about to tell you is of the utmost importance; never talk to anyone without them. Never go any-where without them, and trust no one else. These men are handpicked by someone I trust. Nobody else knows you're coming, and we want to keep it that way. You will be introduced as an FBI profiler, and your credentials are in this package." He handed me an envelope.

"Now I have important functions to attend to. Again, Mick Anderson, my government thanks you for your help in this matter, and you will be rewarded handsomely if you succeed." He tapped on the glass; the door was opened. I shook his hand, stepped out of the vehicle, and was led to the airplane.

The captain of the team introduced himself as Aleksei Ypovich, a twelve-year member of the Spetsnaz, which is the Russian special forces. All the team members came from the special forces, but not all were as high ranking as Aleksei. I was quickly introduced to the rest of the people on the plane. Two minutes later I couldn't remember a single name other than Aleksei. These men had excellent English skills, probably learned from a young age. They were big guys, but not huge. There were two women as well. They seemed well trained, and ready for any situation.

# Chapter 27:
# Not Welcome

It was a long flight, but they had great French toast, butter syrup, eggs, and sausage. I watched TV and got to know the people who would be my security detail.

My seat was made of the finest leather. It converted into a bed with the touch of a button. High-speed internet was available on the plane, so I emailed my wife pictures and kept her up to date on what was going on. This aircraft was used by the ambassador and was very luxurious. So far it was an excellent example of how the other half lived. It beat flying commercial.

That all changed the minute we landed at Sheremetyevo Airport in Moscow.

As soon as the door opened, military people poured in. They wanted to see everyone's papers immediately. Aleksei showed him the orders from the central government. The guy who appeared to be in charge wasn't impressed by this and yelled something in Russian.

I asked Aleksei what he'd yelled, and he replied, "It means, 'He doesn't give a fuck.' Someone is 'up his ass,' as you say in America." They continued to yell back and forth in Russian. Eventually they relented after Aleksei screamed at them and began dialing his phone. Three Ford Expeditions, five Chevy Suburbans and one Ford Taurus police car approached the plane. They were all painted black, with blacked-out glass you couldn't see through. There was no chrome or other color anywhere on the vehicle, even the wheels were black.

I said, "Cool, you guys have US vehicles."

But Who Will Save The Children

Aleksei said, "Yes, they're a status symbol here. The cool stuff you can't see is that the first and the last Fords have multi-barrel machine guns. They pop out of the top when there's trouble, or if we just want to impress the ladies." He grinned, and I could tell he was happy with his "toys."

"Where to now?" I asked.

"We have a room full of collected evidence. I was told you need to see and touch the evidence, so it's all laid out by child. It's a big room; take all the time you need." We were whisked away; the drivers turned on the police lights and quickly drove across town.

We arrived at a large building with about twenty cars outside in the parking lot.

Aleksei screamed, "Shit."

I asked "What's going on?"

Aleksei replied, "Sorry, I just saw a car that belongs to one of the worst police captains on the force. He is inept and just got the job because of friends in high places. We have to tiptoe around him, otherwise he will try to challenge our mission. His name is Mikhail Posivic."

The entire team went in the building. Waiting for us was the man who had Aleksei concerned. He had medals all over his uniform, and you could tell he had a narcissistic personality. He had to be in the center of everyone, with all their attention on him. He looked up and saw us enter.

"Aleksei!" he yelled. "We have been waiting on you. Did you bring the 'chosen one' with you?" He said this in near-perfect English. Aleksei sternly replied, "We have work to do, Mikhail. As you know, we're on a time-sensitive mission. I've brought this man all the way from America, and he needs to see the evidence right now."

"So, you have brought an American spy to our country, and you expect me to allow this? I think not. I have friends who will be most interested in your betrayal," said Mikhail.

Aleksei did something I considered extremely funny. He pulled out his cell phone, raised it in the air so everyone could see, and started walking quickly toward Mikhail.

143

Aleksei, screamed, "Here, you may use my cell phone and call them. I am confident my friends are far more important and powerful, but be my guest, Mikhail. My friends wrote these detailed orders which brought this man from America to assist us in solving these kidnappings. You tried to solve these kidnappings for nearly a month, but your incompetence hasn't produced a single suspect. My orders are to let this man inspect all the evidence. If you have a problem with that, then go ahead and call anyone you want. Right now, we need everyone out. Our mission has top priority."

Mikhail was furious and yelled, "When this mission of yours fails, and it will fail, I'll make sure you never have a job in my police force. You may have friends now, but they'll abandon you quickly when they realize your actions worsened the situation. I'll give you until tomorrow, then seal up the building, friends or no friends."

For some reason I felt like being an asshole at that very instant. I waved and said, "By-by Mikhail." Aleksei and some of the soldiers started laughing.

After they left, I spent an hour looking through all the clothing, books, toys, and electronics collected. I had zero feelings in my fingers. I told Aleksei this, and he seemed shocked.

"But you're supposed to be able to see and feel things. I risked my career to get you over here."

I told him, "Either they're too far away, or something in this building is preventing me from sensing their location."

Aleksei thought for a moment then said, "This building is bomb proof, even against nuclear weapons, and was used during the cold war to make missile parts, so it will have thick steel and concrete. Let's go outside."

Once we exited the building, I proceeded to use my hands as a tracking antenna. I saw the building's fire escape and told Aleksei I wanted to climb it to improve my senses. I was determined to focus on my hands, wanting badly not to disappoint Aleksei. My apprehension was growing exponentially with every second. Once on the top I finally had a weak tingling sensation and told Aleksei, "Good call, Aleksei, you were right. I feel something now. The sensation is weak, very weak, probably many miles away, or else they're in a building like the one we were in. I need to cover a larger area. Can we get a helicopter?"

"I have orders to get you anything you require. I'll have one available in thirty minutes," Aleksei said excitedly.

"Can I bring some of the clothes and other items on the helicopter to keep my focus?" I asked.

"Anything you need," was his answer.

Aleksei was on the phone immediately, yelling in Russian. I have no idea what he was saying but it sounded threatening. My guess is someone on the line was being lazy or didn't understand how important this mission was. He hung up, called another number, and repeated many of the same words to someone else. He hung up and smiled. "Be here in fifteen minutes," he said in a cheerful, yet sinister tone.

About ten minutes later I heard a helicopter in the distance. Turns out it was three helicopters—large ones at that. I'd forgotten; twenty men needed to be transported. The helicopters landed, everyone jumped on board, and off we went.

The Russian helicopters weren't at all nice inside or out. They were basically tin cans that vibrated worse than those cheap beds in cut-rate hotels—the ones where you put a quarter into the machine and the bed vibrates for two minutes. Once airborne, I had no idea if I was feeling something important to the case or just vibrations from this shitty Russian helicopter. The noise, smell, and vibration was about all the fun I could stand.

I had to yell to ask Aleksei, "Have them fly north east. I need to focus to pick something up." We flew a large arc for about five miles. Halfway through I felt a slightly different vibration. I shouted over the rotor blades, "Have them fly more to the east." Then he gave me a headset and motioned for me to put it on. I pushed the button and said, "Your helicopters suck; not sure if you knew that. I was wondering when I'd get a headset. It's difficult to communicate without screaming over the noise from the blades and engine. Why didn't you give me one of these before?"

Aleksei laughed and said, "I forgot, you Americans have overly sensitive ears. You have become soft."

I noticed that both he and the pilots were laughing. I didn't realize the pilots could hear the same conversation, so I said, "If you Russians think having junky helicopters makes you tough, then your understanding of the word 'tough' isn't the same as ours. By the way, I hear these things fall out of the sky far more than they do in America. Is that why you think you're tougher? Every time one actually lands instead of crashing, your mental toughness is built up, right?" I smiled; he didn't.

One of the pilots looked back and gave Aleksei a hand gesture. Aleksei didn't look pleased as he motioned to his men inside the helicopter. They all made quick preparations for something that I wasn't privy to. I asked him what all that meant, and he said, "Nothing important."

Once the helicopter had flown straight for about fifteen minutes, my ring finger started to tingle. I told Aleksei we were within twenty miles; he smiled and gave me a thumbs-up sign. Aleksei got on the radio to request information on where we were going and what might be out there. We had left the city and were flying over a rural area. I got on the radio and said, "We need to go farther to the east." Five minutes later my middle finger started to vibrate, so I told Aleksei, "Ten, maybe fifteen miles."

He said, "Kilometers?"

I laughed and said, "Not kilometers, just miles; my fingers don't work in kilometers."

There was a bunch of chatter in Russian, then we started to descend. "What's going on?" I asked.

"We have another helicopter that has reported problems and must land," he stated.

"Another one? How many are left of the three?"

He didn't say anything, and I took that to mean we were the only one still flying. We circled back and saw the helicopter crash-landing in a cloud of dust. Everyone jumped out OK, but we didn't have enough room or guns on this helicopter to complete the mission if we met any resistance. Besides, these helicopters are so loud they could probably hear us already.

"I'll call for trucks to come get us. Do you think we're close?" asked Aleksei.

"Hard to say, but I'd think we're within ten miles. I feel safer in trucks anyway."

"OK, we will land now and wait. If you need to use the bathroom, just pop the hatch on the bottom of the helicopter and try not to fall out," he said smiling.

I responded, "Over a million out-of-work comedians and you're trying to take their jobs. Real nice."

He said, "I wasn't trying to be a comedian. I guess it's never too late to change careers. You think I am funny?"

I replied, "No, sorry."

An hour later, Aleksei told everyone to get ready to move. I saw the same SUVs that picked us up from the airport approaching. Aleksei finally told me the first helicopter had failed within five minutes! That team was picked up, and now we had all twenty team members accounted for. The temperature was dropping quickly, and now I could see my breath. I had no coat. They gave me a choice of a thick parka, which is far too warm, or wind breaker, far too cold. I wanted the middle bear so to speak, but was out of luck. I took the warm one. We only had one hour of light left, and I was told the temperature would be below zero soon. What I didn't know was they meant Celsius, which meant it would be below 32 degrees Fahrenheit. The team quickly packed the SUVs and continued.

I started singing, "On the road again—I just can't wait to get on the road again," the song made popular by Willie Nelson. I was amazed when everyone else started singing along. These guys are great together, a real team. Aleksei seemed happy with the progress. Many on the team gave me a thumbs-up sign.

We had to move slowly; Russian rural roads are crap. Thirty minutes into the drive I had five fingers vibrating—not throbbing, but I knew we were close. Up ahead there was a large hill. I told Aleksei we were close, and he ordered the vehicles to stop. He had a soldier run up ahead to scout the area. After ten minutes, the scout radioed in. Aleksei, apparently satisfied with the report, had the vehicles continued on.

Once we crested the hill, he ordered all vehicles off of the roadway and into the brush. The team exited the vehicles to survey the valley below with binoculars. About two miles away we saw buildings and vehicles. Aleksei returned to his vehicle. He said something in Russian on the radio. "No lights of any kind," he said to me, then retrieved a laptop.

"What's the laptop for?" I asked.

"Drone will be overhead in a few minutes. We will let it check that area for us using video and infrared sensors," he responded.

"That's bad-ass cool," I said.

It was starting to get dark. I didn't hear or see the drone that Aleksei said was three thousand meters above us. I did the quick math and figured it was around ten-thousand feet. The video feed was displayed on the laptop. It had a split screen—one side video, the other thermal imaging. "Pretty sure you guys stole this technology from us," I said.

Aleksei said, "What makes you so sure America didn't steal it from the Russians?"

I replied, "Because our helicopters don't fall out of the sky as often as yours. It appears you 'found' some of our secrets."

Aleksei paused, then said, "You're probably right, my friend."

The drone showed all the heat traces from the structures in front of us. We counted about forty warm bodies, twenty or so vehicles, and six structures with furnaces on. Aleksei also showed me something else of interest. "Look at these guns, AK-47s and AK-74s, about thirty of them. They're not hunting wildlife with these," he said. "Not good," he added while he spun the computer around so the other men could see the images.

"What is it?" I asked. "What's not good?" The video screen displayed close up images of not only the AKs but very lethal rocket-propelled grenades, or RPGs. This is a shoulder-fired weapon system that fires rockets equipped with an explosive warhead. They're powerful enough to disable a tank if used properly. I counted at least twenty RPGs.

"Any frontal assault on this compound would produce many casualties, more than we can handle," Aleksei said wearily. "This changes our plans. We have enough firepower with us, and the element of surprise. But if some of those warm bodies are the children—well, it could end badly. I am sending scouts down there right now. Within an hour we will have our plan. We will act once we know they're asleep. The drone will be flying around giving us mission-critical information. We need to refine the plan."

He continued, "I think you brought us to the right people. You see, I really put my career on the line asking for help from an American. I am happy that my instincts were correct about you. These people are not normal kidnappers; my guess is paramilitary or ex-soldiers. It's the only way they could get access to those weapons. Since some of the children have important parents, the kidnappers must have a beef with the government. My guess is they want a large ransom, but nobody has informed me if this is true."

I said, "Aleksei, I'm pretty sure you're smart enough to figure this out, but I need to say it anyway. I was told that I cannot trust anyone but your team, so I'd be remiss if I didn't warn you about contacting anyone who may have connections to these people in the police force or military."

He replied, "I know you're concerned, but I have trustworthy members of both branches that we can use. We're on frequencies not used by normal Russian police and military, plus they're encrypted with the best American—umm, I mean Russian technology available. To further increase security, we're using our department's drone, which is flown by my best friend. It has, what you call 'stealth' properties, and our radar cannot follow it."

I asked, "It has wire-guided missiles on board?"

He responded, "Yes, the latest and greatest."

We waited a few hours. The drone footage appeared to show everyone sleeping. A large barn on the property appeared to be the place the children were kept. There were livestock in there as well, but their thermal images were far different from the smaller images.

"Thirty-four small sources," Aleksei said.

That was the correct count of missing children.

The scouts reported in, "All quiet." No guards were patrolling the compound. It was pretty obvious the kidnappers didn't expect anyone would find them.

Aleksei ordered everyone back to the SUVs so we could get closer. They put on night-vision goggles and drove slowly to within about a half mile of the compound. The drive took nearly twenty minutes to travel one and a half miles. The drone and scouts verified we weren't detected. We pulled deep into the brush and trees. Once Aleksei was done looking at the images, he told everyone to continue driving another four hundred meters. We stopped and Aleksei ordered his men to put camouflage curtains over the vehicles. Nobody talked at all; everyone knew their jobs.

Ten minutes later the drone operator told Aleksei, "Target, six o'clock, eight kilos, cover and conceal."

A scout a half mile away confirmed, "Two vehicles, high rate of speed."

Two vehicles were driving down the same road we had just been on. In a few minutes they were about a mile away and moving quickly. Aleksei clicked on his mic to the drone operator and spoke to him in Russian. A targeting line appeared on the screen as it zeroed in on the vehicles. It appeared from the images to be a small van and a pickup truck. They had no markings. Thermal imagery showed two people in the truck and four or five in the small van.

Our team had covered its SUVs with netting to resemble the area around us. The vehicles crested the hill only one hundred yards away at a speed I estimated at seventy miles per hour. We all held our breath.

Aleksei said, "Hopefully they don't notice us."

"No shit, Sherlock," I responded. I don't believe he understood my attempt at humor.

The lead vehicle honked rapidly and flicked its bright lights on and off a few hundred yards from the compound. Thermal imaging of each structure revealed people moving rapidly, lights were turned on, and weapons were distributed. The people inside the trucks jumped out and went into the first building.

"You're sure about security on this operation, right?" I asked.

He looked worried but said, "I trust everyone. If they start moving any children, then I'll be concerned about a breach. In that case we will come up with a different plan, but right now I am confident."

"You have any spare guns, just in case?" I responded. He popped open a compartment that contained six handguns and handed me a nine-millimeter and two magazines without batting an eye or even looking at me.

"Contact two hundred meters, two coming our way." The scout and the drone basically reported the same thing.

Two men, both armed, were walking our way. Everyone froze as we watched the screen and listened to the radio. One scout was in their path, and the drone video showed them walk right past him.

"Shit, that was close," I said.

Aleksei put on goggles that received images from the computer, then he turned off the screen.

Aleksei said, "Snipers ready?" into the radio.

A soft "Roger" was heard twice.

The two men stopped about forty feet from us. Nobody breathed. They appeared to look right at us, then lit up cigarettes. *What are they doing?* I put in the small earplugs so I could listen to everything. The drone pilot radioed in, "Contact, one vehicle, six o'clock, four kilos."

"Son of a bitch," said Aleksei quietly. "It's a big Mercedes, like what an important member of government would drive. Those men who walked up here know this car is coming."

The drone operator said, "Two people in the front, only one in the back seat."

Aleksei said to me, "Someone important, with bodyguards probably. Are you getting anything from that direction Mick?"

With so much excitement I had forgot about my fingers. I turned toward the car coming and held up my hands like a directional antenna.

"Yes, but not nearly as strong as what's in front of us," I replied. "When they get closer, we will know for sure."

This whole experience was nerve racking, to say the least. When I wasn't frightened to death, I thought it was fascinating. I had a bad feeling that any minute this situation would stop being fascinating and start being dangerous.

"Contact, twelve o'clock, two hundred meters, vehicle moving," said one of the scouts.

A truck came quickly up the road and stopped by the two men we were watching. The headlights were pointed right at us. Nobody moved. Finally, the headlights went out, and just the parking lights were left on. I was impressed by the camouflage; they were looking right at us, unaware of our presence.

A minute later the large Mercedes stopped right by the truck. Two men from the truck got out and walked around to the side of the Mercedes. Aleksei had a powerful directional microphone pointed toward the Mercedes. We could hear them speaking in Russian, arguing with the person in the back seat.

Aleksei whispered, "They're arguing about money, the two from the truck want much more money. I can't see who's in the back seat. Do you feel anything from this guy?"

I said, "Yes, but not nearly as strong as what's coming from the compound. My guess he doesn't do the dirty work like the people from the camp."

Aleksei hit the mic and asked his team, "Who's in the back seat?"

"Can't tell, not in position," said a voice.

There was more yelling, then two men joined the people from the truck. Now there were four people near the car.

I asked "What are they saying?"

Aleksei said, "The big one is saying you don't scare us, so either double the money or we kill the kids and take what you already gave us." The guy in the back seat jumped out with an AK-47. He pointed the gun at the men, and they stepped back quickly, hands in the air.

Aleksei said, "I don't believe it. It's Nicolai."

"Who?" I asked.

I heard on the radio from one of the scouts, "Nicolai. It's Nicolai in the car."

The man they identified as Nicolai opened fire with his machine gun, and all four men collapsed.

"Hold your fire," said Aleksei softly.

"Contact, twelve o'clock, two hundred meters, eight people in two trucks. Trucks moving fast and coming your way," said a scout over the radio.

People in the trucks began firing on the Mercedes. It was chaos outside. Aleksei and the team members around me acted like it was no big deal. There were flashes of light from the guns, followed by bullet sparks everywhere. I even heard ricocheting bullets, just like in a Hollywood movie. Men jumped out of the trucks and took cover. The people originally in the Mercedes, now took cover behind the car.

"The car has bullet proof glass," said Aleksei.

The truck's windshield was a mess, holes everywhere. You could hear people screaming in pain; my guess was that out of the original eight in the trucks, at least four were down. After a brief timeout to reload, the firing began again.

"What are our orders?" said a voice over the radio.

"Hold your fire, we need to find out what we're up against," said Aleksei. "Mick, we have bullet proof glass too; we're safe from anything except the rocket-propelled grenades."

"RPG," someone screamed on the radio.

*Whoosh!* I heard and saw it coming right at us; luckily it was aimed at the Mercedes. A large explosion with a great fireball happened only one hundred feet in front of us. The shrapnel was being chased with sparkling lines similar to a firework's show. The sparkling lines went everywhere. We heard pinging sounds as metal fragments hit our SUV.

"Don't worry; we're safe for now," said Aleksei. In the light of the fire, I saw one man staggering toward us. His clothes were on fire and he was missing an entire arm. He finally collapsed.

"Contact, twelve o'clock, two hundred meters. Two trucks at a high rate of speed," said a scout over the radio.

I had a powerful throbbing sensation and told Aleksei, "The guy we want the most is coming toward us now, one of those in the truck coming up the hill."

I saw a person in the truck's headlights, obviously badly injured, attempting to run away. They shot him with a volley from a machine gun, and finally he went down.

"Where's Nicolai?" Aleksei said into the radio.

"Unknown," said someone on the radio.

Even though I knew that now wasn't the time, I blurted out, "Who's this Nicolai?" I asked.

"Nicolai Varchinko, an old friend. I was going to ask him to join our team last year, but he was ordered to go to Moscow. We heard he was mixed up in something, so I didn't bother. I can't believe he was involved in this."

The group of four people pulled someone up from the ground, near where the Mercedes was engulfed in flames. They put him on the hood of the truck. They pointed guns at him and were shouting something in Russian. One guy stepped forward, pointed a pistol at him, and fired.

"Open fire," yelled Aleksei. Tracer fire from four different points started hitting the men right in front of us, and they all went down. At the same time, the scouts near the camp below opened fire on the men guarding the buildings. We jumped out of our SUV and moved behind it. Aleksei had night-vision goggles and scanned the area.

I heard a *whoosh* and saw a trail of fire from the sky. In an instant there was a large explosion of the two trucks 150 feet away. The drone had fired a missile to take out men hiding in the trucks. I felt the shock wave and then was peppered with debris from the explosion. I wasn't trained for this and scampered back into the SUV. This was the craziest day of my life and I won't lie to you: I was very frightened. While I didn't want to take the time to check, I realized the warm fluid running down my leg most probably meant I'd pissed myself. Adrenaline and fear caused my whole body to shake.

Aleksei was calm on the radio. Seemed like it was no big deal—just another firefight. He was ordering his men to do various jobs with the same demeanor and calmness as if he were ordering from McDonald's. Obviously well trained, Aleksei's men went about their business in a quick professional manner. One part of me was scared to death, while the other marveled at their precision. From the light created by the burning Mercedes, I saw Aleksei and four other men running toward the camp.

I heard more machine guns down by the camp as the team broke into the building that housed the children. Over the radio I heard Aleksei: "Get to the children first and secure them. Try to capture some of the criminals alive if possible; we need information." More machine-gun sounds were heard, and then the radio squawked, "Two down. Bring first aid packs." Those were Aleksei's men that were injured.

The drone pilot radioed, "Four making a run for it, behind the main building, what are your orders?"

"Send a missile out in front, don't hit them, try to stop them so we can question those still alive," said Aleksei.

The drone fired another missile. I saw a streak of light from up in the sky, then I heard a *Whoosh*. This was followed quickly by another explosion well away from my location.

"Secured," said a voice over the radio. Then another said the same thing.

I heard Aleksei finally say, "Target secured." I took a gun with me and cautiously exited the SUV. I went over to the remains of the Mercedes. It may have had bullet-proof glass, but the doors weren't RPG proof. The car was nearly torn in two, the roof peeled back like a sardine can. It was still burning.

Two of Aleksei's men were going through the trucks interior while two more were trying to find identification cards on the bodies. They looked up and told me, "You should go back to the truck. We must be sure this area is safe." They didn't have to tell me twice. I hightailed it back to the security of the SUV.

Aleksei instructed the men to go from building to building, and any door locked was to be blown open with plastic explosives. I heard excited chatter in Russian for about a minute, then someone spoke English. They said, "Children in large room, at least thirty." About a minute later I heard Aleksei say to the others to count the children and write down each of their names.

I couldn't reach him to ask if they were all OK, but I was ecstatic that they were found. It was at least ten minutes of horrible waiting until I heard Aleksei tell the other men to bring the children out. I thought, *Out? Does this mean they're OK? Christ, will someone tell me what's going on?* Suddenly I spied a headset radio, less than a foot away from me, that I'd managed to overlook until now. I turned it on and heard Aleksei's voice come out of it, and at the same time I heard him with the earbud.

"Aleksei, please tell me the children are OK," I said into the mic.

After an agonizing ten seconds of waiting, he said, "Dehydrated, some are sick with the flu, but—." The transmission stopped.

"But what?" I asked.

"Contact, five vehicles six o'clock, four kilos," said a voice over the radio.

*Ah, shit. Just when I was about to know the outcome.*

Aleksei finally got on the radio and finished his original comment. "But they're alive, Mick. They're alive."

"About freaking time you finished the original sentence. Thanks for hanging me off a cliff, Aleksei," I said back.

Aleksei replied, "There are no cliffs here, Mick. What do you mean?" I realized the translation wasn't going to be understood.

Then I asked over the radio, "Aleksei, where are the night-vision goggles? I can't see shit."

"Same place as the handguns," came a hurried reply.

*Great, but I don't even know how to turn them on, I thought.* I opened the storage compartment and felt around until I found them. They were far bigger than I thought they'd be. I put them on my head.

"How do I turn them on, Aleksei?"

"Squeeze the fat area by your eyes." Aleksei said. Simple enough; they came on.

*This technology was definitely stolen from America,* I said to myself.

Now I could see everything. "Who's coming?" I shouted into the radio.

"Not sure, waiting on confirmation from drone. We have RPGs now and good defensive positions. Stay in the truck, Mick."

I thought, *No shit, all I have is—.* I stopped my thoughts mid-sentence when I realized I was in one of the SUVs that had a multi-barrel machine gun in the back end. I didn't want to be in a firefight, but if it happened, I figured a handgun wasn't going to cut it.

I turned a few handles, and the divider opened to reveal the gun. Sure enough, it was a multi-barrel machine gun. This weapon appeared to be a Russian copy of the machine gun used on American attack helicopters, just with more buttons and levers. I had no idea how to use it, but I was going to give myself a crash course, right now. This thing was bad-ass, filling the entire rear of the SUV. There was an access door in the ceiling and a hydraulic ram attached to the floor. I couldn't figure out how the access door opened. I was fairly sure I could operate the gun since there weren't many controls. A big red handle on the side appeared to be the charge handle. I saw a selector lever on the left side pointing to a red box position, which I took to mean "safety on." Russian writing was next to the selector lever, so I had to wing it. There was a green line above it, and above that three green lines, and above that a green box. No idea what the different green marks signified, but any green would probably fire the gun.

I finally figured out how to release the roof access panel by turning and lifting four handles. Instantly something near the gun beeped and the gun raised up and out of the SUV, pushing the door to the ground. "Whoops!" I said out loud. I hadn't intended for that to happen. I jumped up, grabbed the handles, and pulled my body high enough to see the mechanisms. *Let's figure out how it fires*, I thought. I could see triggers inside the handles, so it looked fairly straightforward. There was a strap of ammunition already attached on one side, and a burlap bag on the other, presumably to get the spent casings. I really hoped the gun was that easy to operate. I figured I may have to find out.

I hadn't been listening to the chatter on the radio while focusing on the gun. I forced myself to stop looking at the gun and listened very carefully. Aleksei was instructing his men where to position themselves.

"Trucks approaching, less than a kilo," I heard from the drone operator. "Russian marking, two are military type, six wheels, probably 4320s, the rest are KAMAZ."

They must've seen the fires, which would've been pretty hard to miss. I wanted to ask Aleksei if he'd informed his superiors that the site was secured. I kept quiet, though; he certainly knows what to do in this situation.

I held my breath as all the trucks roared by and stopped one hundred feet past my position. I locked the door and returned to the gun and spun it around facing the trucks. I counted fifteen men who got out of the trucks. More were still inside the trucks. They took up positions all over the area. I heard Aleksei tell everyone, "Stay out of sight. If they start firing, we will start firing. I am calling headquarters to determine who they are."

Aleksei had relented and called his superiors on a satellite phone. It was risky, I thought, but he needed to tell them about the mission's success and get reinforcements.

The six-wheel trucks were shining their spotlights all over the compound. I heard the loudspeaker say something in Russian that I didn't understand. Then I heard them say "Nicolai" and then pause, and then say a bunch of other Russian words. It appeared they knew Nicolai was here. I wondered if this is good or really bad. The loudspeaker went off again with similar phrases. I waited patiently for some radio chatter but heard none for about thirty seconds.

Aleksei told the drone operator, "Engage first truck with a missile."

An instant later all hell broke loose.

A streak of light came down from about two thousand feet above. *Whoosh* is what I heard first, followed instantly by a large explosion as the first truck disappeared in a fireball. Pieces rained down all over the area, and I jumped back inside the SUV. Smoking metal fragments, some more than eight inches wide, fell onto and into the SUV.

*I'm in way over my head right now,* I thought.

I heard a whooshing sound followed by another boom as RPGs were fired by our team toward the other truck. Machine guns were going off all over, and tracer fire lit up the sky.

I jumped back to the gun and saw people from the trucks running nearby. I aimed then pulled the trigger; absolutely nothing happened. "OK, what did I forget?" I said out loud. "Safety is on; flip the selector lever." I flipped the lever up to the top and aimed, then pulled the trigger, and again nothing happened. I pulled the charge handle to advance the ammunition strap one round and pulled the trigger, again nothing.

*This thing is starting to piss me off, I thought.* Finally, I figured there must be an additional safety device with the triggers, so I pulled both triggers at the same time. The gun erupted like a fireworks demonstration gone wrong. The combination of a deafening buzz saw and a million roman candles is the best way to describe the event. "Holy shit," I yelled. This was a "come to Jesus" moment that I'll never forget as long as I live.

Tracer ammunition was far brighter than I imagined it would be. I had to rip off the night-vision goggles or face blindness. When I say it was deafeningly loud, that's an understatement; it stung my eardrums like never before.

I spun the barrel back and forth as I watched parts of the trucks disintegrate. Three hundred rounds were probably fired in a few seconds, perhaps more. I could see someone in one of the trucks with a gun like mine, so I directed fire their way. I saw the gun get hit about a hundred times. I don't know if I hit the gunner or not, but it looked like his chances of weathering the storm of bullets was slim.

It all happened so quickly, all I could do was react to what others were doing. I stopped for a second to reassess where I needed to fire. I was petrified that I'd hit one of our team. There were still machine guns firing from the trucks down on my team, so I lit them up as well. With all the tracer fire going different directions, it was a challenge to distinguish good guys from bad. If someone was firing down toward the compound, or toward me, I had to assume they weren't one of the "good guys." I realized there's no way anybody can tell you what to do in a situation like this; you have to use your own judgement and live with the results. I was shaking badly from adrenaline, but once I had both hands on the gun, I was able to control the intense shaking.

It was dark, and I had no idea how to ascertain how many rounds of ammo I had remaining. I saw flashes of light, and the SUV jerked back and forth. *Oh shit,* I thought. *Someone was firing back at me!* I fired two quick bursts toward where I saw the flashes originate. The return fire stopped.

It was quiet, so I grabbed the radio and yelled, "Aleksei, I'm firing the multi-barrel gun up here, is that OK?"

A second later I heard, "A bit late to be asking me, don't you think?"

I thought, *Aleksei has a good point.* I clicked the mic and said, "Now what should I do?"

"Fire at anything that fires at you. Watch your ammo though."

I didn't have a clue what I was doing, so I just prayed I didn't hurt any good guys. I started to look for the goggles, which proved to be difficult inside a pitch-black vehicle during a firefight. I felt around in the general direction I'd tossed them. After about ten seconds of blind searching, I was able to locate the goggles and put them on.

Now able to see, so I surveyed the area. Bodies were everywhere. Nothing was moving. I looked at where I'd originally fired on the truck; it was a tattered mess with a large ragged hole. *Whoops! I guess I left the gun aimed there too long,* I thought. The machine gun on the truck was beat up pretty well. I felt certain it wasn't functional anymore.

I saw two men crawling behind one of the trucks only one hundred or so feet away. Each had an RPG in his hands. I called Aleksei and said, "Two guys with RPGs up here crawling, what do you want me to do?"

"If they're dressed in green then you need to stop them; if not then they're our guys."

"I can't fucking tell; night vision doesn't show colors," I yelled back.

A few seconds later he said, "Are they moving toward the compound or away?"

"Compound," I said.

"OK, carefully look around both directions; make sure nobody else is visible. You need to stop them up there because those RPGs could kill us and the kids. It's very important that you be careful; that thing has tracers, and they'll show your position immediately. Hit them then swing the barrel back and forth around to make sure nobody can fire back, got it? Also, push the power button on the goggles three times to set them in automatic mode or you will go blind from your own tracer light."

*Wish I had known that little trick before I nearly blinded myself before,* I thought.

I did what I was told. I figured it was them or me. I pulled both triggers and aimed toward their location, vaporizing the men with the RPGs.

"Can the drone pilot see any others?" I asked.

The drone pilot told me, "They all have hot spots, even the dead ones. If they don't move, I can't tell if they're alive or dead. Fire on anything you see moving up there."

I looked down at the ammo reel that feeds the strip of bullets into the machine. I couldn't gauge how many were left, but I noticed another one right next to it. I stopped and tried to figure out how to change it when the time came. I found a release handle and examined the way it would come out; simple enough. Hopefully I wouldn't need it.

"Hold your fire, Mick. I'm sending a team up there, understood?"

"Copy that," I said in my best military speak.

The drone pilot said, "Contact, two hot spots moving about forty meters at ten o'clock from the SUV."

I looked around. Like an idiot I responded, "Where's ten o'clock?" and instantly felt like a dismal failure.

"Behind you is six, in front is twelve, do the math," said the drone operator.

*Geez, aren't we testy all of a sudden?* I thought, knowing full well I shouldn't have needed to ask.

I couldn't see them. My guess is they were behind something. Then I saw the flashes and heard "pinging" sounds on my SUV. About twenty rounds hit the vehicle I was in. I saw the impact points on the side windows right in front of my face; thank God for bullet proof glass. The bad guys knew where I was for sure. Ignoring the whole "hold your fire" thing, I grabbed the handles and pulled the trigger in their general direction. Once I found the correct placement, I moved the gun back and forth. Then the gun went silent. *Ut oh, somethings wrong,* I thought.

My mind decided now would be a good time to retrieve a memory of when Scott and I went to a firing range. I was shooting Scott's rifle and suddenly it stopped firing. I tried to be funny, so I looked at Scott and said in a child-like phrase, "Why it no go boom-boom anymore?" It had run out of ammunition. In an attempt to bring myself back to the present-day issues, I slapped myself in the face and said out loud, "Well, Einstein, perhaps this gun is also out of ammo."

When I worked for the Army, I had fired many machine guns. I never fired them at night, and of course, nobody ever fired back at me while I tried to reload the gun. Now I was a bit lost. I pulled the release handle on the drum, lifted it out, and threw it to the side. In one motion I put the new one in and grabbed the strip that was the beginning of the new reel. I needed to load the strip of ammunition into some sort of gear, but first I had to find it. Next problem; how does the cover come off to load the strip? I pulled on everything, twisted, nothing worked. Then I saw a circular object and pulled, and the cover popped up. I put the track of ammo on the gear and thought, *Now what?* "Pull the charge handle, dumbass," I said out loud. I did, and the gear moved until the first bullet was near top center. I closed the lid and hoped it worked.

"Contact, nine o'clock, ten kilos, multiple helicopters," said the drone operator. I did some quick math to determine their location, and saw dim lights in the sky off to my left.

"Those are our reinforcements," said Aleksei. He'd called in the cavalry. Now that the children were found, we needed all the help we could get to end this fight.

It was quiet—eerily so. I had no idea if any bad guys were nearby, hidden from view. I saw a few bodies near the destroyed trucks that appeared to be badly injured but still moving their arms and legs. They didn't appear to be a threat, but I kept my eyes on them anyway.

I could hear the helicopters coming now. In a minute they were right on top of us. These weren't the normal helicopters. They had guns and missiles all over their exterior. I recognized their shape from the movie *Red Dawn*. Pretty amazing how big they were compared to a American attack helicopters. They circled above while a troop transport helicopter landed nearby.

"Mick, stay in the truck until I get everything worked out, understood? Flip the firing selector switch to red."

"Copy that," I said in an idiotic attempt to sound military again. I flipped the selector lever on the gun back to red and waited.

In ten minutes, I heard on the radio, "OK, Mick, I am coming to you. I'll knock on the door when I get to you." I found out that once you're on an adrenaline high, it becomes challenging to calm down. I was wound up but had no choice but to twiddle my thumbs for ten minutes while I waited. Then came the knock on the door. I could see it was Aleksei when he shined a flashlight on his face. I jumped out. What a relief to have this be over.

"Everything OK, Aleksei?"

He said, "As good as possible. Two injured on my team, waiting on air ambulance now. They look like they'll recover." Aleksei studied my face for a second, then said, "And you, Mick—are you OK?"

I answered with a shaky, "I think so, just wound up."

Aleksei said, "Just so you know, Mick, we could've defeated them without you going all John Wayne, but thanks for the help. I am impressed you knew how to operate the gun."

"I didn't. Taught myself. Figured now was as good a time as any," I replied.

About ten of our original team were going through the area to make sure no more bad guys remained. New people arrived as well, and started looking at bodies and putting out the fires. About fifty people were in the area.

I didn't feel any throbbing in my fingers, but to be sure I opened my palms and moved around in a circle. I was relieved to feel no sensations. I asked Aleksei, "Who was this Nicolai? Why'd you open fire so quickly?"

He said, "Nicolai is—well, was—a good friend. He was a good man, and a fierce warrior, well, up until two years ago. Everyone on the team knew him. We also knew he'd had problems with drugs, but the last time I saw him it appeared he was getting back on track. I wanted to give him a shot to be on our team."

"Last year he was in a car accident. His passenger was a daughter of a high ranking official, and she was killed. He was arrested for driving while under the influence and was sent to prison. It was supposed to be for ten years, but after only one year he was released. Rumor has it that a friend of the family, and one of the highest ranking generals in the army, was able to get him out early. The general's name is Scesovich."

Aleksei paused, then said, "General Scesovich was a well-respected military man. Six months after getting Nicolai released, the general was charged with corruption and a host of other charges. The army found out he had a mansion, boats, expensive cars, and liked prostitutes. All of this on an equivalent salary of about seventy-five-thousand US dollars. General Scesovich also had a drinking problem. We learned that defense arms manufacturers were being shaken down to get contracts. It was tragic to watch a good man get corrupted. He was on his way to the top if he stayed out of trouble. They sentenced him to twenty-five years of hard labor. The military let him go home to get his affairs in order before reporting back two days later. That was six months ago. He never showed up. His wife told everyone he was so distraught that he killed himself in the mountains near a cabin he owned. Nobody found the body, but with one to two meters of snow it would be difficult to find him. The military was waiting until the snow melted to retrieve the body. Now we know the wife lied."

Aleksei gave another soldier an order in Russian. Then he added, "It appears they hatched this plan to kidnap a bunch of children and hold them for ransom. The general wasn't suspected because we thought he was dead. Nicolai didn't even enter our radar on this. Turns out the accomplices were only paid twenty thousand dollars each. While this is quite a bit of money in Russia, once they heard the total ransom payments would be in the ten-million-dollar range, they wanted much, much more. We happened to come upon them arguing about the amounts. They threatened Nicolai, and he shot them. The criminals holding the kids were justifiably upset, and they fought back. I don't know the reason the general came tonight; I don't think he knew about you or our team, but I am not sure. With a force that large, it's clear they came to get the children and move them. You know the rest of the story."

After a pause to drink some water, Aleksei said, "Once I realized the kids were in grave danger, I told everyone to open fire. We had no other option. The general had nothing to lose, so I had to assume the children would be killed. It was a no-win situation if I let it continue. I have to say I was impressed with your ability to find these children. Those families owe you big time. I owe you as well. Honestly, Mick, my career was going nowhere. I was bored with my job and saw this case as a way to bring a spark back into my life. I took a chance, a really big chance, to get my superiors to look into your abilities. Nobody believed me—well, until the Russian ambassador to the US found out his children were kidnapped, and then my plan was brought to the top and approved immediately. Like the book *Animal Farm* where everyone is equal but some are more equal—you know that story?"

I said, "Wait—What? Do you mean the man I met with in Washington, the Antonov guy—his kid was kidnapped?"

Aleksei responded, "Yes, both of his kids, actually. They're twins, and both were taken. They'll be OK. He is on my list of people to call. Now that I think about it, he should be called first. I'll call the number and let you tell him, since you know him better than I do, I've only seen him from a distance in Washington."

Aleksei dialed the number.

"How do you say his name again?" I asked.

"Anatoly Antonov."

It rang a few times and a voice answered, "Antonov."

I said, "Mr. Antonov, this is Mick Anderson. I'm the guy from America. I have great news. We found your children, and they're OK."

I heard frantic Russian voices on the other end and a woman screaming. This went on for about thirty seconds before Mr. Antonov returned to the phone. He said, "Thank you from my family. We're so happy. Can you tell me the condition of the rest of the children?"

I replied, "I believe they'll all be OK. The team leader, Aleksei Ypovich, and I wanted to let you know first." He started crying on the phone, and I could hear people in the background crying and screaming as well.

About thirty seconds went by, then he continued, "Mr. Anderson, we owe you a debt of gratitude that I fear I'll never be able to fully pay. You have made us eternally happy. My family was overcome with grief for two weeks and you have made us very happy."

I said, "You're welcome. Let me let you talk to the team leader, Aleksei Ypovich. He would like to talk to you for just a minute."

I quickly handed the phone to him. They spoke in Russian for about two minutes. The only thing I understood was "California." When he ended the call, Aleksei had tears in his eyes.

"Thank you, Mick. The ambassador told me I'll be promoted and given a large bonus. Also, my team and I have been given a vacation to any-where we want. Guess where we're going? To the USA in about two weeks. You must celebrate with us. I want to see California. The ambassador is getting everything lined up. Everyone on the team is getting a bonus as well. The trip won't cost us a dime—Russia is paying for everything. Mick, this is one of the best days of my life."

I felt like I had accomplished something so amazing that it was hard to put into words. We had saved thirty-four children from certain death. On the other hand, I was forced to protect myself and others from harm, which meant I had to take people's lives. That feeling was so repulsive to me that it almost overshadowed the positive outcome of the mission.

Aleksei, still euphoric from the events, finally noticed that I wasn't saying anything. Tears began to flow down my face. Aleksei said quietly, "I know what you're feeling, but what you did was heroic. The fact that you feel this way now means you're a good man. Nobody should take a person's life and think nothing of it. You did take a life, but you saved thirty-four children, and don't forget, you saved their families from the horror of los-ing a child. You also saved my team. In an operation like this, we expect to lose three or four good soldiers, and your actions prevented that. Not one of our team was killed. Let your emotions flow; no one will blame or judge you because every one of my warriors has felt the same way. It took me a month to recover from my first battle. It's difficult to take a life, even for the right reasons. Now you will avoid lethal violence, if at all possible, in the future. You will recover from this and be a better person because of it."

Aleksei said I'd get something called, "adrenaline disorder" from my first intense combat operation. He told me expect uncontrolled shaking for about a half hour. I didn't believe him at first, especially since I had talked on the phone minutes ago. He said once the adrenaline wore off, the realization of what had happened would hit me. He was pretty close; I did start to shake, similar to how you feel when you're freezing cold. This continued for over a half hour before I recovered enough to perform even simple tasks, such as talking and walking. Another half hour went by before I could talk coherently and think logically again. It was the weirdest sensation, and thankfully I recovered fully about two hours later.

Aleksei finished his duties with the other soldiers and assembled his team around me. One by one they shook my hand and said, "Thank you". Aleksei also told the team the news they were going to America to visit California. They cheered.

I told Aleksei, "This is totally up to you, but can I give you some advice?"

He replied, "Sure, Mick."

"Rent a car and take Highway 1 in California from Los Angeles to San Francisco. It will take five days, but you will see the best sights in the world."

Aleksei said, "Oh, I must've forgotten to tell you this. You are coming with us, so the whole team will experience this together."

"OK, but my wife is coming along, so I'll have to be on my best behavior."

"Oh, that's unfortunate. You see, I will be bringing Russian vodka, so that may not be possible, my friend," he said, laughing.

Aleksei made some phone calls, and after he was done, he gave the phone to me and said, "Call your wife. Tell here you have some interesting stories to tell."

I called Michelle. With tears streaming down my face, I told her we were able to find the children, and all would be OK. I also told her that the Russian government had given me a bonus, and even gave the rest of the team a bonus. "I miss you and will be home in a few days. And by the way, we are going on a vacation with the team in California in two weeks."

She said, "Mick, I'm really proud of you. Now hurry home and be safe. It will be nice to go on a vacation after everything we have been through lately."

Aleksei told me that I'd be going back on the helicopter with three of his men. There was a plane waiting at the airport to bring me home. He said they had a lot of work to do to figure out who else was involved, but that my services we no longer necessary.

He added, "I can't thank you enough, my friend. We will see you in two weeks in California. I have your number and will call you with an update."

I was put on one of the attack helicopters for the flight to the airport. There was a man on both sides manning the same type of multi-barrel machine gun that I had fired. We flew in a protective diamond formation for the two giant helicopters that were bringing the children back. The pilot spoke almost no English, so it was pretty quiet. He did thank me and offered me a shot of vodka before departing. I guess most passengers get a bit scared, so I took the shot, then a few more. It didn't ease the pain as I had hoped.

We were only a mile from the airport when warning lights and buzzers appeared on the dashboard. "Shit, here we go again," I said out loud. We were forced to land. I wanted to call Aleksei and tell him another Russian helicopter fell out of the sky but decided against it. We waited only a few minutes for the police cars to arrive to drive me to the plane. Never a dull moment in Russia.

I boarded the airplane and fell asleep almost immediately. It wasn't a restful sleep, unfortunately, as visions of the mission popped into every dream.

## Chapter 28:
### Welcome Home

James P. Douglas, the US spymaster, was waiting for me when I arrived.

I walked off the Russian jet, and he said, "Welcome home. Have a seat in the Tahoe; we need to talk." A man scanned me for electronic devices then took my phone. They analyzed the phone for listening devices and then put it into a sound proof box. I jumped in and we drove away. "We have many questions, Mr. Anderson, many questions. We will be going to my office at the CIA headquarters in Langley for an informal discussion of the events that transpired in Russia. Congratulations. We already knew your mission was a success, and we feel this will help American and Russian cooperation in the future."

After a few seconds he continued, "But I see you had a bit of trouble over there. It couldn't have been easy to jump into a firefight, Mick. We're proud of you."

I asked, "How did you know I was in a firefight?"

He smiled then replied, "We were watching from above. Here, I can pull the whole thing up on my phone if you want to watch it again. It was pretty chaotic, and you handled yourself amazingly well." Then he started laughing and said, "We really had to laugh when you asked Aleksei if it was OK to fire the gun, especially after you had already fired eight hundred and four rounds. Yes, our analysts can count the number of rounds from the video. Sorry to laugh, but that was priceless!"

I said, "You heard all that? I was scared shitless. I feel lucky to be alive."

He smiled again and said, "The Russians 'borrowed' some of our communication technology, so we listen in when it may be of interest to the United States."

He offered his phone to me, and I declined to watch. He said, "OK, how about I just email the video to you? Just make sure to declare the $350,000 you earned from the Russians as foreign income on your taxes, OK, Mick?"

"Rats, you know about that, huh?" I said in return.

"We know about everything, Mick. How did you handle the helicopter crash landing near the airport? It looked pretty scary." He smiled and said, "We even saw the pictures you sent from the airplane ride over. I love French toast as well."

We arrived at CIA headquarters within half an hour. It was a somber moment when I walked past the memorial wall. This wall has a star for each fallen hero killed while on a CIA mission. After staring at the wall for a few seconds, I was put through another barrage of electronic tests to make sure I wasn't in possession of any listening devices.

"OK, Mick, you're clean. Let's talk about how you can help the United States now."

## Chapter 29:
# We Have a Spy

"**M**ick, we have a problem. Someone is stealing top-secret information from us.

We need help finding these people. We want to hire you to find them. In exchange, we will make sure the IRS forgets about the $350,000 from the Russians and the $75,000 you received from the software guy, Mr. Swanson. I'm going to assign you to our building to look around and see if your fingers detect anything."

I said grimly, "You know about that too, huh?"

Mr. Douglas replied, "We know everything. Do I have to keep saying that? How about you just assume I know everything you know, and let's skip the small talk."

"How much will you pay me?" I asked.

"You don't want to help your country for free?" came his quick reply.

"I need to pay my bills, you do understand that, correct?"

"OK, we will come up with an acceptable amount. Maybe we will just take the money the Russians gave you, then give it back to you tax free."

"No, that won't work. Get serious if you want me to help," I said.

"Just kidding, Mick. We will make it worth your while."

I told him, "OK, but I want my wife flown in immediately."

To my amazement, he said, "Your wife is being picked up right now. A private jet will get her here tonight."

"Well, alright. Now I'm impressed."

"I detect bad people who want to harm children," I told Mr. Douglas. "I'm not sure my services will do much good, Mr. Douglas, but I'll give it a try. Usually, I touch someone or some of their belongings to get a feeling. In this case, there's no missing person, and quite frankly I'm unsure what to do."

"While I understand this is a stretch," said Mr. Douglas, "I feel your senses pick up more than you realize. Perhaps we just need to exercise your mind to find out if it works."

I replied, "I just don't want you to expect a miracle. I don't have any experience sensing espionage. How do we proceed?"

Mr. Douglas said, "For starters, how about you sit at an entrance point in the morning to scan everyone who comes through the door? Then at the end of the day, everyone who leaves." I knew this would probably be a waste of time and wouldn't work, but getting the IRS off my back would be worth it. So, I told him that would be fine.

Later that evening my wife was brought by limousine to the hotel. It was great to see her after such a wild week. She wanted to tell me all about the security people who came to the door. "They told me to come with them. I told them to take a hike, but they said, 'You have to fly to Washington. Your husband is there and has requested your presence.'" She explained they had people take the dog and cat to the doggie day care. Then she was put in a limo, taken to the airport, and put on a private jet direct to Washington, D.C. All in all, a pretty good experience.

The next morning, I was picked up by Mr. Douglas's people. I arrived at seven fifteen a.m. at the Pentagon. I was introduced to the security director, Wayne Morris. He gave me a security guard uniform and a disguise, then had me sit in the desk near the doors. I wasn't expecting to accomplish much, actually, but I'd give it the old college try.

"If you detect anything you're to alert the security people by switching on a red light, here on the desk," said Mr. Morris.

Since many people came through the door at once, this didn't seem practical, but we had no other ideas. If I turned on the light, security would stop everyone and make them go back through the metal detectors again. Mr. Morris decided they would all have to go through only one detector. That way I could zero in on the person with better precision.

Talk about boring, I didn't get anything in the morning at all. People came and went constantly but I had no sensations. I called Mr. Douglas and told him that nothing was detected. He sounded disappointed and told me to continue the job.

It was three-forty-five in the afternoon, and I needed a nap. My head would nod up and down while I jumped between dreams and reality. "Hey, wake up, new guy," said a loud voice. It was a security officer making sure I stayed diligent. I stayed until six o'clock without a single trace.

That evening my wife and I went on an actual date. So, I was happy the next morning, ready to accomplish something. Once I arrived at work, it was more of the same, but this time I was placed in a room with a one-way mirror that everyone had to walk past. This was better for at least two reasons: 1) I could look at more people, and 2) If I wanted to take a cat nap it would be harder to detect because other security people couldn't see me.

For five days this went on. I really felt my abilities weren't going to help. I didn't feel anything but boredom and frustration. It was Friday, and my thoughts turned to weekend plans, then I nodded off to sleep.

I was sound asleep when I felt my little fingers begin to tingle. I woke up immediately. At first, I was positive it was a dream. Once I verified this wasn't a dream, I focused on my sensations. There were people in the halls, but it wasn't coming from any of them; the feeling was too weak. Then the throbbing slowly moved its way to other fingers. In about five minutes even my thumbs were throbbing. They were close, so I flipped the light switch to alert security. I used my palms to scan left and right.

I got out of the room as fast as I could and tried to zero in on the source. I called Mr. Douglas on his cell phone and told him I'd need some help. He wasn't too far away from the entrance and was coming by the room in a minute with a group of people. I looked down the hall and realized the red light wasn't on. I was using a wireless light switch, and it had failed to work. I realized why; this building was probably reinforced with some special material in the walls that stopped wireless signals. It probably prevented my senses from working between rooms as well. This meant the person I was interested in was much closer than I'd thought.

The vibration wasn't from the people coming in, it was from people trying to get out. I looked left and saw a large number of people coming toward me on their way out. From the quivering in my fingers, I knew it had to be someone in the group. I ran down the hallway to security and told them to contact Wayne Morris, their director. I told them he needed to get back here immediately.

I saw Mr. Douglas at the end of the crowd so I walked toward him. I had my palms up scanning the people headed right for me. One big guy in front physically grabbed me and moved me out of the way; turns out he was a bodyguard for the station chief, Mark Graham. He put his hand on my chest and told me, "Stay out of the way until Chief Graham goes past."

At that moment Mr. Douglas ran to where we were standing. I told him, "Someone in this crowd could be a problem, but this guy won't let me move." Mr. Douglas told the man to let me go, then got on the radio to have security stop the procession of people. I was escorted by Mr. Douglas's bodyguards to the electronic countermeasure and metal detector area. Everyone has to go through these machines, so we told security that only one machine should be used until everyone in the group was through. The large group, about fifty people, weren't pleased. Mr. Douglas and I watched as each person went through the sensors. I was behind him holding my palms up for a split second as each went through the machine.

When the station chief went through, my hands vibrated much worse. I was initially convinced it was him. I told Mr. Douglas I was detecting one of the three men near the machine. He had security hand check each person. Once that was finished, he had the men sit at three separate desks so I could walk between them to help identify the source.

It wasn't the director; that was a big relief for political reasons. I told Mr. Douglas that when I detected the source I'd stand in front of the person and act like I wanted to review his belongings. That person turned out to be Assistant Director Max Stephenson. Mr. Douglas told the station chief that we needed to stop Mr. Stephenson because he was chosen at random for a special inspection of his belongings. Mr. Stephenson was informed about the special inspection, then escorted to a different room for questioning and electronic inspection. I was not sure that my senses had detected espionage or the possibility that he kidnapped a child, but either way he was up to no good.

He was insistent that this was out of line and he needed to get back to his boss, Station Chief Mark Graham. Then Chief Graham walked into the room. Max Stephenson pleaded with his boss to release him, but Chief Graham just told him, "Random tests are mandatory. Don't worry; it will be over soon. You have nothing to hide anyway, right?"

Mr. Douglas had his men take everything out of his briefcase and out of every pocket. They collected his shoes, pens, cell phone, and even his tie. Using a hand wand scanner, they checked the clothing he had on for electronic signals and metal. His men ran everything through a scanner while we watched. An eagle-eyed security guy noticed something on his tie clasp that the rest of us didn't see. When it was magnified, he could see an electronic-looking device embedded in it.

When confronted with the clasp, he denied it contained an electronic device, saying the item was just part of the design. Security brought out a microscope. When they zoomed the object, they saw it was most definitely electronic and appeared to have a camera lens. Mr. Douglas looked over at me and smiled.

"Max Stephenson," he said, "you're under arrest for violations of Title 18 United States Code, conspiracy to commit espionage."

He was placed in handcuffs and led away.

It was chaos for about an hour as we unraveled what had happened. Finally, they were finished with me. Mr. Douglas asked if I wanted to go to lunch with him to discuss my fee. I thought my job was done, so I asked "You paying?"

He laughed and said, "No, I believe it is your turn."

Mr. Douglas wanted to pay a small fee for my services. I, of course, wanted millions. In the end we reached an acceptable settlement, one hundred thousand dollars, tax free. "We will forget you received seventy-five thousand dollars from Mr. Swanson as well," said Mr. Douglas. That's enough for a new race car, so I was happy.

We returned to Langley, and I went to clean out my area. I felt a slight tingle in my little finger. I could hardly believe the sensation. *Can't be, Mick, your job is done*, I insisted to myself. Then my ring fingers started to tingle. I said out loud, "Well, there goes the weekend. I'm not finished yet." I called Mr. Douglas but couldn't get through, so I went to his office. His assistant said he was in an important meeting and couldn't be disturbed, so I left a message. The message said, "We're not finished yet." I had lost the feeling by the time he emerged from his meeting.

"What is it, Mick?" he asked.

"I'm afraid we're not finished, Mr. Douglas. There's more work to do."

# Chapter 30:
## Eight Days

I returned to Langley, this time as a consultant. Mr. Douglas assigned me to an office and gave me fake files to make me appear busy. My job was to walk around the building with him. During the first day I'd get a sensation from time to time that was so weak it couldn't be verified.

This went on for eight days before I sensed something.

I was returning to my office after lunch when my little fingers told me something was up. The problem I had to contend with was the enormous size of the building and the fact it was heavily reinforced, which I believed had created a barrier to my senses. It was difficult to tell if the sensation was in front of me or behind me.

I decided to ask who was on vacation, away at a meeting, or sick the previous week. I was given a list of 112 people. The list included which department they worked in, what floor, and the room number.

I had the data department sort these names by floor and room number so I could go from floor to floor quickly and know who should be there. One hundred twelve names had to be checked. It isn't as simple as it sounds; many people at the Pentagon were constantly moving. Few people stayed in their offices or cubicles all day long. After an entire day, there were twenty-two people remaining that hadn't been available for me to survey. It took eight hours the next day before I was able to confirm that the remaining twenty-two people on the list weren't the problem. I became frustrated that I couldn't find the source. Every single person on the list was checked, all negative.

I told Mr. Douglas that there had to be some people still missing from the list. He had discussions with each of the department heads about people missing the week before. They listed all the names, and each matched up with the lists I already had.

Then I had an idea. In a rare stroke of genius, I asked Mr. Douglas to see if anyone had quit, been fired, or retired the previous week. Specifically, I asked who had missed the previous week but had come in the next Monday to get personal effects. It was the break we needed, and it would eventually explain why I had gone an entire week without any senses.

"The only one missing is Hank Miller, who retired after forty-two years in the service," said Mr. Douglas. "He isn't your guy; I can assure you. I used to work for him; he was very good at his job and patriotic to a fault."

I replied to Mr. Douglas, "He wasn't in the list, and if he came back Monday, he is the only one unaccounted for." I urged Mr. Douglas, "Call him. Tell him you want to bring a special award plaque to his house since you've been so busy."

Mr. Douglas said, "Mick, that's a really good idea. I wanted to see him anyway."

Then I told him, "If I get any sensations, I want you to continue talking to him while we get a search warrant. Do you think that will be OK?"

Mr. Douglas said, "Yes, but I believe we're wasting our time with him. I'll order an award plaque made up today and go over there tomorrow morning." Mr. Douglas called Hank Miller to let him know of the plan. Mr. Miller told him that he was grateful, but it wasn't necessary to go through the effort. Mr. Douglas is used to getting his way, and finally convinced Mr. Miller that the CIA needed to show their appreciation.

At nine a.m., we left Langley to drive to Hank Miller's house. As soon as we were ten miles away, I felt a sensation. I felt the throbbing grow as we drove closer and closer. I was able to direct the driver where to turn just with my hands. My fingers picked Hank Miller's house. I told Mr. Douglas,

"There's no doubt the guy you want is inside." Mr. Douglas called for a warrant, and then he and his team went inside. I waited outside.

Forty-five minutes later, a forensics team arrived with the warrant. I went inside at the same time. Mr. Douglas had finished presenting the award to Hank Miller at about the same time. I could see in Mr. Douglas's eyes that this was going to be a tough situation.

Mr. Douglas introduced Hank Miller to me. I realized even before we shook hands that Hank Miller caused a very strong sensation in my hands.

I said, "Mr. Miller, you are the one I came to see."

Mr. Douglas and I exchanged glances, and I nodded to him. Mr. Douglas excused himself and told me to follow him into the hallway.

Mr. Douglas said to me, "Are you absolutely sure? I mean are you one-hundred percent sure Hank Miller, a public servant for forty-two years, is the man we're after?"

"I'm sure, my fingers never lie. I'm one-hundred percent sure," I replied.

Mr. Douglas sighed, then said, "I wanted so badly for you to be wrong. I was hoping my old friend could retire in peace."

An FBI agent handed the paperwork to Mr. Douglas, and he reviewed it. Then he found Hank and said, "Let's go into this room and have a talk."

Once inside the room, Mr. Douglas said to Hank Miller, "My old friend, I'm afraid I have some bad news. An ongoing investigation at Langley has recently uncovered evidence of espionage. The evidence appears to indicate that you were involved in espionage. I'm sorry to have to tell you this while celebrating your retirement, but we have to act. As you're aware, when a situation like this occurs, we're required to follow specific procedures and protocols. This is a search warrant which gives us access to search your house, cars, and storage areas."

He handed the warrant to Hank Miller, then asked him, "Do you want to tell me anything now or wait until we take you to Langley?"

Hank was quiet for some time; he looked at the search warrant but didn't appear to read it. Tears began to form in his eyes. He bowed his head down, then put his face in his hands and began to weep. I knew I was right; he's the person who committed this crime, but it was still tough to watch him break down and cry. He was a broken man who appeared to age twenty years right in front of our eyes.

Family and friends were still arriving to celebrate his retirement. It was a joyous day that was about to be destroyed. After four or five members of his family walked by the room, curious as to the reason that Hank was crying, I told Mr. Douglas we needed to close the door before everyone started asking questions. He agreed.

Hank Miller finally looked up at Mr. Douglas and said, "My wife and family had nothing to do with any of this. If you keep them out of this, I'll tell you what you need to know." He started sobbing, this time very loudly. I felt for the man; however, my senses demonstrated he had done something to cause substantial damage to the United States. His arrest had no winners, only a trail of shattered lives.

He asked if he could tell his wife in private. Mr. Douglas nodded and said, "That's fine; we'll bring her in." I didn't think it was a good idea, but kept quiet. Agents brought his wife into the room, and we left.

Once we were outside the office, I told Mr. Douglas, "I don't think that's a good idea. What if he has a gun hidden? We shouldn't leave them alone."

Mr. Douglas acted rather indignant at my statement, and waved me off with his hands. In an irritated voice, he said, "There won't be a problem. We will give him a few minutes of peace with his wife before we take him to Langley. I'm not going to arrest my long-time friend in front of his family and friends."

A few minutes later, my senses changed. This change concerned me enough to insist we check on the Millers. Mr. Douglas knocked on the door and then went in.

"Goddamn it," yelled Mr. Douglas as he walked into the room.

We went in behind him and saw the bodies of both Hank Miller and his wife. They were sitting on the couch; neither was moving. In each of their hands was a bottle of cloudy water. It appeared they'd committed suicide. Could it be that she's involved as well?

Mr. Douglas said, "Damnit; this is my fault. My judgement was clouded by friendship."

One of the security people noticed a notebook in front of Hank and gave it to Mr. Douglas. It was an older, well-worn notebook. Inside were names, dates, and events of nearly thirty years of spying.

"He's the last person I suspected. He hid in plain sight, right under our noses." Mr. Douglas had the forensics people come in and take the notebook into evidence.

"Mr. Douglas," I said, "I've got more bad news. Normally, when a person I'm sensing dies, the sensation ceases. Look at my hands; they're still throbbing. Someone else is involved, and they're here as well. While the sensation did change, it's still very strong."

He called the security detail to block the exits to the house. "No one leaves."

I put my palms up and scanned the twenty or so people in the room. It didn't take long to zero in on one man. I pointed to him and told Mr. Douglas's bodyguard, "The guy wearing the Hawaiian shirt." The man in the Hawaiian shirt saw me point in his direction, then he casually walked toward the back of the room where a door was located. Nobody tried to stop him. I heard the door open, then someone outside yell, "Don't move; put your hands up."

Security tackled him about ten feet from the house. I went outside and verified we had the right person. I returned inside to verify that the sensations grew weaker. I told Mr. Douglas, "We got him." I made a believer out of everyone that day, including myself. I found out that really bad people create these "hyper senses." It doesn't matter the crime.

I'd known quite a few people were skeptical. I'm used to this now and won't take it personally. After we finished, a surprising number of people came up to me, shook my hand, and said, "Good job."

We found out "Hawaiian shirt guy," was the main contact to send secrets to both China and Russia. He owned a paper company, a seemingly mundane operation that was an excellent front for his spying operation. Investigators found a hidden basement in his store. Evidence of long-term spying and "James Bond" electronic devices were found. It appeared he'd been the builder of the miniature cameras and listening devices used at Langley. Mr. Douglas shared that the camera and microphone were only a millimeter wide and voice activated and controlled.

Mr. Douglas told me there would be a bonus check soon. Then he said, "From time to time, expect a phone call. Your services will be required about every six months. And by the way, Mick, you can't ever be too busy to help. Is that clear enough, or should I repeat that statement?"

"Yes, boss," I replied.

He told me, "Spend a week in Washington, D.C., at our expense. I'll get you and your wife into the White House tomorrow for a secret meeting with Number 1."

I said, "Number 1—who's that?"

"Who do you think?"

The next day my wife and I met with Number 1. This was the first time I'd met the President. There were no pictures, no autographs, no press—for a reason. I was instructed not to tell anyone that I'd met her because they'd ask too many questions.

## Chapter 31:

# *Crazy Russians*

I was riding a natural "high" from solving these cases. Uncle Sam had just paid me $150,000, tax free, for taking down three spies, and I was feeling pretty good. The only problem was getting recognized wherever we traveled, so disguises were required. I felt a vacation was in order—after all, I had earned it. Aleksei had said his government was giving his team an all-expense paid trip anywhere they wanted to go, and they wanted to go to California. He called me to explain the arrangements. They paid for our tickets to San Diego and our rental car, plus all expenses during the trip.

I met Aleksei and the rest of the Russian team at the airport in San Diego. They had arranged five vans for themselves, and my wife and I rented a convertible. We had a week of fun planned. The weather for the entire week would be close to perfect; only one day had a chance of rain. We planned on driving up Highway 1, all the way past San Francisco.

I could tell it was going to be a full-time job to control their primal urges.

It was great to see them all in a non-combat environment. They were in awe of the California experience. I was unsure of how to entertain the two women on the team. One of them was named Nadia, and she was missing a few fingers. I asked Aleksei what had happened, and he shrugged and said, "She is now an expert in explosives. While she learned her craft, well, let's just say she lost a few things. I'll tell you this; if you want something blown up, she's your man—well, you understand."

The two soldiers shot during the firefight had been released from the hospital the day before. Aleksei told me they needed to take it easy. I got the feeling they hadn't gotten that memo. Even with a cast on one arm and

184

a boot on one leg, one guy had to be restrained from harassing a scantily dressed woman.

Aleksei also told me that we were being followed. I didn't notice anyone, but he is trained to spot such a situation. Finally, he said, "It's your guys, not ours."

I wasn't sure how he knew, but I accepted his opinion. I told him, "Forget it; don't do anything illegal and we'll be fine. I have the blessings from the top of the CIA."

Because it was late, we drove up to La Jolla, near Torrey Pines, and found a hotel. I wanted the team to try hang gliding at Torrey Pines Gliderport the following day.

We arrived at ten o'clock sharp, ready for gliding. The cliffs are amazing, about one hundred scary feet straight down to the ocean. They took a required class to learn what would happen during flight. After training, they acted like they were old pros and could fly without an instructor. These are seasoned soldiers, as calm in combat as most of us are while we sleep. Tough as nails and fearless, right? No—not even close. They screamed like six-year-old girls at a birthday party when they flew off the edge of the cliff. I was thankful that a trained pilot was flying each glider. They finally stopped screaming after a few minutes. I felt bad for the instructor pilots. We could hear each of the men screaming for a half mile. I made each man and woman take a GoPro camera with them for memories. Only the women kept quiet; they actually looked unimpressed with the whole experience.

Afterward we ate dinner at Torrey Pines Golf Course. I chose this location because the view is amazing. Later on, we went bar hopping. Believe me, it was all I could do to keep them in line. My wife and I were having fun, but we had to act like parents all the time. We found ourselves scolding these men and their behavior constantly.

"Don't touch her."

"No, she doesn't want you to grab her butt."

"Stop! That woman doesn't want you to fondle her breasts."

"You two, stop fighting."

It was like raising a bunch of two-year-olds all over again. Now I know what it's like to work at a children's daycare. Day one was a success; nobody died or got arrested. My wife and I were beat. Raising twenty adults is a tough job.

Day two started off driving through places like Laguna Beach, Newport Beach, Huntington Beach, and Long Beach, where we stopped for lunch. It was like watching kids in a candy store; each mile brought smiles and excitement. We went to the beach, and everyone played volleyball. Smiles all around, even from the women.

I found out a Monday Night Football game was taking place in Los Angeles. We braved the traffic, and in two hours we were at the stadium. Since money wasn't an issue, we bought tickets from scalpers. The teams playing that evening were the Kansas City Chiefs and the Los Angeles Rams. I was aware that they'd seen football games on television, but I knew they hadn't seen them up close.

So, I made a phone call to Mr. Douglas requesting help getting us on the field. I didn't think it would happen, but a few minutes later I received a call from Jack Strough at the LA Rams' front office. He said to meet him at a certain exit and we would be given a few minutes on the field. We were able to watch the teams warm up for ten minutes.

For the first time the normally loud and obnoxious soldiers were silent when the players ran past. A 280-pound, six-foot eight-inch defensive end in full pads shocked even the largest member of Aleksei's team. There was no false bravado; Aleksei's team thought they were pretty good athletes, but they had to admit they were no match for the football players.

Aleksei and his team had no idea how complex the sport of football was until they saw it live. Because they had no favorites, they ended up cheering for both teams. They loved the action, the hits, and the sixty-yard passes. Kansas City won on a sixty-yard touchdown pass from Patrick Mahomes to Tyreek Hill with two seconds left.

Day two had been a success. I was worn out. We found a hotel about ten miles north and I went right to sleep.

About four in the morning, I got a phone call that no parent or even pseudo parent wants to get. It was from the police department; my guys had been arrested for drunk and disorderly behavior. I didn't even know they'd gone out.

I called Mr. Douglas and explained the problem. He told me, "I'll take care of it."

I drove to the jail and picked them up in the van. They tried to tell me all about it, but I just shouted "Quiet!" just like a parent. I wanted to say, "Just wait until I tell your father about your behavior, young man," just like my mother used to say to me when I was in trouble. I'd have given them a time out, but it would've taken longer to explain the concept than it was worth.

Day three was all about Hollywood. Once they finally woke up and got over some nasty hangovers, we went on tours of the area and the studios. We even drove up by the giant Hollywood sign so they could take pictures as close as legally possible. They saw a few Hollywood stars filming a movie, but wanted to meet Jennifer Aniston. A phone call to Mr. Douglas was all we needed to get an invitation onto the set. We took pictures with Jennifer Aniston, who turned out to be very nice. A few men had her autograph their backs with sharpies. She played along nicely. Several of the men thought they could be stars if they were given a chance. I told them they could be extras in a film about Russian soldiers if they made one. Day three, while it had a rocky start, turned out to be a success.

Day four was a long, scenic drive up to Pismo Beach. We went on the pier, and they bought frisbees and took pictures with other people's dogs. We went bar hopping and ate at really nice restaurants. They tried taking pictures of each other in dangerous poses right on the edges of cliffs. We were having a great time, and everyone was smiling. They kept thanking me for the trip even though I didn't pay for it, just tagged along. I didn't have to discipline anyone that day; a nice change of pace.

We went to F. McClintic's Saloon and Dining House for dinner. It was everything I could do to keep the boys in line. I felt like a babysitter again. The bill for twenty-one people was almost four thousand dollars with tip! They ordered quite a few drinks. I was just happy I didn't have to pay for it. Everyone was in a great mood, it was wonderful.

We paid and were getting ready to leave when Aleksei's phone rang. I watched my friend's facial expression go from joy to rage in a matter of thirty seconds.

# Chapter 32:
## Aleksei's Son

He was speaking quickly in Russian, and although I couldn't understand him, I knew it was bad. One of the team, Mirkivok, came over and told me that Aleksei was saying something about his son. When he finally hung up, he put his head in his hands and started to cry.

He finally said, "My son has been taken and my wife attacked." Then their phones started to ring as well. It was from their superiors, telling them to cut their trip short and return at once. The entire team was ordered back to LAX, the Los Angeles International Airport, where a Russian jet would be arriving in three hours.

Aleksei didn't know anything else. He looked at me with tears in his eyes, put both of his hands on my shoulders, and said, "I need your help, my friend. Can you get my son back? He is my whole world. Please help me, Mick."

I replied, "Of course, Aleksei. I'll return with you." The team tried to console him, but it didn't help. His son was close to six thousand miles away, and there was nothing he could do.

Aleksei was told by his superiors this was a retaliation attack. Aleksei didn't want to assume anything; he just wanted to return. The Russians jumped into the vans and my wife and I into our rental car. We sped back to LAX in record time. On the way they called some of their Russian contacts to meet them at the airport and return all the vehicles back to the rental agencies.

I contacted Mr. Douglas and told him of the issue and asked for guidance. He said, "Go ahead. I'll alert the FBI and customs in Los Angeles to fast-track you out of the country. But, Mick, this will be the last time you go to Russia. I can't have one of our most important assets in harm's way. I will have people watching."

We were met at the airport by customs, FBI, and police agents. After we were searched and sent through customs, we were allowed to depart. I've come to the conclusion that what James Douglas wants, he gets. The entire team was impressed with the efficiency of the US government when red tape is eliminated.

We were cleared quickly and took off. Once in the air, we were in constant contact with Russian agents about the case. We received pictures via email, and they were put on a large-screen TV so everyone could brainstorm ideas. Decisions had to be made well before we landed, and Aleksei created an action plan on the monitor.

Although they spoke in Russian, I was able to follow the basics. Aleksei divided the team into five groups of four people. He decided which group would go to which location. Aleksei gave each group a series of questions to pursue to gain intelligence. He printed the questions that needed to be answered. In English, he authorized the team to forcibly extract the information, with every tool they possessed.

The plan followed a series of actions depending on what intelligence was learned. He printed a flow chart. He wasn't screwing around. Everything that needed to be learned and reactions that would follow were going to happen his way.

*God help anyone who gets in Aleksei's way.*

He called the one person he hated, Mikhail Posivic, the captain of the police department. Aleksei had a long conversation in Russian with him. Afterward he told me, "Mikhail was sorry to hear about my son and wife and will allow my team to use any resources he has. Once we land, he will be waiting with police escort to the evidence building, the one you and I were in a few weeks ago. He seems to have lost his hostility to us after you solved the kidnappings. I hope so, because if he gives me any shit, I'll drive over him with a bulldozer. I am not going to fuck around with this guy. If he does what he says I'll be grateful, and if not, I'll make sure his career is over." I didn't need to say anything back.

In a moment I asked a question. "We have an airworthy helicopter standing by?"

"Yes, my friend, you will get anything you need," Aleksei said back.

"I'll work as quickly as possible, Aleksei, but I need to make a suggestion. I'd like the evidence brought to the airport. It'll speed up the response by at least an hour."

"Yes, that's a great idea, Mick. I'll make it happen," he said as he reached for his phone. He called Mikhail and told him what to do. "It will be there waiting in the helicopter. I'll get the team back together and give them new orders. The Russian way of handling these types of cases is to do everything by the 'planning book.' Now we will follow your lead then dispatch my people afterward."

A few hours later, Aleksei woke me and said, "In thirty minutes we land." I talked to some of the team for a few minutes, then I felt a weird sensation in my fingers. I was puzzled; just as quickly as I'd felt it, the sensation went away. I told Aleksei what I'd felt immediately. We were still about ten minutes from landing. He suspected that maybe we'd passed over the area where the suspects were located and recorded our location. "Perhaps we will begin in that area," Aleksei said. I wasn't so sure, the feeling had come and gone so quickly. Aleksei asked the pilots the exact location we were flying over and wrote it in his book.

After landing, we immediately went to a private hanger where the evidence was waiting. I grabbed everything and went outside by myself so there would be no distractions. My fingers felt a sensation from Aleksei's son's bookbag, but it was very weak. Strangely, it was getting weaker. Eventually it went away completely.

I told Aleksei, "Let's go toward where I originally sensed something."

The helicopter engines had been started before we even arrived, so we immediately took off. I asked to sit in the front so I could direct them better. Aleksei gave me a headset immediately.

Once airborne I told them to go as fast as possible. The sensation kept getting weaker and weaker, though. Eventually it went away. I told them to fly in a circle, but I felt nothing. The direction indicated had been west, but for some reason I lost it.

I went back to the evidence and handled it all again. Aleksei told me there was more evidence, but it was from his wife. I wish we had that as well, but it was back at the airport. I had to focus solely on the child's evidence. After fifteen more minutes and no results, I insisted we go back to the airport and get his wife's evidence.

A policeman was waiting with her evidence as we landed. I ripped open the bag and pulled out her purse and bloody sweater. We immediately took off. After a few minutes of interruptions, I was finally able to focus on my fingers. I was rewarded with a sensation and told them to turn around.

We flew for only fifteen minutes before I felt the sensations getting stronger. I asked Aleksei if the SUVs were coming along as well, and he told me, "Not unless we need them. We have all the firepower we need with us, and a drone is following the helicopters."

Five minutes later I told everyone, "Less than five miles now: be ready." They looked a bit confused, so Aleksei did the math to tell them, "Eight kilos." This was understood. They loaded their guns and checked equipment.

"Dead ahead, Aleksei. Should we send in the drone first?"

Aleksei looked at me and thought for a few seconds. "No, we've got to go in hard and fast. I can't waste any more time." I was a bit worried that four helicopters would make too much noise. Aleksei wasn't, and told me, "By the time they knew where we're coming from, it will be too late."

We were flying at a low altitude, less than one hundred feet above the ground. Ahead of us, about a half mile, was a series of buildings with five vehicles—two vans and three trucks.

"There, Aleksei, right in front of us about a half mile." Aleksei yelled some commands in Russian and everyone stood up, the side doors were opened, and the machine guns were manned. A few seconds later I heard on the radio some excited chatter.

I saw flashes of light from the building only one hundred yards away and heard pinging sounds. *Holy shit; they're firing at us.* Then I saw tracer fire coming at us and heard rapid pinging sounds. The left-side machine gunner was hit on his left arm. The helicopter took evasive action, and the right-side machine gunner opened up with a stream of bullets and tracers. I saw four people firing up at us. One man held a larger machine gun, and for a second, I thought I was watching the movie *Rambo*. He was holding the machine gun from the waist and firing. The right-side gunner cut him down.

Almost immediately I started to lose sensation in my fingers, which meant one of the bad guys was dead. *Damnit, we need these people alive.*

I yelled to Aleksei, "Hold your fire. We want them alive."

Aleksei said, "Yes, we need them alive to find my son."

The helicopters landed, and everyone rushed out except for the pilot and myself. After dropping the team off, we took off and circled to provide close air support. The gunner who had been hit used a first aid kit and bandaged himself. *Jesus these guys are tough,* I thought.

The two gunners kept talking in Russian and looking at me. I finally told them, "I don't speak Russian."

The right-side gunner said, "Bad guys better hope Aleksei's son is OK, or he will chop them into little pieces—very slowly."

I said, "That's OK with me," then gave them both a thumbs-up sign.

I heard frantic radio calls in Russian. The helicopter rotated toward a truck trying to drive away near a bunch of trees. The helicopter fired a stream of bullets toward it, eventually hitting the engine area. A large plume of steam and smoke emerged from the engine compartment, then it burst into flames. The truck stopped moving. The pilot was who'd aimed and fired the gun, so I gave him a thumbs-up sign. As we swung around sideways the left gunner fired a burst to stop the two people running. He didn't hit them; just tried to change their minds about running any farther.

We hovered only fifty feet away. The gunner motioned them to put their hands up. They did so quickly. Seconds later, two soldiers from our team appeared and put them in hand cuffs.

A few minutes later I heard Aleksei say in English, "All clear." The drone pilot told Aleksei that there were no other targets in the area. He told the pilot of the helicopter to land. They motioned me to get out. I saw Aleksei with four people in handcuffs. He was screaming in Russian. The right-side gunner was at my side translating their exchanges.

"Aleksei is asking where his son is located. They're telling him that their leader is the only one who knows."Aleksei took out his gun and fired it into the first guy's knee. He screamed in agony, then threw up. Then he went to the next guy and asked him the same question. This man shook his head back and forth, but Aleksei didn't shoot him. He motioned for something from one of the other soldiers. That soldier brought out a bat-tery-powered drill from the garage. Aleksei asked him again then pro-ceeded to drill a hole right through the guy's kneecap. While it was hard to watch, I certainly didn't feel bad for them. Those people chose their life; Aleksei was making them pay for poor decisions. The third man was asked the same question, and this guy finally talked for about thirty seconds. He said something that made Aleksei kneel down.

"What's the guy saying?" I asked.

"He told Aleksei that their leader is Ivan Volkov, but they're not sure if it's his real name. He isn't sure if his son is still alive. These men are scared of Ivan because he killed two of the men just for arguing with him. He's easy to spot, he has a crazy tattoo covering his entire upper body that the prisoners called, 'Ognennaya Tatuirovka D'yavola' which loosely translates to 'devil's fire tattoo.' He told Aleksei that the bodies are in the van behind the building on the right."

Aleksei jumped up and ran to the van. He opened the door, and there were two adult bodies inside. They had been shot four times each. One in the crotch, one in the knee, one in the chest, and one between the eyes. It was a horrific sight. Aleksei was beyond angry now. He walked back to the man who was talking. He grabbed him and yelled something to one of his men. The soldier grabbed the guy and pushed him to the helicopter. The side gunner yanked him inside while the guy screamed. He went to the fourth guy and yelled questions. When the guy didn't answer quick enough, he pulled his pistol out and cocked the trigger. This seemed to be all the motivation he needed to begin talking.

After about forty-five seconds, Aleksei walked over to me and said, "We need to find him. Are you getting anything?"

"I'm sorry, Aleksei—nothing since the guy with the machine gun was taken out. These guys are just pawns. Can you ask them if the Ivan guy was going to the airport? We also need to know what Ivan touched or ate while he was here so I might get a read from it. What kind of car did he drive and who hired these guys?" He went back over to the last guy and started shouting questions. Aleksei pointed his gun at the guy's crotch and cocked the gun again. Finally, after a bunch of yelling in Russian, Aleksei put his gun away. Aleksei told a few men something, and they ran into one of the buildings. Then Aleksei ran over to me and said, "He said the location where my son is being held is about thirty kilos away. Ivan left several hours ago, but they don't know where he went. They're bringing you a soda can and a cup he used. We must leave. A few of my team will stay here with the prisoners, but we need to go now."

We jumped on the helicopter with two of the prisoners who'd given Aleksei information. Like the gunner said, Aleksei will do whatever is necessary to find his son.

# Chapter 33:
## *Help Me Mick*

We took off and flew for about fifteen minutes at full speed. I was discouraged because I wasn't getting any reading from the cup or soda can. Aleksei was on the radio barking orders. It was tough to watch my new friend suffer so much. His son was missing, and I was unable to find the people responsible.

We were flying about five hundred feet above the ground. He grabbed the two prisoners and pushed them toward the open door of the helicopter. He yelled something in Russian and pointed to the ground. They were screaming and looking down. I have no idea what was being said, but I guessed it went something like this: "Show me where to go or I'll throw you out of the helicopter." They knew he was serious and gave Aleksei directions. Eventually we arrived near a farm house in a rural area. We landed, and the team went out and searched the buildings. We took off again for close air support and to scan the area. I still had no sensations in my hands.

I heard frantic radio chatter then saw the gunner who was my translator put his head down.

I asked, "What's going on?" He said, "It's really bad news. They've found Aleksei's son, but he's been killed."

My heart sank. We were having fun in California while Aleksei's family was being tortured. Worse yet, I had no answers for them. We hadn't been able to find him in time and the team was devastated. Then the gunner told me, "They'd also found an old couple shot to death, probably the owners of the house."

It was disheartening that I hadn't been able to help my friend find his child in time.

I'd felt I'd let the team down and allowed some twisted, sick piece of shit escape capture. What could I say to Aleksei at a time like this? I was determined to find this monster and make sure he didn't escape justice again.

We flew in a big circle one more time looking for vehicles. The drone was overhead scanning with thermal sensors but found nothing. We landed and went inside. Aleksei was holding his son's body and crying. His son looked to be seven or eight years old. Who could do something like this to an innocent young boy?

My anger continued to rise, but I had a job to do. *Find something you can touch to help locate this guy, Mick.* I found a cup and then a handgun that appeared to be the murder weapon. The handgun was a real German Walther P38 from World War II. From the age of the couple that lived here, my guess is the old man had brought it back from the war. We put on gloves so prints could be retrieved from both items. One of the team members took fingerprints using a scanner. Once completed, they were sent to the crime lab for analysis. We were hoping this bastard was in their system, but it would take time to receive an answer. *I have to find this guy and help my new friend get closure.* After the prints were taken, I held the gun but felt no senses.

I said, "Can we find out what car the old people drove?" They called in to headquarters to get this information. Then I said, "Have the police search for any vehicles they owned at the airport in Moscow. Also, have them check security footage at the airport. I have a weird sense that he flew out when we flew in."

I needed to keep busy. Depression will make you lethargic, and I worked best under stress. Finally, we received word that the guy we were looking for was Klavdii Popov. I was told he was one of the most feared men in Russia. He was well connected—part of the Russian mob. He specialized in murder for hire, terrorizing government officials, and drug trafficking. It was reported that his other job was to oversee the really depraved part of the Russian mob's business, which is to find young girls and boys for prostitution. Unfortunately, there was no information about where he lived, but quite a few known accomplices. They would start a nationwide investigation immediately.

Aleksei was suffering inside, but he knew the best chance to catch Popov was right now. He developed a plan to investigate his contacts and put an all-points bulletin to Interpol and the FBI. He sent groups of three men to each contact to gain information. He even contacted his least favorite person again, Mikhail Posivic, the captain of the police department, to ask for additional help in finding Popov. Everything was moving forward; we just needed a bit of luck to catch him.

Aleksei told me, "Once we locate this piece of shit, there will be no mercy. He will tell me who hired him or I'll cut him into little pieces. I'll make it my life's mission to destroy everyone involved." Then he said, "I need you to be the best you can be for me, and for my son. Is there anything you need to assist you?"

I told him, "I'll do my best to help. If there's something needed, I'll let you know. Let's get to work and catch these people."

We made the two co-conspirators watch endless hours of security footage from the airport. Finally, we had a hit. A man matching Popov's description was seen boarding a private jet which filed a flight plan to Finland. It had taken off fifteen minutes before we landed. That explained the sensation I'd had in the airplane. The jet belonged to a large company in Russia. Aleksei grilled the men about where in Finland he was going, but they had no answers. Aleksei sent some men to investigate the company and the flight.

Aleksei yelled for me, and for one of the team members, named Recvic. Aleksei told me, "You, Recvic, and I are going to Finland immediately. If you find something, we will call in help from Finland's Utti Jaeger Regiment." I'd heard of them; they were Finland's special forces. "I know a captain on the force, and I'll call him right now to make sure he can help."

Once Aleksei was off the phone, we jumped in the helicopter and flew to the airport; a jet was waiting for us. When we'd landed, a van was waiting to pick us up. We met with Captain Otto Lehtinen, Aleksei's contact. He gave Aleksei all the intelligence available on Popov's movements once he entered Finland. Unfortunately, there wasn't much to go on.

I had the items we'd collected from the house, but I still wasn't getting anything strong enough to pinpoint. Aleksei asked for a helicopter to make the search easier. It only took ten minutes for one to arrive. It was a Life Flight helicopter, a brilliant idea. Bad guys wouldn't be concerned when a Life Flight helicopter flew overhead. The pilot, whose name I couldn't quite understand, knew only five words in English: yes, no, boobs, John Wayne, and Playboy. To make it easier to communicate, I just called him Boris, and he called me John Wayne.

We flew around in expanding circles. It was half an hour before I'd felt anything at all. It was weak and disappointing because I couldn't get a handle on the direction. About fifteen minutes later, it seemed to be strongest near the city of Vantaa. I told Aleksei this wasn't strong enough to be Popov, but maybe it was someone involved. We continued to the north side of Vantaa, and finally my fingers gave us a direction to follow. Five minutes later we flew over a house nestled in the hills. We didn't want to arouse suspicion so Aleksei had the pilot fly another two miles while he thought of scenarios.

We had no vehicles to use, but I'd had an idea. I asked Aleksei, "How about we fake a malfunction on the return flight and land near the house? With the element of surprise, we would jump out and overtake anyone in the house before they knew what happened."

Aleksei agreed. We waited another minute then headed back toward the house.

It only took a minute to be close enough to the house to put the plan in action. To simulate an engine failure the pilot spun down in slow circles. Once the helicopter was about one hundred feet above the ground, we saw three people come out of the house and watch what they thought was an impending helicopter crash. Aleksei told the pilot to aim for the driveway about fifty feet from the house. He came in fast, with a hard landing that was perfect.

The men from the house slowly approached the helicopter. When the men were within forty feet, Aleksei and Recvic jumped out with automatic rifles. The men quickly raised their hands and were placed in cuffs. The ruse had worked to perfection.

My fingers were tingling but not throbbing. Unfortunately, this meant these men were connected, but not as significant. I was disappointed that the mastermind wasn't here, but maybe those men could tell us more. Aleksei went through the house and took their phones and one laptop. He radioed in for another crime team to take the place apart to look for further evidence.

While we waited, Aleksei took each man into the house and questioned them. From time to time, painful screaming could be heard. I couldn't tell what Aleksei was saying, and my helicopter pilot didn't know enough English to explain it to me.

Finally, Recvic returned and told me, "Aleksei use hammer." Then he made a downward motion like he was hammering something each time screaming was heard. It took almost an hour for the forensics team to arrive, which was just about perfect for Aleksei to finish questioning the people in the house.Aleksei came out finally and said something to the pilot that I wasn't able to understand. Then he said to me, "We will be leaving in two minutes. I have new information that may help us." I noticed he had blood on his shirt and face. It didn't appear he was bleeding, so I'd guessed the people screaming were missing some blood. The pilot started the engine.

We waited another minute until the other forensics team arrived. After a brief question-and-answer period, Aleksei ran back to the helicopter with Boris. We took off with the phones and laptop. Aleksei told me, "There's a safe house in Moscow we need to investigate. These three said some of their friends would be there. We have their phones and laptop, which we will bring to our technical people. My team will stake out the safe house and track every person entering or leaving. I need your help, my friend. Can I ask you to help watch the house, in case you sense anything?"

I told him, "Yes, of course. Anything I can do to help you catch these people, I'll do." He shook my hand. I looked into his eyes and saw a determined man. "We have to find these guys and end them," I said to Aleksei.

"I'll eliminate them, Mick, not capture them. I don't want them to live out their lives in jail."

We flew back to the airport where a private jet was waiting for the trip back to Moscow. A few hours of sleep weren't enough, but they were all we could get.

# Chapter 34:
## The Search

We arrived back in Moscow and took the phones and computers to the Foreign Intelligence Service building. Aleksei also called a few contacts from the KGB to assist. Five vehicles arrived, and Aleksei met with each person, then entered the building. I wasn't allowed into the building, so Aleksei instructed Recvic to take me to a restaurant and wait. He'd contact us when they're finished.

Recvic told me to get the pelmeni. I thought it was some kind of exotic Russian food, but when it arrived it looked like common dumplings. I said, "Dumplings?" Recvic didn't understand and just pointed at the plate and said, "Eat, eat." After I'd finished the pelmeni and about a gallon of water, Aleksei called. We met back at the building. Aleksei looked tired; his shirt and pants were crumpled, and his hair was a mess. I could tell he needed some sleep, but he insisted we continue.

If I could sum up Aleksei's demeanor in one sentence, it would be, "Poke it with a sharp stick and channel the fury."

Aleksei had been poked, and now someone would certainly pay for that.

There would be no safe place for the man who'd killed his child. I'd never met anyone so focused. About a dozen cars arrived outside the restaurant. Captain Mikhail Posivic made a grand entrance.

I said to Aleksei and Recvic, "Not this shit now; we don't have time."

Aleksei said, "Let's see what he can do to help. If he becomes a problem, then I'll go ballistic."

To our surprise, Captain Posivic said in heavily accented English, "Here are ten of my best men. Use them for any purpose you see fit. You can have them for as long as necessary to find who killed your son. We have provided five vehicles to use as well."

Aleksei thanked Posivic and shook his hand. Posivic put his hand on Aleksei's shoulder and quietly said something in Russian. Whatever was said must've been useful because Aleksei said, "Thank you," and shook his hand again.

Aleksei knew two of the men assigned to him and took them aside. He motioned for me to meet these men. "Boris and Severic are good men. I've worked with them in the past. They'll ride with us in an unmarked police van." We shook hands. They knew a little English, but I knew it wouldn't be easy for us to communicate.

Aleksei told us to get into the van then barked orders to the rest of the men. They all jumped into different vehicles and drove off. Aleksei jumped in the van and told the driver something in Russian. He turned around and said, "We're going to a small airport where a helicopter is waiting. The KGB traced thirteen cell phone numbers and each team is assigned to bring in everyone at those addresses. We're going to fly three helicopters and ten men to one site about forty kilometers away. That's where the last ping was registered."

We arrived at the airport, and the helicopters were ready and waiting. Aleksei's team was using fake ambulance helicopters again since the ruse worked so well the first time. I jumped in the helicopter. It took off before I could get my seat belt buckled.

Aleksei gave me a pistol and holster. "Just in case you want to shoot anyone again," he said. He gave me a slight smile, just enough to show he's human. It was a quick flight, and before I knew it, we were skimming the tree tops in an effort to conceal our arrival.

Aleksei was on the radio to the drone operator. "Three vehicles and eight to ten people on site," he told me. "Are you sensing anything?" he said while pointing to my hands. I hadn't been able to tell; the noise and adrenaline had made me stop thinking about it.

"Let me focus and see," I told him. I closed my eyes and focused on my fingers and started to rotate my open palms. There was no sensation. I looked toward Aleksei, and shook my head back and forth, and said, "I don't feel anything, Aleksei. I need something to hold. Hopefully there will be something at the house to get the sensation started."

Aleksei looked away. Immediately I'd felt like I'd let him down.

"It's OK, Mick; we'll get something at the house for you to use," he said, still looking away.

The helicopters stormed in and landed in a diamond formation. Everyone jumped out and ran to the house from three different directions. Aleksei's team broke down the doors and side windows and rushed into the house. Loud screaming was heard. No shots were fired, and soon eight people were brought out of the house in handcuffs and forced to sit on the lawn. The team members searched the house and cars for electronics. They tagged each phone and computer, took fingerprints, and used electronic sensors to look for hidden rooms and tunnels.

I went into the house to see what I could find, but Aleksei told me to wait until they had taken fingerprints, tagged and photographed the house. In less than a minute they had everyone's information. Five minutes later Aleksei told me to go back into the house.

"Do whatever you need to do now, Mick," said Aleksei. I went through the house touching everything. Aleksei was screaming questions to the people outside. The last room was being examined with an electronic sensor which revealed a false wall. Two of the team returned with axes and started to knock a hole in the wall. While they finished, I grabbed a few of the pillows on the bed and felt a jolt in my hands. Whoever slept here was the one we wanted.

I wanted to tell Aleksei, but he was now busy with interrogations. I used my hands in an attempt to sense direction, but was unable to find any. I ran over to Boris, the original team member who knew English, and told him, "The man we're looking for has been here. Can you tell Aleksei?"

Boris went outside and told Aleksei. More frantic yelling in Russian was heard. I went back into the room to see a giant hole where the false wall was detected. Inside was a shortwave radio, guns, RPGs, and a tunnel entrance. I asked one of the men if I could hold the items for a second and they told me, "Nyet." I'd have to wait for them to process the items first. It was frustrating to wait, but I understood. Aleksei would tell me when to proceed. Four men went into the tunnel entrance. It appeared to go under the house, which meant some, if not all of the rooms, had an access panel to the tunnel.

Rather than wander through the house and risk getting in the way, I walked outside to watch Aleksei. Aleksei was informed about the tunnel, radio, and weapons. Aleksei asked a question of the prisoners and then gave the men a few seconds to answer. If he received no answer, he slapped them and asked again. If they argued or wouldn't answer, out came the hammer. He shook the hammer at them and asked the question again. Aleksei was very calm—until he wasn't. I couldn't understand what he said in Russian, but I understood the gist of the questions.

Boris came over and translated for me. Then he made a chopping motion with his hand just before Aleksei took the hammer and proceeded to thump the big toe of the man who appeared to be the leader. It hurt to watch. The man screamed in agony. Rather than ask the ring leader the question again, he went to the person to his right. Shaking the hammer in a menacing fashion, he asked the man a similar question. When the man refused to answer, Aleksei yelled for Boris to bring something over. Boris retrieved a block of cement. With help from Boris, Aleksei took the man's hand and pulled it up on top of the block. I was surprised by the sound a hammer makes when it impacts a thumb. I wasn't allowed much time to ponder this because the man's screaming interrupted my train of thought.

Aleksei pushed the screaming man back, then proceeded to the person on his right and grabbed his hand. Aleksei lifted up the hammer and asked another question. This person screamed and immediately started answering questions. Boris looked at me and gave the thumbs-up sign. Another team member wrote down everything the man said.

I said, "Boris, this wouldn't be allowed in America. But I don't give a damn what happens to these animals. They made their decisions, and now they have to pay the price. To be perfectly honest, I'm glad he used a hammer."

Boris was somewhat confused about what I said, but he replied, "When animals misbehave, we need to make them change. Aleksei is just helping them to change."Boris listened to what the person was telling Aleksei. Then he told me, "That guy admitted that a man he called the angel of death or doom; I can't quite tell—is Popov, and he was here a few days ago. He and another man will return next week. They're to call him and say something about a restaurant. If this man says the restaurant is 'good,' Popov will return. If he shouldn't come back, then he is to reply, 'The food is bad.' This man was chosen because his voice is very high and couldn't be duplicated easily."

I told Boris, "Why don't we made a recording of the right response to play if he calls?"

"Good idea. I tell Aleksei after he finishes."

One of the team members yelled, "Mr. Mick, you're being called on the radio."

Boris and I looked at each other, and I said, "Who'd be calling me on one of your radios?" I grabbed the mic and said, "This is Mick."

The voice was somewhat garbled, and the person on the other end said, "Mick, this is James Douglas. We have information that your wife is ill. Please contact St. Francis Hospital in Peoria, Illinois."

Boris looked at me and asked, "You know this man?"

I replied, "Yes. I need to find a way to call the hospital. Do you have a satellite phone? I need some way to look up the phone number as well." Boris replied, "Leave it to me. I'll only need a minute." He went to the helicopter and I heard him speaking Russian on the radio. A minute later he brought me a sat phone with the number already entered. I pushed 'send,' and about thirty seconds later the phone rang.

After a few minutes spent trying to find the right person, I reached a doctor. "Your wife was in an automobile accident three days ago," he said. "We've tried to reach you, but the phone number we had went to voicemail. A man from the State Department called us and said you were out of the country. He said they would reach you. She is in critical condition, Mr. Anderson, but is stable. She's been in a coma for three days because of a head injury. She also sustained several broken ribs. How soon will you be back in the US?"

Stunned, all I could say was, "Please tell me she'll be OK. I'll find the next flight from Russia immediately."

The doctor replied, "We're uncertain because of the coma. We do see increased brain activity today, a good sign. Regardless, she has a long road ahead for recovery. I've seen people in worse condition recover completely, but say a prayer because only God knows for sure."

Boris looked at me and said, "You need to discuss this with Aleksei immediately. I'll make the flight arrangements right now."

# Chapter 35:
## *Rushing Home*

Boris told me the "big plane" was being used by the ambassador. He assured me alternate travel plans back to the USA would be handled. A helicopter would take me back to the airport, and I'd fly immediately from there to the United States.

I boarded a plane that flew from Moscow to Helsinki, Finland, for the first leg of the flight. I had a two-hour layover before I flew to New York. I was able to use my cell phone to call the hospital for an update.

The doctor I spoke to said there was little change in my wife's condition.

I had nothing else to do, so I called Aleksei. He said, "Nothing new yet." I told him to keep me informed. Waiting for a flight is nerve-racking when you must get home quickly. I decided to run around the airport after watching several other people exercising.

I finally boarded the flight to New York. This was the first time I was able to sleep for several days. On the nine-hour flight, I slept about eight and a half hours. The passenger next to me was a young woman with orange and pink hair. When I awoke, she told me I snored—very loudly. I felt bad, but at least one of us was able to sleep.

The next flight, to Chicago, was only a half hour from leaving. The same young woman with orange and pink hair was on that flight as well. She walked rapidly up to me, still appearing to be angry. I was surprised when she said, "You're that guy who found the kidnapped kids, right?"

I put my finger up to my lips and said, "Shhh" in an attempt to keep her quieter. "Yes, I was able to find some kidnapped children," I replied quietly. She wanted a picture with me, for her mother. She told me her mother had followed the story closely and she would've loved to meet me.

Two flights later, I finally arrived in Peoria. My son was waiting for me at the airport and we drove immediately to the hospital.

It was disheartening to watch the woman you love trapped in a coma. Hoses and wires were attached all over her body. Machines beeped and hummed. She was intubated so a machine breathed for her. Her hair was shaved because of the head wounds. Stiches made a path from her ear to the top of her head in a semicircular shape. She was bruised all over her entire body, some areas worse than others, but it was obvious her body had been badly battered.

Sixteen hours after my arrival, my wife awoke from her medically induced coma. She'd been in this coma for four days. I was relieved she knew who I was. A detective, named Harry Tillerson, arrived within thirty minutes. He wanted to know if he could question her about the day of the accident. I told him she was in and out of consciousness so any questioning would have to wait. Detective Tillerson said, "Mr. Anderson, the accident was a hit and run. It was on Riekena Road, not far from your house."

I said, "That doesn't make sense. Why would she go on the back roads?"

Tillerson said, "Mr. Anderson, there was construction on Lancaster Road, which required everyone in your neighborhood to divert through Riekena Road. Unfortunately, as of today, we have found no witnesses. Also, because her vehicle ended up in a deep ravine, we're unsure how much time had passed before she was found. You couldn't see the vehicle from the road. A hunter called it in."

He continued, "We recovered one badly damaged black truck, abandoned in the woods about a mile from the accident. The driver hasn't been located at this time. The truck had been reported stolen two days before the accident. Forensics has the truck now. We believe it's the truck used in the accident based on paint transfer."

After pausing to see my reaction, he asked, "Have you been to your house yet?"

I replied, "No, I've been here since I flew in. Why do you ask?"

"Your house was set on fire, and it appears to have been burglarized. They trashed everything. Either you have the worst luck, or someone is trying to destroy everything you care about."

"Jesus, what is going on?" I replied. I felt dizzy and had to sit down.

I decided in that instant not to trust anyone, even the police, with my new address. We were selling the house that apparently had been trashed, so there wasn't anything of value there for a burglar. This was no accident; it must be revenge; but why?He told me a police officer would be posted in front of her room for the rest of the day, and that he would return tomorrow for some follow-up questions.

Two doctors arrived—one was the surgeon, and the other was a neurologist. I stood up to greet them, still unsteady. The surgeon spoke first and told me, "Mr. Anderson, I'm Dr. Butler. Your wife was pretty badly injured, as you can see. She had a closed head injury, and we don't yet know what the long-term effects will be. The good news is she came out of the coma on her own. The nurse told me she knew who you were—an excellent sign. During the surgery, we were forced to drill a hole in her head to relieve the increased brain pressure. After that we operated on her broken collarbone, and a broken left arm. She has eight fractured ribs, but we're unable to fix six of those, they must heal on their own."

I didn't know how to respond, so I just said, "Thank you for all you have done."

The other doctor said, "Mr. Anderson, I'm sorry for the news. I know you're devastated. My name is Dr. Cohleen, and I'll be working with your wife to improve her brain functions while she heals. My staff will help her with motor skills, speech, and memory. The fact that she is awake, and recognizes your face, should speed her recovery. She's made amazing progress in only four days."

I started to feel dizzy. Both doctors recognized that I was having problems standing and held onto my arms. They slowly guided me into a chair. Everything felt like slow motion. After about forty-five seconds I started to regain my composure.

"We didn't want to overwhelm you, Mr. Anderson. Try to relax and breathe. If you pass out, you could be badly injured. Take it easy; we don't want to treat both of you," said Dr. Butler.

I spent the rest of the day in Michelle's hospital room. She likes horses, so I read her stories and showed her pictures from several horse magazines. Doctors and nurses checked on her every hour and said she was healing well. They brought a portable bed for me so I could stay the night.

The next morning Detective Tillerson returned with more questions. He asked where I had been at the time of the crash.

"I was in Russia," I responded.

He looked surprised and said, "The country of Russia? What for?"

I said, "Trying to find kidnapped kids."

I don't think Detective Tillerson initially believed me. He responded, "In Russia? Well, OK, we just need to check everyone's alibis—pretty standard questions. Do you have someone who can vouch for your whereabouts for the last week?"

"Call the state department, or the CIA, they know where I am at all times. I can get you some numbers to call."

"OK," said Tillerson, "we have to check. Also, do you have any idea where your wife was going?"

"Based on where the accident happened, my guess is to a local horse farm. She likes to help out with horses whenever she can," I replied.

My wife opened her eyes and in a whisper she told us, "Mick, I remember. I was followed from our house by two pickup trucks. I think a black or dark blue, with dark tint on the windows. They passed me, then put on their brakes. I tried to drive away, but one ran into the back of my car and the other pushed me off of the road. I went into the trees near the sharp bend in the road. It's by the farm with the border collie dog you like so much."

I was infuriated. I knew exactly where she crashed, and the ravine is thirty feet deep. My wife and I had talked about that part of the road should've had concrete barriers because the drop off was only ten feet from the roadway.

Tillerson told me they now had a witness who told him two trucks were chasing a black SUV near the farm about a half mile from the accident location. The witness thought it was kids chasing each other and didn't hear the crash.

"So, Mr. Anderson, who do you think wanted to harm your wife?"

"I don't know, Tillerson, but I aim to find out. You may not know who I am, or what I'm capable of doing, but you will soon enough."

Tillerson said, "Hold on, we don't want anyone taking the law into their own hands. If you know something, or know who they are, you need to tell us. I know some things from the television reports, but I don't really know what to believe. You're right, I don't know what you're capable of, but we need to follow the law."

"OK, then I want you to call someone and get my wife twenty-four-hour protection. Then you and I are going on a mission to find these guys, understood?"

Tillerson replied, "Exactly how are you going to find them?"

"PFM, Tillerson. PFM."

Tillerson replied, "What's PFM?"

I said, "Pure fucking magic, at least according to some people. It's what I do, Tillerson." Then I added, "First, I need to see her SUV. It should have some of her personal items. I need to hold onto some items of hers to see if my senses can be triggered."

# Chapter 36:
## *Rip Their Balls Off*

I was beyond determined now. Someone had injured my wife, and I wanted to rip their balls off then feed them to the pigs on a nearby farm.

Once a policeman was posted outside my wife's room, I was ready to go. Tillerson took me to the impound lot where my wife's SUV was stored. It was badly damaged, Tillerson hadn't told me it was a roll-over accident. The roof was crushed; she was lucky to be alive. I saw a large impact point on the driver's door. It was smashed in a semicircular pattern, which would be consistent with impacting a tree. The driver's window was vaporized, and blood was on the front seats, the deployed air bag, dashboard and all over the inside and outside of the door. There was blood on the headliner and sun visors. A tree branch was impaled through the windshield and into the deployed air bag. There was blood on the tree branch. I walked around back and saw the smashed rear bumper and hatch, with dark blue paint traces. The passenger side was smashed in as well, and had black paint markings. Even though her SUV was black, you could see the other vehicle's color was slightly different. Rage was beginning to build inside of me; this was deliberate. The only good sign was Michelle's memory was correct. She told us the right color of the vehicles involved.

As in in my other cases, I needed something important to the person I was trying to help. I hoped Michelle's case would be no different. I wanted her workout bag that's always kept in the back. Clothing and towels should be in the bag. There wasn't anything left inside, so I asked Tillerson where her personal effects had been taken.

Tillerson told me, "This is how we found it, nothing but loose change and a few empty bottles of water. No purse, no identification, and almost no garbage. Nothing was in the glove box either. It almost appeared that it had been cleaned out recently. We had to track her name down using the VIN, which only told us your name. Is she always this neat, or is it possible the someone cleaned out the car?"

"No, the car is usually not clean on the inside. The storage compartment should've been full of papers, and there should've been coffee cups and spoons on the floor. Since there was no purse or workout bag, they must've planned to attack her and make it look like a robbery."

Tillerson said, "Who wants to hurt your wife, Mr. Anderson?"

I said, "I really don't know. It could be anyone related to the cases I recently solved, or even cases I'm currently working on. I need to get back to my house and get a few things to help me figure it out. Let's go."

We pulled into my old house's driveway. The damage to the house was devastating. The roof was partially collapsed, and black burn marks could be seen all over the exterior. Yellow crime scene tape surrounded the whole house. I was getting angrier and angrier by the second. If I didn't figure a way to control my anger, I wouldn't be able to find the people responsible.I knew there was one area where I'd find some of her clothing and other personal effects. I told Tillerson, "We have a hidden storage area on each side of the rear bedroom, behind the two closets." We walked into the remains of the house, and I quickly realized the stairs weren't safe. I'd have to find another way to get into the bedroom, so I went to the backyard where we kept several ladders behind the storage shed. I found the largest one and carried it up to the rear of the house. Tillerson held the ladder so I could climb through the same window the fire fighters had broken to fight the fire.

I went inside; the floor was still passable. The smell of gasoline was very strong. Every room had been set on fire, and luckily this room was probably the first the fire fighters had watered down. The first piece of furniture I saw was the burned-out remains of Michelle's antique dresser. She'd told me her great-grandparents bought it around the year 1900. I pushed it out of the way. It was a bit strange; for some reason my mind was overly concerned about the dresser. I thought it's best to wait until she felt better before I told her about the dresser. She'd blow a fuse if I told her now.

One of the closet doors was badly burned, and I yanked it out of my way. Behind it was a smooth wall that had five hidden latches. I found the first one, flipped it up, and continued until all five were unlatched. I gave the door a shove, and the whole back of the closet opened up about two feet. I'd designed a rocker switch to automatically turn on a light when the door opened, but the power was cut off, and it was pitch black inside the storage area. I yelled for Tillerson to throw a flashlight up through the window.

I nearly lost count of how many times he tried to get the flashlight through a three-foot window. Poor guy; it appeared he didn't have an athletic bone in his body. He finally got angry and heaved it my direction. Instead of going through the window, it went through the burned-out wall. I was able to find enough safe rafters to walk on to retrieve the flash light. Not the smoothest police operation, but at least there was progress.

Now that I had a flashlight, I went inside the hidden storage area and retrieved a few of Michelle's prized possessions. I picked the high school jacket that she'd tried on a month before, the horse saddle she used as a kid, and her wedding dress. If I was to get any sensations, then these were the objects to use.

I calmed myself down and began my normal routine. First, touch each of the pieces of clothing, pause for about twenty seconds, and concentrate. I started with the wedding dress, but it hadn't been worn in twenty years, and I there was no sensation. I chuckled as a few of the memories from that day returned. The horse saddle didn't give me anything either. The high school jacket was my last hope. I took a deep breath and said a little prayer. I put the jacket on, and immediately started to feel something in my hands. "Outstanding," I said. I put the dress and saddle back where I found them, grabbed the jacket and carefully went down the ladder.

"Let's go! You'll need to call for backup, lots of backup, and right now," I said in an urgent tone.

"Where are we going?" asked Tillerson.

"We're going to catch these guys."

We drove to the main road, on-to Lancaster Road, then to the Coyote Creek Golf course and waited for backup. Within a minute four police cruisers arrived. I assembled the officers and told them my plan. "Everyone will follow us. I think they're within ten miles of our location, or less. Once we get close our plans may change, but this is how I want to proceed. When I determine that we're within a half mile, we will need to survey the location, then make our final decisions. They'll be armed, so be ready for a quick firefight. I need a vest. Let's go."

One of the police officers asked why a civilian was telling them what to do. I told him, "Because I know how to find them, and how dangerous they'll likely be."

Tillerson told everyone, "The people we're going to find likely tried to kill his wife. He has special skills that you may or may not know about, but I trust him, and I'm running the operation. I'm calling for the Peoria SWAT team and an undercover agent to be meet us."

We jumped in the cars and proceeded to drive around for ten minutes before I made everyone stop. We were now in Peoria, no more than a quarter of a mile from a hotel. "That hotel," I said to Tillerson. He radioed to everyone.

We couldn't see the vehicle, so an unmarked police car from an undercover unit joined us. He was sent in to survey the parking area. He reported back that no matching vehicles were found in the parking lot. I told Tillerson to have him drive around the block and check side streets. We only waited about two minutes and he radioed back, "One blue GMC pickup found two streets over, front end damaged. Calling in plates now." My heart started pounding, I was excited and angry at the same time.

The undercover officer radioed, "Plates are reported stolen seven days ago." Tillerson radioed to find out the ETA on the SWAT team. The reply was ten minutes.

"That's too long to wait," I said. Tillerson said his hands were tied; they were equipped for this, and we weren't.

The undercover officer radioed, "Alert—four men approaching vehi-cle." A few seconds later we heard popping sounds.

The radio crackled, "Shots fired; shots fired! Dispatch, let them know an undercover is on scene."

Tillerson yelled, "Get out; you don't go with us." I could tell he was serious, so I followed orders and got out quickly.

Four police cruisers raced to the side street, and more popping sounds could be heard. There were a few seconds of quiet then twenty to thirty shots were fired. Police sirens sounded in the distance.

I thought I was in pretty good shape, but it seemed as if ten minutes passed before I arrived at the scene. I was out of breath and had to bend over and rest a few seconds. I noticed a lot of carnage. It looked like a war zone, broken windows, flattened tires, and bullet holes in fenders, wind-shields, and a few mail boxes. I counted four people in handcuffs on the ground. They were all bleeding, and only one was moving.

Police were combing the area to make sure it was safe. I saw Tillerson; he waved me forward. "Three dead, Mick. Nothing we could do; they wouldn't drop their weapons and surrender. I think the survivor will make it. You're not to approach. Do not say anything to him, understood?"

"Yeah, yeah, whatever, just keep me in the loop, OK?"

"Copy that," is all he said.

# Chapter 37:
## *Hired By Who?*

It took four hours before Tillerson could tell me anything.

"Survivor was critical; we couldn't interview him. The phones we recovered are being investigated. The phone numbers they called are to someone who works for a pretty well-connected family in Chicago. This family is well known to local and federal agencies for ties to the Russian mob. We believe they were hired to hurt your family. One of dead guys is a well-known 'enforcer' and probably the main architect, at least according to my source. We think it was ordered by the Russian mob."

"Who? The Russian mob? You've got to be fucking with me, Tillerson," I said.

He said, "No, I'm not. It worries me enough to put undercover agents at your children's residences as we speak."

He stared at me for a few seconds, then said, "Mr. Anderson, we never would've caught these guys without your help. Care to tell me how you knew where they were?"

I replied, "I have special abilities, Tillerson, but you already knew that."

"I've heard about your ability to find children, but I need to know if this is legitimate. My superiors will want to rule you out as a co-conspirator."

"Jesus, Tillerson, I don't have time for this shit. How about you call Detective Dooley from the Chicago PD and he can fill you in? He and I solved many cases together in Chicago. Some you have heard about, but most you haven't."

I pulled out my phone and said, "Call fat-ass." The phone said, "Calling fat-ass." He answered on the first ring. "I'm busy Mick, what the hell do you need?" I said, "Hey Dooley, I need some help. My wife was injured in a car accident and it looks intentional. I need you to talk to this Peoria, Illinois detective, please."

I handed Tillerson the phone. They talked for about a minute before I heard him say, "So, is it safe to assume that he has no ties to the Russian mob?" A few seconds later he said, "Well, it seems odd that he was in Russia twice in the last month, that's all." About a minute went by before he said, "OK, thank you detective, I appreciate your time." He wrote the phone number and name of Dooley in his little book and handed me the phone back.

"OK, I feel better," said Tillerson.

I responded calmly, "Tillerson, my gut is telling me those thirty-four children I found in the middle of Russia were somehow linked to the Russian mob. That would explain why Aleksei's son was killed."

"Who's Aleksei?"

"He was the soldier the Russian ambassador selected to be the team leader for the mission to find those children. He's a Russian special forces commander, and a friend. The team they assembled used a real 'Wrath of God' scorched earth policy to find him. Quite a few bad people ended up dead."

I continued, "Tillerson, I need you to be assured that I had no part in my wife's attack, so believe it or not, I want you to contact the director of the CIA. I'm serious when I say this; he can vouch for my whereabouts during that operation, and also the one I just returned from. You won't get through unless you mention my name. We won't accomplish anything unless I can work without suspicion." I told him to use his own channels to find the phone number and person he needed to talk to.

"I have to check on you, Mr. Anderson. It's required. I hope you can understand that you're a complete unknown to us, so I'll have to investigate what you say."

"Fine, I really don't give a shit. I just need to find the people responsible, and quickly," I said. "What's our next step? I think we need to go to Chicago and let me use my skills to direct you to the source."

Tillerson raised his voice, "Wait a minute, you're not going anywhere. First, we haven't cleared you, and second, we have other people we need to investigate. The trail may end here in Peoria, but once we verify it leads elsewhere, then, and only then, will we be taking a trip up to Chicago. Let me be clear; you don't go anywhere near Chicago."

I responded, "Fine, I don't need to, I'll have fat-ass use his people to check them out."

Tillerson said, "No, I can't allow you to compromise our investigation. Let us do our job, we know what we're doing."

I pointed a finger right at his face and screamed back, "I'll give you two days, then I do things my way." I turned around and left without letting him continue the conversation.

An officer drove me back to the hospital. An hour later I received a call with no return number on the screen. It was Mr. Douglas. He said, "James Douglas here. What the fuck have you gotten yourself into, Mick?" He sounded more rude than normal, as if I interrupted his favorite movie.

I replied, "It's bad, Mr. Douglas. My wife—."

He interrupted, "Save it. I've told you we'll always know more than you do, so let's save the small talk. I'll have eleven of my agents landing in one hour in Poria or Peoria, or however the fuck you pronounce that city's name. My people have already told the mayor, the chief of police, the state troopers, and the local FBI that my men are in charge. If we need to go to Chicago, I'll let only a select few know we're coming. Shit leaks like a sieve there. You will be part of everything we do, Mick, and I'll put the full weight of my office on your side. Now you're welcome; I have to go."

I tried to say thank you, but the line was dead. I like his style, to the point, no wasted time.

I called Tillerson. He picked up and once he realized it was me on the line, he yelled, "What kind of shit storm did you create? I told you to stay out of the investigation. Now I have the FBI, the CIA, the fucking Pentagon, and even people in the fucking White House telling me to stand down and let their people handle it. What the fuck did you do?"

I tried to be as calm as possible, "Not one god damn thing, but you have to remember I have special talents—talents used by agencies far, far above your pay grade. They're aware of everything I do, and take a special interest in me and my family. They reached out to me, not the other way around. I didn't contact anyone. They just know; it's their job to keep tabs on me."

# Chapter 38:
## *Cavalry Arrives*

I was picked up by Tillerson, who of course was still bitter. "My officers and detectives are going to be errand boys now, I hope you're happy, Mr. Anderson."

I said, "I don't care how this gets solved. I'm sorry you feel short-changed, but these people will get results. They don't have the same red-tape restrictions. Together we will solve this and return your life back to normal. They'll teach you a few new tricks along the way. It'll be a win-win for everyone; I guarantee it. Just trust me for a few days."

Five unmarked police vehicles were driven up to the airport for the agents to use. We watched as a private jet landed and then taxied to an unused hanger. Eleven people walked off the plane. They walked right up to me and Tillerson, and one of them said, "Detective Tillerson, I'm Special Agent Sam White, and I'll be heading this investigation. Here is the special directive order, which states that my team is in charge."

As Tillerson reviewed the order, Agent White said, "These orders have been signed by the president of the United States. Copies have been sent to your superiors and their superiors. We don't want to step on any toes; we're here to work together, understand?"

Tillerson said in a resigned voice, "Understood. My superiors have made several of us available for anything you may need."

Special Agent White said, "Excellent. Let's not waste time, then. My team needs to see what you have so far, so take them to your office."

A helicopter arrived overhead, circled once, then landed one hundred feet away.

Special Agent White said to me, "It's nice to finally meet you, Mick. I've heard great things about you from Mr. Douglas. Just like him, I don't like to waste time. Now you and I'll go in that helicopter; I want to talk to you in private, and let you know a few things."

Once inside the helicopter, we both put on headphones. Special Agent White said, "So, tell me what you're thinking and what you know." I started to explain why I went back to Russia and he cut me off.

Agent White barked, "I know all that. What I want to know is what has happened since you got home, and what's your gut is telling you?"

I said, "It has been a blur. My gut is telling me the Russian mob is responsible for my wife's accident and are after me and my family. They burned down my house as well. We have another house that nobody knows about, which has been untouched."

Agent White, in an indignant tone reminiscent of Mr. Douglas, said, "Yeah, we know about the house on Largent Creek. If Aleksei's son and your family are targets, it will be because of what you did in Russia. If so, then we will go fishing for bigger fish to fry in Chicago and in New York."

"What's in New York?" I asked.

"Chicago's Russian mob is run by a nephew of the leader of the real Russian mob; the one in Russia. They answer to New York's Russian mob, which pulls all the strings for the country." I heard a beep, and Agent White said, "Hold on, have to take a call."

He talked for under a minute then continued, "OK, so yesterday we intercepted phone calls which tells us Chicago acted alone, without proper authorization from the Russian mob connections in New York. This has ruffled some feathers in New York. Now we find out that the actual Russian mob in Russia went around New York, direct to Chicago, and demanded action against you. You weren't home, so they went after your wife. New York prefers to keep things quiet, but this jackass in Chicago has a vendetta against you. Now I think we know why."

"OK, why?" I asked.

"Does the name Vladimir Varchinko ring a bell?" Agent White asked.

"Not at all. Should it?" I replied.

"Well, he is a big shot with the Russian mob. He has a step son named Nicolai. Does that name ring a bell?"

"Do you mean the Nicolai who was killed in Russia?" I asked.

Agent White said, "Yes, that one. You see, Vladimir Varchinko thinks you killed his step son—well, you and Aleksei. We believe he ordered Aleksei's son to be kidnapped and his wife attacked. He was going to do the same to your family, but your children are not young anymore. I think they chose your wife instead. We intercepted some phone calls. One of the calls was from the people hired to kill you and your wife. They thought she was dead. Turns out they didn't finish the job. We believe they were ordered to stay until they finished the job. Hate to state the obvious, but they really want to punish you."

"But we didn't kill him. He was killed by the kidnappers," I said.

"Yes, we know all of that, and we have the tapes from the satellite that was parked overhead tasked with watching your every move."

After a brief pause, he said, "You see, we have a problem, Mick. When I say 'We,' I mean you, me, and the United States government. As you can imagine, the United States is constantly monitoring many things in Russia. We're now able to do surveillance with technology the Russians don't know we have. The president wants to solve this crime and help you get justice against the Russian mob. She just doesn't want to show the Russians our tapes. She needs to protect our abilities and sources. It's a national security issue."

"Are you sure they don't know?" I asked. "After all, I was involved in an espionage case at the Pentagon for several weeks. It appeared quite a few secrets were released over the years."

White responded, "Quite sure. You did an amazing job. Nobody else but you could've found the source, and we were all impressed."

Agent White stared at me for about ten seconds, then spoke. "I know I can trust you Mick—you have proven to be reliable—so I'll tell you what this is. I know you won't repeat it, and if you do, well, we'll deny it and then kill you. Our intelligence agencies have something called 'Look Through.' This is a game-changing technology that lets us look through walls and roofs like they're not even there. We used this Look Through technology when we investigated your movements in Russia. For example, the video shows those kidnapped children in the barn sleeping. It's so clear you would swear there was no roof on the barn. It shows the soldiers with guns sitting in the invisible house next to the barn. Most importantly, it shows Nicolai Varchinko sitting in the rear seat of the invisible Mercedes when he drove up. You would swear it was a convertible Mercedes, the image is so clear. We're the only ones with this technology—not the Russians, not the Chinese, just the United States."

"Wow!" was all I could say. "You wouldn't really kill me, would you?"

He just stared at me. "Let's continue our conversation about the video, Mick, and not about some unpleasant thing that could happen," said Agent White indignantly.

Agent White reviewed his phone for a second, then continued, "So, this video shows Nicolai getting out of an invisible car and shooting those soldiers. It also shows an RPG hitting the invisible car and blowing it up, injuring Nicolai Varchinko. We see the other soldiers lifting Mr. Varchinko up onto the roof of an invisible truck and shooting him to death. We were even able to hack into the Russian facial recognition database and find out their names. They're not active-duty Russian military; however, everyone in that operation had served with Nicolai."

I asked, "How were you able to get facial imaging? They never look up."

His response was, "Jesus, Mick, for a smart guy you really ask a lot of dumb questions. Do you remember they slept in the big barn type building—you know that building where our Look Through technology makes it appear there was no roof?"

I chuckled, "Duh." I fully understood.

He replied, "Ya, Duh." He rolled his eyes and sighed.

He paused for a second to catch his breath. "And, Mick Anderson, we see you; firing a Russian multi-barrel machine gun from the back of an invisible SUV. I don't think you realized how close to death you were at that instant. You did a great job preventing six soldiers from killing you. Did you realize you killed one guy who had an RPG aimed right at you?"

I said, "No, I didn't. It's regrettable that I was forced to end their lives. I'm still not over it. I never saw the one with the RPG aimed at me."

"He was hiding behind the invisible truck. You were lucky. If you had waited one more instant, he would've fired and surely ended your life."

It was a lot to take in. I didn't really know what the next step would be. Agent White said, "Mick, the agents here in Peoria are just a distraction. We've already found the guy in Chicago who ordered the hit. His name is Mikhail Andreas. He's addicted to crack, crazy as shit, and very dangerous."

He continued, "Now this guy loves going to the clubs and picking up woman. He also loves to smack them around. Quite a few have had trips to the hospital after an evening with him. Needless to say, he's a real dirt bag. My people in Chicago are going to deal with this tonight. We know where he is; we're just looking for the right time. I authorized the Look Through satellite to visit Chicago yesterday. Everything is coming together nicely."

He stopped for a second to take a drink, then continued to talk. "We expect that tonight he will get high on crack, or drunk, pick up a woman he hasn't seen before, and smack her around. She'll fight back, which will make him angry. She'll have amazing skills that will confuse him. He'll become more aggressive and try to tackle her, but she'll knock him off balance. Then during the struggle, he'll accidently fall onto the edge of his magnificent mahogany desk and become disoriented. The poor woman that he attacked will have her dress torn, will be bleeding, and she'll have bruises. When the time is right, she'll scream for help, causing his body guards to rush in just at the right time to witness him stumbling around, obviously drunk. They'll watch in horror as his stumbling body accidentally crashes through a giant window of his tenth floor luxury condo, and unfortunately, he falls to his death. These five bodyguards will be excellent witnesses. It'll certainly be a strange accident, because those windows aren't supposed to break. It'll be noted, however, that an unfortunate accident happened earlier in the day. The company that washes the outside windows for the entire building had an equipment failure, causing the scaffolding to fall into, of all places, his window, damaging it just enough to make it unstable. This'll be in the management report today, and a replacement window is scheduled to be installed the day after tomorrow. It'll be unfortunate that the window will arrive just shy of twenty-four hours too late."

He continued, "Nobody will miss this piece of shit, and it will be chalked up to a bad-luck fall. I not saying that this will happen, mind you, but it just might be a possibility. You just don't know when such seemingly unrelated events might cause a tragedy."

I said, "Well, accidents do happen."

Agent White said, "Yes, indeed they do. We still need to deal with Vladimir Varchinko in Russia. We haven't determine how—yet."

"Show him the tape," I said. "You should be able to put authentic Russian markings all over it. It should be easy to make it look like the video was shot by a Russian drone."

"Hmmm—I hadn't thought of that. That's an excellent idea Mr. Anderson. I'm a bit disappointed that for two days my best analysts worked on a solution, and not one of them thought of this. I guess it's time to stick my foot in their asses." I thought about it for a few seconds. "Wait a second. There was a real Russian drone flying overhead. Let's use that video."

Agent White said, "Do you mean this one?" He took out his phone and showed the footage.

"Holy shit you have it already?" I asked.

Agent White replied, "Didn't Mr. Douglas already tell you we know everything?" He laughed as he fast-forwarded the video to the correct time.

"There it is, but it isn't as clear," I said.

"Yes, we're aware of that. You can't see who killed him, one of the good guys or one of the bad. They don't have our zoom or image-cleaning capabilities, and we did this from 'Space Force One'. My people are working on cleaning it up to be more presentable, but I like your idea of using ours with Russian marking better."

I said, "What's Space Force One?"

Agent White, apparently understanding that he'd said too much, replied, "I have no idea what it is you're talking about." He gave me a wink and that was it. He told me they would drop me off near the police station so Tillerson could take me home after our investigators get done.

# Chapter 39:
## Plan in Motion

The next morning, I received a call from Special Agent White. "Did you see the news?" he asked.

"No, what news?"

Agent White responded, "Some drunk guy took a dive from the tenth floor of an upscale condo in downtown Chicago last night. They're calling it a very unfortunate accident."

I said, "That's unfortunate. Should we send flowers to the funeral?"

"I'll be there in fifteen minutes. Be ready," said Agent White. Exactly fifteen minutes later, two black Cadillac Escalades pulled up, and an agent jumped out. He took an electronic wand and scanned me for listening devices, patted me down for weapons, took my phone, then opened the rear door. I jumped in.

Special Agent White handed me his phone; a video was on the screen. "Hit the play button," he said.

I watched as a video showed a man and woman fighting. They appeared to be hovering because I couldn't see a floor or ceiling. The video was shot from the side—a building next door, I assumed. I saw the man attempting to dance with the woman. He tried to fondle her breasts, then reach between her legs; she pushed him away. A few seconds later he struck the woman's face and grabbed her dress, trying to tear it off. She punched him in the throat. It appeared this wasn't a lucky punch; she knew what she was doing. He staggered backward, clenching his throat, while she calmly followed him around the room. Every few seconds she'd slap his face. She grabbed him by the shirt and did some judo move that flipped him over like a rag doll. He fell back against something, probably an invisible desk. You could see blood at the top of his head. He got up and swung his arms wildly back and forth, missing her every time. She looked like a boxer, bobbing and weaving away from each punch. When he attempted to tackle her, she skillfully side stepped out of the way at the last second, causing him to fall onto the imaginary floor. After three or four attempts to attack her, she did some kind of spinning round house kick that landed square on the side of his face. It snapped his head sideways. He fell backward into the wall and fell to the floor, bent over unnaturally. He didn't move for about twenty seconds. There was audio as well. Once he started to regain consciousness, she pulled him up to a standing position. We heard her scream four times, "Help me, someone help me!" She grabbed an arm and swung him around in circles about five times. Her acting wasn't Oscar-worthy, but still respectable. Just as five people rushed into the room, she let go and dove for cover.

The reason she dove for cover wasn't apparent at first, then I saw why. He had a gun in his hand.

He yelled, "I am going to kill you, bitch."

Dazed and disoriented, he started shooting while staggering sideways toward the window. She was fortunate that he was completely off balance.

"He had a gun!" I said, loudly.

"Yes, that caught us off guard. She was lucky he was disoriented, or it would've been bad. She saw the gun and dove behind something." The video shows the man aiming the gun toward the woman. An instant later, just as he hit the window, I counted four flashes from his gun, and debris fell from the invisible ceiling and wall behind her. It was crazy to watch. The five men, presumably his bodyguards, who had run into the room witnessed Mikhail Andreas slamming into the window. At that instant, the window vaporized, and he fell out. They witnessed what appeared to be an obviously drunk man with a gun falling through a large window to his death. To anyone on the outside, without the aid of this video, it looked like a crazed drunk guy shooting at a woman, then falling out of a window in an unfortunate accident.

A second later, the video showed another image of a bloody man lying on the remains of a mini-van. The vehicle, parked under his window, was completely crushed where the man's body had landed on it.

"Bummer of an accident, huh?" I asked.

Agent White said, "Life is such a mystery. When it's your time, it's your time. Nothing you can do about it."

"What about the security tapes from inside the condo?" I asked.

He said, "We took care of those the day before. Their machine was reportedly always on the fritz and was scheduled to be replaced tomorrow. There are no tapes."

He took his phone back and said, "There's a half-hearted investigation going on right now. My sources tell me the preliminary toxicity tests showed large amounts of alcohol and cocaine in his system. They have the cracked window report from the management of the condo, and the repair order that was filed yesterday for a replacement window. They also have the new security tape machine, which was scheduled to be installed today. It all adds up to an unfortunate accident. They interviewed the woman, but her bruises, bleeding mouth, and torn dress were all the proof they needed that she was innocent. She'd even told the police that one of his rounds might've hit the window before he fell through. There'd been so many police reports on him, it was just a matter of time."

# Chapter 40:
## The Russians

The next day Agent White met with me again. "Mick, there's some other news you need to hear," he told me. "The Russian police have a mole in the Russian mob. We were able to locate him today and provide an impressive video. This video, reportedly taken by the Russian drone flying overhead, shows the hostage rescue.

It has the correct Russian markings and shows Nicolai getting shot by a disgraced member of the military who used to serve with him. The video even points to the person, and an arrow identifies him by name."

"Do we know if it was delivered to the correct person?" I asked.

Agent White took out his phone and showed me the video, using Look Through technology. It not only shows the delivery of the video but shows Vladimir Varchinko himself reviewing it with five other members of his organization.

"As a bonus," said Agent White, "we found another mob connection we were previously unaware of. We intercepted a phone call between an angry Vladimir Varchinko and a Russian general named Boris Kuzmich. This Boris guy was off our radar, and most probably the Russians' as well. Now we know he is connected to the mob. Our plan is to have this audio tape accidentally fall into the hands of the Russian government."

I replied, "Outstanding. I'm confused, though. Don't they normally use highly encrypted communications?"

Agent White's response was, "Indeed they do, but Look Through also has targeted microphone technology that can listen without detection from surveillance countermeasures. Not bad from a half mile away, wouldn't you say, Mick?"

"What'd he say to the General?" I asked. Agent White removed a printed paper from his coat and handed it to me. On the top it read in bold red lettering, "TOP SECRET." Just below was written "Transcript of RC1," and it read:

*"TARGET 1: Your information was fucking wrong, the guy that shot my Nicolai wasn't active military, it wasn't Aleksei Ypovich, and it sure as shit wasn't the American. You're a stupid fuck, your incorrect intelligence caused us to kidnap that kid, and that dumb fuck Popov killed him. Now there's a nation-wide manhunt for everyone involved. They're destroying my business. You inept piece of shit, this is all your fault."*

*"I told my nephew in America to send someone to kill the American, but instead they killed the wife. Now I hear my nephew fell out of a window in his apartment and died because he was fucked up on drugs. This is the biggest fucking mess I've ever been in thanks to you. You fucking dumb fuck."*

The last paragraph had a more ominous tone:

*"If you wake up dead, you'll know why."*

"Just…wow," I said. "If that's legitimate, then we have our answers, and my family should be safer now."

Agent White said, "True, but for the next month you will be shadowed by a few of my men, and your family will have one agent. I can't let this interfere with the work you will do for us. I believe we will keep you busy for some time."

"OK, next question. Except for the Look Through technology, can I share any of this with Aleksei?"

Agent White said, "No, absolutely not! We want the Russians to take care of the general. You may still help Aleksei catch Popov, but the classified information is off limits. You don't want to wake up dead."

"OK, critique this communication to Aleksei for me. I'll say, 'Aleksei, I have confirmation that Popov is the one we're looking for, and I can help you continue the search.' Does that sound OK?"

His response was, "Fine. No more though."

I thanked Agent White for his help, and he shook my hand and told me, "No problem. I've work to do now, so get out." My door was opened, and I walked away.

I knew my phone calls were being monitored. I called Aleksei and told him exactly what I was told to say. His response was predictable: "How were you able to confirm this?"

I said the information came to me anonymously. I told him I'd be coming back to wherever he was in one to two weeks, after my wife was released from the hospital. He thanked me, and we hung up.

I returned to the hospital. My wife was up and walking—an amazing recovery. She wanted to go home, but the pain from the broken ribs and the head injury meant she would've to remain hospitalized at least a week more.

I got the computer out, and we hooked it up to her TV so we could watch Netflix and horse shows for hours on end. I felt better about life and the prospects for a more normal existence in the near future.

Of course, events would unfold that would never let that happen.

# Chapter 41:

## *Not Alone*

A week and a half later I received a phone call from an unknown number. I figured it was Mr. Douglas or Special Agent Sam White. To my surprise, it was both of them.

Mr. Douglas said, "Mick, do you like science fiction?"

I said, "In movies, sure."

He replied, "How about in real life?"

I wasn't sure what the hell he was talking about, so I replied, "OK, I'll bite. What do you mean?"

"I mean we're landing in Peoria right now. Your security detail is about to tell you to go with them to the airport. Do as they say." He hung up, short and to the point, just like most of his conversations.

I met them at the unused hanger just as before. I was scanned for electronic signals by one of the agents. He gave me the thumbs-up sign and told me to board the airplane. Mr. Douglas said, "Mick, great to see you, how is the wife?"

"Great, but you already knew that, right?"

"Of course," said Mr. Douglas, "we just wanted to be nice."

Mr. Douglas continued, "Mick, we think it's time for you to know something. You're not alone."

*Interesting way to start a conversation*, I thought. I said nothing but had a feeling this would get very interesting.

"You don't look surprised, Mick. Why is that?"

I replied, "I'm not sure why; nothing surprises me anymore. I've been curious since the first case I solved in Chicago. Figured there had to be other people with weird specialties all over the world."

Mr. Douglas leaned over close to me and said, "You may be surprised to find out that the FBI, and even us at the CIA, were keeping tabs on your family since well before you were born."

I looked at Mr. Douglas with my best concerned and confused expression, but didn't say anything. I knew this conversation was about to get even more interesting than any that proceeded it.

Mr. Douglas continued, "You see, Mick, my father also worked for the FBI. He started in Kansas City, Missouri. I didn't know anything about you, or your family, until about twenty-five years ago. That all changed when I found an old safe hidden behind a false wall in my parent's basement. My father was in a nursing home and couldn't remember the combination, so I had a safe cracker from the FBI open the safe. Inside were many documents about important cases he worked on while at the FBI. Apparently, my father met your parents when they lived in Kansas City."

He paused to gauge my reaction but I had none. Then he continued, "The reason I ask is my father wrote in his journal detailing his first meeting with your mother. It was a party for a mutual friend. My father said that your mother told him, "Your wife doesn't like your tie." My father said, "What? My wife just told me she liked it. It's my favorite tie." Your mother replied, "I know, I overheard the conversation. She is just saying that so you won't be suspicious when she throws it away tomorrow." My father thought your mother was joking. The following day an interesting thing happened, that tie went missing. When confronted about the missing tie, my mother finally admitted she hated the tie and tossed it. My father immediately went to see your father and mother. He had to find out how she knew."

"I just know when someone is lying," is all your mother said. Your father reportedly concurred, saying, "I can tell you from experience, there's no doubt about her ability to tell if someone is lying."

Mr. Douglas laughed, then said, "According to the journal, my father gave your mother several tests to see if she could tell if my father was lying about something. Your mother was right every time. The following day your mother was hired by the FBI."

His journal states, "I assigned her an employee number, it was "YBNL2ME", which stood for, 'You Better Not Lie 2 Me.'"

He took a drink, then leaned in closer. "Mick, your mother helped my father close many cases in Kansas City, all before you were born. Your mother's name was mentioned in several of my father's journals as having special abilities to sense if a suspect had been deceptive during an interrogation. According to his journal, your mother would sit on the other side of a one-way mirror, with the palms of her hands on the glass. During the interrogation she would knock loudly on the glass if she felt the suspect had just lied. After four or five times of being caught, the suspect would realize they couldn't get away with lying, and amazingly, began to tell the truth. My father told me something amazing a month before he passed away. He said, "Her abilities are so powerful that once suspects knew they couldn't lie, they nervously looked at the window after every sentence they spoke. If there was no knock, they would excitedly say, 'See, I'm telling the truth.' My father really enjoyed working with your mother. My father marveled at her ability, repeatedly saying her gift was magic."

He continued, "My father knew I was working on many difficult national security issues. He specifically told me, 'Use every asset the CIA has and find her. If she is still alive, hire her. If not, maybe someone in that family inherited the gift.'"

"I was sorry to hear that your mother passed away. Not just because I wanted to hire her, but because I know the heartbreak I'd felt after losing my mother," he said.

I was at a loss for words for a few seconds. "Holy shit!" I exclaimed. "That information just confirmed some of my own observations. It also answered lingering questions I've had about my mom's ability to know when I was lying. That's crazy to hear she worked for the FBI. What kind of cases did she work on with your father?"

Mr. Douglas said, "The first case was a high-profile family whose child was kidnapped, then killed. Other cases were bank robberies, fraud, bribery, and other high-profile murder investigations. It appears that your mother was consulted on many other cases as well. My father told me he was promoted because he closed so many cases, but said it was all due to your mother. When my father was promoted to FBI headquarters in Washington, D.C., your mother decided it was time to have more children. According to the journal, a few years later your parents moved to Des Moines, Iowa, and that was the last time your family's name was mentioned in my father's journals."

After taking a sip of coffee, Mr. Douglas said, "Mick, the CIA has an entire department that investigates unusual police reports. We call it the Green Flag group. They have an extensive computer database, and I put your brother and sister's names into our Green Flag list. Anytime one of you appeared in any police, TV, or newspaper stories, you were flagged and an alert was triggered. Your file contains a couple of minor traffic tickets, a few car crashes while in college, and a very interesting report about you tackling a suspect who was running from police after damaging vehicles near Creighton University. While interesting, it wasn't what we were looking for."

He paused to review a text message on his phone. Then he said, "I helped your sister get a job at Offutt Air Force base. This may freak you out, but I was one of the FBI agents that came to your door to interview your parents when your sister was hired at Offutt. You answered the door, do you remember?"

I remember answering the door, but didn't remember him. To my defense, I was preoccupied with my own issues and not much of a people person. I said, "Not really."

Mr. Douglas said, "I had a buzz hair-cut and looked different, so I'm not surprised. You took one look at our badges, then yelled for your mom and dad, then walked away. I was honored to finally meet your mother. I watched your mother flip her palms up when I said I was from the FBI. It was so cool to see her in action. I could tell she believed me immediately. I didn't tell her that my father knew her, but I think she put two and two together rather quickly. I was ever so careful about what I said, because she flipped her palms up, almost imperceptibly, every time I spoke. She was probing me. Had I not been looking for this behavior, I'd certainly have missed it. We told her that everything in the house had to be investigated and pictures were taken of every room; she agreed. I remember you had pictures of race cars on your wall, and I asked what you were working on. You responded that it was a computer program to calculate performance differences based on weather changes for race cars."

I said, "I do kind of remember that."

Mr. Douglas nonchalantly stated, "We had to be sure, so I put something on your computer that allows us to look at your hard drive a few days later. We did that to every computer in the house to be thorough. We don't let just anyone work for the Department of Defense. Besides, everyone signed a waiver to allow us to inspect computers, cameras, photos, and phone records."

I said, "I didn't sign anything!"

"Maybe you did, maybe you didn't, not important," said Mr. Douglas. He continued, "The following year, I helped you get that Army programming job right after you graduated from Creighton. You weren't the best choice, but you probably already figured that out. You did a great job, and the targeting communication algorithm you created is still being used today. Again, it was impressive, but not earth shattering. But then we found out about the incident at the mall."

I interrupted, "Do you mean Northwoods Mall, a long time ago?"

Mr. Douglas stared at me for a second and said, "Yes, so you do remember the incident at the mall?"

I replied, "How could I forget? It scared the hell out of me then, and is still confusing to this day."

He continued, "That incident was one that tripped a Green Flag alert. Here is a copy of the report from both the officer, and a detective named Brett Stinson." He handed it to me. In capital letters, it said, "THE WITNESS STATES HE NEVER SAW THE SUSPECT ENTER THE CAR. HE SAID HE FEELS HEAT FROM A GREAT DISTANCE."

I said, "That isn't what I told him; it was something to the effect that I had a medical condition that allows me to sense heat from a distance."

Mr. Douglas interrupted, "Mick, I don't give a shit; your actual statement isn't important. What's important is these are the kind of statements that get flagged by our analysts."

Mr. Douglas took another sip of coffee, then said, "Because of what I knew about your mother, it seemed interesting enough to investigate. So, I sent a team of investigators to ask some follow-up questions and find out if you really had abilities the CIA and the FBI could use. Perhaps you remember my investigators. They followed you to some bar and tested your capabilities. They called you "Captain Thermometer" or something similar. One of them hid behind a wall, and you were able to figure out exactly where he was. The other one just put his arms on the wall, and you knew exactly where his arms were on the other side. Do you remember?"

I did remember. "Yes, two guys made fun of me. They'd heard I could sense heat through walls from my friend Dan. They bet me a hundred dollars that I couldn't find them. I made one hundred dollars for about thirty seconds worth of work. After they left, I asked my friend Dan who they were, and he had no clue, nor did anybody else."

"They video-taped the event. Want to see it?" said Agent White.

"Nope, I remember it," I said. "Next you're going to tell me the pretty girl named Wendy Lou from Georgia was part of your investigators."

Agent White said, "You have an impressive memory, Mick. Perhaps you mean Wendy Lou Archibald, who looked like this." He showed me his phone with the girl's picture on it.

In a resigned voice I said, "Yes, that's her. Damn you people, I really thought she liked me. I tried to find her after that, but she just vanished."

Agent White said, "That one cost us two hundred dollars because she didn't believe you the first time."

I said, "I felt bad, but she'd insisted I take the money. I remember her saying, "Here, take the money, a bet's a bet.""

Then he dropped a bombshell. "Do you want to know what she does for the CIA now?"

I said, "Sure."

He brought his phone out and said, "Hit the play button."

I didn't have to; it was the video of the woman who took down the Russian mob guy in Chicago. "Holy shit! She was such a cute little thing; who knew she'd had such lethal skills?"

Mr. Douglas said, "We knew because we trained her. Her CIA code name is QTP, which stands for Queen Throat Punch. She can kill you with that punch, so whatever you do, don't make her mad. The throat punch in the video was only about ten percent of her ability."

Agent White said, "The FBI code name we gave her is CF1, which stands for Cute and Feisty, Number One. Yes, she is very attractive, and expertly lethal."

Mr. Douglas continued, "Mick, at that time I didn't give a shit if you could sense temperature, because, as you're aware, we have thermometers for that purpose. To be perfectly honest, Mick, I felt like your abilities were pretty much worthless to us. I'd hoped someone in your family had inherited your mother's gift, so I kept everyone on the Green Flag list, just in case. I looked like a genius, though, when all hell broke loose in Chicago and you solved three kidnapping cases in two months. Because of those impressive results, I ordered agents to keep you under surveillance. When the Russians requested your help, I was a bit hesitant to agree. I changed my mind because I know the ambassador personally. Once our intelligence found out his twin sons were kidnapped, I moved quickly to help. I had no idea your life was in danger, or I wouldn't have allowed it, but you survived. You actually showed amazing courage. Now, it's obvious to us at the CIA and the FBI, that your gift is different than your mother's, but still extraordinary."

He paused again, and offered me a drink. I declined. He continued, "So, Mick, now it's time to take what you have to the next level. I want you to meet the others. Next week we have a meeting with the Gatekeepers in Washington, D.C., and want you to join."

I interrupted, "Gatekeepers—what do you mean?"

Mr. Douglas replied, "Others like you, and, well, *not* like you. Each of the Gatekeepers has their own special abilities. These are God granted abilities that can't be taught. We assess these abilities, and then they're honed and improved for a minimum of a year before a person can join. At these meetings we see what new abilities the Gatekeepers want to demonstrate. We go over problem areas in the USA and other countries and get their input. Everyone you will meet has been with us for at least five years; they're extremely intelligent, the best of the best. We get them together at Langley every few months for discussions and tactical ideas."

Special Agent White said, "We're making an experience exception for you; your abilities are already proven. We feel your ability to find those really sick and twisted criminals is critical to the United States, and the Gatekeepers, so we're making an exception." Mr. Douglas said, "It really seems like science fiction, but I assure you, it's entirely real. I think you'll enjoy it; these people have extraordinary powers that are different from yours, but just as interesting. There have been others we originally thought could be like you, but they all failed to deliver. You're the first verified 'scanner' we have ever seen."

I asked, "What do you mean? What's a 'scanner'?"

"Just what it sounds like—you scan people and things. We get the name from the scanners used on *Star Trek*. Many have tried, and all failed—except you. You're the first of your kind that we're aware of, and we will pay you a lot of money to use that ability to find spies, solve crimes, and generally help the United States be a better place."

Mr. Douglas said, in his most nonchalant voice, "We have some people who read minds, others who can make objects move, people who can talk to animals, a few who can distort their bodies to conform to objects, people who can mimic another person's voice perfectly, people so strong they can leap twenty feet into the air, people with the ability to discharge electricity from their bodies, weird stuff like that."

Agent White said, "You were specifically chosen because we want you to meet with a husband-and-wife team who sense the future. They've foretold events in the past, but they were limited to bits and pieces of information. We think together you can stop terrorists and other major crimes before they happen. I know it sounds crazy, but it's real. And the president wants you to be part of the Gatekeepers. So, what'd you say?"

"If I get to see strange people then, damnit, I'm all in. I'll ask my wife, just to be sure. I'm scheduled to leave next week to go back to Russia; I promised my friend I'd help him catch that cocksucker, Popov."

Mr. Douglas said, "And we're eager to help in any way we can—covertly of course. We want justice for him as well. We will have agents following you, and will be watching from above. Anything that happens to you is of interest to us at the CIA. Can we ask a favor, Mick?"

"Sure, what is it?"

"Don't get yourself in a gun battle this time," said Mr. Douglas.

Mr. Douglas paused, then said, "By the way, can you tell if someone is lying?"

I said, "Not that I know of, well, unless it's obvious. Why? Are you lying about all of this?"

Mr. Douglas said, "No, Mick, I'm not. It's all real. So, how about your brother or sisters, can they?"

I said, "I don't really know, why don't you ask them yourself?"

Mr. Douglas said, "It isn't something you ask."

After a few seconds he paused, then said, "I think we will schedule a trip for your entire family to Jamaica, where some of my operatives will try to figure out who in your family has the "You Better Not Lie 2 Me" gift. We have ways of determining what they're capable of, even if they don't know their own abilities. Our research tells us this kind of thing runs in families, and we need a lie detector that's as good as your mother on our team. We will do this after you return, and once your crazy life settles down. It will be all expenses paid; a thank you from the U.S. government."

# Chapter 42:
## *Gatekeepers*

Nothing can prepare a person for what I saw.

I was driven to CIA headquarters and led into a room where approximately twenty people were seated in a giant circle. I was instructed to stand in the middle, where a podium was setup, and tell everyone a little bit about myself.

I began with my name and where I was from. I was interrupted by my own voice, which appeared to move about the room. One by one they introduced themselves, in my own voice, without moving their lips. "OK, enough," I said. "Nice ventriloquist act, very funny."

Then I realized I wasn't leaning on a podium but a person with a few pieces of wood attached to them. If the podium hadn't moved by itself, I never would have known. Out of the podium popped a man, who tossed the two pieces of wood on the floor next to me. He turned and said, "Hello, Mick Anderson. Or is it King Mick." What made is so fascinating was the fact that it was my voice he used.

For the next two minutes my story was told, in my own voice, by everyone in the room. Freaky was an understatement. A man stood up then proceeded to jump toward me from twenty feet away, landing only inches from me. He reached out his hand and said, "Welcome, Mick. We've all been impressed with your abilities." In a flash, he jumped backwards, performing a double reverse flip while in the air, and landed a foot from his seat.

My phone was lifted out of my jacket pocket and flew about ten feet, into the hands of an older woman. She used my phone to make a call. I heard a phone ring in my other pocket. I don't have two phones and had no idea how it got there. I pulled the phone out and answered it. It was my voice on the other line, all done by the same woman. She said, "Nice to meet you. Can I have my phone back?" I said yes, and my phone flew back to my pocket and hers flew back to her. It was a circus; I wasn't sure it was real, but I played along.

A woman's voice shouted, "In thirty-two seconds your wife will call you to ask where your car keys are; even though she was the last one to drive it. Tell her she left them under her horse magazines, near the couch. She'll want to know why her old high school letter jacket is on the dinner chair. She'll then tell you your bank balance is $643,567.88 and will be so excited she'll want to buy a horse that she saw on page eighty-eight of the fourth horse magazine down in the stack, also by the couch. She wants the one with the red saddle."

I stood there dumb founded, unsure how I was supposed to answer. Thirty seconds later my phone rang, it was my wife Michelle—at least I hoped it was Michelle. To verify this, I asked her a question only she could answer: "What was the name of that one friend who fell off your horse in grade school?" She thought for a second and said, "Martha Bridgewater." This was correct. She asked why I wanted to know, and I replied, "Just to make sure it was you."

"Who else would it be? By the way, the agents just dropped me off at the house. Do you know where your car keys are? And yes, I know I was the last one to drive it."

I said, "Under your horse magazines, near the couch."

I heard papers rustling for a few seconds, then she said, "How did you know they were under the magazines? You're right, I need to hang my keys in one place when I come home." After a brief pause, she said, "Hey, my high school jacket is on the chair in the dining room. It was at the old house before. Care to explain why?"

I said, "I used it to find the people who ran you off the road."

Then in an excited voice she said, "Have you seen the bank balance? Hold on, I want to read it to you. It's $643,567.88 right now. You said we could buy a horse once we had enough money, and I found one I like."

I just hung my head down and said, "Is it on page eighty-eight of the fourth magazine down in the stack near the couch? The one with the red saddle?"

"You're starting to freak me out, Mick," said Michelle. I heard her fumble through the magazines for a few seconds before saying, "What the hell is going on, Mick? How'd you know?"

I replied, "I didn't; someone here told me it would be the kind of horse my wife would like."

Then a man's voice called out, "Aunt Mary will call you in twenty seconds, Michelle."

Michelle said, "Who's that, and how do they know my aunt Mary will call?"

"Long story, sweetie—a very long story."

Then Michelle said she wanted to rest and would call back later. Just when she was about to hang up, she said, "Umm, whoever said that is right. My aunt Mary is calling, but you must tell me all about this later. Love you." She hung up.

I was still trying to process the situation when I heard, "Welcome to the jungle, Mr. King Anderson. Watch out for snakes."

I thought, *Enough of the freakshow already.*

A paper airplane flew toward me and I caught it. There was something written on the paper. I read: "Enough of the freakshow already."

"OK, alright," I said. "Can we get on with the meeting?"

A voice inside my head said, "This meeting is done. We wanted to meet you." I covered my ears and the voice kept talking. "You see, Mick, the Gatekeepers are here to help you. Virtually anything you need, we can accomplish. No problem is too big or too small for us." I looked around the room. It was completely empty. No chairs, no people; empty.

The voice continued, "For example, my skill is telepathic communication. Only those with special gifts are invited to join. Welcome to the Gatekeepers."

In an instant the room was full of people eating, drinking and talking. Two people walked up to me and introduced themselves. "We're your team," said the man. "I'm Dr. Richard Freeman, and this is my wife, Dr. Virginia Freeman. We're the futurists, and if we work together, there's a good chance we can prevent some catastrophic crimes. We're the voices who told you when your wife would call. While we don't always get it right, there are times when our premonitions of the future are quite good. We just can't see the faces and exactly where it will happen. That's where you come in."

Virginia said, "We need to know who to focus on, and you can help us with this problem. Our results have been nearly perfect if we know the people involved. We feel you can identify the correct people with your scanner."

Richard said, "We've told Mr. Douglas that something major is going to happen within one week, and we need your senses to find out what and who's involved. Will you assist us?"

I said, "Absolutely. It will be a new use of my senses."

Virginia said, "No, not really. It involves twelve children. We don't know why, but both of us feel the same. We just need to know which children, or who plans to do them harm."

Richard said, "This is the only time we can be together. Usually, for safety reasons, they don't allow Gatekeepers to be on the outside together, or fly together. The only place to physically meet is here at Langley. You may call as often as necessary; our phone numbers are already on your phone under the name 'Freemans.'"

Virginia said, "We think the event will happen nearby, and we'd like you to be driven around or flown around in a helicopter to scan for anything you feel will help us pinpoint the people who are planning this."

"OK," I said, "can we start tomorrow?"

"As soon as possible," was their answer.

"Good, because I leave for Russia in less than four days."

# Chapter 43:
## *The Twelve*

I started the next morning at seven o'clock. A helicopter picked me up at Ronald Reagan Airport. The pilot's name was Randy Nicholson. He's a military pilot who'd flown Apache attack helicopters during the Iraq war.

Randy was apparently working on his standup comedy routines, because when I first got in the helicopter, he acted like this was the first time he'd ever flown. "Hey, do you know what's this lever does? I think we should pull on it and see," he said. I was a bit concerned at first but quickly realized it was just fun and games to him.

After we'd flown around for about ten minutes, he told me, "I'm tired. You fly it while I take a nap."

Then he let go of the controls. The helicopter started to drop, not real fast but enough to get my attention. Grabbing the controls quickly, he said, "I thought you knew how to fly this thing." He laughed. I didn't.

My plan was to fly around the city in a wide arc to cover as much ground as possible for our first mission. Unlike most aircraft, we had permission to fly over restricted airspace. I counted more than one-hundred grade schools and high schools on the map we took with us. Flying over each of them would make for a long day. Little did I know, it wasn't possible to accomplish this in one day.

We flew around for two hours. I was able to pick up some sensation, but just not the kind that makes you realize something evil is nearby.

After returning to the airport for fuel and pit stops, we went back up. Since the first trip was just an overview of Washington, D.C., and nothing significant showed up, this time we decided to fly over schools. This went on for another two hours, and all we were able to mark off only about half. With no results again and running low on fuel, we went back to the airport.

I called the Freemans to discuss the lack of findings and to listen to their translation of what they'd felt. Richard said, "We both see the number twelve, and we see children. We believe the children are at a school."

I replied, "That's a pretty vague vision. Anything else?"

"We saw a man. He has a beard and a pony tail; that's all we can agree on." That really wasn't helpful, but it's all I had to go on.

After eating lunch, Randy and I went back up. He said, "Where to?"

I said, "I'm not really sure, we need to find twelve children and rescue them from a man who has a beard and ponytail. And we need to do this within the next week. Where'd you suggest we go?" We took off and continued over schools. There're quite a few elementary schools and high schools in this area—more than I'd imagined. Even from the air you still have to crisscross the city and surrounding areas to hit them all. I'd hoped we could eliminate the city schools by the end of the day. We used a map and marked an "X" when we flew around a school to cross it off. I really thought our progress would be quicker, but we couldn't just fly over the school; we had to fly an ascending circle to cover the area as well. I'd felt, at this pace, it would take another day to cover the county school districts, maybe more.

Randy said, "You want to fly it. This time for real, it isn't that difficult?"

I said, "Sure, I've always wanted to fly a helicopter."

I'd watched him take off and noticed the controls he used to turn and hover. He explained each control's function, then showed me the effects each had by itself, and when used in conjunction with other controls.

He was right; flying a helicopter in steady flight is simple. Pull up on the stick in the middle, and the helicopter climbs; push it down, and it descends. Foot controls and the stick allow it to change directions. "Take offs and landings are difficult, and of course hovering takes a long time to master," said Randy. It was fun, but after fifteen minutes, I told Randy to take over. He didn't respond, so I tapped him on the shoulder. Always the jokester, he acted like I'd woke him up from a nap.

After two more hours we returned to the airport and called it a day. We hadn't found anything, and after six hours in one seat your butt goes numb. I told him, "Seven o'clock sharp tomorrow." He replied, "a.m. or p.m.?" then laughed. I was disappointed, tired, and hungry. I hate days like this, long and tedious with no positive results.

The next day we mapped out the remaining schools in the city. I asked about Randy's family and his job. He had five children, ages four to sixteen years old. His wife was a teacher at Kelly Miller Middle School.

"Middle school?" I asked.

He said, "Yes, the middle school near our house."

I said, "I don't have middle schools on my list, only elementary and high schools. We need to look up and check middle schools, plus the ones we missed."

We both sighed heavily. This was going to be extra tedious now. I was concerned as well; I was scheduled to leave for Russian in a few days. I certainly didn't want to miss helping my friend, Aleksei, search for his son's killers.

We flew in two-hour shifts again, this time traveling faster to make up for lost time. Since we needed fuel every two hours, I asked if he could land at a different airport, one that was closer to our current location. I calculated the time savings since it was taking at least an extra fifteen minutes to go back and forth from Ronald Reagan Airport each time. That was nearly an hour each day of wasted time. He called his superiors to make sure it was OK. They granted him permission to use any local airport or military installations.

We were able to cover the remaining city schools this way. Tired and disappointed, with no results to show for it, we returned. I told Randy we would cover the remaining schools, which were outside the city, the next day. He said, "Great. There's an airport about thirty-five minutes away. My wife is taking a teacher credentials test near there; it would be a great place to stop for the evening."

After a few seconds, he said, "Do you like Mexican restaurants?"

I replied, "Sure do."

He said, "There's a great Mexican restaurant near there as well. You can meet the wife and have some dinner." Sounded good to me, especially since I hadn't found a good restaurant near the hotel that served Mexican.

The next morning, we flew around marking off schools. I was able to fly the helicopter about one hour of the four we were airborne before lunch. I'd flown airplanes before, but flying helicopters presents its own challenges. Randy even let me land when we stopped for lunch. I'd thought I did pretty well; the look on his face told me otherwise. Regardless, it helped me focus and get my mind off the negative results so far.

We decided to call it a day at four thirty. Close to the airport was one more high school to mark off before then. I was flying the helicopter, the GPS said we were near a town called Friendly. As we neared the high school, I was startled by a tingling in my fingers. It wasn't very strong, but it was the first one I'd had and it caught my attention. I told Randy to take the controls and hover. We hovered over the school for about two minutes while I attempted to see if it was real, or the vibration from the helicopter. I couldn't tell, so we flew around a bit. I lost the feeling; either it'd been nothing, or whatever triggered it was now out of my sensory range.

We landed at a little airport called Potomac in Ft. Washington, Maryland. His wife was waiting for us in her car. Randy introduced his wife, Gail. She'd just finished her teaching credentials at Friendly High School.

They told me the Mexican restaurant was fifteen minutes from the airport. "Great," I said. "I'm really hungry."

We arrived at the restaurant. Workmen were fixing the sign, so all I could read was, "Nin" and, under it, was "Mexican Cantina." The hostess seated us, and immediately a server brought chips and salsa. I love salsa, and this restaurant had the best. It was spicy; but not obnoxious, with chunky ingredients. I was hungry and filled up on the chips and salsa. The food was really good.

I'd sensed a tiny tingling in my fingers from time to time, but it was so weak it was tough to tell if the feeling was real. When I couldn't decipher what I was feeling, I put the area into my memory bank and finished my meal.

After dinner, his wife drove us back to the airport, and we flew back to Ronald Reagan Airport. Tomorrow would be another day to check any remaining areas and perhaps fly around Friendly High School again.

The next day I ate breakfast at the hotel. It was six o'clock in the morning, and I was the only one in the restaurant. While I was flipping through channels, I stopped at a news story about area high school basketball teams, and one of those interviewed was a center from Friendly High School. He was averaging twenty-eight points and five blocked shots a game. Impressive.

An hour later, I met Randy at the airport, and he said, "Where to, boss?"

"Let's do some sightseeing. We're out of schools to investigate."

He said, "How about the private ones—did we get those?" I hadn't even thought about those. When I'd asked Mr. Douglas to give me a list of schools, his analysts must've missed those, along with the middle schools. Disappointed, I quickly realized that I should've done my own research. We called and got a list of the private and religious schools in the area and found out there are about thirty.

Randy let me take off. It's much more challenging than I'd thought it would be. The spinning blades, called rotors, caused the helicopter to turn from torque. Power is automatically applied as you lift off, which causes even more rotor torque. You have to counteract that effect with the rear rotors, and they're controlled by pedals. There's a fine line between "just right" and "way fucking wrong." The helicopter swung one way, then I overcompensated and swung it the other way. I finally got it fifty feet off the ground and was able to push the stick forward. This caused the helicopter to move forward, ending the seesaw battle of torque and improper foot work. I was sweating profusely from anxiety after less than a minute of flying. Clearly, I needed more training.

"I don't want to do that again," I said to Randy.

He replied, "Thank God; you suck at it."

In just over two hours we were able to cover the private schools, but with zero results. I said, "Let's fly over toward Friendly again. I want to check it out once more."

Randy said, "You just want to eat at that Mexican restaurant again."

*Partially true*, I thought.

As we flew over Friendly, I felt no sensation. I was hungry and we needed fuel, so we landed at Potomac. I called ahead for an Uber to take us to the restaurant. "My treat," I said to Randy. He gave me the thumbs-up sign.

We had an uneventful lunch. A Lyft driver picked us up when the Uber couldn't get back in time. We took off and returned to Ronald Reagan Airport. We were out of ideas. I called Mr. Douglas and filled him in. Then I called the Freemans to discuss the results. We brainstormed for about half an hour, but to no avail. They were convinced it was twelve children at a school, and I couldn't find anything in this entire area.

I'd checked everything that made sense. The next morning, we decided just to fly around the area in a fifty-mile circle, crisscrossing every ten miles. We spent over four hours with absolutely nothing to show for it. After we'd finished, I called Mr. Douglas. I explained that we had spent the better part of three days flying all over a one-hundred-mile circle. He simply told me, "You did everything you could. We should have a conference call with the Freemans tomorrow morning." I reminded him that I was going to Russia tomorrow at eleven a.m., but this would be on my mind until it was resolved.

We had our conference call in the morning. I had the Freemans restate their visions so it would be fresh in my mind. I felt dismal; I'd fully expected to solve this case. At ten forty-five I boarded the plane. I was tired and a bit depressed about the failures of the week. Part of me was excited to get to Russia and help my friend get justice. I was one of the last to board the airplane, and I sat next to a woman who was just ending a phone call. I said, "Good morning," and she returned the greeting. I got my neck cushion out of my bag and tried to make myself comfortable. I realized my car keys were in my pocket and silently cursed myself for not placing them in the bag before sitting down. The keys always dig into my skin, and now the flight would be uncomfortable until I could get them out of my pocket. I checked my other pocket, and it only had a napkin from the restaurant. I placed it on my lap; I'd give it to the flight attendant when trash was picked up.

Ten minutes later we left the terminal and started to move to the runway. "I see from your napkin that you went to my favorite Mexican restaurant. I know the owners well and eat there often. I love their food. It has a strange name for a Mexican restaurant, but great food."

Since I don't know Spanish and my mind was elsewhere, I just shrugged. Realizing it might appear rude, and since it would be a long flight, I said, "I don't know Spanish. What's it mean?"

She said, "It's really an interesting story. The owners, Francisco and Teresa, have eight children, but they wanted more. Unfortunately, she'd had several miscarriages after that, and they were told by the doctors that she'd be unable to have any more children. She was really depressed, and felt she'd jinxed the family."

She paused a second to cough, then continued, "In an effort to cheer her up, her husband wanted her to decide what to name their new restaurant. She decided to call the restaurant after the size of the family she wanted. It's called Doce Niños, which means, 'Twelve Children,' and that made her happier."

I yelled, "I need to get off this plane!"

# Chapter 44:
## *I Want Off, Now*

The lady said, "Wait, where are you going? You can't leave your seat. What did I say that offended you?"

I hurriedly said, "Nothing. I'm sorry, but you just solved a huge problem for me, and I can't thank you enough. I'm working on an investigation and we were missing some key information. You just helped connect the dots, so to speak."

I left my seat and told the flight attendant that I had to get off the airplane.

She said, "Sir, you must get back to your seat now. We can't allow you up here. Besides, we have already started taxiing, and we're only seconds from takeoff. Please go back to your seat now or I'll have you detained."

I know I sounded like a lunatic, but I couldn't worry about that at this instant. I made the flight attendants even more angry when I pulled out my phone and called Mr. Douglas. The flight attendants joined in and scolded me for using my phone. Then several of the passengers began to yell. The passengers had no idea what I was doing; for all they knew, I could've been a terrorist. Naturally, they were shocked and angry that their normal airplane routines were now in turmoil. A few got out of their seats and raced toward me, screaming, "Air marshal." I only had a second or two before I'd be detained. Just as I was being tackled by an air marshal, Mr. Douglas answered. I yelled into the phone, "Stop the plane, Zulu 15, I've found the twelve children."

The code word phrase "Zulu 15," is only to be used when all hell breaks loose and we need CIA help.

The air marshals and the flight attendants have practiced this numerous times. I was placed in handcuffs. They'd thought everything was under control. Unfortunately, they had no idea who they were dealing with. When Mr. Douglas wants something—it happens; quickly. The flight attendant called the cockpit from her wall phone. She quickly explained what'd happened. A minute later she hung up.

I told the flight attendant, whose name was Crystal, that in thirty seconds her flight attendant phone would buzz. She'd be told to have the air marshal release me from custody.

She rolled her eyes and said, "I don't think so."

The air marshal said, "You're going to be arrested for four offenses." He started to name them off for everyone, then got interrupted by the flight attendant's phone buzzing.

I looked at her and said, "I told you so."

"Yes, captain?" she answered. "OK. Wait, what? Are you kidding me? Oh, my word, I can't believe this. Yes, captain, right away." She handed the phone to the air marshal.

"This is air marshal Bruce Johnson," he said into the phone. I knew what would come next. I could tell the air marshal wasn't happy when he said, "OK, but…no. Well, OK, if you…but sir…yes, sir, I will."

The air marshal spun me around and said, "We're to release you. I don't know who you are, but you have powerful friends. I can't believe I have to do this."

One minute later the captain got on the intercom and told everyone what I already knew. They were tuning the plane around. I heard groans from the passengers.

I said, "You don't understand why, but you've just saved at least twelve children from certain death. I'm investigating a crime and just found the link I needed to prevent a mass murderer from committing a tragic crime."

I stood up and spoke loudly to the passengers. "I'm terribly sorry for the inconvenience. I'm investigating a serial killer and hopefully I've just found the evidence we needed to solve the crime and prevent many children from being murdered. Again, I'm sorry, but there's no other way." I heard a loud murmur as the passengers digested the information provided.

I walked back to where I'd been sitting and pointed to the lady who was seated next to me and announced, "This is the real hero. Thank you. The Spanish translation helped in more ways than you realize." I grabbed my bag and walked back up front.

The captain came over the announcement system and told the passengers, "We're sorry, but we have been ordered to stop and let a passenger depart. He is an FBI agent. The good news is we're not going back to the terminal; they're coming for him here, so our delay will be five minutes or less."

I saw flashing lights on the tarmac as three police cars raced toward us. Behind the police vehicles was a truck that had a step platform built into the back. The captain was right; I'd walk off the plane on the taxi way.

A minute later there was a knock on the door. The flight attendants opened the door, and the stairs were pushed closer to the plane. The passengers clapped, I wasn't sure if it the reason was because I was getting off the plane or because the delay was short. Four police officers, hands on their guns, were on the stairs. I don't know what they'd been told, but they were certainly ready for anything. I thanked the air marshal and the flight attendants and waved to everyone.

"We have been instructed to escort you wherever you need to go," said one of the police officers. He was loud enough to be heard throughout the plane. The passengers understood I was serious, not some nut-bag crazy guy.

I called Mr. Douglas and thanked him. I told him I'd contact the Freemans and tell them the good news.

Mr. Douglas said, "What good news? You haven't even told me."

I said, "It's about a restaurant located twenty miles away. I'll tell you more at your office." After hanging up, I called the Freemans. "I found it; I'll give you more information in twenty minutes. Meet me at Mr. Douglas's office ASAP."

# Chapter 45:
## Let's Try This Again

We met twenty-five minutes later at Mr. Douglas's office. The Freemans arrived, and so did Special Agent Sam White.

"I figured it out—well, with the help of a passenger on the plane seated next to me."

They stared at me, and then Mr. Douglas signaled for more information by rotating his arms. I continued, "The Mexican restaurant called Doce Niños in the city of Friendly, Maryland. Doce Niños, translated into English, means "twelve children." I think that's where the Freemans' predicted terrorist event will take place."

They looked at me, expecting more. I said, "It has to be there. The restaurant is busy all the time, so we need to scope it out for anyone who has long hair in a pony tail. I don't think we need to look at schools. Besides, the only sensation I received was in that area."

Then I said to the Freemans, "I believe you were correct about the twelve children and the school. I was at that restaurant, and they have a mural on the wall that depicts Friendly High School. On the wall were pictures of students. I might be wrong about this, but my memory tells me there are twelve pictures on the wall of Friendly High School students, all in a circle around the mural."

Mr. Douglas said to Special Agent White, "You get some men over there now, and have them take Mick. Take pictures and video of the immediate area while we get background on everyone who works there. Is there anything else, Mick?"

I said, "No, not at this time."

Mr. Douglas then said, "By the way, Mick, here is an FBI identification for you to carry. It will give you more freedom in the future with law enforcement and allow you to carry a firearm in all fifty states and Washington, D.C. Hopefully it will save some frantic phone calls in the future."

Then he asked the Freemans, "How about you—do either of you have anything to add?" Richard said, "I think you're on to something. Keep us in the loop."

Mr. Douglas said, "Of course. Now get out. I've work to do." His ability to turn off a conversation was epic.

# Chapter 46:
## Bomb?

We took a caravan of police vehicles to the restaurant. Within about ten minutes, I felt something in my fingers. I called back to Agent White and said, "Can we get a bomb disposal person to come to the restaurant, just in case?"

He said, "Let me see who's available and call you back."

The closer we got, the more worried I became. My fingers never lie, and currently they're shouting warnings that became louder and louder with each passing mile. I didn't understand why these sensations weren't happening before, and I really hoped we wouldn't be too late. We were about half a mile from the restaurant when I noticed the throbbing in my fingers had diminished. It was still strong but not as overpowering as before. I was getting multiple sensations from several directions. This had to mean more than one person was involved.

We arrived at the restaurant. It was packed, just as I thought it would be.

I could tell evil was near, but my fingers sensed it wasn't only here but also somewhere close by.

I had a strong sensory signal nearby, but it didn't trigger the common "electrocution" event. Regardless, I had to go with the visions predicted by Drs. Richard and Virginia Freeman. If their visions proved incorrect, then I would go with my senses.

I asked for the manager. When he arrived, I told him, "We have reason to believe there may be someone who intends to either blow up your restaurant or attempt to kill people." Then I asked, "Does a guy with a beard and pony tail work here?"

I think he was a little shell-shocked at first, and then he said, "Yes, we have an employee named Omar who matches your description."

I walked around the corner, and my fingers began to quiver. I saw the mural of the high school with pictures of students in a circle around it. I quickly started counting the pictures; there were twelve. Under the last one was a man sitting alone at a table. He had a large red backpack next to him, and he wasn't eating. He also had a beard and pony-tail and was swaying back and forth in his chair. The bag was much larger than a regular bookbag.

I went back and told them, "Pull the fire alarm. I think this guy has a bomb." They just stared at me. I said, "Never mind. I'll do it." I saw the red fire alarm control on the wall nearby and pulled it. The sirens went off, and people began to scream. I yelled, "Fire in the kitchen, everyone out."

People scurried out the door in a quick fashion, except for a few young people who thought they would ride it out. I yelled again, "Hey, kid, that means you—everyone out!" They got out of their chairs, muttering under their breath, "I don't even see smoke." Thirty seconds later the restaurant was clear, only one person was still inside—the man with the backpack.

We all went outside, and the police called for backup. We heard sirens in the distance and realized the fire department would've been alerted automatically. I told one of the officers to keep them away.

Then I told the remaining officers, "If he comes out, keep your guns on him; you may have to shoot him."

I grabbed the manager and said, "What does this Omar guy look like?"

He said, "Brown skin but not Mexican, long hair in a pony tail. He isn't a big guy at all. About five foot eight inches, probably one hundred and sixty pounds."

"Did he get weird lately? Religious nut?"

He said, "Maybe a little. He still came to work on time and did his job as a cook. Never had a problem in the two years he's worked for us. Lately he started to tell employees that America was no good, that the way it treats people from other countries was wrong." After a brief pause, he said, "I really wasn't concerned; he didn't seem angry."

I heard more sirens as the cavalry arrived. Among them was a bomb-sniffing dog accompanied by a bomb disposal officer. We explained to him what was going on. His first job was to let the dog go near the restaurant; the dog would signal if he found explosives.

The dog went around the building, quiet at first. Once he was near the wall where Omar was, he barked and pointed by scraping his foot on the ground in the direction of the wall. The bomb disposal officer called the dog back and said, "You have a bomb! Get everyone farther back." Thankfully, everyone was out of the building.

My phone rang. I figured it would be Mr. Douglas, and it was. "What's this shitshow I'm hearing about; this guy has a bomb?"

I took his statement as a question and said, "Yes."

Mr. Douglas said in his usual manner, "I know, Mick; it's a rhetorical question, I already knew the answer. I want to know what you're doing about it."

I said, "I pulled the fire alarm to get everyone out of the restaurant. I believe we're at a safe distance now. I'm waiting on instructions from the police or whoever comes to a scene like this."

Mr. Douglas said, "I know all that. I'm watching from above. You did a good job. That quick thinking may have saved many lives. You make sure you stay in the loop. Don't let anybody push you around. Your badge will prevent that." He hung up, short but sweet as is normal.

A police captain showed up and started ordering everyone around. He looked at me and said, "Who are you, and why are you here?"

I pulled out my new badge and said, "Mick Anderson, FBI." After I'd said that phrase, I'd felt completely ridiculous. It was awkward and unnatural.

He said, "OK, then, I'm Captain Rich Berg. Get me up to speed on the situation." I told him everything that had happened since we arrived. He said, "But who told you there'd be someone with a bomb here?"

*Excellent question*, I thought, so I fibbed a bit. "We heard some chatter about a possible bomb attack and traced it to this restaurant. The guy's name is Omar, and he has a backpack that the bomb squad's dog picked up on." I added, "It's your crime scene; we just want to be in the loop about every decision."

He said, "So you can tear me apart if it goes wrong?"

I said, "I know how you must feel, but you have people in place that can handle the situation. Just do your job, and I promise we won't judge you. Do what you have been trained to do. The FBI will be here to assist you shortly, if you need us." I thought that sounded pretty good.

He shook my hand and said, "You must be new to the FBI; nobody is that nice to us normally." He turned to look around, and said, "OK," and then yelled, "Where are my sharpshooters?" to no one in particular. We all kind of looked baffled. Then he said, "Let's get a perimeter around the entire area. I need my bullhorn."

He looked over at me. I didn't know what he wanted so I just gave him the thumbs-up sign.

"OK, let's try to talk him out of the building," I said. I felt pretty stupid because they have the training; all I'm doing is quoting TV shows. I surveyed the area. There were about fifty police cars and quite a few gawkers. Several police officers were stringing yellow tape as quickly as they could. It was a bit chaotic, but they had trained for this, so I figured it should smooth out soon. I just tried to stay out of the way and let them work.

He yelled into the bullhorn, "This is the police. Come out with your hands up. Leave the backpack inside and come out. Nobody will hurt you if you give yourself up."

Nothing happened. We could see through the window that he was still sitting at the table. He appeared to have a phone next to his face. The police radio broadcast a message to Captain Berg. "There's a man on the phone who says he is the guy in the restaurant. He called 9-1-1. Should we patch him through?"

Captain Berg said, "Absolutely."

"I don't want to die; this wasn't my idea," the voice said.

As soon as the caller finished his sentence, I ran to the bomb squad officer and said, "We need to check the crowd." When he looked at me for what I considered too long of a period, I yelled, "Now!" I had a bad feeling this could be a setup. "We need you to use the dog and go through the crowd as quickly as possible. Do you have any other bomb-sniffing dogs?"

The officer said, "No, but doesn't the FBI have them?"

*Now I really felt stupid. He's right; don't we have them?* I called Mr. Douglas. He answered on the first ring, and I told him, "It could be a setup, Mr. Douglas. Send more bomb-sniffing dogs and trained explosive experts ASAP."

He said, "Already in motion, consider it done," and hung up.

I called the Freemans and got them up to speed on what we found so far. I asked, "Is it possible this could be a setup to get a crowd nearby?"

They both agreed it was, and Virginia added, "Anything is possible, of course, but we have not sensed this scenario. I don't know, Mick. You need to start scanning the crowd."

Not much help, I thought. I started to scan in the least obvious way, which wasn't a simple thing to do. I told them, "My senses are picking up something very strong, just not at this location. They're close, probably less than a mile. I'm concerned we're missing something."

I started to feel a bit helpless and checked myself. If I'm amped up, I could miss something simple. *Calm yourself down, Mick; just breath and focus,* I told myself. I started to look around the crowd for people doing something weird—whatever that looks like. I grabbed a few police officers and told them to mingle into the crowd and keep their eyes open.

"For what," one said.

"Anything weird. You have been trained on this, correct?"

"Not really," said another.

*OK, great, what am I going to tell them to look for?* I thought.

"Look for backpacks, especially those that have been put on the ground. Look for people leaving; nobody should be leaving a scene this interesting. Now go!"

I went back to Captain Berg and asked what the man inside had told him. He summarized the conversation: "He is depressed about how his life has been going. His girlfriend left him and took his son, his job wasn't rewarding, and he had investigated radical religions. Recently, someone convinced him to strap a bomb around himself and blow it up near a large crowd. They told him that he would become a famous martyr, and everyone would remember him. We're tracking his movements and getting a search warrant for his apartment and car. He didn't share anything further."

"Great, I have your officers combing the crowd, and the bomb sniffing dog is going through as well, I hope you don't mind."

He replied, "You think it's a setup? There's someone else is in the crowd who will actually explode the bomb?"

I said, "Could be a strong possibility. This guy isn't the type of religious zealot you normally see who's ready to risk their life. It could be a phone-controlled bomb inside, or even in one of the cars outside. It could even be someone wearing a bomb in the crowd—hard to say. I have them looking for people with backpacks, bags, boxes, and investigating any people leaving the scene."

"Wow, for someone who said it was my crime scene, you certainly seem to be taking over."

I didn't like that comment and just said, "You're one person, there're many jobs, and I—well, we at the FBI—can help. If you feel I'm stepping on your toes, bring it up with my superiors later. For now, let's get this situation controlled as best as possible."

He said, "Fair enough. I believe your direction of my officers is just fine."

I wanted to ask him, *Then why the hell did you get shitty with me?* But I decided to keep quiet.

"Backpack, left near a car, pretty large," came a message on the radio. I yelled for the bomb squad guy to check it out. "Tell what-ever police offi-cer who called it in to identify themselves and location, and move everyone away from it. Make sure we're actually talking to a police officer."

There was a flurry of activity near the backpack. A student was tell-ing a police officer it was just his book bag, but we weren't taking chances. The bomb squad officer sent the dog over to sniff it, but there was no alert. The officer went over and examined it, opened it up, and realized it was just books. There was a collective sigh of relief from everyone in law enforcement.

I was certain we needed to watch the crowd. As more officers arrived, they were directed to make a presence in the crowd. I told them to ask questions, see if anyone saw anything suspicious, and just keep looking.

Another bomb-sniffing dog and more detecting equipment arrived. They went to work on checking cars in the parking lot and people in the crowd. It still didn't feel right. I couldn't quite place my reservations, but it just didn't feel right. I kept thinking of the vision Dr. Freeman had foretold. They were convinced a school was involved, but I had found a bomber at a restaurant. Once the crowd and building checks nearby were underway, I grabbed the bomb squad guy and asked him to take his dog to the school, just to be sure. He didn't understand, so I told him, "We need to check for diversions; perhaps the school could also be a target."

He finished checking his current location, then loaded his van with equipment and his dog. He said, "I'll contact you directly. What's your name?"

I said in my most professional fake FBI voice, "Agent Mick Anderson." I felt it was wrong in some way to tell others I was an FBI agent, but appar-ently it's the truth. The day before I was just Mick Anderson, and now I was FBI Agent Mick Anderson. Weird.

I had a second to think and focus. I decided that my hands and fingers should tell me where to look. I scanned back and forth until I locked on a direction. I grabbed binoculars and looked at all the buildings in that direction, first nearby, then farther out. I was looking for something that appeared to be out of place. It didn't take long to locate someone of interest about a half mile away. What caught my eye was a group of three men, one with a walkie talkie and the other two with binoculars, standing on a balcony. The people on the balcony could see us, and they had a clear line of sight to the high school. I grabbed one of the sharpshooters and told him to take a look and give me his opinion.

"This is interesting," is all he said. He clicked his mic and said, "Captain, we need to investigate three suspicious individuals on balcony half a click at eleven o'clock, sixth floor."

I guessed that when they setup a perimeter, the front door was twelve o'clock, because everyone looked in the correct direction, almost simultaneously. Captain Berg ordered four police cruisers to investigate, but without sirens or lights, approaching from the back side of the building. It seemed like an excellent decision to keep it low-key for now.

I know the CIA and FBI can intercept radio traffic, so I called Mr. Douglas. When he answered, I asked if he could intercept walkie talkie channels nearby. He said, "No problem. Tell me where to have them look." I asked Captain Berg where on the map the people on the balcony were. It had coordinates listed on the map, so I told Mr. Douglas to concentrate within a two-mile range. Mr. Douglas said, "OK, call you back in a minute."

There was some commotion, then I heard a policeman yell, "We have movement in the restaurant!" I looked up as the person inside the restaurant started walking toward to door. The large bag was left at the table. He stopped at the door but didn't go out. Captain Berg, still in contact with him, asked "Are you willing to come out now?"

All eyes were directed to the front door as the suspect opened it. He started to walk out and said something that I couldn't quite understand. I was pretty sure he said, "I don't want them to kill me."

Captain Berg said, "Just keep your hands up when you come out and nobody will hurt you."

The suspect said a chilling statement: "Not you. I'm worried about them."

Captain Berg said, "Who are you referring to?"

In an obviously petrified voice, he said, "They have my family. If I go outside, they'll detonate both bombs." I trained the binoculars on the door, trying to peer through the glass. The reflection of the sun made that impossible, so I moved. I ran about seventy feet to an area where the sun wasn't creating a blinding reflection. Finally, I was able to look at the man's clothing. Nothing out of the ordinary. I looked behind him at the book bag and thought I saw an antenna, possibly a walkie talkie. Using the binoculars, I swung around back to the men on the balcony. They were now more animated, moving their arms up and down.

My phone rang. I hoped it was Mr. Douglas, and it was. "Besides the police bands, only one other one is transmitting. You're right," said Mr. Douglas. I told him to hold on; I wanted others to hear.

I ran back to where Captain Berg was standing. I put the phone on speaker so Captain Berg could hear. Mr. Douglas said, "The broadcast is centered exactly where the apartment complex is located. They're speaking Arabic. Our translator told me they're saying the man in the restaurant must not to fail in his mission. They're yelling at him to push the button and punish the Americans. If he doesn't finish the mission, they will. His family will be OK if he finishes the mission. If he doesn't they'll blow up all three bombs. They want him to put the backpack on and run as close to the police as possible. If he doesn't, his family will face the consequences."

I took the phone and walked about twenty feet so I could talk in private. I told Mr. Douglas we had people on a balcony who I believed were part of the plot and asked what to do. He said, "Captain Berg is a veteran; I'm sure he has officers ready to breach the room where these men are located. Make sure the snipers cover from the outside. Additional FBI Agents will be there in a minute."

Captain Berg clicked his mic and said, "Sergeant Berg, are your officers ready?"

The radio crackled, "Ready, everyone is in place, awaiting orders."

"You're cleared to breach," replied Captain Berg.

I looked at the Captain and asked, "Berg? Is he related to you?" I never got an answer as chaotic sounds came over the police radio.

"Three-two-one, go!" said an officer on the radio. I assumed they were outside the room where the three men were watching from the balcony. We all held our breath.

An instant later, Captain Berg told Omar, "I want you to wait inside the restaurant. We need to find where the other bomb is located. Do you know where it is?"

In a shaky voice, he said, "There's one in a van, not sure where. There is one around me, one in the backpack, and one at my ex-girlfriend's house. She and my son are prisoners, and they're threatening to blow them up if I don't do this."

In all the excitement I had forgotten about my fingers. I wasn't exactly sure, but I thought I'd felt something. This feeling was interrupted when police radio chatter became more important.

At least one officer had left their mic on and transmitting. They did this to quickly alert the sharpshooters if there was no other way to prevent a catastrophic event. I had the binoculars trained on the balcony and saw chaos, then heard screaming from officers and the people inside the room. I saw a man on the balcony holding something in his hand. The other two men dropped to their knees as instructed, but not this man. "Bomb!" was screamed by one of the officers. An instant later another officer yelled, "Suspect on balcony has bomb strapped to his body, won't put device in hand down, advise."

"I have the shot," said another voice, I assumed it was the sharpshooter.

Captain Berg clicked the mic and said, "Clear to engage, I repeat, you're clear to engage. Take him down."

I saw the man on the balcony lurch forward then fall backward over the railing. We were so far away it took over a second before I heard the crack from the sharpshooter's gun. From my vantage point it appeared the balcony was fifty feet from the ground. He fell probably ten feet then disappeared in a fiery explosion. I felt the shockwave and heard the explosion instantly. I was almost knocked off my feet. It took us a few seconds to realize what had happened. The man exploded his bomb as he fell, and apparently triggered the backpack in the restaurant at the same time.

Debris was falling everywhere; dust clouds filled the air. There's no visibility, just choking dust. Since it wasn't windy, the dust cloud didn't dissipate. Two officers radioed that they had been injured by debris. I was amazed that was the extent of injuries.

Eventually the dust cleared enough to see the restaurant, or what was left of it. We were very lucky. If we hadn't been able to get everyone out of the restaurant before the explosion, there would've seventy people dead and probably twenty-five badly injured.

I grabbed the binoculars and looked at the building where the men had been on the balcony. There was quite a bit of damage to the building. I said a little prayer to protect the officers and innocent civilians. The balcony was gone. The side of the building, just below where the balcony had been, now had a hole that was ten to fifteen feet wide. Flames poured skyward from that location. Captain Berg asked for an injury report, and we all waited.

Reports started coming in. "Four officers injured; none are dead. Civilians unknown at this time," said some officer on the radio. I assumed this was from the building about a half mile away. Officers approached the restaurant with guns drawn. I really didn't see the reason; nobody inside would've survived that explosion.

Captain Berg was on the radio asking about his son. Now I understood why he didn't have time to answer my question about the other officer named Berg. It was his son who was in charge of the men who breached the room. I looked at his face; he was trembling. "He is injured but will make it," said an officer on the radio. Captain Berg took a deep breath and let out a sigh. I had no idea what to say at a time like this, so I kept my mouth shut. He looked at me for a few seconds. The glazed look in his eyes told me he had lost his focus and control of the situation.

I finally said, "Captain, your officers need direction, they're looking for guidance. What are your orders?"

"I know, just give me a second to catch my breath."

Men arrived with black windbreakers that had FBI on the front and back. "Where are Captain Berg and Agent Anderson?" said the first one.

I pointed to Captain Berg and then said, "I'm Anderson."

One of the men said, "Captain, the FBI would like your permission to gather evidence and inspect the bomb area." Captain Berg, apparently lost in his thoughts, just waved them forward; he knew he had lost control of the situation. He wasn't used to extreme chaos, so he gladly gave up control. Nobody was chastising him; the situation required an immediate decision. I believe he will be commended for his handling of this no-win situation.

The agents looked at me and said, "You need to come with us."

I said, "Hold on, I need to make a phone call and then see your IDs." They looked at me like I was nuts, but I didn't care. I called Mr. Douglas and told him I was with some FBI agents. I wanted to verify their identities before we went any further. I looked at badges and names and told them to Mr. Douglas. It took only a few seconds to verify each person. I said, "OK you're verified."

The first one said, "Can we get to work now?"

I said, "Absolutely, let's go."

My adrenaline level was still exceptionally high. Even so, I'd felt a sensation in my fingers that began to get really annoying. It wasn't just the adrenaline spike that happens after experiencing an explosion. I told them to hold on; we needed to investigate further. Once more they looked at me like I was nuts as I scanned with my open palms.

I could tell they hadn't been briefed on my capabilities, so I took my phone out and called Special Agent White. I talked to him for a second, then handed the phone to one of the agents. They talked for a few seconds, and then the agent said, "I understand. Yes sir." He handed the phone back to me.

Agent White said, "They're ordered to do whatever the hell you want them to, understand?" He hung up, short and sweet as usual.

The agents introduced themselves as Special Agent Pierce Fletcher and Special Agent Brody Schneider. Schneider told me he was a bomb technician. Fletcher said, "We're to shadow you and do as you ask. So, what are your orders?"

I told them, "You will see me do weird things. Just stay with me." I started to scan again. Whatever was creating my sensations was moving. "If you're unaware of my abilities, I can sense things, usually evil people. Right now, I'm sensing something evil that's coming closer to us. I need you to follow me." My fingers started throbbing, which meant they were probably within a quarter of a mile. Police vehicles were entering and leaving the area. It was chaos, as would be expected. The evil had to be coming from one of the vehicles approaching us. I focused on each vehicle; there were four patrol cars, and a police van, followed by a patrol vehicle and another police van, all heading our way.

I told the agents, "There are seven police vehicles coming our way, and one of these vehicles isn't as it seems. The deceased guy in the restaurant said something about a van, so focus on the two vans."

All of the police vehicles followed each other into parking lots near the restaurant. I used the binoculars to quickly look at the driver in each police car. Nothing looked out of the ordinary. I took particular note of the van drivers. They looked the part and were too close together for me to sense exactly which one to focus on. I told the agents, "One of those vans has someone inside intent on doing something evil, and they may have a bomb. If either of those vans turns a different location, I'll be able to tell you which one it is."

They were still three-hundred yards away. Agent Fletcher said, "You can tell one of the vans has a bomb in it—from here?"

I was hyper aware right now, and just quipped, "Yes, follow me. I added,

"We may need a sharpshooter, any of you have a rifle?"

"We both have ARs in our cars," said Agent Fletcher.

"Get them now. Right away," I replied.

They ran back to their vehicles, which were only about twenty feet away. The vans were moving slowly because the number of vehicles in the way. My fingers were pretty sure it was the first van, but I let it play out a few seconds more; I couldn't be wrong in a case like this. It would be shoot first, ask questions later if I determined which van had the bomb.

The agents returned. "Make sure they're loaded," I said. It may seem stupid, but when situations happen that are chaotic, some basic things are forgotten. I expected them to be loaded, so when both agents had to pull the charging handles, I was a bit shocked. I thought to ask them later why they weren't ready to fire, but now wasn't the time.

"You have the first van Fletcher, and Agent Schneider, you aim toward the second one." I removed my weapon as well. I yelled to an officer nearby to use his radio. He came over, and I took the mic. I yelled, "Captain Berg, alert your men that we may have a bomber in a police vehicle coming into the area." I forgot to tell them the direction, so I had to do some quick math. I clicked the mic again and said, "First police van at ten o'clock." About fifty officers started to look toward that direction.

A saw the van move away from the procession of vehicles. The driver went straight rather than turn with the rest. My fingers told me I was right about this guy. I yelled, "It's the first van!"

I'd waited too long. He drove faster now, behind a row of trees and shrubs lining the side street. I looked ahead to an entrance into this area and saw one about 120 yards away. I told the agents and the officer, "There's no reason for that van to be coming in from another street like that. He's the one. If he turns in that entrance, he will probably try to drive close to all of these officers and blow up the van. We must prevent that from happening."

One of the agents said, "Are you one hundred percent sure? I don't want to fire on a fellow officer."

I needed a foolproof way to confirm my suspicion, but how? There would be only seconds to act. I needed a way to stop the van from entering the area or we're all as good as dead. I saw a police cruiser start to drive that direction; there was no time now. We had to act. "Shoot out the van's tires!" They looked at me, and again I shouted, "That's an order, shoot the van's tires." I'm sure it sounded silly; hell, I wasn't even sure of the proper terminology. It worked, though; they fired a few shots. I saw sparks on the pavement near the van and the branches of a few shrubs fly into the air. The officers stopped for a second to see if they'd hit their targets. "Keep firing," I yelled.

I heard a gun go off nearby, but it wasn't a rifle. I looked and saw a policeman firing at the van with a hand gun. I thought he was nuts. "Dude, seriously, you're firing a nine-millimeter hand gun at a van one hundred yards away?" From that distance I wasn't even sure the bullet would punch a hole in a tire. Hitting a quickly moving van would be hard enough with a rifle, but a hand gun wasn't going to cut it.

The van kept coming, now picking up speed. I looked at the other agents; they looked back. They were looking for guidance or an order to stop the van, and I wasn't qualified to issue such an order. Decisions had to be made, but what if I was wrong? This was the first time I doubted the feelings in my hands; however, I didn't have the luxury of time to reconsider. I snapped myself back to reality. I had to trust those feelings; they hadn't been wrong yet. I yelled, "Shoot the driver!" A hail of gunfire erupted. Sparks flew off the pavement, tree branches fell to the ground, and the side windows were blown into a million pieces. The windshield started to disintegrate as the officers found their range.

The van veered off course and ran over a fire hydrant, continuing on until it crashed into a nearby building. I yelled, "Cease fire and find cover." We all held our breath, waiting to see what would happen.

The engine was racing, the accelerator obviously stuck at full throttle, and the rear tires were still spinning. Smoke and steam spewed out of the radiator and from under the van. To everyone's relief there was no explosion. Water was spraying everywhere. I had no idea that a broken hydrant could cause water to shoot fifty feet into the air; perhaps if there was an explosion, the water could help put the fire out. I took an instant to say a prayer that the driver really was evil and not a police officer.

"Nobody is to go near the van," I yelled. The entire time I kept thinking, *Why the fuck do they think I should be in charge?* After a second, I thought, *why do I think I'm in charge?*

More officers converged on our area. They inched closer, so I yelled again, "Stay back—it isn't safe." If this was a huge bomb, we would all be dead in an instant, even at this range.

I felt a huge relief when I took a breath and focused on my hands, pointing them toward the van. I had almost no feeling, an excellent indicator that preventing the van from entering the area was the correct decision. I told the agents and officer nearby that the suspect was almost certainly dead. I really shouldn't have said this; from the look on their faces I realized they were wondering how I knew from three hundred feet away. I nearly laughed when my thoughts turned to, *Go ahead Mick, tell them your telepathic hands and fingers can see that far. I'm sure they'll believe you.* I kept that my little secret; no reason to confuse them any further.

My phone rang. It was Special Agent White. I really thought it would be Mr. Douglas. "Did you just order them to shoot up a police vehicle?" he asked.

I replied, "Yes, he wouldn't stop. Pretty sure it wasn't a policeman inside. Well, at least I'm praying it wasn't."

"Goddamn, Mick, I hope you're right."

I asked, "Are you watching from a drone or—?"

I was interrupted by Mr. Douglas, who was also on the call. "Of course, I am. Now wave to the nice satellite, Mick."

I waved. "You didn't really have to wave, Mick," said Mr. Douglas.

I said, "What now? I want someone else in charge. Where are the bomb squad people?"

Mr. Douglas said, "Nope, you're in charge. You sent one to the high school, remember? The other one is about one-hundred feet to your left. Get him over there to check the van. Keep everyone back, even farther than your location. I don't need to tell you what to do; your Gatekeeper instincts are all you need to follow."

The phone went dead. Well, shit, I haven't been a Gatekeeper, or an FBI agent, long enough to know what to do. I really wanted to ask more questions on procedures and what should be done next.

I yelled for the bomb squad officer. A man ran at full speed to where I was standing. I looked at his name tag which read: SGT Stevens – Bomb Squad. I didn't know what to say, so I asked, "What should we do next, Officer Stevens?"

He looked at me a bit dumbfounded, looked around, then quietly said, "Umm, well, I normally follow orders. You appear to be in charge; what do you want me to do?"

I just thought to myself, *Shit! I've no idea what to tell him to do.* I finally said, "Well, if you think it's safe enough to check out the van, then do that."

His response was pretty funny. "Safe?" he said, "Nothing we do is safe, and this is no different. We don't know if he is going to push a trigger or if it could be remotely detonated. I follow orders, unless I know a bomb is about to explode. I've no idea here, so what are your orders?"

I told him, "The man is dead; he won't be pushing anything."

His response was predictable, "How do you know?"

"If he weren't, we'd all be dead, Officer Stevens," I replied.

I quickly realized I don't like giving orders, especially in a perilous time such as this. I'd be sick if anyone died or was injured because of a mistake I'd made. I looked around. Now one hundred officers' faces were watching me. They were looking for someone to make a decision. I said, "We need to know what we're facing, and right now you're the only one who has the ability. Go over there and either diffuse that bomb or tell me how big of a hole it will cause if you can't."

I yelled, "Everyone else get back." They moved about twenty feet in unison. I yelled, "No, goddamn it, way back, and now!" They moved about 150 feet and stopped. *To hell with it, I thought; it would have to do.* Smoke was rising from the engine area and the rear tires. We really needed to shut the engine down to prevent a fire.

I decided to scan the area again, just to be sure I hadn't missed anything. Luckily, I didn't have any strong sensations. I needed to contact the other bomb squad officer and see if he found anything at the school. I asked to use a radio to contact him, but I didn't even know his name. I yelled, "What's the other bomb squad officer's name? Does anyone know his name?"

"Peterson," someone yelled.

I clicked the mic and said, "Officer Peterson, status?"

A few seconds later he replied, "Dog was triggered by a suspicious vehicle at school. Gray Dodge minivan, license plates are missing, but it does have a temporary tag. I'll give update in a few minutes."

Six black SUVs drove into the area. The police, already hyped up, pointed their weapons toward them. Special Agent Fletcher said, "Keep calm everyone, they're FBI forensics agents." The officers looked at me to see if it was true; I didn't know one way or the other. The people jumped out of the SUVs with FBI on their body armor. One man yelled, "Where's Agent Anderson?" A few men pointed to me.

The man introduced himself. "Station Chief Mike Robinson, FBI forensics. I was told to find you by our chief, Sam White. Can you bring me up to speed?" I told him what I knew but was interrupted by the radio. It was the bomb technician, Stevens. I looked over at the van. Smoke was billowing out of the engine and tires. I heard a loud pop, followed by tire debris flying rearward behind the vehicle. The tire had spun in place for so long that it finally blew.

Officer Stevens said over the radio, "It's OK, just a tire. By the way, this isn't a real police van; it has no steel prisoner divider. I see one deceased male, about twenty to thirty years old. There are two fifty-five-gallon drums in the back with wires hanging out. The man is holding a switch with a light on it. I think your officers got him before he could push it. I'm attempting entry, and will report more in a minute."

The radio crackled when Officer Peterson called in from the school. "False alarm at the school. No bomb, but they did have a bunch of fireworks in the minivan. Owner arrived, said there was a party later so he had fireworks brought in from another state. He checks out. We're checking around the school now; will report back when finished."

The fake police van now received my focus. The engine, badly overheating, started loud knocking noises. It was just a matter of time before the engine locked up from overheating. I was more worried about a bearing seizing inside the engine, especially on any of the connecting rods. If that happened it would break the connecting rod, which would punch a hole through the oil pan and engine block. In the worst-case scenario, oil would pour out of the engine, right on to the super-heated exhaust system. The hot oil, which would've had plenty of gasoline fumes mixed in from the overheating engine, would result in a fire. If we couldn't put the fire out, the explosives would detonate within a few minutes.

I took proactive action since I was apparently in charge. I clicked the mic and asked for the person in charge of the fire fighters located near the restaurant. A Captain Demers responded. I told him, "I need several fire extinguishers brought to the smoking van, just in case a fire breaks out."

He responded, "Roger, on their way."

Three fire fighters, each carrying two bulky fire extinguishers, ran toward the van. I could see Officer Stevens still examining the door for booby traps. He clicked the mic and said, "Thanks." At that instant, the engine made a loud banging sound followed quickly by a screeching sound, and then it stopped abruptly with a loud *thunk*; fire poured out from underneath the front end. The worst-case scenario came true. We needed to act fast or people were going to die.

The firefighters weren't too far away; they rushed forward and activated the extinguishers. Officer Stevens also grabbed one; there was no time to waste. If the fire wasn't put out in less than a minute, I'd have no choice but to give the order to evacuate.

I clicked the mic and told Captain Demers we needed more extinguishers, but he had already figured that out. He sent nine men toward the van. We held our breath as the fire retardant, steam, and smoke obscured the van. I counted the seconds. Once I counted to forty seconds, I clicked the mic and said, "I need a status on the fire, right now."

A few seconds later Officer Stevens told everyone, "Fire is out, under control. Sending fire personnel back to their holding area." We all took a collective sigh of relief.

My phone rang; it was Mr. Douglas again. "OK, we're watching from above, what's your contingency plan if the bomb can't be defused?"

I hadn't really thought of it, so I said, "Not sure. I was going to move three quarters of the police and first responders back about a quarter of a mile, but I hadn't decided anything else. What else do we need to do?"

"Good; everyone but the most experienced should be out of harm's way. Make sure nobody from the media is within a quarter of a mile. Have all churches and schools evacuated within a two miles range. Another thing, Mick, we're hearing chatter of another bomb, perhaps two."

I asked, "Are the Freemans telling you something new?"

He responded, "No, just intelligence from other areas."

I hung up, clicked the mic, and repeated the suggestions to the police officers. About ninety percent of them either left the area or went to check on schools and churches. I wasn't getting any pushback from anyone; they did what they were told.

Officer Stevens's voice came over the radio. "Done checking the doors; robot ready to open doors when I'm far enough away." I saw him running back toward us carrying a case. He was between us and the van when he stopped. He opened the case and flipped an antenna up, then got to work moving controls. We watched through binoculars as the robot pulled the door handle with the steel arm. The door opened slowly. We all took a deep breath; no explosion. Officer Stevens used the robot arm with a camera attached to peer into the van and inspect the device.

"I see no booby traps. Suspending robot, going in manual."

All I could think of was it takes big balls to do his job. He was well trained and fearless. He walked back to the van and he peered in. Using an extended mirror, he took a look around the fifty-five-gallon drums. He said into the radio, "Unknown device on top, battery wired to both drums, pretty sure if I take power away it will be disarmed. Can you hear me, Officer Peterson?"

Officer Peterson said, "Roger. Peterson here."

Officer Stevens said, "I'm taking pictures of the top of the device. You should have them in a minute. Just need to know if it's safe to remove power."

A minute later Officer Peterson told Officer Stevens to remove power. "Roger," said Officer Stevens.

A few anxious moments later, Officer Stevens clicked his mic and said, "Device is diffused; removing electronics now." We heard people nearby start clapping. A few seconds later, Officer Stevens came out of the van and bowed to their clapping and cheering.

My phone rang, and I answered without even looking. It was Mr. Douglas. "Hey Mick, great job," said Mr. Douglas.

I replied, "You're kidding, right? I didn't do anything. Everyone is cheering; it's a big relief. I need someone else to clean up here. I want to scan some additional areas; my hands are telling me we're not done."

I told Special Agent Fletcher to take over. I told two officers I needed a lift to check the school and other areas. I said into the mic, "Great job everyone. Really proud of your professionalism." We took off toward the school.

I really wanted to get out of there before I screwed up something that would haunt me for the rest of my life.

# Chapter 47:
## *Where To Sir?*

Officers Springer and Johnson were my drivers. They asked, "Where to, sir?"

I told them, "We will start with the high school." It only took a minute to get there.

Officer Peterson met us in the parking lot. "I have nothing, sir; place is clear."

I said, "OK, but we need to check a few more places." I called Mr. Douglas and asked if there was any new intelligence on the location or number of bombs.

He said, "We're diffusing another bomb at Omar's apartment. Other than that, a school or a church is the best intel we have. We're poring over everything, but that's the best we have for you at this instant." Another dead end.

My fingers had an extremely weak sensation. It was difficult to get a direction. I called the Freemans and asked if any other visions had materialized. "Sorry, nothing new," said Richard. "But we thought you found what we'd predicted already?"

I said, "We found bombs, but my fingers are not convinced we have eliminated the threat."

With nothing else to go on, I decided to call Mr. Douglas back. I wanted a helicopter to speed up our timeline. He told me to find the nearest airport, and a helicopter would meet me there. I told the officers to take me back to Potomac, in Ft. Washington, Maryland. Waiting for me was Randy Nicholson, the same pilot I'd used before. It's good to see a familiar face.

In his usual joking manner, he said, "I had a rough night; I think I'm still drunk. Mind if I sleep in the back while you fly it? If you have any problems or think we're going to crash, feel free to wake me up." He started to climb in the back, so I pulled the collective lever, and the helicopter started to take off. He changed his mind and quickly jumped back into the pilot seat.

I said, laughing, "I thought you were taking a nap? I've got this, go ahead and take your nap."

He responded, "No, on second thought I feel more awake now. I'll take over. Your last take off made me air sick."

We made a big arc around the city again. This time I picked up a sensation within ten minutes. I pointed to the west and said, "Go west, young man." He rolled his eyes. I started to feel my ring fingers throb. I told Randy it was less than ten miles away now. Soon, all of my fingers were buzzing. I asked what the group of building were straight ahead. Randy said, "That's Georgetown University, the oldest university in Washington, D.C."

We flew another thirty seconds, and I knew whatever we were looking for was at that school. I called Mr. Douglas. "We need officers to meet us at Georgetown University, and bring the bomb squad."

I told Randy to put us down in a parking lot if possible. We flew over the main school building and realized the parking lots were almost full; people were everywhere. "Wonder what's going on," I said to Randy. He thought about it a few seconds, then said, "I think they're having commencement ceremonies today." There's no way to land in any parking lot, so I pointed to a field nearby. We were about to land when I realized my fingers weren't buzzing as badly. I shouted, "Take it back up, something isn't right!"

We flew in the direction my fingers were sensing. We didn't have to go very far before my fingers started to throb. The person or persons we needed to find were in a moving vehicle. Traffic was light at that time of day, so there were no bottlenecks. We flew two hundred feet above the street, allowing me to pinpoint the location as being one or both of the vehicles below us. I told Randy, "Right below us, either the semi-truck or that blue van." I called Mr. Douglas and told him what I knew so far. I really needed to be closer to the ground, but my gut was telling me we needed to focus on the blue van.

The large blue van turned, and my sensations followed it. I called Mr. Douglas back and told him, "I need you to track the large blue van, looks like a Mercedes van, but it could be a Dodge version of the same van. It's going east on North Road."

He said, "OK, we're scanning traffic cameras now; we see it."

As we flew in front of the vehicle, I finally saw the vehicle's grill through binoculars. "It's a Dodge Sprinter van and has something that says Capital on the side," I told Mr. Douglas.

He said, "We see it. That van has 'The Capital Flower Shop' printed on the sides. What do you want us to do?"

I thought about this for a second. *What could we do?* "I don't know, but they're the source of the sensations from my fingers. I'm more worried about why they just left Georgetown University earlier. Georgetown has a large event going on right now. We need to check that location as well. I want you to stop the van and find out who they are."

Mr. Douglas replied, "OK, we will have the van stopped, and the bomb squad will check it out."

"Great, so what do you want us to do?" I asked.

He said, "Stay as top cover, in case they bolt."

We saw flashing lights and soon heard sirens as police vehicles converged on the van's location. When they were within a quarter of a mile, they turned off their sirens. The van turned onto Tondorf Road and approached Prospect. It turned east on Prospect Road, where fifteen police vehicles were waiting. The police had surrounded the van before it even came to a stop, and they pulled the passengers out instantly. I was stunned the people in the van came out peacefully. I think the speed at which officers descended on the van, along with the overwhelming show of force, prevented any thought of escape. We had to wait an excruciatingly long time for information while we hovered over the area.

Finally, a policeman came over the radio and said, "Van is secure; forensics is moving in. Two middle eastern men in custody; no IDs. They have walkie talkies and cell phones." I called Mr. Douglas, who, of course, already knew this information. He was able to tell me that the commencement was scheduled for later that day at Healy Lawn, at Georgetown University.He also told me that Georgetown's School of Medicine commencement was scheduled to be held in Constitution Hall, near the White House, at seven o'clock that evening.

I had Randy fly over Healy Hall so I could scan it. I didn't feel anything, so we turned toward Constitution Hall. As we flew closer, my fingers started to vibrate. I called Mr. Douglas back and yelled, "Get a bunch of police over to Constitution Hall, and bring the bomb squad."

He asked, "Are you sure it isn't back at Georgetown?"

I shouted, "No, I'm not sensing anything near Georgetown now, but I'm one hundred percent sure about Constitution Hall."

Since Constitution Hall is close to the White House, there are hundreds of Secret Service agents and Capitol Police available. They also have quite a few bomb-sniffing dogs and bomb experts. I saw flashing lights a few seconds later. I counted well over twenty police cars swarming Constitution Hall as we arrived overhead. They're pretty serious about security, and more than one aimed their machine guns upward at us. They must've been alerted to our arrival, because they finally put their guns down. I saw another van that was similar as we flew nearby. Police had surrounded it.

I knew it wasn't a good idea to look toward the White House, but I couldn't stop myself. There was a flurry of activity on the roof. Snipers trained their weapons on our helicopter, and multi-barrel machine guns pointed up at us. Trap doors swung open, and a rack with three missiles poked out. These missiles were on an apparatus that spun around to face our helicopter. I think I piddled on myself just a bit.

Over the radio we received an ominous call: "White House Secret Service to unidentified helicopter, please identify." It was a show of force.

They know every single aircraft in the area well before they get anywhere near the White House.

Randy clicked the mic and said, "FBI Helicopter Whisky Tango Alpha 426—special clearance mission."

They made it abundantly clear that we weren't to proceed any further. "Whisky Tango Alpha 426, be advised, you have clearance only to the street you're above. If you continue your aircraft will enter the White House Restricted No Fly Zone." Then, loudly and firmly, the voice he said, "This will be your only warning. If you continue, we will fire on your aircraft. Do you understand?"

Randy replied, "Roger, understood, turning back one-hundred meters."

We wisely heeded their warnings and turned around, hovering on the far side of Constitution Hall. As we retreated, I was able to see the missile rack and multi-barrel machine guns continue to track us. Randy and I looked at each other, then I spoke: "Let's not do that again."

He smiled and said, "They get their panties in a wad pretty quickly at the White House, especially when the president is there."

I laughed and told Randy, "It's OK, I've met the president. We're tight, like best friends." I made the twisting finger motion with my hand to signify the validity of my statement. Randy rolled his eyes. I said, "Hey, I'm serious. I really have met her."

More seriously, I said, "I need to get down there to help search. Where can we land?"

Randy replied, "The police have closed off traffic. Let's land behind them." He clicked the mic and told the officers we were coming in to land.

"Where are you going to land?" was the police response.

Randy said, "Either on top of your police cars or just behind. Your choice." I saw a police officer waving a few of the cars to move out of the way, and we landed.

I met with the police lieutenant Dave Morris; he was in charge of the operation. While we waited for the bomb technicians to arrive, we reviewed security camera videos. It appeared that the van had been delivering flowers all morning. The company was under contract with Georgetown University and Constitution Hall to provide floral services.

We watched carefully and soon realized some of the flower planters were very heavy. They required a wheeled dolly to be transported from the van. This seemed odd to Lieutenant Morris and me, since other flower planters of the same size were brought in by one person. The security tapes revealed half of the heavy planters delivered were upstairs and the other half to a basement office area. This basement area turned out to be directly underneath the main hall.

I scanned the entire group of bomb squad officers just to be sure we were safe. Then I told them to let their dogs check the entire area. We needed to find each of the heavy flower vases first since it seemed like the best start. FBI agents searched the entire hall and found an additional six heavy planters. Each of these heavy planters was stationed near an outside wall, one every fifty feet.

It didn't take long for the dogs to finish. Nothing was found, which was a huge disappointment for everyone. I felt all eyes were on me, since I was the reason all hell had broken loose in this building. These planters were at least twice as thick as the light planters. It seemed odd they needed to be this thick and this heavy. My "spider senses" just couldn't believe that these were normal planters, so we inspected each flower pot by hand. Large plastic mats were brought in to carefully pull each plant out and sift through the soil. The first five quickly yielded no results. After reviewing the security footage, we knew the additional six heavy planters had been delivered the day before. We finally found the last one in a hallway in the basement. Not a trace of explosives was detected. I still wasn't convinced.

After an hour of checking the other planters, we had nothing to show for our efforts. The manager and the event planner for Constitution Hall were getting angry. They wanted us to finish so they could setup for the evening's graduation ceremonies.

I was getting weird looks from the agents on site. I heard whispers about this being "a wild goose chase." One of the FBI agents told police officers to put the planters back together and clean up. I was unable to provide any reason why we should wait, so I watched while a police officer was placing the plants back into one of the planters. I heard an officer grunt while trying to lift the planter and then yell, "Shit, it cut me!" Had I not been within earshot, we would've missed an important clue. Since smooth planters don't normally have a sharp edge or an object in the design that's sharp enough to cut a person's skin, I became intrigued. I told him to put it down, then felt around the planter until I saw two pieces of bronze tabs that appeared to have been installed inside the planter. These tabs were small and hardly noticeable. Because the tabs were the same color as the paint on that area of the planter, it took careful examination even to see them.

At first, I didn't understand the significance of these bronze tabs, especially since they were several inches apart. I reviewed the other items the floral shop included with the planters and found my answer. Included with each of the heavy planters were automatic watering machines. They had an electrical box that hung over the planter, a water jug with about a gallon of water, a timer, and wiring to an electrical plug. According to the hall manager, these automatic watering machines are supposed to provide a small amount of water every six hours. He told us, "It's a great system; we just add water to the jug every four days."

We examined the electrical box and noticed it had tabs exactly lined up with the tabs on the planter. I immediately ordered these planters to be removed, along with all the equipment included. I called Mr. Douglas and explained what I wanted done. After we talked, I ordered everything to be delivered under guard to the FBI forensics lab in Washington, D.C.

My senses knew something was wrong. I was amazed when the answer was finally revealed. The FBI technicians put each planter into an X-ray machine. The X-ray showed wiring and encased components fabricated into a mesh of support structure. After each planter was carefully broken apart, it became obvious why the bomb-sniffing dogs couldn't sense the bombs; they were completely encased and air tight, the outside was painted with a chemical that irritated a K-9's nasal membranes, so they just avoided them.

We'd easily have missed these bombs had it not been for the police-man getting cut by the metal tab, and my determination to trust my fingers and hands.

A bomb analysis expert with the FBI, named Shelly Ferguson, told me the bombs would've caused hundreds of casualties. She was mostly concerned about the bombs perfectly placed next to the outside walls. She said the explosions would've weakened the walls and allowed the ceiling to collapse on everyone in a matter of a few seconds. She estimated everyone inside would've been injured, and ninety percent of the injuries would've been fatal.

Mr. Douglas had a search warrant for the floral shop. They found twenty-seven additional heavy planters that were scheduled to be deliv-ered to Georgetown and five other historical buildings in the Washington, D.C., area. One other employee was arrested. The rest of the employees were completely innocent, hard-working Americans who were tasked with delivering flowers to many locations. The three men who'd been arrested wouldn't talk, but they didn't really need to. We had foiled a terrorist plot that would've injured and killed people on an immense scale. It would've been headline news all over the world.

After we relaxed a few minutes, I realized that these same bombs could be at Georgetown. We sent FBI agents to Georgetown, and they conducted exhaustive searches on the buildings. They found another innocent-looking planter outside an underground artifact storage room, located under the original building of Georgetown University. No auto-matic watering device had been attached yet. Thankfully, only one was located. The rest were to be delivered within the hour, according to the schedule, at which time the automatic watering devices with timers were to be installed. These devices seemed innocent to virtually everyone. Built in the late 1790s, the building was robust, but a large enough bomb would've destroyed it as well.

This new tactic had everyone in security details frightened. Mr. Douglas reported that nearly fifty more were found, already in government buildings and other sites. That day, the CIA, Secret Service, and FBI would announce new procedures using X-rays and ultrasound machines to scan each flower vase, pot, or planter in Washington, D.C. The expanded this requirement to include all federal buildings in the United States and our embassies overseas.

I felt a sense of pride that comes from a job well done. I was happy no innocent people were harmed and life would return to normal. News outlets inevitably covered the commotion. To prevent panic, the FBI decided to have a press conference. They didn't disclose the bombs, but told the reporters that this was an FBI specialized training event. Mr. Douglas told me the press accepted the information, at least for now. He wanted it low-key to give the FBI time to find additional evidence of a wider plot, and to track down the country that had paid for it.

# Chapter 48:
## *Coincidence?*

After two days of meetings about the terror plots, I was cleared to leave for Russia to help my friend, Aleksei find and punish those responsible for his son's death. I was actually pretty excited about helping my new friend. These were bad people; they'd hurt my friend, killed his son, and attacked my wife. My senses were becoming more precise as I learned to control my focus. We would get them, and soon. Popov, the most wanted man in Russia, was first on the list, and I really wanted to put an end to his reign of terror.

This time my wife wanted to go as well. She'd recovered about sixty percent from her injuries and insisted she was well enough to travel. Besides, she'd always wanted to see Europe. I agreed to take her along; after all, she'd been putting up with our new life so well, she deserved a trip. We'd have security with us the entire time. Our flight itinerary was Washington, D.C., to London, then on to Berlin, Germany. From Berlin we flew to Helsinki, Finland. The last leg of our flight was to Moscow. Aleksei and his team would be waiting to pick us up.

While waiting in line at the Helsinki airport coffee shop, I noticed two men ahead of us. It was impossible not to notice them; they were drunk. My wife described them as obnoxious, loud, and vulgar. These two men had small containers of alcohol that they were downing with regularity; a strong aroma of hard liquor permeated the air. One whiff had been enough to sting my nostrils. They were speaking English, and it was clear they were from America. I was in no mood to make any new drunk friends, so I kept quiet. One of the men looked back in my direction several times. He looked puzzled for a minute, then said, "Hey buddy, by chance are you an American?"

I replied, "Yes."

The man continued, "You look familiar. I've seen you before, just can't remember where. Where are you from?"

I said, "Near Peoria, Illinois."

He erupted, "Wait a minute, I've seen you on TV." He looked at his friend and said, "I knew I recognized this guy. I saw him on the news."

Now highly animated, he snapped his fingers and pointed at me in an effort to recall the memory.

"You're the guy that found some kidnapped girl near Chicago, and some children's bodies in Aurora," he said. Then he paused a second and said, "Aren't you?"

His friend intently studied my face, then said, "Yeah, now I remember. We saw some of your interviews. Both of us are from Aurora, Illinois. We work for Caterpillar. Hey, you also got shot, right?" Excited that he remembered something important, the first man reached out his hand to shake mine, then said, "My name is Marty Edgington, and this is Bill Schneider."

I was a bit hesitant, but reached out to shake his hand. As soon as our hands touched, I felt a little jolt. I tried to keep my composure but needed to know why I was sensing something negative from this man.

The sensation I received was unusual—strong but with no electrocution feeling. I needed more information, so I replied, "Yes, I was fortunate to help the police find a kidnapped child near Chicago. And yes, I was shot by one of the kidnappers. A few months later, I helped the police solve a forty-year-old murder case in Aurora."

Marty replied in an excited voice, "I knew it."

"Marty and Bill, let me ask you something. Where have you guys been traveling?" I asked.

Marty replied, "Russia and Finland. We are powertrain engineers on the newer Caterpillar 8000 series mining truck."

I said, "Interesting. I bet you meet all kinds of people in that business."

Marty said, "Oh, we certainly do. There are quite a few interesting people in mining operations. The owners and operators refuse to follow our guidelines; often removing or disconnecting our safety sensors in an effort to move more weight. So, we're here to train the operators and also test a new truck with more capability. Hopefully we can stop them from ruining our equipment."

I tried to keep the conversation moving by asking, "So, how did you like the two countries? You guys have any strange encounters while traveling?"

The two looked at each other, then Bill Schneider said, "Everything has been great—well up until we left Saint Petersburg."

I asked, "What happened there?"

Marty replied, "Bill and I damn near got killed—that's what happened."

Bill said, "Some crazy idiot was running out of the airport while we were going in. I didn't see him until it was too late. I tried to get out of his way, but he crashed into me, then tripped over our luggage trying to run away. He got up and went absolutely nuts. The guy screamed something in Russian and took a swing at me, and before I knew it, he grabbed me and threw me on the ground. I thought he broke my arm. When Marty tried to help, the guy grabbed him by the throat with one hand. Show him your throat, Marty."

Marty undid his tie and shirt button to show deep blue and red bruising around his throat.

Bill continued, "Thank God the police noticed and came to help. It took five policemen to stop this guy from killing us. He had to be on drugs—guy was nuts. They cuffed him, but he still got up and started running away with one policeman on his back. An additional six or seven policemen arrived just in time to restrain this guy. They had to hogtie his legs so he couldn't get up. He was so angry he was frothing at the mouth. His shirt was torn apart during the scuffle, and there was a crazy tattoo on his chest and back."

"Marty and Bill, this is very important, and I need you to listen closely," I said. "I'm part of a team that's chasing someone who matches the description of the man that attacked you. If this is the same man, then he is wanted for multiple murders and must be stopped. I need you to answer some questions and I need you to be very specific. Understood?"

They nodded in agreement.

I said, "First, was this at the airport in Saint Petersburg?"

They both nodded yes.

"OK, how long ago did this happen?"

They looked at each other, and Bill said, "Eight hours ago." Marty added, "Ya, give or take."

"Did the police take a statement from you?" Again, they both nodded.

Marty said, "We gave them a quick statement of what happened, but we needed to get through security and get to our flight here. Once we went through security, we went to the bar and got a bit drunk. We don't really know what happened after that."

I said, "OK, so just for your information, if this is the same guy I'm trying to find, then both of you are fortunate to be alive. I appreciate this information. Police forces around the world have been looking for him. Hopefully your information helps us keep him in jail for good."

I quickly called Aleksei's phone. He answered, "Mick, sorry, change of plans. I hope you're not in Moscow already because I can't pick you up. We received information about Popov and his gang's location, and I had to leave Moscow."

I said, "Aleksei, I need your full attention, OK?"

He said, "What is it?"

"I have information that the man we're searching for was possibly arrested at the airport in Saint Petersburg four hours ago."

There was silence for a second. Aleksei said, "Wow, that's interesting, Mick. You see, I was finally able to get some answers from one of the people we arrested. The man we were interrogating was on his way to Saint Petersburg to meet with Popov. My entire team is on helicopters right now on our way to Saint Petersburg to investigate. We're only twenty minutes away. At first, I thought it might be, what you call 'bull shit,' but your additional information tells me this could be the break we're looking for. I'll contact their police and see if they still have him. Thank you, my friend. At a later time, you must tell me how you found this information. Goodbye."

I decided to watch the news. The international news station popped up a live "special alert" news story about a prison break. At first, I didn't really understand what was going on because it was in Swedish. Then someone switched the TV channel to an English news channel. The same story was on this channel. My interest was piqued when the reporter said the jail is located in Saint Petersburg, Russia. My wife was talking on her phone during the news story, so I wasn't able to get all the details. I opened my laptop to try to find the story on-line.

Twenty minutes later, my phone rang; it was Aleksei. "Did you hear about the prison break in Saint Petersburg?"

I told him, "The news just announced it. What do you know?"

He said, "We arrived at the airport about fifteen minutes ago. Saint Petersburg police officers had picked us up from the airport when it came over the radio. All hell is breaking loose." I heard him shouting orders for a few seconds, then he said to me, "Mick, about one hundred ex-military stormed the prison. They blew holes in the outside walls on two sides. Almost everyone inside was freed, and I think Popov was one of them." After a pause, he said, "There's a huge gun battle going on right now. They have KAMAZ vehicles, which are equipped with anti-tank rounds, and they're destroying the police response. They're basically taking over that part of the town. The police can't stop them; they have far too much fire-power. Our military has been called in. My unit is going back up in the helicopters to engage them. Wish us luck."

*Luck,* I thought—*what an odd thing for him to say.* There was some reservation in his voice, like he knew it's going to be a difficult mission. It was an ominous statement, especially from a warrior like Aleksei. I said, "Good luck, then. I'll be there as soon as possible and help in any way I can." That was the end of our phone call.

I watched the story unfold on-line. Amateur video showed smoke pouring out of the jail. Tracer fire could be seen coming from large, military-like vehicles. These had no markings on them—a sign they weren't police. There were explosions in buildings as the trucks stormed through residential streets. The police were outgunned and stood no chance. Aleksei and his team would hopefully even the odds.

Fox News's website had a "Breaking News" banner on the screen. An instant later a reporter explained that a major event was happening in Russia. "Live in Saint Petersburg is resident Antov Kasich with cell phone video of a prison break happening right now. Antov, what can you tell us?"

The person on the phone told an exciting story. "There are military-looking people with big trucks fighting with police officers. They blew holes in the jail. Now they appear to be driving to the airport." He showed video of the smoke and a close-up picture of one of the six-wheel trucks with men firing machine guns out of the back, while others were firing RPGs at the police vehicles trying to block their path. The video appeared to be taken from a roof. The trucks were coming toward him. The video showed one of the people on the truck firing upward toward the caller, and sparks could be seen nearby. The video then showed the caller gasping for breath and saying something in Russian.

A second later the caller said, "I don't think I got shot, but that was close. Let me check to make sure I'm OK." A few seconds later he yelled, "We see helicopters now; they're firing on the trucks." You could hear the heavy machine guns and cannons on the helicopters. Video showed the helicopters firing, tracer rounds were as bright as the sun. The helicopters zoomed in, firing long bursts, then banked left or right away from the truck's return fire. After the fourth helicopter flew by, the grainy images showed a missile fired from the helicopter. As the camera spun around, the truck in the front exploded, bodies and equipment flying up into the air. I believe Aleksei ordered them to wait until the trucks cleared the densely populated city streets, then when they finally came out into the open, the helicopters opened fire. Now that the remaining trucks were trapped, the helicopters fired more missiles. Eventually all the trucks were destroyed. The video was both interesting and exciting; you could literally feel the danger. The caller was breathing heavily but kept the camera pointed toward the trucks.

The men on the trucks who weren't killed now tried to escape. The helicopters, hovering, fired thousands of rounds from their multi-barrel machine guns toward the men hiding behind the burning trucks. Some tried to run down alleyways but were soon cut down. Eventually smoke from the burning trucks obscured the visibility to the point the caller stopped filming. The caller yelled, "Those helicopters came at the right time. That was crazy."

Then the caller turned on the video again as a helicopter hovered nearby. I recognized one of the people on the helicopter immediately. It was Nadia, the soldier who specialized in explosives. Nadia had her rifle pointing right at the caller. It was obvious he'd had his hands up. A few tense seconds went by, then the helicopter flew away, apparently accepting the caller as an innocent bystander.

The caller yelled into the phone, "That was close! I think I'll leave the roof now." A few seconds later the reporter came back on the screen, and the news channel cut to a commercial. Damn commercials—just when it was getting good.

My wife prodded me, "Hey, they're calling our zone to board the flight."

"Shit," I said. In all the excitement I forgot to change flights. I told her, "I have to get us to Saint Petersburg instead." I went to the counter and asked if there was a flight to Saint Petersburg anytime soon. Moscow wouldn't do us much good since Aleksei wasn't there, and I didn't feel safe without he and the team nearby. After a few seconds of furious typing, which reminded me of the airport counter agent on the movie *Meet the Fockers*, she told me a flight was leaving in fifteen minutes on the other side of the airport. I had her switch reservations, and we ran as quickly as possible to the other gate. They were on the final boarding call when we got to the counter. They printed our tickets, and we boarded. We were the last ones on the flight and were seated all the way in the back. Out of breath, I called Aleksei to check the progress. The phone went right to voicemail. I left this message: "We're on a flight to Saint Petersburg. Be there in one hour."

I left my phone on, in silent mode, just in case Aleksei called. I texted him to see what was happening, but received no response. I was tired but couldn't sleep; my excitement level was too high. Mr. Douglas had given me a special Wi-Fi card that he assured me would function anywhere. I was surprised it worked inside the airplane at thirty-two thousand feet. I went to the international news site and read about the ongoing prison break in Saint Petersburg. Video from many sources showed various angles of the same explosions. One brave soul even took an amazing video of the helicopters attacking the trucks. He was so close that the explosions shattered his window.

The reporter stated the siege on the prison had ended, while the screen showed grim images of bodies strewn all over the street. It was reported that more than seventy people were dead, mostly the attackers. Five policemen had died in the ensuing firefight. One person interviewed said something in Russian that was translated in the captions in English, "Bullets were flying everywhere, explosions, dead bodies, it was chaos. Then the helicopters fired missiles that blew up the trucks and the attackers." She showed the cameraman a vehicle destroyed nearby; holes were visible. Those weren't from bullets, I surmised; the holes were too large. These appeared to be the twenty-three-millimeter cannon rounds probably fired by the helicopters.

The news switched to a video clip of the helicopters now flying in circles over an area where smoke was visible. The reporter stated there was another firefight going on in this neighborhood. They stopped talking for a few seconds, instead they showed the tracers light up the sky, then a few seconds later, you could hear the *braaaap* sound of the multi-barrel machine guns. These multi-barrel machine guns fire over three thousand rounds per minute, so whatever is in the way won't be a threat for very long. I counted four helicopters, so that meant two others were at another location.

We finally arrived in Saint Petersburg, Russia. We were eager to get on our way, but the Russian customs officer put us into another room for further inspection. I called Aleksei, and was still routed to voice mail, so I left this message: "Help get us through customs. They want to inspect everything we have."

We were given the third degree by the two customs officers, both named Ivan. We went around and around about the purpose of our visit to Russia. It was tedious—so many repetitive questions. Finally, I told them to call to the Russian ambassador to the United States; surely that would help. It didn't; they had no idea who that was. *Come on, Aleksei, help me out,* I thought.

After twenty seemingly endless minutes, I heard a commotion outside the room. The two Ivans looked confused. Before they could even open the door to investigate, Aleksei charged in. He pointed to the officers, said his name, and showed them his badge. Then he pointed at them and shouted something ominous in Russian. He told us, "Let's go, we have work to do." Then in the middle of all the shouting he turned to my wife and said in a calm voice, "So how are you feeling, Michelle? It's so nice to see you again, my name is Aleksei, and I'll be your guide today. So, sit back and enjoy the ride."

She smiled and said, "Well, I guess I'm fine. Nice to see you as well."

I told the Ivans, "Thank you," and out the door we went. It's nice to have friends in high places.

"What's happening now, Aleksei?" I asked as we walked.

He said, "We have not found Popov yet. Eighty-one of his men were killed, and six police officers. We surprised the attackers. They weren't expecting anyone nearby to have attack helicopters, so it was a blood bath. You think you can find him?"

I said, "Get me close and let me touch something he wore or used. I'll find him within the hour if he is still in the city." I was feeling cocky, focused, and ready to go.

Some of the team were with Aleksei, including Nadia. She was chosen to stay with Michelle. I don't think she was happy about it. I put my hands on her shoulders and told her sincerely, "I'm trusting you with my world. She is everything to me. Thank you."

She said in a heavy Russian accent, "You know I didn't want to do this, but I'll keep her safe for you. You must find Popov, though." She said something in Russian, then made the sign of slitting a throat. I was mildly concerned because I wasn't sure if the gesture was intended for Popov or for me.

I replied, "You know I'll do my best."

She handed my wife her handgun. My wife asked, "You have anything smaller?" Nadia looked at me, and then rolled her eyes. I kissed my wife, and they left.

We jumped in the police vehicles and went to the jail. The rest of the team was waiting. I was informed that nearly five hundred prisoners had escaped. The police and military had already re-captured about three hundred. Smoke poured out of the walls of the prison in several places as the firefighters fought to control the fires. I saw the first hole; it was about ten feet across. Aleksei had radioed ahead to have the team pull out the pillow, sheets, and clothing from Popov's jail cell. It had been placed in plastic bags and labeled. The bags were waiting for me in a truck outside the jail.

I went through each item. I was so focused that it only took about ten seconds per item to know if a sensation was felt. I didn't get a strong sensation from anything except the blanket, and even that was weak. I reviewed the items and realized the clothing he was wearing when he was arrested wasn't among the items delivered to me. "Where are the clothes he was wearing when arrested?" Aleksei summoned the warden and asked him. I didn't understand what he said, but I guessed that clothing had been thrown away. Aleksei said, "They threw it away; it was torn up and bloody.

He says it might be in a dumpster, so we will go look." I hoped they would find it; otherwise, the search would be far more difficult.

We went to the dumpster area. The dumpsters were virtually empty. The warden called the trash company and found out the trash had been picked up a few hours before. The trash company said that truck was coming in now, and they would put the contents in a separate area so we could search the contents. While I wasn't fond of going through the trash, it's our only choice.

We arrived at the trash company within ten minutes. They were still spreading the contents out. I thought we'd have to go dumpster diving, so this was a welcome surprise. It only took ten minutes of searching before one of the police officers found a plastic bag with torn clothing. It had been tagged with a date and name but wasn't that of Popov. The warden looked at the bag and said it was the correct clothing. Popov had given them a fake name.

I took the shirt out and inspected it. There was a slight sensation from the shirt immediately. I decided to put the shirt on to increase the chance of a sensory improvement. This was the tactic I'd used with my wife's high school letter jacket, and it really helped.

My little fingers started to tingle immediately. "Aleksei," I said. "I can sense he is within ten to fifteen miles. Let me get a direction so we can get this guy." I closed my eyes and tried to block out all the distractions. Calmly I scanned left, then right, finally turning all the way around. I opened my eyes and said, "Got him."

Aleksei looked at me with a relieved smile. I needed to get justice for Aleksei's son. Aleksei asked, "Should I get the helicopter?"

I said, "No, I think we need to have them on standby, but I don't want to spook him. We need to get a vehicle that doesn't look like a police car. How about we get some taxis to be less visible?"

Aleksei said, "Anything you need."

I focused on the direction while Aleksei contacted the police chief to find some taxis. I said, "I've sensed the general direction now; it's east of us."

"OK, taxi company is about five kilometers away. We can take two taxis, and the rest of the team will go to the helicopters," Aleksei said.

I replied, "I have an idea. Once we have the location figured out, we will have the helicopters patrol a completely different location as a decoy until needed. Will that work for you?"

Aleksei said, "Yes, that might be a good idea. I know they'll have people looking out for police. If they feel no threat from the helicopters or police, they may be easier to surprise."

We drove to the taxi company. Two team members put on company uniforms to make the ruse more believable. There were three of us in each taxi, all in the back seat. We put hand grenades, extra ammunition, AK-47s, and two RPGs in the trunks. The team members had AK-47s, but I just got a hand gun. I tried to joke with Aleksei by saying, "But I want the multi-barrel machine gun I had before."

Aleksei said, "Listen, John Wayne, you used up one thousand rounds in about twenty seconds. You put a half a meter hole in a truck, and then hit, what, six people? I think we will just give you the handgun for now."

I laughed, and so did the other five people in the taxi. We had the other taxi go a different but parallel route to avoid detection and seem less suspicious. As a backup, a beat-up, older SUV would follow a block behind with six team members and far more firepower.

We started driving toward the direction my fingers were sensing. It took just five minutes before I began to feel my ring fingers tingle. I knew we were getting close when my entire hand was vibrating ten minutes later. I told Aleksei to turn down a street, but he said, "No, go straight." I was about to ask why when he said, "I recognized someone back there, a man I served with. He was disguised as a homeless person. Then I saw the end of a Kalashnikov hidden in his cart."

All I could say was, "Wow, that would've been bad."

He said, "Correct." Then he said, "I was trying to figure out why a homeless man needs a machine gun. Then I noticed four other people who had ear pieces, also disguised as homeless guys. They're the lookouts, and eventually they would've recognized us."

Aleksei called the team in the old SUV and told them to divert immediately. He then called the team in the helicopters and said something in Russian. He told me, "I told them to start flying in the airport sector, well away from us for now. I am trying to figure out where we can take you until this is all over. It won't be safe for you here."

I was confused and unsure how to respond. I badly wanted to help find this guy for Aleksei and wasn't sure if they could do it on their own. On the other hand, Aleksei was right; I wasn't trained for urban warfare. I might've been more of a hindrance than a help in this situation.

"OK," I said, "can we get someone to take me to where my wife is?"

He said, "Sure, let me call you a taxi."

Everyone in the car had a healthy laugh at my expense. I guessed that meant I wouldn't be taken to see Michelle.

Ahead of us was a large hotel. Aleksei told me, "We will drop you off here. You have a gun and here are a few extra clips in case you get attacked." They pulled over and let me out. I told Aleksei that I'd continue to scan, and to let me know if he needed my help.

He said, "We're going to that building about a quarter mile away to survey the area. I'll call if needed."

I went inside the hotel, and immediately noticed an advertisement for a bar on the roof. I took the elevator to the roof, which was the eighth floor. When the elevator doors opened, I found myself in a room with many people and thumping American hip-hop music. The music was so loud I couldn't concentrate on my fingers. I had to escape the music vibrations or I'd be unable to focus. I found the exit door to the outdoor rooftop seating and went outside. It was much quieter. I walked around until I was able to see the area where my senses had picked up Popov. It was less than a two hundred yards away. I could see most of the street and noticed the homeless people milling about. I couldn't tell the lookouts from the rest of the homeless. Perhaps none were homeless. In the distance I saw the helicopters flying in a figure eight near the airport. I counted only five. I scanned the entire area then walked around to the back of the building to look behind me. I finally saw the last one helicopter about two miles away. It was low, and was heading in my direction slowly.

Since this was the perfect lookout, I thought the bad guys might be using it as well. I decided to watch the people nearby. Most were couples. I took my phone out and acted like I was a tourist, innocently taking pictures, trying not to attract attention. I noticed one guy in the corner. He wasn't drinking, and he never took his eyes off the area where I saw the homeless people. I took a picture of him. When I noticed his earpiece, I decided to text his picture to Aleksei. The message read, "He seems too interested in that area, and he has an earpiece."

Aleksei called me immediately. "Where are you, Mick?"

I said, "There's a bar on the roof of the hotel, and it has an excellent view of the area."

He said, "You think he's a bad guy?"

"Yes, I'm positive. The helicopter you have behind us will be seen by this man if it continues to advance. I think you need to turn it around for now."

He said, "OK, I'll call you back in a few minutes."

The waitress came up to me and said something in Russian. She had a short skirt and a blouse with a deep plunging neckline. It left little to the imagination. I didn't want to stare, but I'm human, so it was difficult. I acted like I was still on the phone because I didn't understand her. I figured she was asking me what I wanted to order. The man next to me had a beer, so I pointed to his drink, then held up my hand with two fingers up. I hoped she understood that I wanted to order two beers. I figured that ordering two beers would look like I was expecting another person, and be less conspicuous. She seemed happy enough, wrote something in her order book, spun around, and walked away. Her short skirt barely covered her butt. Every man in the place, and quite a few women, watched her walk away. I had to laugh when a few women smacked their dates after they caught them staring at the waitress.

I tried to act like I was looking straight ahead while keeping my eye on the people in the street to my left. I noticed quite a bit of activity as more and more people appeared. These new people entering the street didn't have the "homeless shuffle" walk that many long-term homeless people develop. They had the correct clothing and pushed grocery carts holding clothing and other possessions just as other homeless people did, but they appeared to be trying too hard to fit in. What drew my attention to these new people were the expressions and mannerisms of the actual homeless when they walked by. When you watch an actual homeless person walk by another on the street, they hardly react to each other. Here, some of the homeless people were watching the new people, a dead giveaway that the new people weren't as they seemed.

I called Aleksei when two of the new people moved quickly to strategic areas of the street. There were three men with grocery carts on each side of the street every fifty feet. They all started moving clothing in their baskets until I saw the butt end of a machine gun in each one. As quietly as possible, I said, "I see machine guns in every one of the grocery carts."

Apparently alerted to possible problems, the real homeless people looked puzzled and a bit scared, and immediately scurried away.

Aleksei said, "Get off the roof, then. We're going in. The helicopters will be overhead in less than two minutes. I'll call you when we have control."

I walked back inside the bar to tell the waitress I had to leave. It dawned on me though, exactly how would I tell her since I know almost no Russian? I saw her by the bar. I didn't even know how much the beers would cost, so I handed her one hundred rubles and pointed toward the exit. The expression on her face told me that was wrong. She yelled at me in Russian. I didn't know what she was yelling, but perhaps she may have thought I was trying to buy sex. I said, "I have to go. This is for the beers. Is this enough?"

She seemed to calm down. "You're American?" she asked.

I said, "Yes. Sorry if I confused you."

She said, "You think I'm a prostitute?"

I said, "No, I have to leave and wanted to pay for the beers. Are those mine?"

She started laughing. "I'm just messing with you. Yes, they're yours."

I took one and drank nearly half in one giant gulp. I put it on the counter just as a helicopter flew by the building. I realized the music was about the same beat as the rotor blades on the helicopter, so nobody inside had heard it coming. I looked out the doors to see the man I had been watching yelling into a walkie-talkie. I'd had suspicions that he was one of the bad guys, but now I had proof.

Everyone inside immediately wanted to go outside and see what was happening. I didn't think it was safe. There was loud cannon and machine guns from the helicopter, and flashes of light similar to a disco ball. Another helicopter hovered about one hundred feet above the roof. Napkins and other debris were swept up by the wind forces of the helicopter and flew everywhere. The plastic chairs used outside started to lift off the ground, and the ones that didn't topple over flew off the edge of the building onto the street below. Many of the woman came back inside when their skirts were flipped up by the wind gusts. A flash of blinding light signaled an escalation of the firefight as a helicopter just above us fired a missile. Everyone except the drunks or the insanely stupid ran back inside.

I kept my eye on the man with the walkie-talkie. He eventually came back inside. The elevators going down were hopelessly slow, so he took the stairs down to the ground. I followed behind with a group of people. Once he exited the building, he ran to the next street toward the homeless encampment. I followed behind but stopped when he kept looking back. I decided to scan with my fingers and focus on my special senses.

I felt strong sensations, but not all my fingers were buzzing. I had to be close; the man we were searching for was less than a mile away. A few moments later strong explosions and gunfire came from the direction where I'd last seen the man from the bar.

My phone rang. It was Aleksei. "Mick, get to the parking lot in the back of the hotel. We will pick you up in the helicopter. It isn't safe there."

"No shit," I replied.

I ran to the back of the hotel toward the parking lot just as a helicopter was landing. I sprinted the one hundred yards or so and jumped in, hitting my head on the doorway and almost knocking myself out. I received a nice cut on my head, a large bump, and laughter from the team members and Aleksei for my efforts. We took off immediately at full power to get out of the range of small arms fire from below. As we lifted off, I felt something smack my arm.

Aleksei said, "Mick, a bullet went through your jacket."

"Bullshit," I said.

He pointed to my arm. I looked down to see my sleeve with a tear in the arm that wasn't there a second ago. I didn't get hit, but it barely missed me. Then he pointed to the wall on the other side of the helicopter. I shiny dot was visible. He shouted, "It went through your jacket and hit the wall." He stood up and pried the bullet from the bullet proof padding and handed it to me. "Kalashnikov 7.62 round."

"We're in, how do you Americans say it, mopping-up operations right now. There are only twenty or so remaining enemy fighters. We haven't found Popov, so we need you to tell us where to go."

I said, "Aleksei, the sensation is stronger back toward the homeless area. Go back that way."

Aleksei said, "OK, just need to give the team a few more minutes to make it safe, and we will."

We patrolled the area from about one thousand feet above the buildings to make sure we were out of small-arms fire range. When the team on the ground told us it was clear, we went into land. I was having a tough time telling the difference between the vibration from the helicopter and the vibration from my senses. As soon as I jumped out of the helicopter, I could tell we weren't in the right place.

I told Aleksei that Popov was in the next building. We landed nearby and the entire team rushed in, cleared the area, and then I checked again. While the sensation was strong, it appeared it was moving. Small-arms fire rained down on us from a building to our left. Nobody was hit, but it scared the crap out of me. A helicopter patrolling nearby ended the threat with a burst of its cannon.

I ran to where Aleksei was, and tried to focus. I could sense Popov was still moving, but how? Helicopters were patrolling, soldiers were in the streets, and nothing moved without being checked out thoroughly. It didn't make sense at first.

Then I realized this could be a diversion. It would make sense to use the firefight and massive explosions to divert everyone's attention while Popov escaped below through a tunnel. I knew Aleksei was busy searching for more threats, but I wanted to make sure he considered this scenario.

"Hey," I said, "I sense Popov is moving, but there's no way he could with so many soldiers out looking for him. This may be a diversion. Is there a tunnel below Popov could be using?"

He said, "Mick, that's possible. He is still moving toward the river?"

I said, "I have no idea where the river is located, but he is heading the same way as the street in front points."

Aleksei dialed a number and spoke in Russian for a minute. "OK, we have an idea what he is doing. We're going to the end of the tunnel that spills into the Neva River. There's an opening there, and he may be trying to escape that way."

I said, "Have a helicopter innocently fly over that area and see if there are a few boats waiting there with heat signatures from the motors and people."

"Great idea."

He clicked his radio and was about to say something when I said, "Wait! I bet they're monitoring our communications; we need a more secure way." Aleksei used his phone to call the helicopter pilot and tell him the orders. Aleksei pointed to six men and gave them orders, then grabbed me and said, "In ten seconds we're going to run to the helicopter. Try not to get shot."

I looked at him and said, "Try not to get shot? Is this a joke?"

Aleksei replied, "No joke. I want you to weave back and forth as you run."

*Oh, shit. This still isn't safe,* I thought.

His hand counted to five, then he grabbed me, and we all ran to the helicopter. We were all weaving back and forth. Shots rang out from several location that were quickly dealt with by the team members manning various locations. Several bullets ricochet off the ground, sending sparks flying. I dove into the helicopter. Once the door was closed, we were in full vertical acceleration. I yelled to Aleksei, "That's about all the fun I can stand." I'm not sure he understood, but he still managed a hesitant laugh.

Aleksei said, "Another helicopter picked up heat signatures and armed men on the boats in the river. There are ten men and two innocent fishing boats waiting. We have been cleared to engage with missiles. We're going to hit them with five helicopters at once, and hopefully they won't be able to alert Popov."

We were in the air only two minutes when the helicopter made an abrupt left turn. There was a blinding light and loud whooshing sound as we fired several missiles. I had no idea our helicopter would be involved. I think I pissed myself. We banked hard right, then left in what I assumed to be evasive maneuvers. The team looked out the front window at the light show. Trails of fire from the missiles headed toward the water. I could see other trails of fire from missiles fired by other helicopters as well. Two seconds later, multiple blinding flashes lit up the sky. Large boiling fireballs with debris flying in the air filled the area. A few seconds later the helicopter reverberated as the automatic twenty-three-millimeter cannons mounted on the winglets opened fire. Tracer fire allowed everyone to see the path the rounds took on their way to earth. Sparks flew on the pavement, then a few vehicles parked in a parking lot exploded as the gunner found his targets.

The other helicopters landed in a parking lot and off-loaded the soldiers and other team members. Aleksei said, "We're not landing; I have to protect you now. My team will clear the area of enemy soldiers, then go into the tunnels. I need you to tell me if he is close."

My heart was racing, and focusing on my hands was difficult. I told Aleksei that I needed to calm down and focus to see where Popov was at that moment. It took several anxious moments, but finally I was able to discern between the vibration of the helicopter and the sensations from my fingers. I could see the street direction we were using before and realized Popov was no longer going toward the river. I yelled at Aleksei, "I think we need to go toward that old building straight ahead."

Aleksei called someone on his phone. Then he yelled something in Russian to the pilots. We made an abrupt right-hand turn and basically fell out of the sky. It was an emergency descent. Aleksei yelled over the rotor noise, "I have a car coming for me. Once I'm dropped off, you'll go with the helicopter for safety—and no, you can't go with us, Mick." Part of me was disappointed that I wasn't invited along, but the majority of me realized it was time for the soldiers to do, "soldier shit."

We landed with a giant *thump*. The door opened, and Aleksei jumped out and slammed the door shut. We made an emergency ascent and then a rapid turn to the left to get away from the parking lot and back over the river as quickly as possible.

One of the pilots yelled my name. I looked up to see him holding night-vision goggles. "Aleksei say to give you these."

I grabbed them. I didn't have to ask how to turn them on this time. I watched as several vehicles sped toward the building. Once they were close, the team jumped out and went in many different directions. We were moving away from the building, and I was unable to see.

"Hey, I can't see anymore," I said.

The pilot said, "Aleksei said we're too loud, must move back. You can watch on weapons control monitor."

I took the goggles off and watched as one of the pilots moved the display toward Aleksei's men. You could see them plain as day. We were probably a mile to a mile and a half away, and you could see some of the team member's faces. We sat there and waited for nearly five minutes before anything happened. I started to get a sensation in my fingers.

The pilot gave me a headset. "Aleksei said to give you this also."

I put it on and listened. I heard Aleksei say: "Stand by, there's movement in the building. Looks like a homeless guy."

I watched the monitor. If this person actually was homeless, he was one of the largest homeless guys I'd ever seen. His grocery cart looked brand new. I clicked the mic and said, "Then he's the largest homeless guy I've ever seen."

Aleksei's voice came over the radio: "He's mine. Nobody engages him but me, understood?" It was an explicit warning to the other team members to stay away.

Aleksei was waiting near a group of trees as the disguised man walked nearby. He was pushing the cart slowly. Aleksei yelled something in Russian that made the man stop in his tracks. I asked the pilot what Aleksei said. The pilot said, "Shhh." I was impatient and wanted to know the answer.

In an instant, Popov—the disguised man—opened his coat and started firing a small machine gun. Aleksei fired back. Popov grabbed his neck, and stumbled around, still firing wildly. Eventually he fell to his knees, then to the ground.

We immediately began a high-speed run toward where Aleksei and the men were located. I could see Aleksei standing over the man, his gun pointing right at his head. Other team members began to appear in the picture.

"Can you tell me what Aleksei said to him before the shooting started?"

The pilot said, "I can't tell for sure, but it was something about his son."

I replied, "What did Popov say back?"

The pilot said, "All I could hear was Popov saying, 'How did you find me? You shouldn't be here, but it's better that I kill you both.'"

"What did Aleksei say after he shot him?"

The pilot said, "Something about hell was all I could hear."

I lost my sensation of Popov, so I knew he was dead. Aleksei walked away from the man and sat down. A few of the team members were going through the man's pockets and removing cell phones and other items, while others went through the building.

"We land now," said the pilot.

When the doors opened, I could see a few of the team members hugging Aleksei. I waited on the helicopter. I could see Aleksei was crying, obviously emotionally spent. He eventually walked over to the helicopter. I got out and we hugged. He was still crying.

"Thank you, my friend," he said. "I thought when he was finally neutralized, I'd feel better, but I still have a hole in my heart."

I could only say one sentence: "Now is the time for healing, and living again."

I was glad Popov was gone. He was a shitty, defective human who got what he deserved. I knew Popov's death wouldn't bring back Aleksei's son, but it would prevent this horrible man from killing any more people.

After Aleksei calmed down, I told him, "Call your wife. Tell her you love her and can't wait to see her. Make her feel special, then tell her you got that son of a bitch."

Aleksei shook my hand, then gave me a long hug. Aleksei, tears in his eyes, said, "No, we got that son of a bitch. I couldn't have done it without your help. I'll be indebted to you for the rest of my life."

I replied, "Think nothing of it. I'm proud to call you a friend, Aleksei, I'll always be there to help you and your family. This won't bring your son back, but it will allow you and your wife to heal and move on with your lives, as best you can."

My job was done. I called my wife to tell her the news. "Thank God," she said. "Now get back here safely so we can go do something fun."

The team rounded up the rest of Popov's crew. Aleksei told me there was irrefutable evidence that Popov was working with several politicians high up in the central government. It would take years to clean up the mess and find everyone responsible.

Once everything was completed, the entire team went out for a late dinner at a small restaurant nearby. Aleksei looked tired once the adrenaline wore off. His team did their best to cheer him up. Aleksei took his wallet out and passed around a picture of his son. Once it made the lap around, a toast was declared. There wasn't a dry eye at the table. It was an emotional tribute to a young boy who would've been very proud of his father.

After an hour had passed, it was time to leave. I shook hands with the entire team, then Aleksei took me to the airport.

I asked Aleksei a question: "What did you yell to Popov?"

He said, "Today would've been my son's ninth birthday."

"What did Popov say back?"

Aleksei said, "He wanted to know how I found him. He was told I should be in Moscow. Then, the instant before he pulled out his gun, he said something like, 'That's OK, because I get to kill both you and your son, then kill your wife.'"

"That was a messed-up thing to say to someone. What'd you say when you stood over him?" I asked.

Aleksei smiled a bit and said, "I told him I'd see him in hell, then kill him again. I'll do this over and over again, for all eternity. He died less than a minute later. His last vision was me, standing over him, with a picture of my son in front of his face."

Now that this was finally over, part of me was sad to have to leave. I'll miss my friend. In such a short time, we'd bonded like brothers. As my friend Scott always tells me, "We're brothers from another mother."

# Chapter 49:
## Shake My Hand

We stayed a week in Europe, visiting old World War II battlefields, historic cities, and beaches. We hated to go, but it was time to fly back to America. During a stopover in Germany, my phone rang. It was Mr. Douglas. "When you arrive in the country, you're going to stay in Chicago, not back to your home. We have something we need you to look at. And before you complain, you, and your wife will stay on the top floor of the Ritz-Carlton in downtown Chicago." The phone call ended before I could say anything. That's a fancy hotel; something important must be happening.

When we landed in Chicago, Mr. Douglas was waiting. I was scanned for electronic devices, and my phone was put through a series of tests before it was returned to me. Mr. Douglas said, "I have a cold case involving a murdered FBI agent. I want you to review some evidence and then do your scanning thing." He told me about the case then gave me the reading material, murder book, and new evidence information.

The case involved his old partner who was killed in the line of duty nearly twenty years ago. "This case has haunted me for nearly two decades," he said. "I want the person responsible dead, but arrested will have to do. We have some new evidence and faces to investigate."

After a pause, Mr. Douglas added nonchalantly, "Oh, I almost forgot—you also have a TV interview tomorrow."

"I do?" I replied. He didn't respond for at least 30 seconds.

Finally, he said, "Will you look at that? Mick, take a look at the billboard up there." I looked and saw my face and a TV station logo. It disappeared before I could read it.

"They're advertising your TV interview all over, even on national channels." Mr. Douglas said.

I was asked to do television interviews nearly every week. I almost never accepted. They were so predictable and so clueless about anything but what's on their teleprompter. The press always wanted to know what cases I was working to solve, and talk about how I was able to assist the police. They always started with, "So, tell me about your ability to sense things. How does that work?" I got tired of this, so I simply didn't do interviews. I had a life too; I needed family time and time for my software company. I need a distraction from my new life and enjoyed the race track. Racers don't really care about your personal life; they want to have a good time with friends. Fellow racers tell me all the time that I'm no better than anyone else, and I liked that. I knew these abilities I currently possess might be gone someday, but I'd still have my other life that I loved, and friends that I enjoy.

I'd found out who arranged the interview when a television producer called our hotel room later that evening. She told me Mr. Douglas was the person who'd contacted the national TV news company to setup an exclusive interview. I thought it was strange, but there were ulterior motives. The interview had been advertised constantly on TV channels for the entire week I was in Russia. Mr. Douglas wanted me to talk to the reporter and discuss his partner's case. I accepted, mostly because Mr. Douglas told me I was going to do the interview—whether I liked it or not. Apparently, you don't say no to Mr. Douglas.

The room we were given overlooked Lake Michigan. It was a pretty cool view at night. The next morning I'd run down to get a bite to eat at a corner coffee shop before our meeting. I'd just received my food when I noticed my fingers had started to vibrate. I sat down and finished eating quickly. I had to get Michelle some food and coffee to go since she was sleeping in this morning. I felt the intensity of my fingers change and knew someone evil was nearby.

My fingers trembled just as I received Michelle's food and coffee. I was trying to juggle the food and cup of coffee without spilling either while

315

still focusing on my fingers. I felt the electrocution event building, so I sat down quickly. I'd been able to focus and reduce the effects of the electrocution over time. It was a major achievement and allowed me to be in public without embarrassing myself. The event came and then passed with just some deep breathing. Once it finished, I noticed a man walking toward me.

"I want to shake your hand," said the strange man with a long beard, his hand extended. I was a bit surprised since I was in a full disguise. My disguise usually worked well and prevented photographers and reporters from following in public places. I was startled that this man seemed to know who I was. Nobody should've known I was there except a few key people in Mr. Douglas's and Agent White's office.

"Why?" I said, trying to act confused while not looking at this man. My fingers were quivering. I knew something wasn't quite right about this guy, and I hadn't even touched him. I wasn't sure why I needed to fear this man, but I learned long ago that my fingers never lie.

This guy was evidently a lunatic, and I could tell nothing good would come from a conversation with him.

He stuck his hand out even further and repeated his request. "Mickey Kingston Anderson, I just want to shake your hand."

Only someone who had put forth an extreme amount of effort to investigate my life would know my middle name and what I looked like with my normal disguise. I needed to get as far away from this lunatic as possible, so I said, "You have the wrong guy." I turned away immediately.

In a thunderous voice, which made everyone in the coffee shop turn to notice, he yelled, "If it isn't the latest phenom, Mickey Kingston Anderson. To what do we peasants owe this honor of your presence?" I said nothing and left the coffee shop.

I had a meeting with Mr. Douglas in an hour and a TV interview scheduled later that evening. I was here to work and didn't have time to deal with this freak. I called Mr. Douglas and said I was being followed. I wanted him to review the security video of the coffee shop to see who this guy was. He told me he would get right on it. I said, "This guy is a bad dude;

we need to find him." I went about my business for the remainder of the day and tried to forget about him.

The interview that evening was indeed something special. They had a studio audience, which was a bit out of the ordinary. I didn't understand why, at least at first. My life was such a whirlwind that I'd forgotten today was a year to the day when I solved my first case. It was a wonderful surprise when Stacey Robinson and her family walked on stage a few minutes into the interview. I enjoyed seeing the family again. As you can imagine, this was an emotional reunion. We cried as the memories of that eventful week returned.

The studio audience became emotional as well. I could see most of them wiping their eyes along with us. Afterward they gave us a standing ovation. It was a wonderful experience. I really felt my abilities had made a difference in this family's lives, and I had an enormous sense of pride for fighting through these challenges' life had hurled at me for four decades.

I was also surprised to see Mike Dooley, the detective I first worked with. I started to call him "Fat-ass" but stopped myself just in time. He was still fat, but he had been promoted to the rank of captain, so out of respect, I didn't call him fat-ass. He told everyone how we'd met, and that he didn't believe me at first. Then he stated, "Our department has closed well over forty cold and active cases with Mick Anderson's help." The audience applauded for about twenty seconds.

I hadn't even bothered to count all of the cases I've worked on. Honestly, only those first three cases were the ones that I'd never forget; those cases put me on a course that forever changed my life. Dooley and I had become good friends, even though we called each other vulgar names whenever we had a conversation.

Toward the end, the reporter brought up the case Mr. Douglas wanted to discuss. An FBI agent had been murdered, in cold blood twenty years ago. The agent's picture was put on screen for twenty seconds. The reporter wanted to know if we had any new leads. I had reviewed the evidence but hadn't even held any clothing or items yet. I said, "Yes, we have some new leads we're following up. We hope to be able to announce progress on this case soon. We're also asking the public for help." After a few more minutes, the interview was completed.

After the interview was over, Stacey Robinson, my wife, and I stayed to sign autographs. We also took extra time just to talk to people. I felt something wasn't right, and right on cue my fingers began tingling and vibrating. About ten minutes later they were quivering. I scanned the crown of people, then noticed a man in the back with a long beard. He looked like the weirdo from the coffee shop I'd visited earlier that morning. I excused myself and went over to Captain Dooley. I said, "Dooley; we got another weird one. My fingers don't like the guy in the back." I didn't want to deal with the weirdos, but it was difficult to avoid them. This guy definitely gave me the willies.

Dooley said the man had walked out of the entrance a minute later. I told him, "My spider senses are tingling; see if we can get video of him." I also called Mr. Douglas and told him to review the security video from the TV station. "This guy is following me, and I'm getting weird senses from him. He is the same guy from this morning."

"Mick," said Mr. Douglas, "He looks like a homeless man, we haven't been able to identify him with his beard and hat. Do you want the police to grab him?"

"I would like him detained to find out who he is, can you make that happen?" I replied.

"Of course," said Mr. Douglas.

After about an hour we ended the evening, and Stacey and I hugged. I would see her again, I was sure. The media loves this kind of reunion; it's great for ratings and fun for us as well. Then I said farewell to my friend, Captain Dooley. Before we went out the door, I said, "I don't see the weirdo anymore, but I sense he is close by. Let me know what you find." Because it was raining heavily my wife stayed inside to talk to Dooley and Stacey's family while I found the car.My fingers were quivering as I reached for the studio door. I left the building even though my mind told me it was a bad idea. Just five feet from the car, I heard a man cough, as if he wanted to clear his throat in order to get my attention. The man yelled, "Are you Mick

Anderson? You are! Hey, I want to shake your hand." I turned to see the weirdo from the coffee shop. I said, "I'm really busy, and it's raining. I have to get back to the family. Perhaps another day."

"You should shake my hand, it's just the polite thing to do," said the man.

I turned back toward my car and opened the door. I felt a sharp pain in my back, and the world around me began to spin. Everything went into slow motion. The last image I saw was that of the man who'd insisted I shake his hand. He was standing over me. I heard him say, "You just wouldn't shake my hand, would you, Mick? You might've been able to save him, and perhaps yourself, if you'd just shook my hand."

## Chapter 50:
# Don't You Die, Mick

"Darkness is just the absence of light. The lack of light doesn't necessarily mean the end," said the voice. A flash of light appeared. Had my mother been able to pull me back? A brief flash of light, then darkness once again.

Then I heard a familiar voice—mine.

*Don't you fucking die on me, Mick.*

I felt a warmth come over me. I was back in the room of Gatekeepers; they were telling me not to give up. "Fight back with every ounce of energy you have. You must find and then climb the ladder that has three lights on each rung. Don't climb any other ladder you see. We have done what we can for you; now fight like the Gatekeeper you are."

I began to see images of ladders. They all had lights on them, some more than others. Some had three lights on a few rungs, the rest only had two or four. There seemed to be thousands of ladders. After an extensive search, I was finally able to locate the ladder with three lights on all the rungs, and I started to climb it. It was a long ladder. I counted as I went up, unsure why. After climbing 110 rungs, a light flashed in my face. A voice said, "Ten more to go." I continued climbing.

I saw another image; it was my body being treated in a hospital emergency room. It appeared that I was watching from the ceiling, looking down on my own body. There was activity everywhere in the room. A nurse, running into the room with medical supplies, slipped on blood, slammed into the "crash cart," and knocked it over. Tools, syringes, bandages, medicine, and blood bags crashed to the floor. "We've got a pulse," yelled the doctor, still holding the paddles of the defibrillator he had just used to shock my body back to life. "Get another crash cart. I need more units of blood stat. Is surgery ready to go? As soon as we get blood into him, transport immediately."

There were no more images, just darkness. I could still hear them say, "We're losing him! Clear the body, I'm shocking him again."

The Gatekeepers reappeared. "Think of your best day on earth—a time when you laughed the most. We want you to laugh, right now, as hard as you can. Laughing will help you fight for your life."

I heard a doctor yell, "Blood is in. Let's get him to surgery now!"

I was awakened to a bright light and someone snapping their fingers. "Do you see the light? Mr. Anderson, can you see the light?"

I tried to speak and say yes, but nothing came out. I blinked my eyes a few times. "Holy shit! I think he just blinked his eyes," yelled a familiar voice. It was fat-ass. *Why was Dooley yelling? Where the hell was I?*

I heard someone else's voice, "Welcome back, Mr. Anderson, can you see me?" I blinked a few times and turned my head to look at the direction of the person. Nobody was there. I turned the other direction and saw my wife, Michelle. The voice said, "Do you see your wife, Mr. Anderson?" I blinked my eyes. I heard screams, which startled me. "I'm Dr. Winters. You are in the hospital. Blink if you understand." I blinked my eyes twice. I realized the screams were from my wife. *Hopefully they were screams of joy,* I thought.

I was in and out of consciousness for the next two days. When I awoke, my wife told me I'd had been shot by some deranged gunman. The day I was brought in, the doctors told her that it would be a miracle if I survived. According to the doctors and nurses, I had made amazing progress. It took another disappointing day, though, before I was able to move my arms and legs on command.

I was still trying to figure out what had happened to me. From time to time, strange memories flashed into my head. I kept thinking of Scott's son, Ely, but I couldn't understand why.

A few hours later more memories appeared in my mind. I think that Ely, my best friend's son, had been in the room with me. I remembered a man whistling our high school fight song—but why? I'd been unable to remember anything else.

The next day Dr. Winters felt I had made enough progress to try physical therapy. My hands were healing quickly. The bandages were removed, and I could see the stiches used to repair the damaged area. Dr. Winters told me I was fortunate; the bullet went through my hands in the perfect place—between the thumb and index finger. It didn't damage the hands as badly as it looked. It broke some bones but missed important tendons. It looked terrible, but he said my hands would heal completely. *Why am I in the hospital for a bullet wound to my hand? There must be more wrong with me than a non-lethal hand wound,* I thought.

I was still discouraged that I was unable to talk, or remember anything else. It was a welcome relief when one of the Gatekeepers arrived who could communicate telepathically. You have no idea how tough it is when you aren't able to talk.

At first, he told me that Ely, my best friend Scott's son, was still missing, and presumed kidnapped. The day Ely went missing a voice mail was left on Scott's home phone which said that his son would never be coming home again. The caller disguised his voice. The Gatekeeper informed me that Ely's blood proved that he had been in the same room where I had been found. He also told me that when I felt up to it, investigators wanted to question me about anything I remembered. He told me nothing positive had happened since then, there were no new leads, and the kidnapper had vanished. He did tell me the FBI had everyone possible working on Ely's case.

*That explains the memories I had been having, I thought. What does the high school fight song have to do with this?*

I already knew about the injury to my hands. Now I wanted to know what other injuries I had suffered. He informed me that I had been shot twice, one on the left side of my head, and another bullet had struck my chest. *He shot me twice?* The Gatekeeper just nodded, "No, counting your

hands, he shot you three times." *I need to get this son of a bitch.* He nodded again.

*How serious are my injuries?*

He frowned and said, "Well, you coded five times. Your injuries literally couldn't be any worse, or you'd been unable to survive. We were able
to track your phone location. Your phone had been tossed on the side of
the road about five miles from where we eventually found you. We caught
a lucky break when someone called the police to report they'd been forced
off the road by another vehicle as that vehicle exited a nearby driveway.
They didn't find the car, but drove down the driveway and found you only
twenty minutes later. Unfortunately, it took ten minutes before paramedics
arrived. They determined you were dead but kept at it, and eventually your
heart restarted. You owe the paramedics, doctors, and nurses a beer when
this is all over. Your heart stopped on arrival. That was ten days ago, Mick."

*Ten days ago? I can't believe it has been that long ago. I'd heard your
voices about not giving up. Did you really tell me to go to the ladder with
three lights on it?*

His response was, "Trust in threes. The strongest shape is a triangle,"
he said, "and the Gatekeepers use this image amongst ourselves to transfer the load between members. You see, Mick, we all have special powers, but we still need a total of three Gatekeepers to do most of our work.
You, Dr. Richard Freeman, and Dr. Virginia Freeman worked together to
solve a potentially catastrophic bomb plot. You wouldn't have been able
to solve it without their help, and they couldn't solve it without yours. I
read minds, but unless other Gatekeepers tell me who to shadow, I don't
know whose mind to read. Other Gatekeepers have been injured just as
severely as you over the last one hundred years, and they'd relayed stories
back to us from the other side. We know from their experiences that there
are ladders seemingly floating. These ladders represent choices. Choosing
the correct one determines if your will to live is stronger than your injuries.
Three Gatekeepers are able to communicate telepathically, so even though
you weren't conscious, you heard instructions on how to proceed. We can't
always save someone, but the power of the Gatekeeper family is immense

when we come together. Your survival from these horrific injuries is due to the Gatekeepers' formidable will to live. Most people would've perished with similar wounds."

My wife came in, smiled, then kissed me. She asked the Gatekeeper, "And who are you?"

He answered, "I'm Steven Donnelly from the FBI. I've worked with your husband on several cases."

I hadn't remembered his name until then. Even though the wounds to my hands were excruciatingly painful, if I didn't find a way to communicate, I'd go nuts. I asked him for a pen and notebook so I could write down questions for my wife. They waited patiently as I carefully wrote a list of questions.

She looked at them with astonishment, and she asked me, "Mick, did you really write this?"

I tried to talk but nothing came out, so I nodded my head.

She responded, "How? Your penmanship was never like this."

We were interrupted when the doctor walked in. Michelle handed him the notebook. He took one look at the note and said, "Who wrote this?" My wife pointed to me. I didn't understand what the big deal was; all I wanted to know was how she was doing, how the children were dealing with it, and how bad did I look.

Agent Donnelly said, "I watched him write it."

The doctor asked, "Who are you?"

He responded, "Special Agent Steven Donnelly from the FBI."

My wife was still intrigued by the note and asked me to write my name on another piece of paper. I did, and handed it back to them. She swayed back and forth, then said, "I'm feeling dizzy." She immediately sat down.

*What's the big deal about the note?* I asked the Gatekeeper. He turned the notebook around and showed it to me.

It was written in calligraphy—flawless flowing letters that looked like they had been created by a computer. I thought they were kidding. *How could I have written like that?* I had no idea it would come out that way, nor did I notice it while writing. The doctor told my wife that sometimes after a head injury, a patient acquires new abilities while losing others. I had the lost the ability to speak but had gained weird writing skills.

There was a knock on the door. Mr. Douglas and Special Agent Sam White walked in. It was nice to see them. They gave me a fist bump and Agent White said, "Mick, we have the FBI and CIA investigating. We will find the man that did this to you." As usual, they'd said very little, and quickly ended the conversation. Still, I'd felt better because someone high up in the government cared enough to visit.

# Chapter 51:
## *The Answer Why*

A doctor and nurse came into the room. They announced that I needed to rest, and told everyone to leave. I didn't want to rest; I was wide awake and ready for answers. The nurse injected a sedative into the IV line that was in my arm. I tried to fight the sleepiness, but it was a lost cause. I drifted off to sleep.

While I was asleep, memories of that day flooded my mind. I began to replay in my mind a vivid dream, with detailed events of what had transpired that day. I remembered someone wanted to shake my hand, and that person had whistled the high school fight song. It was someone from high school—but who? Random memories began to fill my mind. My head was covered by something dark, and I was held down by duct tape and couldn't get away. This man told me that because I wouldn't shake his hands, this was all my fault. This same man had fired a bullet through my hands. He had a knife. Had I hit the man? Yes, I had. I could see his whole body, but his face was blacked out. I remembered a phrase he said to me, "I liked you in high school. You talked to me when others wouldn't." Memories of Ely, duct taped to a chair, blood in his hair and collar, and the frightened look in his eyes made me lash out in anger. Ely screamed for his mommy and daddy. I screamed back to him in my dream, *I'm coming to save you Ely. I have to help Ely. Think, Mick. You must remember who took Ely.*

I was awakened by several nurses. They had rushed in because the monitors attached to my body had signaled that my heart had stopped beating, and I wasn't breathing. Apparently, during my dream, I had flailed by arms around all over, tearing the sensor wires off and triggering alarms. I had nearly fallen out of the bed.

At that instant I'd remembered who it was. *Benji Cunningham*, I thought.

The door opened again. My wife, Agent Donnelly, and Mr. Douglas rushed in to see what had happened to me.

"It's OK," said one of the nurses. "He disconnected his sensor wires."

The wires were reattached, and the alarms were turned off. Everyone looked relieved. There was a knock on the door. In walked my best friend Scott, Ely's father. He was in tears, and looked like he hadn't slept or shaved in a week. Mr. Douglas asked if it would be OK if Scott could talk to me. I nodded. Mr. Douglas asked the nurses and doctor if we could be alone. They checked me over for another minute then left. Mr. Douglas asked my wife, "We need to discuss the case. Can you give us a few minutes alone, please?" My wife kissed me, and then left.

Scott looked at me and said, "I just wanted to see how you were doing, Mick. They tell me you can't talk. I just want to say that none of this is your fault. I know you love Ely and want to protect him."

I looked at the Gatekeeper, and he said, "I'm Agent Donnelly from the FBI. We're working with Mick to find your son. The information we have is that he was alive when Mick was shot. The FBI is investigating, and Mick has given us new leads to follow up. Mick wants you to know we will find him and bring your son home."

I grabbed the notebook and wrote: "Scott, I'm so sorry. I know who took him. It was Benji Cunningham, the weird guy from high school." I handed the notebook to Scott.

Scott looked at the note and said, "When did you learn to write like this? You're saying Benji Cunningham is the man who took Ely? Mick, Benji stopped by my house the day before we went to Chicago. I hadn't seen him since your thirtieth birthday-slash-Christmas party."

I grabbed the notebook and wrote: "Benji was at that Christmas party?"

Scott said, "Yes, don't you remember? He arrived just before you threw the drink into the downstairs ceiling. I think he was just coming down the stairs when it happened."

He paused for a second to collect his thoughts, then continued, "I remember because I didn't invite him, he just showed up. Your glass explosion showered him in alcohol and glass fragments, so he went to the bathroom to clean up. He was angry, and I think he left shortly afterward."

I thought to myself, *Halle-fucking-Lujah*, which caused a stern eye from the Gatekeeper. *Whoops, I'd forgotten he could read my mind.* I pointed to the notebook so I could write more information.

I wrote: "I have the ability to sense evil people, as you know. My body tells me someone evil is nearby by making me feel like I am being electrocuted. I didn't understand this phenomenon until last year. I'm positive the reason I had those spasms at your party was because Benji was nearby. That night has always haunted and embarrassed me, but it all makes sense now. I've felt the same electrocution feeling many times, not just at your Christmas party. It means there many evil people who must've lived close to me."

Scott reviewed the lengthy letter and said, "You know, his mother lived up the street from you in Peoria Heights, right?"

I started to cry. I'd lived through hell for decades, unsure why my life was such a complete mess. The whole time I was sensing evil, and the most-vile being Benji. He went to the same high school and probably drove by my house quite often during those years. Then when I moved after my divorce to another town, his mother lived right up the street from me. The memories were almost too much to bear. Jesus, I'd thought about suicide so many times because I misunderstood the significance of those events. Every day was horrible; all I thought about was when the next embarrassing moment would occur. I was constantly asking myself why I had to suffer for so long. It didn't seem fair.Even badly injured, this gave me a real spark of hope. In an instant, my memory banks went into overdrive. I had to analyze each time an embarrassing situation happened to me. Was Benji around during all those disasters? I couldn't say for sure that all of them were related to Benji, but that doesn't mean that other people, perhaps just as evil, weren't the reason.

The Gatekeeper looked at me and said out loud, "Your life has been given new meaning. You have now been given the answers to explain the struggles you experienced. Many of us struggled during the early years, unsure of our destiny. You were no different. God only gives us what we can handle, but it seems he believed you could handle quite a bit."

Scott looked at me and said, "Mick, what's this dude talking about?"

I wrote in the notebook, "He is a specialist; his job is to get my senses working as quickly as possible. I promise, Scott, we will find your son, and then get that piece of shit, Benji."

There was a knock on the door. Captain Dooley, the Bobs, Stan Holliday, the ex-football player and now FBI agent, came in. They all said, "Hi" and gave me fist bumps. It was great to see them. Dooley said, "We really thought you were dead—you had us scared. You look like shit. Gonna have a nasty scar where the bullet hit your head." I wanted a mirror to see for myself, but that would have to wait.

I grabbed the notebook and wrote: "Dooley, this is my friend Scott; his son is Ely."

Dooley noticed the paper. "When did you learn to write like this?"

I wrote: "Oh that? It's just something I picked up when the bullet entered my brain. I'm trying to impress you with a speedy recovery."

Dooley told me, "I've met him Mick. We were introduced over a week ago when you were brought in." He paused, then said, "It's my understanding you know the attacker; his name is Benji Cunningham?"

I looked at the Gatekeeper and thought, *How do they know; had I told them already?*

He tapped my shoulder and pointed to a microphone on the desk. He said, "Microphone in room. With a head injury as bad as yours, it isn't uncommon for people to tell their story even without knowing it. Scream a name in their sleep, or suddenly awaken and yell out a name, that kind of stuff. They were listening and recording all of your conversations."

I started to remember things from that day I was shot. I grabbed the notebook and wrote: "Dooley, I need you to look up an old murder case as well. Benji confessed to killing two girls. It happened in Peoria. I understand it's not in your jurisdiction, but perhaps you can help by getting a detective to reopen the case. I remember that these twin girls were abducted and murdered. Their bodies were put into an old fair ride and not found for a month. Fisher was their last name, and I think it was twenty to thirty years ago."

After Dooley read the note, I grabbed the notebook from him. I wrote: "Scott told me Benji's mother lived on the same street as I did, East Terrace View Lane in Peoria Heights. His actual name is Bartholomew Cunningham. I remember her name is Grace. Benji's mom picked us up from a football game in high school, and instead of calling her Mom, Benji called her by her first name, Grace. I thought it was so weird at the time, so her name is stuck in my memory banks. Benji was weird like that, always had a screw loose."

I motioned for the notebook after thirty seconds. I wrote: "Scott, I'm so sorry that I couldn't bring Ely home. Now that I'm awake, we will make this our top priority."

He replied, "It isn't your fault, King; I'm just so distraught. I know you did everything in your power to rescue him. You know I love you like a brother."

Mr. Douglas had already received information about Bartholomew Cunningham's cell phone. He reviewed his phone and told us, "We've tracked his cell phone, it's in New York. At this instance, it's moving on a highway near Poughkeepsie. I've already told them to find and stop the vehicle."

Everyone stared at Mr. Douglas's phone while we anxiously waited for information. Twenty minutes later his phone rang. He talked for a few minutes, then hung up. He looked pissed off.

"False alarm," he said, "the phone was stuck to the underside of a Wal-Mart trailer using double sided tape. The truck driver picked up the trailer in Chicago four days ago. According to phone records it has been there the entire time to throw us off."

# Chapter 52:

## I've Lost It

It had been thirteen days since I was brought into the hospital. I still couldn't talk and my senses were gone. The doctors said my wounds were healing just fine. I looked like a freak, with my face and head still black and blue from extensive bruising. I feared the bullet fired through my hands had destroyed the ability to use my senses to find Ely before Benji murdered him.

When it became obvious that I'd be unable to help Ely or law enforcement, my feelings of worthlessness and severe depression started all over again. Scott checked in on my progress each day, and I had visits from detectives who updated me on the progress of the case, but I couldn't help in any way. I was so depressed that it was difficult to stop myself from crying at least five times an hour.

I was scheduled for plastic surgery to repair the bullet wound on my head the following day. I hoped this might bring a spark back into my life. Physical therapy on my hands, arms, and legs was going well. Soon they would get me out of bed to see if I could walk. The next day the surgery was performed. After surgery the surgeon informed my wife and I that the wound to my head would look much better in a few days. All I'd see after it healed was a small depression, and only I'd notice. She told me the butt implants my wife had requested turned out great as well. Nobody smiled, so I tried to feel my butt, not sure if they were serious or not. My wife and the doctor started laughing.

"No, Mr. Anderson, we didn't do a butt implant—just joking." She removed the stiches on my chest wound and my hands and said they were healing nicely.

Captain Dooley came to see me. With him were two FBI agents. The senior agent was Bruce Pappas. The younger agent was Robert Blue. I thought it was funny that Agent Blue was here to assist me. It had to be tough going through life as Bob Blue, and for some reason the song by Johnny Cash called, *A Boy Named Sue*, popped into my head. Agent Blue was a sturdy big guy, probably had to fight his way through constant insults growing up. My mind wandered as usual. The movie *Old School* with Will Ferrell loaded into my memory banks to distract me. There was an old man in the film that Will Ferrell called "My Boy Blue." I chuckled to myself, then realized I had wasted precious time. In a few seconds my brain returned its focus on the task at hand.

Agent Blue showed me a copy of a letter that had been addressed to me at the hospital. According to the agents, it appeared to be sent by Benji. The message wasn't clear; the sentences were jumbled up, almost like it was a code. Only the last line was immediately readable; it said, "The devil is in the details."

A distant memory popped into my mind. I grabbed the notebook and wrote: "Get me a high school yearbook from my senior year right away." For some odd reason I remembered something in our high school senior yearbook. Each senior was allowed to include one line about where they wanted to be in twenty-five years. I remembered something strange Benji had said in the yearbook. One of the agents called the high school and requested a scanned version. One wasn't available, but an original was still at the high school in the vault. The agent asked if someone from the police could review it, and the request was approved.

It took an hour for a detective in Peoria, Illinois to go to the school and review the book. I was shocked when he called and said nobody by that name was in the yearbook. I wrote a message for the agents: "Then they gave him the wrong year." Sure enough, once they gave him the correct year, he read off Benji's answer to the question. "Where do you see yourself in 25 years?" His answer was: "Fishing the Dirty Devil River in Utah."

I grabbed the notebook and wrote: "The devil is in the details; he is testing us. I'd bet my right nut that he is near the Dirty Devil River in Utah. Let me fire up the computer and get a map of that area."

The map showed that most of the river is extremely remote, with virtually no visitors and limited access. To stay there any length of time you would need survival gear and an RV. Benji would need supplies at constant intervals. A young boy would attract attention in a remote place because people would be naturally concerned about the child's welfare.

The more I thought about it, the more I questioned my theory. I wondered if it might be a trick. The reason I remembered Benji's line in the yearbook so clearly was he didn't like to fish. We had multiple high school field trips during our senior year, and one was to a nearby lake. Some of us went fishing, but not Benji. He just sat on the dock, determined to harass us. He yelled derogatory comments the whole time. One comment I remembered was, "Fishing is dumb. You're wasting your time trying to catch a fish that's smarter than you are." He seriously considered fishing to be dumb, so when I read his senior statement it surprised me. I thought he was weird, and his statement just reinforced that opinion.

His letter didn't make sense, so I started focusing on possible misinformation. The FBI was using code breakers to help us figure it out, but so far, they hadn't come up with anything. I could see Benji sending a letter riddled with clues that were completely false. It might not contain anything at all—just be a time waster to send us on a wild goose chase.

I remembered something else and grabbed the notebook from Agent Blue. I wrote: "His father was in the air force, find out where he was stationed." It only took a minute for a reply. His father had been stationed at Nellis Air Force base in Las Vegas, Nevada. That seemed like a dead end. I wrote several things down. "1. What was the nickname of his unit? 2. What was the name of his airplane? 3. Did they ever fly missions to Utah?" Agent Blue tore the paper out of the book and went into the hall to find out.

There was a knock at the door. The nurse walked in. In a cheery voice that could only mean her shift had just begun, she said, "How are we, Mr. Anderson?"

I said, "Doing better today, thank you."

She said, "Well that's just wonderful. Let's check your vitals."

Captain Dooley, who had been immersed in some magazine, stood up and said, "Hold the fuck on. Mick, did you just talk?"

I was so focused on the case I didn't even realize that what I said could be heard. "Holy shit!" I exclaimed. "I can talk. Holy shit, I can talk again!"

Dooley said, "Great, now you won't shut up."

I replied, "Fuck you, Dooley. I can talk again!"

The nurse used a call button to summon the doctor. A few minutes later, two doctors came into the room. "I hear you're talking again," said one doctor.

I answered, "Yes, what a relief. Now when can I leave the hospital?"

The doctor replied, "Hold on, Mr. Anderson; you have a long way to go. We don't even know if you can walk." They checked my vitals and shined lights into my eyes. The second doctor just exclaimed, "Excellent."

"So, if I can walk, then I can leave, is that what you're saying?"

The doctor replied, "No. You have just suffered a traumatic brain injury. You won't be going anywhere for some time."

Just then my wife ran in, obviously out of breath. "They called me and said you could talk."

Trying to be funny, I said, "No sweetie, not yet."

A few seconds later, Mr. Douglas entered the room. "What's this I hear? You can talk?"

I replied, "Yes, I can, but the doctors won't let me leave."

Mr. Douglas said, "Out-fucking-standing. You can leave when they tell you, not before, Mick."

The room was nearly full when Agent Blue walked in, unaware of what happened in his absence. He looked around and said, "What'd I miss?" We all started laughing.

I said, "Nothing, what'd you find out?"

He carried on like nothing had happened. "I have additional information. Did you know Benji Cunningham was adopted?"

I answered, "Well, that explains a few things. His parents were nice people, but the mother seemed tense around Benji. I didn't see the father much, but now that you mention it, there was no family resemblance. What else did you find out?"

Agent Blue stopped and said, "Wait, I thought you couldn't talk." We all laughed again.

"I woke up finally. Go ahead and continue." I replied.

"Well, apparently I missed more than I thought. OK, that's interesting. So, I have a friend at the defense department. He was able to go around the normal red tape to get us information. Ben Cunningham, Benji's father, is deceased, killed in an accident while on duty five years ago. He was seventy-two years old and still on active duty. There's only one reason someone of his age would still be on active duty—he was someone strategically important to the air force."

Agent Blue paused to review his notes, then said, "Officially, he was listed as a fighter pilot, and his unit was called the Green Mountain Boys. The odd thing he told me was Ben Cunningham wasn't even a fighter pilot, and wasn't stationed at Nellis Air Force Base—ever. He told me Mr. Cunningham worked on top-secret missile programs at White Sands in New Mexico and Green River in Utah. He said the group is part of the Tactical Nuclear Missile Program called GCG, which people in the military call God Complex Group. I believe Mr. Cunningham was listed as a pilot on that fighter squadron to possibly deflect attention from what he really did."

I said, "Then it's quite possible that the family took vacations to Utah. I'd think that while growing up, Benji was shown some top-secret areas by his father, perhaps hidden bunkers, stuff like that. I believe we need to check out these areas in Utah first. Mr. Douglas, can we get a few drones to do some aerial surveillance?"

Mr. Douglas said, "I don't normally use military assets for non-military use, but I believe the new jet-powered Reaper drone III's group at Nellis could use some real-world training in Utah. I might be able to pull some strings and get five, which should cover virtually the entire state in one or two days."

I said, "Outstanding. Let's concentrate on retired air force bases and other defunct military bases in that state, and also the Dirty Devil River area. I'm not sure how to identify where they'll be or what they'll be driving, but those cameras can see faces from twenty thousand feet pretty easily, and they have facial recognition software, right, Mr. Douglas?"

Mr. Douglas said, "I don't have the foggiest idea what you're talking about." Then he winked at me. He added, "I need to call home and tell them I'll be late." He stepped out of the room. I took that to mean he was calling someone to make drone arrangements.

A few minutes later my friend Scott came in the room. "Your wife texted me that you can talk—is that true?"

I said, "No, not yet, but I'll let you know when I can."

He smiled, "King, do you always have to be a dick?"

I replied, "You know it, brother."

I told him what we'd found out so far. "So, you think my son is in Utah?"

I replied, "I have a feeling that's where we'll find him. I believe Ely is alive, otherwise the letter from Benji would've been full of gloating. You remember what a dick he was when he was right about something and we were wrong."

Scott replied, "And you think you can find him and get Ely back alive, even if your hands and fingers aren't working?"

I said, "Scott, even though I can't sense anything yet, we have every asset possible looking for him. Even the military is involved. If Benji is out there, we'll find him."

I added, "Here, give me a hand. I want to try walking."

I was amazed that although I was still shaky, I could actually walk with some assistance. The pain level was pretty high, but I had to get better and find Benji, regardless of the pain. I was exhausted after only a minute of trying to walk. While my mind appeared to be sharp, thirteen days of not moving had taken its toll on my body. I didn't have any stamina. I was tired, so I told everyone that I needed some rest.

When I awoke, the clock said 3:23 a.m. I was now wide awake after over nine hours of sleep. I decided to see if I could walk by myself. I used a table with wheels nearby to steady myself and made it to the hallway. Over the objections of the nurse, I walked up and down the hallway for over an hour. She told me it wasn't safe; I didn't give a damn. I was tired but pushed myself until I couldn't walk anymore. I went back to the room to take a nap. Every six hours I forced myself to get up and walk at least an hour.

The following day was busy as the FBI and Mr. Douglas phoned to tell me the status of the investigation. Mr. Douglas sent video to my phone from the drones. I'd hoped he would use the Look Through technology to assist us, like we used in Chicago, but because of national security issues I was forbidden to ask about it on the phone or text messaging. I knew he would allow the use once they determined a suitable reason.

I was now walking without help. I even walked up and down the stairs to test my stamina. I desperately wanted to leave the hospital, but the doctors said it was too soon. They'd done everything they could for me, and now I felt strong enough to leave. The doctors kept saying, "Let's see how you are tomorrow."

I said, "Screw tomorrow, I need to leave today."

I used my hands to scan but had no sensations. Another interesting sign that I was indeed recovering, came when I could no longer write in calligraphy. I'd really missed it; watching people's reactions to my notes was priceless. It's a good sign, though. In only fifteen days I had recovered everything except my ability to use my hands and fingers.

The next day I was able to run through the halls. It wasn't pretty, but I was running. When I showed the doctors my abilities, they told me I could be released later that day. I contacted Michelle and Scott to tell them the news. Then I called Mr. Douglas and told him. I also asked about a meeting with the Gatekeepers to enlist their help as soon as possible. He told me he would set it up for the next day in Washington, D.C. I asked him, "Do you give them the facts of the case, or do I?"

He said, "They already know everything you could tell them. Be there tomorrow at nine o'clock sharp."

I called Michelle and told her to pack a bag for both of us; we were going to Washington, D.C., the next day. Being pragmatic, she asked, "Did you get plane reservations already?"

I said, "No, but I think one of the FBI jets is here. They'll take us." I called Agent Blue and said, "I need a ride to Washington, D.C., tomorrow at six o'clock in the morning. Can you help with that?"

He said, "How about we go tonight? Wheels up at eight o'clock." It's nice to have friends in high places, and we flew to Washington, D.C., later that evening.

# Chapter 53:
## I Need Your Help

I arrived at Langley at eight in the morning. I met with Mr. Douglas and Special Agent White for about twenty minutes. We went together to the meeting room where the Gatekeepers were waiting.

"I need your help!" I shouted as the door closed. I wanted everyone there to know how important this was to me. The man who had visited me in the hospital, Agent Donnelly from the FBI, spoke first. "We're glad to see you have recovered. We know the situation and already have discussed ideas. The Freemans have had a vision that should be helpful."

Dr. Richard Freeman said, "We had a vision that the boy was still alive. We sensed desert or barren conditions, but we also see a large tree and a mountain behind."

Dr. Virginia Freeman said, "While we can't understand the meaning, we also see an 'E' and a 'G' in lettering on the building that's near the area."

Agent Donnelly told me, "We'll have two Gatekeepers go with you if you'd like. I'm aware that Mr. Douglas has made some military people available to you as well."

I replied, "I need all the help I can get. Who wants to go?"

Agent Donnelly said, "I believe the correct choice is myself and Agent Tweener. His specialty is tracking suspects with his amazing vision. He can see things you and I can't."

"Excellent. When can you leave?" I asked.

"Our bags are packed; we're ready to go," replied Agent Donnelly.

I started singing the old Peter, Paul, and Mary song, "Leaving on a Jet Plane," which made everyone else laugh. "Let's roll. There's a jet waiting," I added.

Agent Donnelly asked, "Where are we going?"

I replied, "I hear Utah and Nevada are pretty at this time of the year."

My wife was assigned a security person, and she would stay in Washington, D.C., until my return.

We flew direct to Hill Air Force Base near Ogden, Utah. Once we arrived, Mr. Douglas called to update me on information he had just learned. He said, "We've got an alert to all law enforcement agencies in Utah and Nevada about the missing boy. Green River Utah police said a man and young boy, matching the descriptions of Benji and Ely, were sighted in town. The RV they were traveling in had engine problems, and the two were picked up by a family returning to Green River. The family said the boy wouldn't talk. Both the man and the boy had military haircuts. The man said they were on their way to explore the Dirty Devil River. The RV was towed into a local repair shop. The man rented a vehicle using the credit card and Florida ID of Robert Cunningham. FBI agents arrived there today and are checking DNA samples inside the RV. There's no signal from the GPS on the rental car; either it isn't functioning, or it has been disabled. They're driving a new Chevy Tahoe, red or maroon in color.

I wanted to take the jet, but Mr. Douglas thought the helicopter would be more useful once we arrived. It took us just under two hours to get clearance and fly to Green River. A Utah State Police SUV was waiting for us at the small airport. The officer dropped us off at the repair shop where two FBI agents were processing the RV. To speed up DNA testing, Scott and his wife had given the FBI their own DNA samples to compare with Ely's. Crime scene technicians had also found samples of Benji's and Ely's DNA from items in the house Benji used in Chicago. All we needed was a partial match on the string of DNA, and that would take just a few hours.

While we waited, I watched the crime scene people painstakingly go inch by inch through the RV. I tried to scan using my hands and fingers, but I received nothing. I was pretty sure this was Benji's RV after seeing another fuel tank mounted inside the RV. It was right under the couch behind the driver and it appeared to hold over one-hundred gallons of additional fuel. No rational person would fit an extremely dangerous fuel tank where occupants would sit.

"We found urine stains on the driver's side carpet, on the door panel, and on the outside of the driver's side window. We think he urinated into a cup then tried to throw it out of the window at highway speeds. The air pressure difference probably sprayed it back into the vehicle," said one of the agents. "This will make a DNA test easy, and much quicker."

Mr. Douglas called and said, "Wave to the nice drone." I looked up but couldn't see anything in the sky. I waved anyway. Mr. Douglas said, "Your head looks much better than it did a week ago. Mick, I need to talk to Donnelly for a minute; hand him the phone." I handed the phone to him and continued scanning the sky for the elusive drone.

Donnelly hung up and said, "The state police had spotted a maroon SUV and chased it into the mountains. We're waiting on what they found. Don't worry, I told Mr. Douglas you were fine—sharp and motivated." I laughed; figures he would double check my progress. A few minutes later Donnelly's phone rang. He talked for just about twenty seconds. "False alarm; it was a few drug runners. They crashed and are in custody. About one hundred pounds of cocaine was seized, so overall not a bad outcome. Just not our guy."

My phone beeped; it was a text message from an unknown number. A video was attached. When I opened the video, it became obvious the video was from Mr. Douglas. It was a video of me looking up into the sky with my hand shielding my eyes. Then it panned out to show damn near the entire state of Utah. The drone had to be over fifty thousand feet above us. No wonder I couldn't see it.

# Chapter 54:
## *Places To Hide*

I still felt useless. Mr. Douglas and Agent White had grown accustomed to my ability to solve difficult cases quickly. I had the best skill set for a job like this, but my injuries forced me to be a spectator. I needed to work on renewing my senses; they needed to be exercised, just like my body. Agent Donnelly told me, "It's possible they'll return; just don't expect it to happen today. Just focus. If it's meant to happen it will, but you won't be able to force it."

I turned my thoughts toward Benji. He'd had a four—or five-hour head start, so he could've been anywhere.

I was certain that Benji needed to get someplace suitable to hide the vehicle. I wanted to get in the helicopter and investigate anything that looked like a decent hiding place.

Suddenly everyone's phones started to ring. Mr. Douglas was calling the entire team at the same time. "Get on the helicopter, we think one of the drones has spotted the vehicle in Nevada."

"Nevada?" I asked. "I guess he could make it there, but he would be taking a huge risk of being caught speeding."

Mr. Douglas said, "Just get on the helicopter. We will provide more information within five minutes."

I looked up the number of miles just to the Nevada line—it was at least 250 miles. Five hours would allow plenty of time to do it. I also checked his vehicle's fuel economy and the size of the gas tank to see how far they could drive without stopping. It was rated at twenty miles per gallon and had a twenty-six-gallon tank. He probably drove near 80 miles per hour, so if we factored fifteen miles per gallon, he could probably go 330 miles before he had to stop.

Once we were airborne, Mr. Douglas called again. He said the Nevada State Police had posted pictures at fuel stations all over Eastern Nevada. A customer at a gas station in Baker, Nevada, remembered a man and a boy that matched the pictures, and they drove a large red SUV. I had a tough time finding Baker and eventually realized it was on Route 50; which was at the edge of their fuel range. This area was rural, mostly used by tourists and thrill seekers. Once he crossed into Nevada, he'd had less of a chance of being spotted. Where would he drive from there?

One town that popped up in my search was called Ely, Nevada. This was also on Route 50, and it was also the name of Scott's son. It was approximately one hour away from Baker. I could see Benji heading that way, but it seemed too easy. I called Mr. Douglas and asked him to send a drone to the Ely, Nevada, area and find out what was out there.

Once he looked up the location, he told me "I can have them out there in probably an hour. They're refueling, last I heard."

I asked, "Can we have the Nevada State Police on those routes to help in our search?"

He said, "I'll try to make that happen. Now that we have possible routes, it will be easier."

If this was indeed Benji, he had an almost insurmountable head start. We would take two hours to get to Baker, probably three to Ely. By that time, he would be gone. Since the area was so rural, my guess was there were few patrol cars available. It was possible that Ely didn't even have a police force.

I really wished we had the jet, and my senses working, but neither was happening. We lumbered along at 180 miles per hour in the air force's HH-60 Pave Hawk helicopter. While not as loud as the Russian helicopters, it was by no means quiet. Our headsets allowed us to communicate with the pilot. I asked him to take a northern route, to line up with Ely instead of Baker. He poked the screen, and the autopilot changed our course.

I looked at my phone to see what was up in that area. I saw an airport, and it appeared to have some covered parking, a perfect hiding place for a vehicle. I saw no place for Benji to go if he abandoned the SUV. This was a long shot either way.

It was getting dark, so I took a nap. I was amazed that the nap lasted two full hours before one of the agents shook me. "Hey, get up, there's a call on the sat phone for you."

They handed the phone to me. I was still groggy when Mr. Douglas yelled into the phone, "Your phone not working?"

I looked at it and saw there was one bar of reception. Then I realized the volume was on mute. "Sorry, dozed off, pretty loud in the chopper. What's up?"

He replied, "Nevada Patrol spotted a red SUV at a grocery store in Ely. It's the one we're looking for. No sign of Benji or the boy, and nobody remembers seeing them."

I thought for a second, then asked, "Do you know if Benji has a pilot's license?"

Mr. Douglas paused for a few seconds, apparently reading something. Then he said, "I don't have an answer for that question; let me find out. Do you think he flew out of Ely?"

I replied, "Just covering every angle. Can we find out what planes went out of the airport today, and their destinations?"

He said, "I'm on it," then hung up.

The pilot told everyone, "Fifteen minutes."

I asked the pilot, "How soon can we take off again?" Everyone looked at me with that "You gotta be kidding" look. I said, "I'm getting the feeling he rented or stole an airplane." Everyone was tired and a bit surprised that I was now bright eyed and raring to go.

Mr. Douglas called me on the satellite phone and said, "We finally found someone who rents airplanes at Ely airport. He said he had a reservation from a week ago that showed up today. The man who rented the plane had no child with him, and he had an ID that said his name was

Ben Weaver. The identification showed his hometown is Newbury Park, California. It may be a dead end."

I said, "Any video of the guy? Did the man renting the airplane watch it take off?"

Mr. Douglas said, "We're trying to find video or photos. Nobody bothered to ask if he witnessed the take off. I'll have my people investigate it."

I said, "While you're at it, any GPS on the plane we can cross-reference with the flight plan?"

We landed at Ely Airport. We needed a bathroom break and fuel. It would take at least forty-five minutes to get the fuel. Hopefully it would be enough time to investigate further. The state police were waiting for us, and we jumped in their vehicle for the short ride to the SUV. Investigators had verified it was the right vehicle and had searched all the stores in the area. Now they were combing through the only surveillance video they could find, which came from a store that sold marijuana. It's the only working camera in that area. They fast-forwarded the video until the SUV came in, but we couldn't tell if there was a child in the vehicle. The man had a hat and sunglasses, and he'd hid himself well. The only thing that caught my eye was the sun glasses; they were unique. I asked, "Could you print off a picture of this, and perhaps another one where the image is zoomed in on the glasses? I want to show this to the guy who rents airplanes."

Since the store didn't have a printer, the investigator asked for a copy. The store made us a copy of the video onto a CD and told us to take it to the Walgreens down the street to get some of the images printed. Twenty minutes later we had twenty different photos. We jumped in the police cruiser and headed to the house of the man who rents planes. He didn't appreciate visitors at nine thirty in the evening and told us so. "It's well past my bedtime."

I apologized but insisted that he review the photos. I asked, "Is this the man who rented your airplane?"

"Yeah, that's the guy. Those are his glasses," said the old man who owned the plane.

"Did you watch him take off?" I asked.

He said, "Sure did. I watch all of them. I watched him land also, just to be sure he knew what he was doing."

I asked, "He returned?"

The old man said, "Yes, I require them to take off, fly a minute, and then land, or I won't rent to them."

"Aren't you concerned they would just steal the plane?" I asked.

"Not at all, they only have three gallons of fuel, which isn't enough to go far," he replied.

"Does your plane have a tracking system?" I asked.

He replied, "No, too old for that."

"How about a flight plan—did he file one with you or the FAA?"

"Yes," said the old man. "He wanted to fly to Provo, do some business, then return tomorrow."

I asked for a detailed map of the area. I told the police, "I bet he dropped Ely off somewhere nearby—a place where he could land a small plane. My guess is he will go back to get him, if he hasn't done that already. I feel he is too narcissistic to just leave the boy to be found. He wants to torment us for as long as possible."

A patrolman spread out a map of the area. He said, "Maybe I can help if you tell me what you're looking for."

I didn't say anything for a minute. "There," I finally said. "Looks like a small airstrip near the Nevada Ely prison." Everyone looked at me with a tilted head, much like a dog will do when it doesn't understand. I said, "I can feel it. He dropped off the kid nearby, drove to Ely, rented the plane, then returned to pick him up." I saw more than one lifted eyebrow as those around me digested my seemingly far-fetched interpretation of the facts.

The patrolman said, "My buddy works at the prison. Let me call and ask him if a plane landed." He walked away at the same time he said into his phone, "Call Billy Reiman." I heard the phone say, "Calling Billy Reiman." He talked for a minute and returned to the group. "Billy said an airplane was spotted a few hours ago. It was getting dark, and the strip is known to kick up quite a bit of dust. They were unable to get a tail number, and the plane didn't stay on the ground long."

I said, "I bet it went north when it took off."

He asked Billy. "Yes, that's correct, it turned north."

I said excitedly, "I know where they're heading! Let's get back to the helicopter."

Agent Donnelly, who'd up to this point been silent, said, "Where do you think they're going?"

I said, "Wendover Air Force Base."

"What makes you so sure?"

I was just about to say, "My Gatekeeper instinct," but caught myself. I pointed to my head, an indication he should just listen to my thoughts. *The Gatekeepers saw a deserted area, with initials 'E' and 'G'. Wendover was the initial base for the Enola Gay B-29 bomber that dropped the first atomic bomb. There are Enola Gay signs around that location, and something tells me we will find 'E' and 'G' inside one of the hangers.* Agent Donnelly just smiled and nodded.

Once we took off, I asked the pilot to make a heading toward Wendover Air Force Base. He didn't ask questions, just found the heading and away we went. I told everyone on board, "I suspected Wendover because it's not an active base anymore but is still historic. Wendover is the place where the Enola Gay B-29 bomber was stationed during its training. The original Enola Gay hanger is still there."

After a second, I continued, "I did quite a bit of research and found out there used to be a missile base nearby called Green River Launch Complex. This base is closed now, but I believe Benji's dad probably worked near there. Also, close by is the Utah Test Range, where missiles were tested. There're many places to hide."

We flew on for a few minutes, and then I had a thought I wanted to share with the team. I said, "I'd bet Benji's dad took him on summer vacations in the area. He probably showed him top secret, restricted access areas. I feel this would be the perfect place to go unnoticed for a few weeks. Knowing Benji, he probably visited several times, stocked up supplies, and either planned this for years, or planned to live here."

I had an idea and called Mr. Douglas. It was late where he was, but he still answered. "I need to find out if Benji, or anyone in the family, owns property in Utah. I needed high-resolution maps of the Wendover, Utah, area as well." He said he would check on it and get back to me.

It didn't take long to get my answer. Mr. Douglas called and told me, "Benji's great grandmother used to own mining land near West Wendover, Nevada. Satellite maps will be emailed to your phone in a few minutes. According to property records, the ranch was called, 'Good and Evil Ranch.' It had been in her family since the 1880s. Benji's father inherited the land and sold it twenty-five years ago."

The high-definition maps appeared on my phone. The area his family used to own was now a landfill. It was remote. You could land an airplane on the road, but it would be difficult to hide it. I called Mr. Douglas back and asked for a drone over that area ASAP. He said it was in flight, heading that way now.

We were only a half hour from West Wendover, Nevada when the phone rang. Mr. Douglas said, "The drone is overhead. You're correct; there's a small airplane near Landfill Road. It's covered with a tarp. The heat signature from the engine tells us the plane landed less than two hours ago. We're searching the surrounding areas. Heat marking on the roads indicate a vehicle drove away recently. The drone is making a low pass to get the tail number of the airplane right now. I'll call back." The phone went dead, just when I was about to ask a question.

A minute went by then the phone rang again. "Can't get a tail number; it's wrapped with thick tarp. Nevada Patrol is en route; we're scanning for vehicles. Not that many vehicles on the roads at this time of night." I interrupted before he could hand up in his usual abrupt way. "Mr. Douglas,

I need to know if there are any weapons storage tunnels in the area, even as far back as World War II. Second, does this property have an actual mine on it?"

Mr. Douglas's reply was, "Don't know. Will find out and call back. Anything else?"

I thought for a moment, then said, "What were you dreaming about before I woke you up?" I started laughing.

Mr. Douglas replied, "Mick Anderson, you know I can end you, right?"

I laughed nervously.

He said, "I don't dream about anything; woman dream about me." He hung up.

I had a chilling thought. If Benji planned this entire event, he either had help or had traveled there before. Instead of calling Mr. Douglas, I just texted him: "Check Benji and his entire family for vehicles, credit card receipts going back two years, and even unlicensed vehicles like small four-wheel off-road vehicles. He didn't just land an airplane in the middle of nowhere without transportation standing by. It may not have been a car either. We need to scan the mountains nearby for smaller heat traces." I knew it would be difficult to find him with nearly an hour head start, but we needed to cover all avenues of escape.

If Benji had been to the property when he was younger, he probably knew of hidden tunnels and mine shafts that had long since been abandoned. His father may have shown him hidden military areas that would be perfect places to hide. Without my sensing capabilities, we were in the dark.

A half hour later we landed near the plane. Investigators had arrived about ten minutes before us and were busy dusting for fingerprints and swabbing the interior and door handles for DNA. This plane's tail number was the same as the one rented in Ely.

One of the investigators found a note before we arrived. They'd just finished taking pictures of the letter and dusting it for fingerprints. An investigator handed the note to me, the front of the note read: "For my best friend, Mick Anderson."

The note read:

*Mick, if you're reading this note, then I've underestimated your resolve to find me. I was even more impressed you lived through our 25th-year reunion party. You must have nine lives.*

*Mick, I wish you good luck in your quest to find where Ely and I are hiding. You're a worthy adversary, but the next part of your search will be much more challenging.*

*Go Trojans!*

The last line was weird. Our high school athletics name was "Trojans." Benji wasn't athletic and rarely attended a football or basketball game. He told us that attending pep rallies was stupid. So why'd he put that line in there? There had to be an ulterior motive.

We were all exhausted, and agreed to get some sleep and return later. The team was driven to a hotel, where I was able to get nearly seven hours of sleep before there was a loud knock on my door. "Time to go," Agent Donnelly shouted.

I talked to Mr. Douglas on the way back to the airplane. "We checked every vehicle on the road with facial recognition—got no hits on your guy, but we did find four stolen vehicles that were abandoned within four miles. Not sure if they're connected; might be a coincidence. No other vehicles were titled in the family name, and no reported purchases of unlicensed off-road vehicles."

We met with the lead investigator from the Nevada State Police, Lieutenant Mera Livingston, and she gave us an update. "We have preliminary confirmation the recovered DNA was from both Mr. Cunningham and Ely. Fingerprints on the letter are Mr. Cunningham's. Fresh foot prints from two individuals, one small set, and one adult set, went north about one hundred yards. We found a desert camouflage tarp near a set of tire tracks leading out of the area. These tire tracks indicate a smaller four-wheel vehicle was parked about one hundred yards away; it was driven northeast to the highway. We believe it was a Jeep Wrangler based on the wheelbase and track. It appears to have driven north on Route 93, but we're unsure."

Mr. Douglas called and said, "We have two drones overhead. Which direction do you want them to go?" I thought about it and said, "One north, the other south. Look for four-wheel smaller off-road vehicles. I have another request: can we find out if anyone in the area worked with Benji's father?"

The helicopter had gone to refuel and was on its way back. It was so dusty we had it land on Route 93 so as not to disturb the scene. Once we took off, I had them head north, into the mountain areas. I kept scanning just in case my senses returned, but I'd felt nothing. It's tough not to get depressed when I have the capability, if it worked, to solve this case quickly.

We flew around looking for anything out of the ordinary. We found no tracks in the sandy and salty ground that pointed to where they were hiding. Benji had a sizeable head start, and could be out of the state by now. Another thought crossed my mind, Benji could've just put the four-wheel vehicle on a trailer. I see Jeeps on trailers all the time; he could hide in plain sight because there's no way to stop each one. I was getting frustrated that more progress wasn't being made.

The helicopter had to go over a mountain range. The pilot told us to hold on because the winds were kicking up. At full power we covered the peak of the mountain. For a brief second, I thought there might be a tingle in my little fingers. The helicopter vibrations at full power could easily have caused the sensation, and as the helicopter returned to a more normal power setting, the sensation was lost. We continued for over an hour before all of us wanted a break. We returned to the airport where the investigators from the Utah and Nevada State Police were waiting.

Lieutenant Livingston said they'd recovered a few strands of Ely's hair. The hair appeared to have been pulled out, complete with roots. That brought back a few memories. I remembered watching TV with Scott and Ely when one of those CSI-type shows was on, showing crime scene investigations. They talked about finding hair with the roots attached for quicker DNA identification. Scott had told Ely, half-jokingly, "Remember, if you ever get kidnapped, pull a few hair follicles out every place you go, so your father can find you." I believe Ely was listening and did exactly what his father had told him.

We continued to discuss possible hiding places nearby that were both remote and underground. After a few minutes, Lieutenant Livingston said, "This might not be important, but my father was a scientist for the air force. He used to work at Green River Launch Complex before it closed. Then he worked at Hill Air Force Base. My father told me that several of his co-workers couldn't go home for holidays because they lived to far away. He always felt bad for them, so he started bringing co-workers home, or to his hunting cave, for Thanksgiving and other holidays so they wouldn't be alone. I was about fifteen when a man came home with my father. This man was unable to return to Illinois for Thanksgiving because of some important launch test. If my father was still alive, I'd ask him who the man was from Illinois. My father's old hunting cave is near Pilot Peak, only twenty miles away. I know he brought plenty of people up there to fish and hunt. The reason I remember the man from Illinois is he used to come about once a month."

I said, "I'm not familiar where this is. Can you show me on a map?" She pulled the map up on her police car's computer and pointed to it.

I asked for the pilot of the helicopter to come over. When he arrived, I asked him, "Is this place on the map anywhere near our flight path last hour?"

He took a minute to orient himself and said, "Yes, probably ten, possibly fifteen miles away. We went west, covered a few mountains in this area, then south. Do you remember when we went over that larger mountain, and I told everyone to hold on because of the high winds?"

I said, "Yes."

He said, "I think we were between ten and fifteen miles away at that point." I asked Lieutenant Livingston, "What's the name of the town?"

She said, "I believe this area is unincorporated, but it may be part of Loray." That didn't mean squat to me, and it didn't fit his note.

She said, "Agent Anderson, the reason I brought this up now is because of the note left in the airplane. It said, 'Go Trojans,' which I thought was odd."

I said, "Yes, that's the nickname of our old high school sports teams. We were the Bergan Trojans."

She said, "Well, that's interesting, because my maiden name is Troyanos, which translated into English is 'Trojans.' Can you show me a picture of Mr. Cunningham's father?"

I called Mr. Douglas and asked for a picture that could be texted or emailed to me. A minute later my phone beeped with a picture. I showed it to Lieutenant Livingston, and she studied it for a minute then said, "I'm almost positive that's the man from Illinois."

"What's your father's full name?" I asked.

She said, "His full name is El rey de los troyanos." I'm able to translate a few Spanish words, and one of them is "rey," which means "King". I knew this word only because Scott called me that sophomore year in high school after his Spanish class. He usually called me King, but one day he started calling me Rey Anderson. After a few days of me ignoring him, he finally translated the word.

I said, "I know 'rey' translates to king."

She said, "Yes, literally translated, his name means The Royal Trojan King. I've been told that our family apparently ruled an entire section of Mexico many centuries ago.

I said, "That cannot be a coincidence, and it can only mean that Benji has been here before. Benji knows my middle name is Kingston. He is at your father's hunting lodge. What can you tell me about it? Can he see us coming long before we get there?"

She said, "There used to be a cabin in front of the mountain, but it was taken down after a fire. There's something cool there that virtually nobody knows about. There's a huge cave built into the side of the mountain. The military used it for storage during World War II. They cut about one hundred feet into the mountain side to keep it cool during the summer and warm during the winter. My father purchased it before I was born. When I was in my teens, it partially collapsed, so he designed and built new support structures inside. He used a state-of-the-art design to reinforce the cave. He added ventilation, water storage tanks, and a sewer system. It's large enough to park trucks and even a boat inside."

I said, "Benji never thought we would figure this out. I'd be amazed if he checked on you, so he never thought our paths would cross. Do you still own the land?"

She said, "Yes, but the generator stopped working ten years ago, and there are no power lines, so I've not been there in years."

I called Mr. Douglas and told him of the new information. He said, "Wow, you actually know something I don't. I'll send the drone and park it overhead."

I told him, "Thank you, but I was hoping for something more technical." This was a reference to the new Look Through technology that I wasn't allowed to speak about over the phone.

He understood the insinuation immediately, and then said, "You were huh? Well, let me see if my wife will let me bring out my new big gun to that hunting lodge and call you back."

The call came about ten minutes later. "My wife said it would be OK to borrow the big gun for your hunting trip in Utah."

I said, "Well, thank you very much, but I need it in Nevada. Still OK?"

He said, "Fine, text me the address of the hunting lodge you think I'll be interested in buying." I got the coordinates from the digital map on the helicopter and texted that information to Mr. Douglas.

A few minutes later I received some bad news. Mr. Douglas said, "My drone overhead received these images." I received a text video from Mr. Douglas of the drone footage. No vehicles, no fresh tracks, and no heat signature at that location. My heart sank, and so did my enthusiasm.

I enlarged the video and looked at the only dirt road nearby. When I enlarged the video, I could see tire tracks about two miles away, but they stopped in the middle of the desert landscape. No vehicles visible, and the tracks didn't reappear afterward. I thought the tracks were erased by rain, so I asked if there had been any recent rainstorms. "We've had no rain for 3 weeks," said a local officer. The tire tracks were far too fresh for that; wind will erase tracks in the sand in a matter of days.

I called Mr. Douglas and asked, "Can you have an analyst look at the tire tracks on coordinates fifteen—fifty?"

He said, "I'll have Mike call you back since I believe you will have more questions."

I received a phone call from a restricted number. The caller said, "This is Mike. You interested in the phantom tire tracks?"

I said, "Impressive, how did you know?"

"Mr. Douglas tells me you're sharp. Most people wouldn't notice tire tracks vanishing, especially since they're so difficult to see and several miles from the target. When the video is enlarged, I see some foot prints that appear to go into the brush. Based on damage to some of the shrubs, it appears something heavy was pulled into the roadway. I think I know what it was. The pattern is similar to a spinning brush apparatus used to sweep road surfaces of dust and debris. If you look closely, you will see an unusually flat appearance in the middle of the roadway. This anomaly begins at fifteen—fifty and continues all the way to coordinates zero—one hundred and fifty. He was diligent, I'll give him that. He figured nobody would look for two miles from the target. What I believe he did was drive back over his tracks for a few miles, then turn well before the main road. If you look closely, you will see his brushed tracks go all the way up to coordinates one hundred by five hundred. Those tracks then go north a quarter of a mile until they disappear near the mountain side. From that point on, there's just rock. No footprints or tracks can be seen. A small four-wheel drive vehicle could make it, provided it had plenty of suspension. If the vehicle is still in that area, we don't see it. Any other questions?"

I thanked him, reviewed the video, then hung up.

I decided to call Scott, Ely's father. I didn't want to give him any false hope, but I needed to let him know we were working hard to find his son. A second reason was that I needed to talk, just to make sure he was OK. Talking to a victim, especially a close friend, gives me the motivation required to focus on my senses. When I hung up, I still didn't feel my senses, but I felt a calm sense of peace that comes from a solid friendship. I'd find Ely, and it'd be soon.

Mr. Douglas called and said, "My wife says the big guns have found something interesting. We see earth-covered doors on the side of the mountain. Gotta say, Mick, your investigative skills are impressive. Texting coordinates now with images."

I replied, "Tell your wife thanks, and ask her if she minds if I borrow a few helicopters with some soldiers who might need some training on hostage rescue."

"My wife says that's fine; they'll be there in thirty minutes. You feeling it?"

I replied, "Not yet, but that could be changing."

The video appeared on my phone. Arrows on the screen pointed to the location. The earth-covered doors were genius. They were complete with shrubs, making the entrance so cleverly concealed that you could walk right by the entrance and not see it. There was a dirt road, mostly covered with vegetation, going up to the area, and a small flat area nearby. In an attempt to hide his tracks, he had damaged some vegetation, but unless you were looking for this, it wouldn't set off any alarm bells. Regular drones wouldn't have seen the doors because of the earth-covering; only Look Through technology could see it.

In thirty minutes, two more troop transport helicopters arrived with ten additional men. Also tagging along was a bad-ass AH-64 Apache attack helicopter. This has a 30-millimeter cannon in the nose that moves wherever the pilot looks. I know all about this gun because, according to Mr. Douglas, the targeting software algorithm I created after college is still being used. I know it can put a round within a two-foot target from a mile away. To say this helicopter is intimidating is an understatement. Up close it's frightening. I started to climb into the first helicopter but was told it wasn't for civilians. I thought about flashing my FBI badge, but quickly realized they wouldn't give a shit.

We jumped into the original helicopter and went north. I didn't want to see outside. I wanted to see if any sensation would appear without a visual clue. Crisscrossing the first mountain produced no senses, and no heat sources were reported by the pilot. My hands were healing quickly, but they had been badly damaged. Perhaps I was expecting too much, too soon. I knew I might never get my senses to return, but if there was ever a time that I needed them back, it was now. I closed my eyes and focused. We went a bit further, and they were just about to fly toward the next mountain when I felt something.

The sensation caught me off guard. I wasn't sure I believed it. I kept my eyes closed and pointed my hands back and forth. *Do you feel something Gatekeeper?* I opened my eyes to see Agent Donnelly staring at me. *Your senses have awakened?*

I looked at him and thought, *I feel something, but am not sure I believe it.*

He said out loud, "Trust in threes. This is your second time. The next one will be game on." I wasn't sure how to take his comment or how he knew about the first time, but I trusted his wisdom.

We went another five minutes with my eyes closed and my hands trying to find something. It wasn't there. "Turn around," I said into the headset. "Go back where we were five minutes ago." A few seconds later I felt the craft bank left. I tried to motivate myself and thought, *Talk to me fingers. Where should we go?*

Three minutes later I was rewarded with another tingle, this time with both hands. I kept my eyes closed and pushed all other distractions out of my mind. Slowly I rotated my hands to the left and felt my ring fingers tingle. I clicked the mic and said, "Turn left about forty degrees." We turned. In thirty seconds, I felt the rest of my fingers start to tingle. I was getting excited now. All of a sudden, I felt a jolt, then nothing. I yelled into the mic to ask the pilot, "Are we near the spot where the target is located?"

The pilot said, "Yes, four miles back and to the left."

I replied, "Keep going, then. They can probably hear us, and I want them to think we've left the area."

Everyone looked at me with shocked faces, except Agent Donnelly. He was cracking a little smile.

I asked the pilot, "How far do we have to go before they can no longer hear us?"

He said, "If I fly away from that side of the mountain, only about a mile."

I told Lieutenant Livingston, "I need some vehicles for all of us. Can you arrange that?" She nodded. Then I said to the pilot, "It will be dark soon, do you have any extra night-vision goggles?" The pilot radioed back, "Roger."

I told the team we would wait until the middle of the night to proceed. We would get as close as possible with the vehicles then go on foot the rest of the way. The soldiers already had night-vision goggles, I wanted extras for the drivers of the vehicles because we would approach with no exterior lights. Thirty minutes after we landed, five Army Humvees arrived.

We set out at two o'clock in the morning and drove to within a mile of the mountain-side location. The Apache helicopter was flying a few miles away, ready to go in an instant. I couldn't hear the helicopter, but I knew it saw us. Everything was in place to proceed. We also had a drone high overhead checking for any movement or heat signatures.

I called Mr. Douglas and told him to guide us toward the door. He said, "About two thousand feet, straight ahead." We approached the mountain-side in the vehicles until we were a quarter of a mile away, then we went on foot. The helicopter pilot would keep us informed of any movement. Although dulled by the injury, my fingers were sensing something. It was a huge relief. The feelings of depression I'd had only a few hours ago were replaced with a calm, yet forceful determination.

When we arrived at the cleared area, I could see an outline of the camouflage used to hide the entrance. The soldiers used a detector to identify listening devices and special goggles to see any laser or infrared triggering devices. There were none. They were just about to move forward when Agent Tweener, the other Gatekeeper, told everyone to stop moving.

Near the door covering he crouched down to examine several of the bushes attached to the door and in front of the entrance. He saw something everyone missed. The bushes were fake, inside were wires and some kind of sensor buried inside. He returned to explain to the team what he'd found.

"Looks like a motion sensor, if the bush moves too far, I believe it will trigger an alarm," said Agent Tweener. Mr. Donnelly smiled, and spoke, "Nice catch, Agent Tweener."

Agent Tweener carefully pulled back the covering approximately a foot, just enough to examine the door but not disturb the sensor attached to the bush a foot away. He informed everyone on the team to avoid touching the bush in front of the entrance.

The covering over the door was impressive. Thick insulation covered the inside, with carbon fiber support brackets attached every foot or so. The entire outside surface was dirt and desert shrubbery held in place by the carbon fiber brackets and nylon netting. It was impressive, well thought out, and extremely effective in hiding the door to the cave. I assumed Benji's dad taught him some survival skills, and military concealment designs.

In my earpiece I heard the Apache pilot tell everyone the now-exposed part of the door was radiating a small heat signature. It was chilly outside, and certainly inside the cave as well, so some type of custom heating system had to be used.

Another soldier pushed a camera cable under the door and viewed the video in his goggles. He whispered, "Checking door for latching and alarms." He slowly examined everything around the door. Once he was satisfied there were no alarms, he turned on the heat sensor. "One adult in a bed, appears to be sleeping. One Jeep Wrangler with some kind of attachment on the rear, multiple rifles, no sign of child. Moving camera higher to view rest of room." We held our breath. He whispered, "Can't get visual on other side of room, unable to verify identity of person sleeping." He did something on his control box, then the images appeared on my goggles. The man appeared to be restless but sleeping. I noticed the exact same sun glasses on a table. I immediately knew it was Benji. On a counter behind the sleeping man were items stacked in a pyramid shape. Benji always stacked things in the shape of a pyramid. I noticed the entire back wall had pyramid stacks of water, canned goods, and toilet paper. He finally rolled over, and I could see enough of his face to positively identify him as Benji. I whispered, "We have confirmation of identity. It's Benji." The captain instructed the soldier on what they would do next. I was left out of this decision making for obvious reasons. Quietly they determined how the door would open and divided the room into sectors. They determined that two people per sector would cover everything but where Benji was sleeping. Three soldiers were tasked with taking care of Benji.

They took their guns off safety, and I chambered a round in my gun. One man lay down, his gun already aimed toward the sleeping man. Then I heard them whisper, "three-two-one, GO!" Two people opened the door while one man jumped under the door and charged toward Benji.

An alarm went off inside the cave. The camera feed revealed Benji, obviously alerted to the door being opened, rolling over with a gun in his hand. An instant later he started firing. The lead soldier was hit in the chest; luckily his Kevlar bullet-proof vest stopped the round. The next shot hit his helmet, nearly knocking it off. He spun away to get out of the line of fire, while the soldier laying prone next to me in the doorway fired two shots. Benji rolled backward off the bed; it appeared he had been hit. The soldiers rushed in as Benji continued to fire under the bed and over the top of it. Bullets pinged off the edge of the doorway, just a foot from where I stood. More shots were fired by the soldier through the mattress before I saw the gun Benji was firing fall from his grasp.

The soldiers went to their assigned areas while the three tasked with securing Benji ran for cover inside the room. It appeared Benji was down but still moving. One soldier ran around the bed and pointed the rifle right at him. He yelled, "Suspect down!" The others ran around the bed, pulling it out of the way to verify Benji had no other hidden weapons. Benji was alive but losing quite a bit of blood.

I waited patiently for confirmation about Ely. I heard the phrase: "Clear" five times. Then I heard a loud 'thunk' sound as a soldier slammed something into the alarm speaker to make it stop blaring. Once it was quiet, I heard a child crying. I decided it was safe enough to go in and find Ely.

Ely was found chained up to a pole about forty feet away. He had a bowl of water, a plate with a half-eaten lunch meat sandwich, and a bucket next to him to use as a toilet. It was disgusting to see how he was treated. He was crying hysterically. It was dark inside the cave, except for our flashlights, so I used a soldier's flashlight to shine a light on my face and said, "Ely, it's your buddy, Uncle Mickey, the one with the race car. I'm here to take you to your Mommy and Daddy."

Ely looked up with tears in his eyes and then jumped into my arms crying and sobbing. "I've got you, son, and I won't let anything happen to you." After about thirty seconds I said, "How about we call your Mommy and Daddy. Would you like to talk to them?" He was still crying but nodded his head. One of the soldiers found the key for the handcuffs and unlocked him.

I took the phone out of my pocket—a difficult task when Ely wouldn't let go. I said into the phone, "Call Scott." The phone replied, "Name not found." I realized I had Scott under the name Shithead. I wasn't sure how to call now; I certainly didn't want to say, "Call Shithead," but I couldn't manually dial the number. I gave up and said, "Call Shithead." The phone replied, "Calling Shithead." I was embarrassed, but this little stunt would be forgiven.

Scott answered on the first ring, even though it was after four in the morning, "Mick? What's going on?"

Ely yelled, "Daddy!"

Scott was overcome. "Oh my God, you found Ely. Is he OK? Please tell me he is alright."

I told him he would be OK. He started screaming and crying. Emerald woke up and took the phone from Scott.

"You've found my little boy? Is he OK?" she said.

I replied, "Yes, he will be OK."

I heard more shouting and crying in a manner that reminded me of the Russian ambassador's call. Soon both Scott and Emerald were crying and yelling into the phone. I could barely hold on to Ely, so I found a chair and sat down. Ely wouldn't let go, and he was heavy, but I didn't mind. For five minutes we mostly cried. I was overcome with emotion. The adrenaline began to wear off, and a feeling of dizziness took over.

Ely, still sobbing, said, "My daddy wants to talk to you."

Scott said, "King, you're my hero, and I owe you big time. You're proof that some people don't need to wear capes to be a super hero."

He started to sob, so Emerald took the phone and said, "Our family thanks you from the bottom of our hearts. Bring my boy home safe, and may God bless you." I gave the phone back to Ely, and he talked for another five minutes before handing the phone back to me. Scott was still sobbing on the other end. Finally, we ended the call.

I brought Ely out of the cave. I told him a doctor wanted to check him out to make sure he was OK. I told Ely that I had to go back into the cave for just another second, but I'd be right back. He didn't want me to go, but I told him, "This nice man needs to check you over. This is important to make sure you're OK." He finally nodded.

I ran into the cave, up to where Benji lay on the floor, and bent down next to him. He was bleeding from two bullet wounds.

In my most cheerful voice, I said, "Benji, you're a hard man to find. Do you still want to shake my hand, Benji?" I stuck out my hand as if I expected him to shake it. I continued, "So now you don't want to shake my hand? Benji, that's kind of rude, especially after all the trouble we went through to find you. Well, Benji, I gotta tell you this; you look a bit under the weather, so I'll make this short."

Benji interrupted me and in a raspy voice he said, "How—did you find me?"

Continuing to use my cheerful voice, I said, "That's a great question, Benji. I'm really glad you asked. Actually, I owe it all to you. I read your letter at the hospital where you wrote: 'The devil is in the details.' I also remembered our senior yearbook, where there was this question: 'Where do you see yourself in twenty-five years.' You answered, 'Fishing the Dirty Devil River in Utah.' But, Benji, I also remembered you hated fishing. Then I investigated your father's employment history, and realized he worked in Utah, so I chose that state to focus on."

I had to pause to wait for him to finish coughing, then continued, "Benji, there's one more thing—and I think you will really appreciate what I am about to say. Do you remember that nice note you left for me—you know the one left on the airplane that concluded with the phrase, 'Go Trojans.' I doubt you knew this, but the daughter of your father's friend and coworker is now a police officer. Actually Benji, she's a lieutenant, and very smart. Her father's last name is Troyano, which she told us is Spanish for Trojan. She told us her father had a hunting cave nearby. Isn't that interesting, Benji? Well, Benji, as you know, I'm able to sense really evil assholes, much like yourself. All I needed was the general area where you were hiding. My senses did the rest. Isn't that a great story, Benji?"

I paused to wait for him to finish coughing up blood so he could hear the rest of the story. I continued, "Now, Benji, I can't take all the credit; it was a team effort. I think you will be impressed how I was able to get the military, and many police agencies, involved in order to hunt your worthless ass down."

I paused, mostly for effect, then said, "I can see in your eyes that you're concerned about Ely, so the great news is he is safe, and heading back home tonight. His parents, my friend Scott and his pretty little wife, Emerald, will be so excited to see him."

Benji was having trouble breathing. His face was changing colors to a darker grey. I told him, "Benji, your time on earth is coming to an end, but I won't be seeing you on the other side. Where you're going won't be a nice place. To be quite honest, Benji, I can't think of anyone who deserves to die more than you. You're nothing more than a fucking piece of shit." I smiled at him. "Any last questions, Benji?"

He was near death. I wanted—no—I needed to be the last thing he saw. He coughed up blood but didn't say anything. He was gasping for air; it wouldn't be long before his body gave up and shut down. He stopped breathing about thirty seconds later. I felt nothing for this useless piece of crap. He wouldn't be missed. Some humans are defective, and Benji was one of them.

I went back outside and picked up Ely. I told him, "That bad man won't hurt you, or anyone else, ever again."

I called Mr. Douglas, and he said, "Great job, I heard all about it."

I asked, "How the hell do you know about this already?"

His smart-ass reply was, "Didn't we go over this a long time ago? I know everything that's important to know. The FBI plane will be there in twenty minutes to take you home to Poria or Peoria or whatever the fuck that city is called. I'm flying out in a few minutes, and we'll see you there."

Ely held on to me the entire time. The police vehicles came to the cave and picked us up. I walked Ely around to each soldier and police officer so he could thank each one. I had Ely give each person a high five or fist bump as well. It seemed to brighten his mood immensely. We jumped into the SUV and went to Wendover Airport just in time to see the jet land.

Ely fell asleep in my arms for the two-and-a-half-hour flight back to Illinois. It was early morning when we landed at Peoria's airport. Scott and Emerald were waiting. TV news crews were everywhere. Ely was frightened of the lights and flash bulbs and wouldn't let go of me until Scott and Emerald took him out of my arms. We were ushered to a private room where my wife met us. The mayor of Peoria was waiting, too, along with twenty or so reporters. Alongside was a woman I recognized from local advertising as a child psychologist.

The mayor said, "I've been told that Ely should talk to a therapist first, before he is brought home. I have a counselor with us who has agreed to talk to Ely." Scott and I looked at each other and said, "No" simultaneously. Scott told the mayor, "Not a fucking chance. We're taking our son home now." Scott was right; Ely needed to be home, in his own bed, with his parents tonight. I hated that a politician would use this event to act like they cared when everyone in the room knew it was a cheap political stunt.

There was a police escort for both of our vehicles. The police would block off Scott's street, and mine, so nobody could bother us. The healing process would begin after Scott and his wife determined it was time. I was happy for them, and I was happy for myself. I'd set a life goal to get Ely back, and it had worked out. I needed this victory to avenge the crimes that were committed against this child and to eliminate the threat Benji posed to everyone around him.

# Chapter 55:
## *Retreat*

I retreated from public life to heal and to be a regular father again. It felt good to know my family accepted the crazy year I'd had. My body had been through so much in a little over a year, and it needed a rest.

Once I had healed enough, Mr. Douglas had an FBI jet pick me up in Peoria, and fly to Washington, D.C., for a meeting with the Gatekeepers. Once in the meeting room, I was placed in the center of a triangle, with the other Gatekeepers around the edges. A piercing spotlight shown on an open chair right in front of me.

Agent Steve Donnelly started the meeting by announcing, "Mick Anderson, when you're ready to return to the Gatekeepers, this spot is yours." I felt tears running down my cheeks, unsure of why. I didn't really know these people all that well, but still felt a fraternal bond to each and every one of them. I was allowed to be part of something that only a few months ago, seemed unimaginable. These amazing people had welcomed me into their inner circle, and saved my life with their insight. Nevertheless, I still felt fragile and unworthy around what I considered were super heroes.

Donnelly continued, "We understand that you feel unworthy because your abilities have been disrupted, but you're a Gatekeeper, which means your God given talents are just as strong, and probably more refined, as they were before your injuries. Just remember: Once a Gatekeeper—forever a Gatekeeper."

After his statement, I'd felt a sense of ease, as if a weight had been lifted from my shoulders. They would wait as long as it took for me to be ready, and I'd return when I was able to contribute.

I left a changed man. I decided to have the FBI jet change course so I could visit Captain Dooley, Detective Miller, and The Bobs, in Chicago. Dooley and I had become good friends, and the other detectives, once cold to me, were happy to see me. For two hours we joked and relived the first three cases. Then Dooley said, "Hey, while you're here, take a look at a few cases."

Detective Miller wheeled a dolly with ten large evidence boxes. They thought it was funny and started laughing. Detective Miller said, "We're just fucking with you Mick."

Dooley then said in a more serious voice, "I do have one case that's bothering me, can you take a look while you're here?"

I said, "Sure, fat ass."

Dooley replied, "I ought to put you in jail for the night just to teach you some respect. From this point on, it's Captain Fat-ass, understand, Mick?"

I replied, "Yes sir, Captain Dooley, Fat-ass, sir."

He flipped me the bird, then brought a box out from behind his desk. He carefully unboxed everything inside. The outside of the box had a label that read: "Frank Dooley."

I asked Dooley, "Is this a relative of yours?"

Dooley said, "Yes, Mick, my brother was murdered twelve years ago. We thought we arrested the right guy, but it turns out he wasn't the actual killer. We do have proof he was there, but I want to find his accomplice and also put him away."

I looked through everything, but my sensing ability was still diminished to the point of being unreliable. I felt the senses were there but were afraid to come back.

I said, "Sorry Captain, can we revisit this again in a month, after I've had time to heal a bit more?"

He shook his head and said, "Sure, Mick. This case isn't going anywhere; take all the time you need." I stayed another half hour, then flew home.

Once home I tried to be a normal husband again. For a few weeks I was checking off the "Honey Do" list of chores around the house. I'd be dragged back into the crazy life again eventually—I was certain of this—but for now my wife was happy to have a somewhat normal husband back with her.

I was overjoyed that Ely and the family had found a way to put this behind them. In less than a month, Ely seemed unaffected by his ordeal and was back to his normal behavior. It took the adults much longer to recover.

Three months after Ely's kidnapping, my wife and I decided to take a trip back to California, and back to Highway 1. It was time to see some scenery before my life went sideways yet again. I asked Scott if he wanted to join us on the trip. I thought his family would have a great time with ours, and I'd felt it would be a rewarding and healing trip. We would see some of the most amazing beaches and mountains that mother nature had to offer as well. Not only did he say yes, but he insisted that it was his treat.

When we arrived for what I hoped was a nice, relaxing trip with my wife, and best friends, a nagging voice inside my head told me something weird was about to happen.

I groaned, for I knew the voice inside my head was always right.

*The End*